CHILDLESS

CHILDLESS

ROTHBURY MAJOR CRIMES: BOOK ONE

JULIANNE FEHER

ISBN: 979-8-9999421-1-1 (Paperback)
ISBN: 979-8-9999421-0-4 (E-book)

Any references to historical events, real people, or real places are used fictitiously. Names, characters, and places are products of the author's imagination.

Front cover image © Eberhard Grossgasteiger/Pexels.
Book design by Julianne Feher.
Interior images @sketchify on Canva.

First printing edition 2025.

Mom, for your unwavering faith.
Dad, for your blind support.

CONTENT WARNING

Childless is intended for mature audiences. It does contain topics some readers may find dark, disturbing, or upsetting to read. I try to handle all topics sensitively; however, please use your discretion before reading. The following topics are found in the book:

Pedophilia (non-descript references, occurs off-page)
Death of children
Sexual abuse of minors (occurs off-page)
Miscarriages & infertility
Murder (occurs off-page)

PROLOGUE

Redacted Copy of Vincent Anthony Watt's Confession
02.07.2019

I, Vincent Anthony Watt being of sound mind and body, at the advisement of my attorney, wish to confess to sins of my past that weigh on my soul.

I confess to the murder of Melody Dawson. ██████

██

██████████████████████████ I confess to the murder of

Kelly McLane. ████████████████████████████████████

██

I confess to the murder of Rebecca Smith. ██████████

██

██████████████████████████ Lastly, I confess to the

murder of Anne Griffin. ████████████

██████████

If we confess our sins, he is faithful and just to forgive us our sins and to cleanse us from all unrighteousness (John 1:9).

Vincent A. Watt

CHAPTER ONE

THURSDAY, OCTOBER 4ᵀᴴ, 2018

Detective Ethan Dumas walked into the closet-sized cold case office, a steaming cup of slightly burned black coffee and a bagel bag gripped in one hand, his backpack in the other. Inconsiderately placed in the doorway were three tattered banker boxes, a hazard without Ethan having properly woken up. With more agility than he knew he possessed, especially given the hour, he sidestepped the stack and only splashed a minimal amount of the sludgy coffee onto his white dress shirt.

"What the hell," he mumbled. He leaned around the boxes to get his breakfast safely on his desk and tossed the backpack into his chair. Taped to the top box's lid was a folded note addressed to "Dumas."

Hope your wife and you are well. Had these still and wanted you to have everything from the cases.—Det. John Coppin

The morning grogginess slowed him down, but he was pretty sure he had heard the name in passing. He couldn't recall if he'd ever worked with Detective Coppin directly, but there was a chance they'd met during a New Haven County joint investigation. He glanced again at the note, confused about what cases he meant. Surely, there was a detective in Southbury PD Coppin could have pushed it on.

Warm breath tickled the side of his neck as he heard Jay Verne's voice right behind his ear. "Is it your birthday?"

Ethan started forward and caught the top of the tower to prevent them all toppling over, his other hand gripped at his heart.

"Verne, maybe try being normal and just say good morning—with some space."

Verne, a junior detective with blue blood roots, ignored his remark and slid into his chair. Their desks butted up together, with little room in their makeshift office for choices in desk arrangement. They spent the day face-to-face with a foot-tall cork board as Ethan's only shield from Verne's antics.

"Who's ruined your morning?" Verne asked, already with his rubber band ball slapping from one palm to the other.

"Presumably, it's for a case." Ethan squeezed past the tower and shoved his backpack to the floor to take a seat. He watched the tower, wary of what this would mean for them.

"What's the case?"

"I just got in when you did."

"The boxes all say Watt. I feel like that means something."

"Probably has to do with the cases," Ethan said, half ignoring Verne as he checked his emails.

"Isn't watt something to do with a light bulb too?"

Verne looked sincere, which Ethan brushed aside. He focused on the few emails in his inbox to avoid delving deeper into Verne's mind. He had reminders of upcoming court cases, a request to buy candy bars for a patrol officer's kid's fundraiser, and nothing about a new assignment.

"This just looks like junk," Verne said. He'd managed to leave his desk and start going through the top box without Ethan even noticing. Clearly, he'd gotten too good at ignoring Verne.

Ethan stood up and plucked the paper from Verne's hand. He placed it back on top and shoved the lid, which barely fit, back on to the box. "Until I know which case this goes to, and if it's ours, we're not touching it. Last thing I need is you getting us in trouble for tampering with who knows what," Ethan said and waved his hand at the tower.

"Why does that name sound so familiar?" Verne mumbled, not acknowledging Ethan's instructions. He had moved back to his desk and propped his feet up on the edge of it, his body angled toward the tower. Ethan made sure the box lid was not going anywhere and then used his side to push the boxes farther into the office and out of the doorway.

Verne's feet came down hard on the office floor. "Oh, Ed did give us this!"

Ethan cringed at the use of Captain Camilleri's first name. It never felt appropriate that Verne was the captain's godson and was casual with him at the station. "When did Camilleri give us this case?"

"Yesterday. I was leaving, he grabbed me on the way to my car and said, 'Jay, got a big one for you. The Watt cases from the eighties. Missing and dead girls.'" Verne's attempt to imitate Camilleri was awful.

"Watt," Ethan repeated. The name tugged at the memory he couldn't quite reach, and he mumbled it again under his breath until it seemed to click into place.

"Like Vincent Watt?" Ethan clarified, as he glanced warily at the boxes. The name struck a bell because he was familiar with the cases. Watt was the classic detective nightmare. His case was one they told you about in the academy as a type of bogeyman. When he'd started working cases as the lead detective, he'd prayed to never get a case like Watt's, and he wasn't a religious guy.

"Vincent Watt, as in the pedophile rapist murderer from the eighties!" Verne said, catching up on who they were talking about. His enthusiasm matched a kid sharing his favorite comic book hero.

Before Ethan could scold him, he was interrupted by a knock on their office door. Verne whipped around in his chair to face the doorway, and Ethan stood up, forcing a smile. Barely filling half the entry, the woman was short and dressed as if on the way to a funeral, apart from the overloaded plate of muffins plastic wrapped in place. Ethan could tell from the overwhelming aroma, and the moisture trapped under the wrap, that they were fresh.

"Good morning!" Ethan offered in an overly enthusiastic tone that made him want to cringe. He was not sure how much of their conversation she had overheard, but he immediately knew he had overcompensated.

"Ethan Dumas?" she asked, with a slight tilt of her head. She looked him over head to toe and then glanced at Verne before returning her gaze to him. Her expression was unreadable, frustrating for a first impression.

Ethan felt acutely aware of the brown coffee spot in the center of his shirt as he stepped forward and extended one hand, while he attempted to shield the spot with his other. "That's me, ma'am. Detective Dumas. How can I help you?"

She took hold of his hand, hers much smaller. Her skin felt like an icy shock to his system. Her face went from unreadable to a wide smile. Up close, Ethan could see she was into her fifties, if not encroaching on sixty, with visible white roots peeking through in contrast to her deep-mocha hair and delicate lines creating a spidery map across her face.

"Fiona Griffin, nice to finally meet you! I've brought you boys some freshly baked muffins. It's important to fuel your minds with breakfast." She held out the plate of muffins balanced in her other hand.

"Thank you. We don't usually get fresh goods like this, at best some grocery store muffins from the day before," Ethan said, laughing to defuse the palpable discomfort that had settled in the room. He was not in the habit of accepting baked goods from strangers. On the contrary, stranger danger was instilled in him at a young age, and his chosen profession had only emphasized the importance of healthy cynicism where strangers were concerned.

Verne did not bother with introductions; he gave her a polite smile and nod before he took the plate from her. Ethan tried to ignore Verne's rustling in the background as he released the muffins from the plastic wrap. He considered telling Verne not to eat them, but he knew it would come off as rude, so he held his tongue and hoped Verne would not be poisoned. Fiona Griffin smiled politely, but she was visibly tense.

"Was there something I could help you with?" Ethan asked, when she had not made a move to further the conversation.

"Yes, I hope so. I was told you're taking on my daughter's case, and I would have felt rude not introducing myself properly. I can't expect you to just pick up where they left off if you don't even know who you're working with." Fiona's smile had not wavered and seemed to be slowly widening with each passing minute.

"Are you connected to those?" Verne pointed at the boxes Ethan had relocated to the corner. He spoke through a mouthful of muffin, spraying crumbs all over his pants that he brushed off shamelessly.

Ethan watched her glance over and her smile momentarily slip. Her mouth puckered like she tasted something bitter, but when their eyes met, she slid back into her smile. "They'll likely contain information about Anne. She's been connected to him, despite police failing to adequately support that connection."

"Have you worked closely with the police since your daughter's disappearance?"

"Somewhat. John helped more than most."

"Detective Coppin?"

She gave him a curt nod.

"I'm sorry to say, the boxes barely beat you here this morning and we were only given the green light yesterday to reopen the cold cases." Ethan glanced sideways at Verne, who halted mid-bite to give him a sheepish shrug.

She began twisting her wedding band around her finger.

"Ms. Griffin—"

"It's missus. But please, just call me Fiona," she interrupted.

"Why don't you take a seat and tell me a little about the work Detective Coppin was doing with you?" He directed her toward the spare chair in their office. "I'd love to hear how I can help you," he added as an amicable gesture.

She nodded and smiled, this time less aggressively, with no teeth; it hardly reached her cheeks and came nowhere close to her eyes. Ethan moved the chair closer to his desk and allowed her to take a seat before he retreated to his own chair. He got situated and looked up to see her studying Verne as he devoured another muffin at a speed that would be a choking hazard for a normal person.

"Mrs. Griffin," he said to draw her attention away from Verne.

"Sorry, I just…" She did not finish her sentence. Ethan nodded, imagined the thoughts and doubts she had witnessing Verne in action. "And it's Fiona."

"Right, of course. So, you were saying, Detective Coppin was helping you investigate your daughter's disappearance."

"He was, back when Anne first went missing. And it's not that he truly stopped, but John isn't an idiot, and he didn't treat me like one either. After the conviction, it was prudent I found closure, and the other families too."

"Watt's conviction?" Ethan asked.

"Yes, Vincent Watt." She spat the name out like it left a bad taste in her mouth. Ethan sat back in his chair and waited. Experience told him it was far better to allow Fiona to dictate the conversation. He glanced in Verne's direction to see he had abandoned the muffins to focus on the conversation. He'd even retrieved a legal pad from one of the many piles on his desk and had a pen poised to take notes.

"Anne was kidnapped from Rothbury Hospital's emergency room in July of 1982. July ninth. For years, there weren't any leads until they arrested him, but nothing ever happened to him for Anne." Her voice cracked and faded out at the end as she seemed to lose the will to finish her words. Her hands and lips began to tremble. Ethan grabbed the box of tissues shoved into the far corner of the desk and aggressively set them down in front of her.

"Take your time," he added to soften the gesture.

She shook a few tissues free from the box, but only gripped them in her hand before she collected herself enough to continue.

"John, and a lot of others, believed Anne was one of his victims—one of ten children originally, but they only convicted him of three. Sometime later, it came to light three others of those ten weren't his victims." She stopped and looked at Ethan. She seemed lost in her thoughts for a bit before she picked back up. "They convicted him for the cases that had enough evidence. They didn't think his lawyers could get him out of those ones, but Anne wasn't one of those cases. They told us, my husband and me, that everything was circumstantial that connected him to Anne. He'd also denied everything, so John said that Anne's case would remain a cold case. It had been a cold case up until they tried to connect him to Anne. All he kept saying was if something did come up, then they may press charges."

Ethan could hear the hatred get heavier with every word she spoke.

"What about you, and your husband? Do you believe Watt is responsible for Anne's disappearance?" Ethan asked.

She smiled, but it was gone so quickly that he may have imagined it. "No—well, I don't." She did not say more, and it seemed like something to delve into another time.

"Did Detective Coppin regularly review Anne's case for new evidence?"

"Another decade was spent trying to find missed evidence, but they found everything they were going to find. Nothing came up to support them pressing forward." She paused, as if she expected Ethan to have something to say to that, but he only nodded once in acknowledgment. He wanted to hear what she had to say and felt the less he hindered her with questions, the more she'd talk.

His silence seemed to encourage her to continue. "After that, time was spent doing private investigation work." She smiled what seemed to be the first genuine smile of her visit. "I became quite the detective myself."

"To clarify, as far as you were made aware, no existing or new evidence was tested as forensic advancements were made?"

"I'm not sure about any of the forensics. I know work was being done, but it's a very slow process when there is little to work with. I was always afraid Anne's case would be tucked away in some basement and forgotten about."

"It's a warehouse, actually," Verne said.

Ethan had nearly forgotten he was in the office with them. He'd been uncharacteristically quiet for most of the time she spoke. Ethan took his interruption as the perfect time to wrap up their conversation. Without the chance to look over the case, he did not want to form a bias based on her view of things. He'd made that mistake before and ended up following everyone else's hunch but his own, and he'd been the one on to something of value. Now, Ethan preferred to let the evidence and facts speak for themselves.

"You've given us a lot to think about. It was nice to meet you Mrs. Gr—Fiona," he said, catching himself. "We need to properly acquaint ourselves with all the cases, but we appreciate what you've told us about Anne's."

He stood up, which drew Verne out of his chair, and then, after a few seconds of them towering over her, Fiona stood. She reached into the small black bag that hung in the crook of her left elbow and retrieved a monogrammed card along with a pen. She wrote her name, address, and phone number on the blank side of the card then held it out to Ethan expectantly. Ethan arched an eyebrow but did not make a comment as he accepted the card and slid it into his shirt pocket.

"We'll be in touch."

Ethan felt like her eyes would drill right through him if she stared much longer. She made a humming noise, her lips slightly parted on the brink of saying more, but then she clamped shut and gave them both a small nod in turn.

"Let me walk you out," Ethan offered, already moving around the desks toward the door.

"That's very sweet of you, Ethan, but I'll show myself out." She hovered for another uncomfortably silent moment, and he stood awkwardly by the door, not sure if insisting would be rude or polite at this point. She smiled at him and then at Verne before maneuvering her way out of their office.

He listened to the echo of her heels as she click-clacked down the corridor until she was through the doors and out of earshot. He shifted his attention from the empty doorway to Verne, once again seated, with his fourth muffin and a lap showered in crumbs to prove it.

"You're just the sweetest, Ethan," Verne mocked through a mouthful of muffin.

Ethan dropped into his chair with a forceful exhale, ignoring Verne, and logged into the database for the digital files. He had little grasp on what the case was beyond Fiona's synopsis and the fact Vincent Watt was infamous. He prided himself on being well versed in the cases they worked, and he felt like he was behind now.

"That was weird, right?" Verne asked, after a few minutes.

"That you ate the muffins she brought without considering the fact you'd never met the woman and didn't know her intentions for being here?"

Verne abandoned the muffin he was working his way through. "Why'd you have to go and ruin a good thing?" he mumbled, as he dumped the remaining muffins into the trash.

"And yes, that was strange," Ethan said, addressing Fiona's visit. "Can't say I've had that happen before." He knew he would need to unload that later, but for now, he wanted to focus on the cases. "Do you know if Camilleri was sending over any hard copy files, evidence, anything from the cold cases?"

Verne dragged himself to his desk and logged in. "Looks like we should expect eight boxes—maybe two per cold case. That's nothing."

"Must be insufficient evidence," Ethan said, retrieving the electronic files that would have to suffice in the meantime. There were four cold cases linked to Vincent Watt. They were now familiar with Anne Griffin's thanks to their unorthodox meet-and-greet with Fiona. Then there were the cases of Melody Dawson, Kelly McLane, and Rebecca Smith, all girls who went missing from Rothbury in the eighties.

"You know what's weird," Ethan said, staring at the victim profiles he had pulled up. "Why did a Southbury detective have material on Rothbury cases?"

Verne drummed his free hand on his desk as he clicked around on his own computer. "The Griffins live in Southbury?" he offered after a few minutes.

"None of the others did, and Anne Griffin went missing from our hospital."

Verne shrugged and leaned back from his computer. "They are only fifteen minutes west on 84. Maybe he was just invested personally. Fiona sure made it sound that way."

Ethan nodded but wrote himself a note anyway to call Detective Coppin and pinned it to the corkboard separating him and Verne. It seemed clarification was safer than assuming anything in the boxes was legally obtained for investigative purposes.

"I'm setting up the board," Verne announced. He pushed himself out of his chair and closed the short distance between himself and the whiteboard to the left of Ethan's desk. He erased the remnants of their last cold case then divided the board into five uneven groups. He scribbled, in practically illegible scratch, the last names of their victims along the tops of the groups and then Watt's name at the top of the last one. "Hit me with what we know!"

Ethan listed off the names and information from the oldest to the most recent case. Rebecca Smith was three when she was taken from her front yard while playing with her older sister June 1st, 1981. The sister gave an overly vague witness statement, which was not shocking, as she was only four, but they had no leads even when her body was found three days later in woods along the Naugatuck River, less than a mile from her home.

Anne Griffin was thirteen months old when she was taken July 9th, 1982 from Rothbury Hospital's ER while her parents slept beside her. There were no eyewitnesses. Her body was never recovered.

Kelly McLane was four when she was taken from a playground on September 8th, 1984, while in her babysitter's care. A little over a week later, her body was found just a short distance farther down the riverbank from where Rebecca Smith's remains had been discovered.

Melody Dawson was five when she was taken from Rothbury Mall, since torn down, on November 17th, 1988. Nearly six weeks passed before a dog found her remains in woods bordering Bradleyville.

An excruciatingly slow hour later, Verne had managed to fill in their board with the basic profiles, leaving minimal room to add to it later, but that was what the wall and thumbtacks were for—as the many pinholes in the drywall proved. He stepped back, clearly admiring his work, despite the spelling errors Ethan would fix later.

"We can split the review work, but you can have Griffin," Verne said and tossed the dry erase marker at his pot of pens, completely missing.

"How gracious of you." Ethan snorted but had expected as much. Verne ran from any signs of overly involved family—he once claimed he was allergic to neediness, which was also why he didn't do girlfriends, kids, or pets. "I'll take Smith as well. That way, we've just split it between older and newer cases."

"That means that stack is all you," Verne said, nodding toward where Ethan had banished the boxes. He turned to look over his shoulder at the wreck. The lid of the box on top was loose from the contents that pushed their way out. Another of the boxes was less box and more silver duct tape at this point. Its seams were all secured by tape that lifted at the edges, as if it had been at the job far too long, ready to dump its mess elsewhere.

"We'll consider those unofficial. I'll look through them over the weekend." Ethan wasn't ready to let that mess out. He wasn't sure it would even fit back in the boxes once he did.

"I could still help you sort through them now."

Ethan shook his head, returning to reading the case files on the computer. Verne made a noise, a combination of a sigh and a cough—

his tell. Ethan looked up, already arching an eyebrow in anticipation for Verne's display.

"I don't see why we shouldn't take advantage of this time to go through the boxes."

"You said you don't want to deal with the Griffin case."

"It's probably not just Griffin case material in there," Verne said. He crossed his arms over his chest, emphasizing the fact he wore shirts a size too small to make himself look more muscular.

"Our first priority is the official case documents."

Verne huffed like a child on the verge of a tantrum, but he didn't push further, which was his admittance of defeat. Ethan grabbed his bagel and ate the cold brick slathered in lukewarm cream cheese while reading through Watt's rap sheet before his final arrest.

Ethan did his best to ignore Verne's repetitive huffing combined with his overly aggressive typing. If he thought he was making a point, he was failing. All he accomplished was annoying Ethan. After resisting for over an hour, Ethan finally relented and gave him the attention he so clearly craved.

"If you hit that keyboard any harder, it will break."

"I am just so bored," Verne said, throwing his head back.

"Some people didn't learn to self-soothe, and it shows," Ethan mumbled.

Verne snapped out of his mood. He could act like a toddler when he wasn't getting his way, but nothing hurt his ego more than when Ethan called him out for it. Ethan checked the time. They'd made a good dent on their initial profiles for understanding the cases, but without the evidence in front of them, they'd hit a wall as to what they could do.

"We need to get our hands on all the boxes from the cases, not just the digitized files."

"I'll call and see how long until we get our boxes," Verne said, pouncing on the opportunity.

Ethan hid the smile that tugged at the corner of his mouth. He'd had other partners before Verne, most of whom were far better at their jobs, less prone to tantrums, and able to work independently. Still, Ethan appreciated the breaks from monotony Verne added to cold cases. He made the work more tolerable than some dull detectives who were paper-pushing pros.

"Heads up!" Verne shouted.

Ethan looked up from his monitor in time to see Verne's rubber band ball catch the edge of his coffee cup and send it flying across his desk and into his lap.

The sludgy coffee didn't get on anything important on his desk. However, his pants and shirt looked like a disaster. Verne stood up, grabbed his ball off Ethan's desk, and dropped himself back into his seat, frozen with a look of horror on his face.

"Some napkins would be nice," Ethan hissed through gritted teeth.

"Right, on it!" Verne ran out of the office, shouting down the hall to move out of his way. Never dull with him.

CHAPTER TWO

THURSDAY, OCTOBER 4TH

Ethan's headlights illuminated the last mile of his drive before he drifted into the driveway a few minutes past six. He stared at the peeling black paint on the garage door, reminded that he'd promised to repaint it this past summer. He wondered if Vanessa remembered his promise as he climbed out of his car.

He made his way to the front door on the uneven stone path that needed to be redone. He moved somewhere between a long stride and a lazy jog, tripped, and cursed under his breath at another project he probably promised to do. Through the distorted glass, he could see the shapes of the hall illuminated all the way through to the kitchen.

He let himself in, kicking his shoes off to the side and abandoning his backpack by the door. He walked down the hall to the kitchen and stopped in the doorway. Vanessa had headphones in and looked foolish dancing in silence with her eyes closed. After a minute, she opened her eyes and screamed. She yanked out her headphones, hand over her heart.

"Jesus!"

"Sadly, just me," he said, dodging her playful swat. "What smells so good?"

"It's chicken pot pie, but since you almost gave me a heart attack, I don't feel like sharing."

Ethan feigned hurt. "You're going to deny me my own mother's recipe?"

Vanessa laughed. "You wouldn't even have that if you weren't such a procrastinator! You'd have thrown all the boxes out without even opening them. You're lucky I insisted on sorting through it all."

Ethan threw his hands up in defeat. Vanessa wrapped her arms around him under his suit jacket, resting her head on his chest. He hugged her back, resting his head on top of hers. He was lucky he'd had Vanessa there when he decided, after a decade of keeping his parent's belongings in storage, to go through them. They died shortly before his twentieth birthday, and at the time, the easiest thing was to lock all their belongings away and pretend they didn't exist.

"You smell like coffee."

"Jay," he said, as she pulled away for the timer.

"You can't blame him for everything."

"Oh no, this was definitely his fault."

She snorted in response. She had a soft spot for Verne. Every now and then, she would insist Ethan invite him for dinner, and reminded Ethan he was young and still making a name for himself. She reminded him often to be patient, even when Verne had frayed Ethan's nerves.

"How was work?" He shed his suit jacket and tossed it on the back of a chair in the kitchen nook.

"Really good! Didn't have to send any kids to the office, and no one said anything that made me concerned for the future of our world."

"Your expectations get alarmingly lower by the year."

"Yeah, because yours are so much better." Vanessa carried the pie over to the table. "How was your day?"

Ethan laughed, thinking it over before he could even say anything. "Well, we got new cases, but they're all related to the same guy, and I can already tell it's going to be a headache. A mom of one of the victims showed up first thing this morning. Verne and I had barely even looked at what the cold cases were, and she's in there giving us muffins—"

"Did you bring me one?"

His phone vibrated, drawing his attention to the rapid-fire texts he was receiving. He fished it out of his pocket and saw Verne had texted him.

> got the msg that boxes arrived at r office

> want 2 go back in

> i dont have plans so we can start 2nite

> slumber party 👯

>> We'll wait until tomorrow

> boo 👎

>> Some of us have a life. You should try it.

> thats offensive 2 my singlehood

"Everything okay?" Vanessa asked, drawing Ethan's attention from his phone.

He smiled sheepishly and put his phone face down on the table. "Sorry, it was Verne about the cases."

Vanessa arched an eyebrow but didn't comment. She preferred the table to be a phone-free spot, but she never commented when a work text or call came in that he couldn't ignore.

"I told him it could wait until tomorrow. Sorry, I'm all yours for tonight. What were we talking about?" he asked, shoveling a forkful of pie into his mouth.

"Muffins."

"Oh right. Verne threw them away after I pointed out he shouldn't accept food from random people when he doesn't even know why they're at the station."

"What a jerk."

Ethan smiled, always amused at Vanessa's PG language. She refused to swear in case she was to slip up in front of her students. Ethan pointed out by that age most of them had probably heard it on TV or at home, but that would not sway her away from "jerk" and "gosh darn it."

"Okay, continue on with your original story since we've established you hate Jay and me."

"I do not hate either of you. I'm just, apparently, the only one with common sense."

"Sure you are."

He gave her a vague summary of meeting Fiona Griffin and avoided any details about Watt. Vanessa could handle some of the crimes he worked, but, like any normal person, she couldn't stomach the gruesome cases. Especially the ones that involved kids. It had taken Ethan over a decade to be able to read the cases without feeling like he was going to throw up every time. Even now, if he was caught off guard by it, there was still a chance his last meal could come up.

After dinner, they spent the evening with reruns of '90s sitcoms on the TV while Vanessa graded essays and Ethan worked on a crossword puzzle on his phone. He tried not to focus too much on the cases and only googled Rebecca Smith's case before he caught himself and stopped. By the time he climbed in bed, he was itching to get his hands on the case boxes.

CHAPTER THREE

FRIDAY, OCTOBER 5TH

First thing Friday morning, they were a disorganized mess in their office, mainly thanks to Verne acting like a child on Christmas morning. He insisted on looking into every box first.

Verne happily announced Melody Dawson's case had decent physical evidence as he rummaged through one of the boxes he had on his desk. The way they had split the cases seemed to be working out more and more in Verne's favor the further they dove.

Ethan had unwisely chosen to crouch down to look through the boxes, surrounding himself with Verne's mess to the point that trying to move was too risky. His toes had gone numb a little while ago anyway, so there was no point. He had balanced a file from the Kelly McLane case on his thighs. The babysitter's statement was essentially worthless. Whatever she had been doing, it clearly wasn't her job. The eyewitnesses at the park had been more aware of Kelly McLane, not that it meant much. No one had seen her leave, and more importantly, no one had seen anyone there that stood out to them.

"Witness statements," Ethan said. He flipped the file closed and stuck an orange sticky note to the front. He had come up with a system for them to quickly identify what may or may not work for them. Verne was enthusiastically slapping green sticky notes on the evidence bags from Melody Dawson's case. Ethan hoped he was sticking to their guidelines, green meaning "most likely to solve the case." All Ethan had managed to place was orange, which was their makeshift red for "probably useless," and that would require following up as best they could.

Ethan pivoted to his left and popped open the box on Anne Griffin's case from storage. The physical evidence was meager—the blanket Anne had been wrapped in, the ER sign-in log from the day prior and the day of her kidnapping, and more that wouldn't provide anything testable. He skipped over it to retrieve one of the files.

"Crack the cases?" Camilleri asked, as he pushed open their office door, almost knocking Ethan on his ass.

Ethan grunted in response, forced to move from his spot and face the leg-tingling consequences of his poor positioning. Verne set down his green sticky notes to entertain the captain.

"We're making progress already. There's some evidence in here that could close cases up like that," he said, snapping his fingers to emphasize his point.

Ethan moved out of the mess he'd made around himself and sat down at his desk, not adding to Verne's validation of Camilleri's desire for every cold case—a speedy, preferably cheap, solve.

"I'm sure I don't have to tell you boys the stakes here," Camilleri warned, perching himself on the corner of Verne's desk. Verne pulled a face behind Camilleri's back as he glanced from Ethan to Camilleri's butt, now planted on top of several of his case files.

"Watt is a big name—the media love a big name." Camilleri kept talking, not waiting for either of them to acknowledge him. "And I don't want to go into too much detail, but Mayor Chippley himself pushed these ones through. He had a rather generous donation during his last campaign, and their only request were these cold cases get reviewed."

"Promising," Ethan mumbled under his breath, studying the cracking rubber trim on his desk.

"What was that?" Camilleri asked.

Ethan looked up, playing dumb, and shrugged like he hadn't said anything.

Camilleri didn't press him, still trying to make his point. "If this is going to go sideways, I want you two to be quick and quiet about it, so it can be forgotten. And if we solve it," he said, pushing himself off Verne's desk, "then there may be promotions for all of us."

"You don't have to worry about us," Verne said, working to unbend one of the files Camilleri had sat on. Camilleri smiled and smacked Verne's shoulder. He had almost made it out of their office when he turned back to look at the mess of boxes. "You two should sort this out. Looks like mishandled evidence waiting to happen."

Ethan waited a few seconds so it wouldn't seem aggressive, and then closed the door firmly behind Camilleri. "Remember when he said we didn't have the budget to digitize every file from all the cold cases?" Ethan said, returning to his desk instead of the pile of boxes.

"We'll be fine. It's like we're old-time detectives, going through all the paperwork," Verne said, lifting the Griffin box onto his desk.

"It concerns me you think that is an old-time detective thing."

"You know what I mean."

Ethan didn't, but he wasn't about to get into it with Verne. He pulled up the contact information for Southbury. He had decided yesterday that he should reach out to Coppin on the off chance he could tell them more than what was in the files. Ethan hadn't touched the boxes he'd dropped off yet, but if Coppin could save him a little time by summarizing what he should be looking for in them, then Ethan would take it. There was always the chance, too, he may have some additional insight to help solve these cases quickly like Camilleri wanted.

He picked up his desk phone and dialed Southbury, signaling at Verne to shut up with a zipper motion across his lips. After a few rings, he was connected to the reception desk, answered by someone who sounded inconvenienced to be doing their job.

"Good afternoon, this is Detective Dumas over at Rothbury PD. I'm looking to get in touch with Detective Coppin—"

"Yeah, one sec." Ethan was cut off before he could explain he knew he was retired but needed contact information. Three minutes and forty-two seconds later, the phone clicked as he was taken off hold. "He retired."

"I'm aware. I was calling for his contact information."

"He doesn't have a desk here anymore because he's retired."

Ethan ran his free hand over his mouth and tried to ignore Verne giggling. He could obviously hear the conversation. "Like I said, I know he retired. I just need a phone number I can reach him at, like a personal cell or landline. Even just a home address?"

"He has a home phone number on file."

He scribbled down the number and mumbled a half-assed thanks before hanging up.

"Don't," he said, before Verne had a chance to poke fun. He dialed Coppin's number, refusing to look at Verne in case he was pulling faces.

The phone rang until the message machine kicked in. An overly chirpy and high-pitched voice practically sang out, "You have reached the Coppin residence. We're sorry to have missed you, but we'll get back to you in a jiffy!" The robotic voice came on after instructing him to leave his name and phone number.

He left his office extension and his cell phone number, reiterating several times the importance that Coppin got back to him as soon as he was home, potentially a little too aggressively, as he heard his voice rising. He set the receiver back in the cradle and took a deep breath before he finally looked across at Verne.

"I've started making a list of evidence I'm going to send out for testing next week," Verne said, clearly thrilled with himself. Ethan was just glad he was helping with the cases. It could have been like the armed robbery that had left two dead they'd worked on five months earlier. Ethan essentially did the entire investigation by himself, and when he'd confronted Verne about it, he'd said it was for the best because Ethan just did it so well.

"That's great. Hopefully, by then, I'll have something from Smith and Griffin too," he said, as he grabbed Anne Griffin's box from the floor. From the depths of the bottom drawer of his desk, he pulled out a fresh yellow legal pad. With a file from Anne's case flipped open on his desk, despite this being one of the ones that was digitized, he copied the basic profile for himself.

Victim: Anne Griffin born on June 13th, 1981, kidnapped July 9th, 1982 from Rothbury Hospital. Cold case as of August 24th, 1992. Parents: Gregory and Fiona Griffin present at time of kidnapping. No body recovered to date.

Flipping a few pages in, he did the same with a file from Rebecca Smith's case, giving himself the basics to have when he was working at home. He already had contact information for Anne Griffin's family, and it didn't seem like he was going to have to do much chasing to get ahold of Fiona Griffin. When it came to Rebecca Smith's family, it wasn't going to be so easy. Both parents were dead—nothing dramatic, it seemed; both had died of natural causes only a few years earlier. Her sister, the one who had witnessed the kidnapping, had a last known address from eleven years ago in Colorado, so Ethan wouldn't hold his breath on getting much out of her.

He read through the entirety of Rebecca Smith's file, shaking his head as he read about the complete misses for evidence collection. It was the early eighties, and the science wasn't there for detectives the way it was now, but still, it was like Rothbury had never dealt with a murder. They had essentially collected nothing from the crime scene, preserved nothing. The crime scene photographs made him want to smack his head against his desk. He could see one of the detectives smoking mere feet from Rebecca Smith's tarped body.

Flipping another case closed, he decided to switch gears, hopefully to something more promising. He flipped to another page on his notepad and began creating a list of everyone he could find referenced in reports, witness statements, evidence, and questions. He combed through Rebecca Smith's files first, from the beginning. If there was any information to help him track them down, he added it next to their name, as well as their relevance to the case. Rebecca Smith's sister was the best witness they could have for this, but she was just a little kid herself when she saw her sister get taken. He'd feel safe wagering, without needing a fancy psychology degree, that the trauma she experienced likely made her forget most, if not all, of that day. Still, he added a little star next to her name.

"You started on your people to stalk lists yet?" Verne asked, as Ethan closed the last file from Rebecca Smith again.

"Just finished Smith's. I'm about to start on Griffin's, and then I'll start seeing who is still around to talk to," Ethan said, ignoring Verne's antics. Half the time, he didn't even notice the weird things that came out of Verne's mouth anymore unless someone else, who wasn't used to Verne, was around and mentioned it.

Putting away the files from Rebecca Smith's case, he pulled out the pathetic stack from Anne Griffin's case. He knew from logic alone that the fact a body was never found made Anne Griffin's the weakest case. While Fiona Griffin seemed to have her beliefs on the case, Ethan had his experience to tell him no body made it significantly more difficult to solve, especially decades later.

The names were far fewer to note in Anne Griffin's case. Alarmingly so, as Ethan realized there was no list of hospital employees working at the time of Anne Griffin's kidnapping. He was able to pull a few names of employees from witness statements, but not nearly enough. He flipped through all the files and swore under his breath when he realized there was also no list of patients who'd been in the hospital or, the very least, the ER, when Anne Griffin was taken.

"I don't like that look," Verne said.

"There isn't an employee list or patient list in these files. I knew Hadeon was a 'cut every corner he could' detective, but this is ridiculous." He slammed the files shut, silently cursing his old boss. Every time Ethan learned something new about him, it only reinforced his belief that he was valid in hating Hadeon during his junior years as a beat cop.

"The boxes might have something. I mean, Coppin was an officer on Griffin's case. Maybe he just misplaced some evidence and paperwork in there and forgot to put it back."

Ethan threw the boxes behind him a weary glance. He appreciated Verne's attempt to hope for the best, but he did not share the optimism.

"Even if it's in there, that raises questions as to why Coppin was taking documents from the case and not returning them." He looked back at Verne, who shrugged.

"Do you have anywhere to start at least?" Verne asked.

Ethan held up his notepad, showing him two columns: one for Rebecca Smith's case and one for Anne Griffin's. The second column was significantly shorter. Verne mirrored him to show Ethan two columns, with random doodles throughout, which were more promising than Ethan's, at least in quantity.

"Do you think Ed will approve overtime so we could come in tomorrow to work on these lists?" Verne asked, setting his notepad down.

Ethan snorted. The idea of Camilleri approving overtime was a joke. Homicide, who often enough had legitimate reasons for needing it, had to fight to get overtime approved. Even with Camilleri's emphasis on how important these cases were to him and the mayor, Ethan wouldn't hold his breath on getting overtime.

"You're right. Guess it'll be a Monday job. I think I'm calling it a night," Verne said.

Ethan picked up his cell—just past six—and figured he could wrap it up for the evening too. He could get home to Vanessa at a decent hour, not that she ever made a big fuss when he came home late. Usually, she just joked she had to figure out what to eat alone.

"You know you have court Monday, right?" Ethan asked, as he shut down his computer and tidied up his desk.

Verne swore, throwing his head back. "Barnes scares me. That was like the worst month of my career, having to work homicide with him."

Ethan tuned out Verne as he went into a self-pitying retelling of why it had been so bad for him. Ethan packed up the supplies he would need for the weekend: his notepad, a half-used stack of sticky notes, fresh files, and a handful of pens. He smiled at the thought of Vanessa commenting, "In case the hundreds we have at home couldn't do the job."

He slung his bag over his shoulder and went for the boxes from Coppin. He got himself into a slight squat, wrapped his arms around to grab the middle box's handles, and lifted with a strained groan that came from deep in his chest. He mentally chanted to himself to lift with the knees. He straightened up long enough to turn and balance the bottom of the box on his desk and let out an embarrassed exhale.

He gave himself a few seconds to regain his pride before he turned to see Verne leaning in the doorway grinning. Ethan looked down at the boxes he was balancing.

"They're full of paper."

"I bet. Plus, you're an old man," Verne said.

"Forty-two isn't old."

"You've got fourteen years on me, so I'd say that qualifies as old." Verne moved around him and grabbed the last box off the ground. "I'll get all the doors for you. Just try not to have a heart attack on the way out."

Ethan mumbled his thanks and led the way out of the office, under the weight of the boxes he carried. He did his best to control his breathing until they were loaded into his trunk. Ethan closed the hatch, and Verne stood beside him, watching the spot where the boxes had been visible.

"I'll get this all organized so we can start tracking people down come Monday."

Despite the hassle it was going to be to sort through the boxes alone, he was slightly relieved Verne had pushed it all on him. There was no action in sorting through decades of paperwork to decide what was relevant or not. He could imagine the complaints of boredom, the exasperated head tosses back from trying to focus too long. Plus, this way, he could still be at home around Vanessa, even if he worked. He didn't even mind that he wouldn't get overtime for it.

"Can I call dibs on interrogating Watt?" Verne asked, as he walked backward through the parking lot, completely oblivious to the cars.

"Watch where you're going! You're in a parking lot!"

"I'm taking that as a yes!" he shouted, as he got to his car.

CHAPTER FOUR

FRIDAY, OCTOBER 5TH

Ethan unloaded the boxes one at a time, carrying them straight through to the family room, which he had determined to be his base for the weekend. He made sure to stack them in the same order they had been stacked in the office in case there had been a purpose to their order. He would wager there was not, but it at least gave him a sense of where to start.

Vanessa pulled in beside his car as he jogged out for the last box. He waved before he hauled the last box out, balanced it on his leg to close the trunk, and then headed inside. As he rounded the corner to the family room too fast, he caught his knuckles on the door frame. He dropped the last box in place and pressed his knuckles to his mouth.

"Shit, that hurt," he mumbled to himself as she walked in.

She held grocery bags in the crook of one elbow and her school bag in the other. Ethan watched her eyes comb over the three boxes he had placed next to the coffee table, which he needed to move out of his way for a clear work area.

"For the new cases?" she asked, as she headed for the kitchen without waiting for his answer. He heard the rustling of the plastic bags in the kitchen.

He joined her as she unloaded the bags and helped to put the items away. They managed to move around one another somewhat gracefully with minimal hip checks. He balanced two towers of cans as he moved to the pantry. "Yeah, the ones I mentioned yesterday. I figured you'd have some grading to do, and Verne wasn't going to enjoy sorting through it, so I'm just going to go through it this weekend."

"I'm glad you don't have to spend your weekend stuck in the office."

She walked over to where he was and wrapped her arms around his neck, giving him a long kiss. She pulled away and slid past him to where she had dropped her school bag and unloaded her work onto the counter.

He was itching to get started on the boxes, despite his own pessimism that he would find nothing useful, but he forced himself to linger at the counter. He asked her how her day went and listened with a smile to her recall her students' alarming lack of U.S. history knowledge. He even held his tongue this time on his thoughts on the education system.

While talking, she pulled off one of the dozen takeout menus held in place by a magnet, whose advertisement for a fertility specialist was peeling off. A few times now, the magnet had failed, scattering the menus across the floor. He was pretty sure the menu for his favorite sushi house was still under the fridge from the last time it failed.

"I'm feeling pizza," she said, waving the paper menu in front of her face. After almost five years of ordering from the same restaurant, they had rarely wavered from their large meatlover pizza with garlic knot crust. The few times they had strayed from their usual, they agreed it was the wrong choice.

"The usual?" she asked, as she pulled out her phone, already dialing their number.

"Obviously." He grinned and pushed himself away from the counter and headed to their room to change. He needed to be in sweatpants for pizza and case work.

* * *

Ethan sat on the floor in the family room, the coffee table relocated to the kitchen to give him more room to spread out. Vanessa had grumbled, while helping him move the table, that she hadn't realized his work required an interior designer.

His empty plate was balanced on the arm of the couch behind him, and the pizza was now out of reach in the kitchen. He would probably eat a few cold slices before bed, once he was willing to traverse his mess.

Vanessa had been warned that by positioning herself in the family room with him, she was trapped. She agreed, though, and was in her armchair with a stack of tests. Tests she forgot to grade for an entire month, she'd explained while waving a slice of pizza around. Ethan had been more captivated by the pizza, which he expected to go flying out of her hand, than her defense of her lapse in grading.

He had created a semi-circle around himself in his efforts to organize what he pulled out of the first box. In a rapidly growing pile to his left were sticky notes. The sheer amount had made him decide to tackle those later. The pile did not include the ones he found stuck to documents and stuffed between the well-handled legal pad pages. He left those in their place.

He separated out the copies of reports, notepads, and other loose papers into a stack to read through later. He was left with a pile of browned newspaper clippings that crunched like leaves if he handled them too roughly. Some were carefully cut out around specific articles, while other times the entire page was saved, folded and unfolded enough that it had produced little holes and tears along the creases.

One of the full sheets was from May of '97, a piece on the fifth-year anniversary of Watt's trial beginning. There was a copy of a courtroom sketch accompanying the article that depicted a very angular and slouched Watt being pointed at by a crying Fiona Griffin.

Ethan flipped over the sheet to find a piece highlighting a local high school softball team's state championship win. He skimmed the highlights of the game and then looked at the team photograph with a caption listing the names of the players. Halfway through the list, a single name popped out, Vanessa Ashby. He looked back at the photograph of the team, though all their faces looked about the same thanks to the newsprint quality. Right in the middle of the second row he found sixteen-year-old Vanessa, beaming with her crooked smile, her arms around her teammates.

"Ness, look at this!" Ethan said, leaning precariously over his stacks to half toss her the article. "I found a piece about your high school softball team."

Vanessa put aside her tests and pulled a face as she picked up the dried newspaper. She flipped to the side about her school, and after a few seconds of frowning at it, her face broke out in a smile much like the one in the photograph.

"Wow, this seems like a lifetime ago." She ran her finger carefully along the photograph, studying her old teammates' faces. "Not to brag, but the softball team hasn't won state since," she said, looking at him.

Ethan smiled, not surprised that she would know that. "You didn't get your team there your last year?" he asked, with a teasing wink, which earned him an eyeroll and a failed attempt to throw the article back at him.

"Why is that even in there? I thought you said those boxes were for your cases?"

Ethan picked it up and carefully placed it back on the pile before pulling out a smaller clipping whose title caught his eye.

"It's on the back of an article about one of the cases," he mumbled, already distracted.

In bold capitals, the words "WHAT ABOUT THE OTHERS?" filled the top of the clipping. The article was an interview with Fiona Griffin and Tracey Pennington, the mother of Travis Pennington, a year after Watt's sentencing. Travis Pennington had been murdered, and police had erroneously accused Watt of his murder. Tracey Pennington hadn't held back, quoted saying, "I believe the detectives took the easiest way out of dealing with a serious issue in their towns. They found one man sick enough to hurt children and decided, instead of finding the others, they'd just blame him for everything and move on."

Tracey Pennington had been right. There had been three male victims at the time, and all three boys' murders were solved; none were remotely linked to Watt. It had seemed far-fetched to believe Watt would have targeted male and female victims, and the MO for their cases weren't even comparable to Watt's—he and Verne had glanced through them yesterday. Ethan wasn't surprised though. The crime scene photographs from Rebecca Smith's case seemed to have set the tone for the entire investigation. He tossed the clipping back into the pile.

"What was that one?" Vanessa asked. He looked over to see she hadn't resumed grading; instead, she watched him with her head slightly cocked to the side.

"An interview with some of the moms," he said, picking up a chunk of the reports to flip through.

"And what are those?" Vanessa followed up and pointed at the stack of sticky notes. She climbed out of her chair, moving with carefully placed steps in-between the mess he had created to reach a clear spot beside him. She dropped onto the floor with her legs crossed under her and helped herself to a handful of them.

"They're notes," Ethan answered, offering no further clarity. He resisted the urge to tell her not to touch anything. It was too late anyway, since she was already shuffling through what she'd taken.

"These make no sense. Like this one, 'voice in sleep,' or this one that says, 'where,' with lots of underlining. There is more underlining on this than ever acceptable." She held up the note she was referring to, which Ethan agreed had an excessive amount.

"What are these cases again?" She had put back the ones she had first grabbed and helped herself to another handful.

"There are four cases, but Verne and I split the load. I've got an unsolved murder from eighty-one and a missing persons case from eighty-two. But most of this box so far has just been about the missing person—baby."

He thumbed through the paperwork, finding the copy of the original Griffin police file he'd spotted while unloading. He wasn't sure why

Coppin had had a copy of it, but it was helpful to have since he hadn't brought the actual case files home. He freed it and slapped it down on the top of the pile.

"What new evidence came up to reopen them all?"

Ethan looked over at her, thrown off by the question, despite her asking it every time he told her he got a new cold case. He was like her personal *Dateline*; that was what she told him on their second date when he had been rambling on about cases. He had been nervous and then realized mid-dinner he was telling this teacher, in far too much detail, about murders he had solved. She'd had a look of horror and disbelief that had halted him in the middle of a story. When he'd apologized, she'd started laughing, which had made him panic, until Vanessa had said, "I could sit here all night with you as my personal *Dateline*." She knew working cold cases didn't thrill him like homicide, but she tried to ask the questions that would at least bring out the excitement in it all. Even when most of the time his answer was vague and boiled down to science and money.

"Politics and money." He spared her the details Camilleri had given him and Verne on the media and attention it could bring.

"Anyone I would know about?"

"You wouldn't know him."

"Try me."

"No."

Vanessa's eyebrows arched, but she didn't say anything. He felt a pang of guilt for his tone, but it was necessary. She would look up his name and get upset when she read the details he knew would be out there. Sometimes, she seemed to understand his work so well, but it was cases like these that reminded him that she had not signed up to live with this stuff. Yes, she married him knowing he was a detective, but he couldn't always unload case stress on her. He had seen and read too much that would give her nightmares and make her feel unsafe. It didn't bother him until he had to censor himself around her. He felt cruel for putting up a wall between them, but he had to remind himself it was for her own peace of mind.

He forced himself to refocus and continue to get his bearings in the cases. It wasn't the first time he investigated cold cases where he wasn't confident in the original case work. Most of the time, the detectives did everything they could with the resources they had available. Then there were the cases like these, where Ethan had to be concerned if corners were cut, especially when the detectives who worked them had been trying to throw all child-related cases from the eighties at Watt. The guy deserved to rot in jail, but if there were others out there he was taking the fall for, Ethan wanted to see them locked up too.

He flipped through the Anne Griffin case to a photocopy of Gregory Griffin's handwritten statement given at Rothbury's station a few hours after Anne was taken.

> *Fiona, Anne, and I arrived at the Rothbury Hospital emergency room at around 10:50pm on July 8th. Anne is extremely sick and has a reoccurring ear infection. We were seen shortly after midnight on July 9th and led into a curtained section of the emergency room. We were told we would be seen shortly, but over an hour went by and we were still waiting. Anne had cried herself to sleep. I had had a long day in court and Fiona had been taking care of Anne all day. We both fell asleep when Anne did, in chairs on either side of the bed she was on. Fiona woke up first, around 1:45am, and started running around shouting Anne's name, which woke me up. Anne was no longer on the bed. We began searching for her and a nurse joined in who had come over when Fiona started yelling. We searched for about 10 minutes, and during that time, another nurse called 911. I was running around to the different desks and stations I saw, but none of the staff saw anything. No one remembered seeing Anne leave the emergency room with someone. By this point, police arrived.*

The statement bore Gregory Griffin's signature along with Coppin's as the officer witness to his statement. Ethan added it to a file he'd started to collect anything worth separating from the boxes. He knew the statement was back in his office, but it was good to have an extra copy for his own file.

It didn't say anything controversial or contradictory to Ethan's understanding of the case and was hardly indicative of Gregory being anything but the victim's father. Still, it was worth referencing during a conversation with him in case there were any changes in his story after a few decades.

The rest of the stack he put aside, recognizing most of it from the digitized files and what was sent over from storage. He let out a body-slouching sigh as he looked at the mess he'd made with just one box and the few scraps of paper he'd deemed worth setting aside from it.

"Oh, wouldn't this be twisty?" Vanessa held up a sticky note in front of her face.

His eyes took a moment to adjust to read the sticky note only a few inches from his own face, the words "psych ward escapee" written in a very neat print in the center of the note. He plucked it from Vanessa's hand to move it farther from his face. It was just another theory, one he imagined fell through like the others that Fiona posed to Coppin. It was one of her more imaginative theories so far.

"The mother has a lot of ideas about what happened to her daughter. Pretty much anything other than what detectives believed," Ethan said, before tossing the sticky note back into the pile with the rest.

"I could always just google this missing girl's name. I bet the case information would come up." Vanessa stood up and not at all gracefully jumped from her spot on the floor next to him to her chair, scattering her stack of tests all over the floor. She pulled a face somewhere between a grimace and a sheepish smile as she leaned down to collect them as they crept into Ethan's mess.

"I don't advise that," Ethan said.

"Picking up the tests?"

"You know what I meant."

"I'm a curious creature, what can I say?" she said with a shrug once she had secured the tests.

"This is one of those times I need you to just trust me. You don't want to read whatever details have managed to find their way to the Internet."

He knew he couldn't stop her if she decided to; Vanessa could be obnoxiously stubborn once she had set her mind to something. She didn't push her case further though. When Ethan looked over at her sometime later, she had resumed her curled-up grading position, completely oblivious to the world around her.

* * *

By Sunday evening, Ethan had added to his list of names, sometimes with contact information that was probably outdated. His hands were covered in paper cuts, his battle wounds for making it through the disaster. Still, Ethan had made it through all three boxes, and he was pleased with himself.

The second box, he'd had little luck. He found typed transcripts of at least three dozen interviews pertaining to Anne Griffin's and Melody Dawson's disappearances. They were not official police interviews, so they would be nearly useless in a trial, but it gave him and Verne some potential leads. Other than those, nothing else out of the three boxes mentioned any of the girls other than Anne. Fiona had led him to believe she and Coppin had done more work than that to investigate the other cases, but nothing else in the boxes suggested as much.

While there was still no sign of the originals, there had been copies of the Rothbury Emergency room visitor logs for July 8th and 9th, 1982, but they weren't nearly as helpful as he'd hoped. Someone had spent a lot of time annotating them. They had been marked up in pen, which was mostly illegible scrawl next to names. What he could make out seemed to be notes on the people. Most of the names had also been redacted, he assumed eliminated from their suspicions. For his own endeavor of tracking down people at the hospital at the time, the log was nearly useless. Even trying to hold it up to the light, the copy was such poor quality and the redactions so dark, he couldn't make out any of the names blacked out. Two dozen or so names not blacked out did stand out, for different reasons. One was the last admitted patient on July 8th, Anthony Watt. Ethan recalled the name during his and Verne's board making, but a quick google search confirmed he was Vincent Watt's father.

The second was Vanessa Ashby. It had sent a chill down his back spotting her name in the box again. There were no notes around her name, like a few other names who also hadn't been blacked out or annotated. It seemed logical from the other notes and blacked-out names that whoever had marked it up had just deemed her unworthy of looking into. He decided it was just a weird coincidence, so he hadn't mentioned it to Vanessa. Ethan knew it would only fuel her desire to look up the cases more, and he was not going to feed into that behavior. He set it aside with the items he deemed worth showing Verne.

While Ethan had spent the weekend unloading his mess, Vanessa had sat in her chair or, occasionally, on the floor when she dragged herself into his mess to offer moral support. He'd had to be careful to ensure she didn't go through anything other than the sticky notes in case there were gruesome details. She hadn't questioned why, and he was grateful it hadn't needed to be explained.

Dinner was the only complete break Ethan took from the cases all weekend—mainly because Vanessa pointed out getting food over potential case-breaking information might be an inconvenience later. The dinner table was also the "no case zone," as designated by Vanessa during their dating years when Ethan had talked about a homicide and her dinner almost came back up. He hadn't thought it was that bad, but after that dinner, he'd learned not to tell her anything in detail.

They stabbed at the takeout salads Vanessa had picked up, their forks making dull thuds against the bottom of the containers.

"Do these kinds of cases scare you?" Vanessa asked, breaking their monotonous chewing. "Like, when you think about our kids one day, do you worry more because you really know people who would want to hurt them?"

"I worry, but I don't think I've ever worked a case so high stakes that we'd be a target. It's not like I'd be handing out our address or telling criminals I have a kid."

This wasn't the first time they'd had this conversation, or a variation of it. If Vanessa knew he was working a case involving kids, she would ask how it affected his fears for the kids they didn't have yet. He would be foolish to not worry, but he didn't lose sleep over it. It was a future problem he would have to consider, and even then, he believed he could handle it. He knew how to protect his family.

"What if you really pissed someone off and then they googled you and then they came after us?"

"No one is going to do that."

"You don't know that."

He reached out and put his hand on top of her free one. "Luckily for you, you're married to a detective who will avenge you and our family if anything were to happen. I already know what I'd tell those assholes: 'I will find you and I will kill you.'" He quoted Liam Neeson's *Taken* line, pretending to be on the phone, cracking himself up as he did. He pulled back in time to avoid the swat.

"You're not funny."

"I love you," he said, grinning.

"Stay here," she instructed as she got up from the table, her salad only half eaten. She headed for their room and then a minute later came back out with her hands behind her back. "Close your eyes."

Ethan gave her a wary look, trying to decide if she was about to get back at him for his joke. "Don't go hitting me because I've got my eyes closed."

"Ethan! Just close your eyes!"

He gave her one last warning look before he did as he was told, and only flinched slightly when she leaned over his shoulder to set something down in front of him.

"Okay, open."

She had set a small red gift box in front of him, finished off with one of those peel-and-stick plastic gold bows. It wasn't their anniversary and, as far as he could remember, there weren't any significant days in October.

"It's not a bomb, you can open it," she said, pushing it closer as she sat back down across from him.

She was beaming, so he figured it must just be a surprise. He pulled the box closer and popped off the lid, tilting it toward him to look inside.

"Surprise!" Vanessa shouted like she had just given him a million-dollar scratch ticket.

He didn't know how long he sat there staring into the box. It felt like an hour as his mind raced. They had been here before, a few times now, and even though he knew he should be excited, he couldn't help the fear that gripped at his stomach. When it clicked in his mind that he needed to react in some way other than staring at it, he pulled her into a hug so she wouldn't see the tears welling up in his eyes. There was a part of him, a part he resented in this moment, that wanted to say they shouldn't get their hopes up yet, but he remained silent. He hated that they knew the pain that could follow the euphoria of two pink lines appearing on a pregnancy test and that there was nothing he could do to prevent it.

CHAPTER FIVE

MONDAY, OCTOBER 8TH

Ethan's knee twitched under his desk, desperate to shake the anxiety that had had a grip on him since Vanessa's pregnancy announcement. He held eye contact with Rick Barnes, a Rothbury homicide detective. Barnes and Verne had a court appearance today, and as usual, Verne had not arrived early as Barnes instructed. Ethan felt he should be entertaining him, but he'd learned from his days in homicide and an excruciating five-hour car ride, silence was better with Barnes.

Verne arrived seventeen minutes late, fumbling with his tie. Verne got it into a poorly shaped knot after a few more seconds, fighting it in the middle of their office.

"You got plans for the case?" Verne asked.

"Yes, I'm going to pay Fiona Griffin a visit, and then call the hospital after."

"Cool," he said, fighting his tie again.

"We need to go," Barnes said, making a point of looking at his watch before leaving their office.

As soon as Barnes was out of sight, Ethan motioned Verne over. "Come here."

Verne huffed but was wise enough to step forward as Ethan stood up. He yanked loose the knot Verne had only managed to worsen and quickly retied it for him. It wasn't Ethan's best work, but he wasn't used to tying ties on other people, and he wasn't about to stand behind Verne to give himself a more natural angle.

"He's a ray of sunshine," Verne whispered.

"You were late. Okay, done. I'll give you an update later, or tomorrow if I don't see you after court."

"He's overreacting a bit; we've still got nearly two hours. The stick is just a little too far up there," Verne said, tugging at the tie a little.

"Verne," Ethan said sternly.

"Right. Let me know how it goes. And thanks for this." Verne motioned to the tie.

Ethan waved him away. Barnes might just murder him if he had to wait any longer.

Ethan leaned back in his desk chair, building up the energy to leave. He'd decided after going through the boxes that the Griffins would be his first stop. He had a few things he wanted to ask. He'd done his best to put a list of questions together and organize his thoughts last night, but he hadn't been able to focus after dinner. To make it worse, he'd spent most of last night worrying about Vanessa and the baby and not nearly enough time sleeping.

He didn't have time to ponder his chance of being a dad, again. He looked around his desk, deciding what he needed to bring with him. He picked up the legal pad he'd taken notes on for the cases thus far and a pen, scribbling on the corner of the page to make sure it worked. He ran through his list of questions, preparing himself for the potential derailing a strong personality like Fiona could pose.

Ethan left the office door unlocked. He knew Verne wouldn't have thought to bring his keys with him to get in after court. He waited for the elevator, hoping to get caught up in conversation and distract him from the baby stress weighing on him. For the three floors down, he stood alone in the elevator, listening to the faint efforts of the machinery.

* * *

The Cape Cod-style homes lined the street in two orderly rows, bundled together in suburb style, with only minute variation in shades of blues and grays to give the faint impression of individuality.

Ethan crossed the street onto the crumbling sidewalk hugged by the Griffins' white picket fence. It broke only for an opening onto a thoughtfully laid stone walkway. The stones were laid for someone with a much smaller stride, and he found himself taking stunted steps to attempt to remain on the path. He stopped trying halfway up and walked beside it in the grass.

Ethan took the two stairs in one step and rang the doorbell. He listened to the echo of hard-soled shoes on hardwood as they approached, gauging if they were Fiona or Gregory Griffin's. He decided they were too soft to be the latter's and was proven right when the door swung back, kept from nailing the wall by Fiona's slender fingers gripping its edge.

She smiled; her cheeks pushed her eyes up into a squint. Ethan held her gaze, expecting some reaction from his unannounced visit. She didn't seem surprised, as she stepped aside and beckoned him in with a swoop of her arm.

"How was your weekend, Ethan?" she asked, with her back to him.

She didn't give him instructions on shoes, but he kicked them off anyway. His mom would roll over in her grave if he wore shoes in someone's house, even if Fiona had hers on. He stayed a few steps behind as she led him down a narrow photo-lined hall.

"Good, thank you," he answered, distracted by the photographs.

Every photograph included Anne Griffin, making none older than 1982. He stopped to examine them as she kept on down the hall. A chubby-cheeked Anne, with her toothy grin, was captured in one. Her arms spread wide toward the camera and her green eyes still bright, despite the decades that had otherwise aged the photograph. Verne probably would have likened it to a shrine and said so in front of her, which made Ethan thankful he wasn't here. He stopped to study a couple more photographs but realized she'd abandoned him in the hall, so he continued into the kitchen.

"I hope I'm not inconveniencing you."

"Not at all! I appreciate you coming over. I know this side of Southbury isn't a quick stop by from your station." She ushered him toward a table set for three, nestled up to a bay window overlooking the Griffins' backyard. She watched him choose one of the three chairs and then moved to the counter, putting together two cups of coffee. "If I had known you were stopping by, I'd have asked Greg to be here, though he likely has something more important to keep him at work," she said, the last part with bite to her tone. "And I'd have made more muffins! Sugar, milk?" she asked, a heaping spoonful of sugar already hovering over one of the mugs.

"I'll just take mine black—please."

She gave him a thin-lipped smile and moved the sugar spoon back to the canister.

Ethan looked away from her to the window ledge lined with more photographs. These ones were only of Fiona and who he assumed was Gregory Griffin. As time progressed through the photographs, the only thing that seemed to change was his wavy hair and Tom Selleck-worthy mustache, which had gone from a deep black to a dark gray that only enhanced the broody look he sported in all of them.

"We traveled a lot for the first decade after," she said from beside him as she placed one of the steaming mugs in front of him. She took a seat to his right and picked up one of the frames in the front. "This was Prague."

She handed the frame to Ethan, and he accepted it, not knowing what else to do. He nodded, wondering if he knew where Prague was. It sounded like a place people threw out there to sound wealthy. He stared at the photograph for what he felt was an appropriate amount of time and then set it down on the table facing her.

"I was not as fond of traveling. I think it helped him to act like nothing had happened to us."

"It is not uncommon for parents to grieve differently."

He thought of Vanessa and how she rarely talked about the pregnancies she'd lost so far. He tip-toed around the topic with her, but she never wanted to have a conversation about it. It was always worse, too, when she was pregnant again. He could only imagine the weight it put on her when he struggled so much.

"And he didn't do anything. I've seen and read a lot. I know the husbands and fathers are considered suspects." She took a sip of her coffee, staring Ethan down over the rim of her mug.

"I'm not here to accuse your husband of anything. Right now, we are looking into potential suspects, as well as reinvestigating the links to Vincent Watt."

The corners of her mouth turned down at the mention of Watt. She had already made her opinion known to them, that she did not believe him responsible for her daughter's disappearance. Going through the boxes this weekend, he had seen theories of who could be responsible, but they were just that. Nothing in the case files or boxes from Coppin gave a solid lead in a direction other than Watt.

"I do have questions about your work with Detective Coppin." Ethan backed away from the subject of Watt for now. He didn't want to push her walls up before he had a chance to ask more of his questions. "I tried to contact him, but he's not getting back to me, so I hoped you could give me some insight for now."

"What is it you'd like to know?" She took a long sip of her coffee.

"When we spoke last week, you mentioned you two were doing private investigative work, of sorts. I went through those boxes, and while I found a lot of potential leads..." Ethan chose his words carefully. "I didn't see much beyond Anne's case and a bit on another of the cold cases. Do you know if Detective Coppin kept additional records elsewhere?"

She seemed to ponder the question before offering him a slight shrug. "I would have assumed they'd be kept with the material on Anne. Not that there was much to keep. I don't want to give you the impression there is case-solving material you're missing."

Ethan would have liked to see it for himself to decide, but he couldn't imagine Coppin would have sat so long on anything that would close any of the cases. He jotted a little note on the margin of the empty page to contact Coppin, again, for potential missing boxes.

"Are you continuing to follow the assumption that Watt took Anne?"

He looked up from his note. He had mentally prepared himself for this question. It was not unusual for the families to be frustrated, even if the detectives' only way to diverge would be pulling new leads out of thin air. Still, they had been on the case for less than a week. Hardly enough time for him to decide whether there were other leads worth following.

"Given the short duration we have been investigating, we have to work with what is there until we can gather more information. It can be difficult to determine new leads after so long, especially given the unusual circumstances surrounding the reopening of these cases."

Ethan didn't need to say more about Mayor Chippley's generous campaign donation. Fiona might be accustomed to hiding her emotions, but Ethan was trained to read people like that. Her understanding of his implications was crystal clear.

She held eye contact over the rim of her mug and let out a small sigh when she'd set it back on the table. "I do hope you are open to investigating other avenues."

"Verne and I are always thorough. I do not believe in cutting corners." He kept his tone even, reminding himself her words weren't an accusation—just a mother who wanted justice for her daughter.

Fiona held his gaze a little longer in silence before she nodded, seemingly satisfied with his proclamation.

"Why don't you believe Watt is responsible?"

"I'd say mother's intuition, but I learned long ago that wasn't enough for your lot."

Ethan arched his eyebrows, reminding himself of Vanessa, but didn't interrupt.

"The detectives didn't do their jobs. They never followed up with everyone at the hospital that night. They ignored my attempts to help in the case, they ignored my recollection of events! One detective had the audacity to tell me my hysteria was a hindrance and to leave the case details to Greg. My husband, who handled this all by pretending nothing was wrong and working whenever he could." She stopped talking for a moment, but Ethan stayed silent. She kept going after she collected herself. "They hadn't paid him any mind for years, even though they knew he'd been at the hospital—hadn't questioned him, hadn't questioned his father. Nothing. Then they get him for his other cases— and don't get me wrong, I'm happy they locked him up—but that was it for Anne. She got lumped in because they figured if he'd committed his horrible acts before she went missing and after she went missing, then he must be responsible for her too."

She paused long enough to take another sip of coffee. Ethan had abandoned his pen on his notepad and leaned back in the chair. The less he hindered her, the greater chance she might say something he could work with. And she had a lot to say.

"As I mentioned before, they did that with other cases. I'm not just a grief-stricken mother coming up with delusional scenarios. They tried to pin him for three other cases that ended up being unrelated. Ryan Kearney, Liam Perez, and Travis Pennington. Not a single connection to Watt. Not even a connection to one another! But they had to wait longer to get justice because detectives decided the crimes seemed connected enough."

Ethan recognized Travis Pennington's name. He recalled finding the clipping of the newspaper interview that Travis's mother had done alongside Fiona. Neither had held back about their feelings on the investigation, and Fiona's stance had not wavered since.

"I understand the original investigative team dismissed you, but didn't Coppin follow up on any of your potential—leads?" He refrained from using the word "ideas." He saw the slightest twitch at the corner of her mouth and suspected they had been referred to in less flattering terms over the years.

"Reopening the cases wasn't an option. Jurisdiction and such, but he tried looking into some of them for me. He just never had the right leverage. Too much time had passed, not enough people wanting to talk about a night that they hardly remembered so many years later. I—we kept running into the same wall. Everyone who did remember the case remembered Watt going down for it, so they tainted their own memories. One nurse even tried to say she saw Watt take Anne out of the hospital," she huffed at the end.

"And that wasn't possible?"

"No. I looked into it myself. She wasn't even working in the emergency room that night."

Ethan made a note to check if any of the names on his list were hospital staff, just in case the hospital took a while getting an employee list over to him. While he was sure Fiona had a point, time and hindsight often tainted a witness's recollection, it could still help them to see if any staff could fill in the gaps of what happened that night.

"What other leads did you have?"

She perked up a little at this question. "I believe it may have been a staff member or potentially a patient at the hospital." She stopped speaking, but her eyes begged him to ask the next question.

"Why is that?"

"I know it's speculative and that I was sleeping, which is my biggest regret in life, that I let myself fall asleep when Anne had stopped crying." Her silence filled the kitchen, and Ethan didn't know if he should let her have her moment or urge her on. Fortunately, she snapped herself back to reality and kept going like she hadn't stopped. "I remember a woman's voice, she was cooing. I remember it even now; it was as if I was aware of her in my sleep, but I was so exhausted it didn't disturb me enough to wake up properly. If it had been a strange man, I would have woken up, I'm sure. And Anne, I think, had started crying, but I was exhausted from her having been sick and in pain and crying so much the days before. The woman made her stop. Greg told me I just dreamed it when I told him after the detectives dismissed me."

She turned to face the window over her yard. She didn't sob or choke up as the tears came. At the right angle, the light danced on the surface of her tears, making it look for a moment as though she had jewels trailing down her cheeks.

Ethan reached out a hesitant hand, gently touching her arm. "If there is anything there, I will find what they missed originally."

He stayed in that position for a few seconds before he pulled back. He wasn't confident there was much there to use as a lead, but he would keep it in mind. If more evidence pointed in that direction, her recollection could give support to considering it.

She remained staring out the window as she dabbed under her eyes with the backs of her hands. Ethan had more questions, but he didn't want to push her to the point she wouldn't be able to talk through her tears. The last thing he wanted was to distress her more about her daughter's disappearance. She seemed to have spent almost four decades doing that on her own.

"I know people think it's crazy I'm still pushing Anne's case." She stared past him, down the hall. Her hand moved up to her chest where a gold "A" hung inches from her heart. "She is alive. Greg thinks I'm deluded for believing that—he's told me as much. I've had people tell me I'm wasting my time, to let her go, that it's been decades now and it's unhealthy. But it's just something I know." She snapped out of her daze and dropped her hand into her lap. "It's hard to be completely alone fighting for Anne."

He nodded along, but he didn't know what else to tell her, and he would not give her false hope. He pitied her. He picked up his pen and scribbled another note to go through witness statements again, as well as hunt down an original copy of the ER sign-in sheets.

"I do have a few more things I'd like to ask you about, if you're up for it," Ethan said.

She wiped at her eyes again and flashed him an uncomfortably forced smile. "I am. I want to help anyway I can."

"Your statement, well, lack thereof, on file. Mr. Griffin gave his statement on the morning Anne was taken, but I didn't see one on file or even in Coppin's copies of the file. Were you never asked to give a statement?"

"I was never asked to give a written one, like Greg, or have my statement taken officially. Detective Hadeon—he's the one who locked in on Watt and decided it was him or no one—Hadeon spoke to me once about my recollection of events, but that was it." She smirked a little, which Ethan found unnerving. "He didn't like me. I overheard him once ask Greg if I was always a handful. Which, of course, is an awful thing to say about a person whose baby was taken, but he didn't seem to think much about me."

"He was an awful person."

Ethan didn't see the point in holding back about him now. He knew it was poor form to speak ill of the dead, but anyone who genuinely knew Hadeon wouldn't have had many nice things to say if they were being honest. The best Ethan came up with at his funeral was he had an impressive tie collection. His widow hadn't taken much comfort in that though.

"Amazing how someone like him stayed a detective for so long. I would look him up from time to time to see what else he was working on, check he wasn't poorly investigating other cases. I was honestly shocked when I read he was made captain."

Ethan held back from expressing his shared surprise when he had found out. The number of internal investigations into him should have shut down the captain track for Hadeon. Apparently, the right amount of dirt on your superiors will get people far. He took a sip of his lukewarm coffee and then attempted to pull the conversation back on track.

"Did Coppin ever take a written statement from you? Even if it was late to be done?"

"When it came up, it was decided mine essentially matched Greg's statement."

"Did it?"

"I suppose it captured the bigger picture."

"What did it leave out?"

"My leads."

He understood why Coppin may not have taken her statement. A statement full of ideas wasn't much use when they needed facts. "Since you've given me your leads to work with, we can probably skip going over the statement again for now."

"Of course, but I'm happy to give it whenever you'd like."

"I would like a chance to speak with your husband. Do you have ideas for when's a good time to catch him?"

"Let me get you one of his cards, that way you can try and catch him at his office. Really, that's your only chance of speaking to him. He's rarely awake if he's at home."

Ethan noted the matter-of-factness in her tone. He hoped he and Vanessa never got to that point. It seemed pointless to still be together if the relationship sizzled to nothing but housemates.

She disappeared through a doorway off the hall he hadn't paid much mind to earlier, and then a minute later reappeared holding out a business card for him. He thanked her. Gregory Griffin's office was in Hartford, about forty minutes or so north of Rothbury. He figured a guy like him, based on what Fiona had said, would require an appointment and not take kindly to a drop-by visit. He tucked it into the breast pocket of his suit for later.

"His secretary can be a difficult one, but you're a detective, so she can't brush you off too easily."

"Noted," Ethan said with a small smile. He stood slowly, his entire body a little stiff from the wooden chair. He grabbed his notepad. "If you think of anything, you know where to find me."

Her lips parted and a small noise came out, but then she stopped, as if she had changed her mind. She pressed her lips together and smiled at him, like she had at the station. She rose from her seat, and they stood there for a moment before he turned to leave.

She caught up his empty hand and gave it a squeeze. "Thank you for working to find Anne."

Her face broke into a wide smile, and for the first time, her smile made it to her eyes.

Ethan didn't know quite what to say, so he gave her a small nod to dismiss himself as he gently pulled his hand free. He showed himself out with her clicking down the hall behind him. He walked beside the stone path on the way out, making it all the way to his car across the street before he looked back over his shoulder. Fiona's face was faintly visible in the window.

CHAPTER SIX

MONDAY, OCTOBER 8TH

Verne was at his desk when Ethan got back from Southbury. Based on the tie dumped on the floor by Verne's feet, the two likely empty Red Bull cans, and the Cheeto fingers Verne held up in the air while typing one handed, Ethan guessed he'd been back in the office for a little while already.

"How was court?" Ethan asked, rounding the desks to take his own seat facing Verne.

"Bullshit. We got there, and then, after an hour of waiting, the lawyer came out and told us they worked out a plea deal and we didn't need to testify anymore. I put on a tie for nothing." He popped another bunch of Cheetos into his mouth, shaking his head as he crunched obnoxiously.

Ethan flipped to the page in his notepad where he'd made his few notes while speaking with Fiona Griffin.

"How's Mrs. Griffin? She try to feed you poisonous muffins again?" Verne asked.

"I never said they were poisonous. I said you shouldn't just take food from strangers. Your dad was a cop. Surely, he taught you stranger danger," Ethan said, as he pulled up his phone contacts to find the Rothbury Hospital's records department number he had saved from a previous case.

"Dad probably missed that one when he was too busy helping my mom give me child of divorce trauma."

Ethan rolled his eyes, used to Verne's child of divorce card. It's also why he was self-proclaimed terrible at sharing, could not commit to a woman, and hated trains after too many trips commuting from Rothbury to Queens, where his mom had moved back after the divorce.

Ethan dialed the records department number, scrolling through admin emails while the obnoxious static music blared through the desk phone speaker.

"Rothbury Hospital Records. How can I help you?" The voice broke through the music abruptly. Before Ethan could form the first syllable, she impatiently repeated herself.

"Hi, yes. I'm Detective Dumas from Rothbury PD. I'm calling for documents in relation to a case I'm working."

There was a distinct pop of chewing gum through the speaker. "I cannot release patient medical files because HIPAA protects—"

"Excuse me, sorry. I don't need medical files. I need a list of hospital staff for two specific dates, and a list of all patients in the hospital for the same two days."

"You'll need a warrant for patient names."

Ethan rubbed the bridge of his nose. He'd expected as much but had hoped he could avoid the headache of more paperwork and mind-numbing red tape. "Yeah, no problem. I'll get the patient names later. However, I'll still need the staff records."

"That's a different department. I'll transfer you."

He held back the sarcastic comment on the tip of his tongue. "That would be great, thank you."

Before the words were completely out of his mouth, the obnoxious hold music had returned. He remained on hold for nearly twenty minutes, as he continued through emails and forwarded as many as he could to others to deal with.

"Thank you for holding, this is Jonathan. How may I help you?"

Ethan felt the tension in his shoulders relax. The gentleman on the line was already more friendly than the oh-so-helpful records department. "Yes, hi, this is Detective Dumas from Rothbury PD. I was transferred from records. I'm looking for a concise list of hospital staff from two specific dates for an investigation I'm working."

"Of course, I'll do my best to help as far as I'm able and get you the information you need. However, we do pride ourselves on both patient and employee safety and security, so may I have your identification number so I can confirm with Rothbury PD?"

"Absolutely," Ethan said, before he recited the information. The music returned, and he leaned back in his chair, wishing Verne had taken the Griffin case instead. Of course, Verne was sitting across from him going through his list of names to contact and finding out most of them were dead, so it seemed they were both having slow starts. Still, this was one of the tedious parts of the job that gave him a glimpse into why some detectives cut corners simply to avoid the amount of time wasted waiting on tiny scraps of information that might be useless anyway.

"I apologize for the wait and appreciate your patience, Detective Dumas. Now that's taken care of, let's get down to business," Jonathan said, after the music cut off again.

"Not a problem. Are you ready for the two dates I'm looking for?"

"Yes, go ahead."

"July 8th and 9th, 1982."

"Oh, I'm so sorry Detective, but that won't be possible."

Ethan rested his forehead on his desk for a moment before answering. "May I ask why?"

"Well, you see, back in 2000, we converted exclusively to digital records. We digitized some of our old records; however, we only went back to 1985—"

"If it's a matter of searching through paper records, I can send an officer."

"Unfortunately, that wouldn't help. All the records prior to 1985 were stored in the hospital's basement. In 2011, the basement suffered major flooding and, I'm afraid, all the records stored down there were destroyed." Jonathan at least sounded apologetic, which he figured was more than he would have got from the record's department.

"Can I assume the patients in the hospital those two days were also lost in the flood?" Ethan asked, half expecting to be told he wasn't allowed that information.

"Yes, we would not have a complete record of patients in the hospital those days."

Ethan finally lifted his head up from the desk. "Well, I appreciate your help."

Before Jonathan could say anything else, Ethan pressed the phone back into the cradle and ended the call. So much for tracking down witnesses from the hospital. This was exactly why poor police work made cold cases even more difficult. Nearly an hour wasted for nothing.

The one glimmer of hope he had to hold onto right now was the copy of the ER log he found in the boxes yesterday, which had to have been made from the original. Maybe Coppin had the original somewhere else. He could hope at least.

"No luck then?" Verne asked, his sharpie squealing as he dragged it across another name.

"I could ask you the same."

"Problem with old cases involving kind of old people. They go and die before I can ask them about it." Verne capped the sharpie and held up his list to show Ethan. A quick count and Verne was left with less than a dozen names.

"That's really it? Everyone else is dead?"

Verne nodded and tossed the notepad on his desk. Ethan flipped back to his own list, which he hadn't started going through yet. If his success rates were anything like Verne's, he'd be lucky to even have that many people left to talk to about the cases.

"I'm going to try calling Coppin again," Ethan announced, flipping the notepad back to the first page. He tried the number that he'd gotten from Southbury PD, but it went to voicemail. He left another message, doing his best not to sound rude but emphasize the urgency in needing him to call back.

"Did you find something in the boxes?" Verne asked. He'd seemingly checked out for the time being and was playing with his rubber band ball while lounging back in his desk chair.

Ethan pulled out the folders he'd brought back from his research this weekend. The boxes were still in his trunk, but he'd worry about unloading those later. He pulled out the copy of the ER log, which for now was the main document he was concerned about. Given the lack of witnesses and any documentation of who was there in general, it was the best piece of information he had for Anne Griffin's case for now.

"This was in the boxes, and there was no original in the case files from records or in the boxes Coppin sent over." Ethan handed the pages over their desks.

Verne leaned forward and took it. He flipped through them, his eyebrows conveying a flurry of emotions before settling on what Ethan imagined was surprise.

"Vanessa Ashby—isn't that our Vanessa?"

Ethan ignored the proclaimed our; Verne had inserted himself like a grown child into their lives, and Vanessa would probably be flattered Verne considered her one of his people. "Yeah, it's wild, right? We might end up having to talk to my in-laws as potential witnesses. If we do, I'll have you lead that. Howard doesn't like me as it is."

Verne continued to read through the log, turning the pages sideways now and then, likely to see the margin notes. Ethan had tried reading some of them when he found it, but a lot of the writing had either faded with time or was so condensed it was hard to make out.

"Safe to guess this guy is related to Watt?" Verne held up the log and pointed out Anthony Watt's name.

"Yeah, his father. It's why they stuck Vincent Watt with the crime. He was at the hospital to pick up his father from the ER around the same window of time Anne Griffin was last seen."

"So, they had an original at some point?"

"I mean, that's a copy and was in the boxes from Coppin, so yeah, at some point from July 9th, 1982 to now, the original disappeared."

"And why couldn't the hospital help with the records?" Verne asked, when he handed back the pages to Ethan.

Ethan tucked them back away in the folder he'd brought them to the office in, adding it to the organizer on his desk. He knew that as far as evidence went, it wouldn't be admissible to show in court without the original. Any lawyer would argue it could be fake, even if the original case was built around the fact Anthony Watt was in the ER that night. Without the evidence and documentation to show that, it was hearsay now.

"They lost everything prior to 1985 in a flood a few years back. So, all I have to go off is the marked-up sign-in log and whatever witness information and statements the original detectives and officers bothered to take." Like other cold cases they'd managed to close, he had to remind himself investigative work was done differently in the past—even if differently just meant wrong.

"It's fine," he said, as he flipped the notepad back to his list of witnesses and individuals connected to Rebecca Smith's and Anne Griffin's cases. "I'll just focus on what I do have. Hopefully, Coppin will be able to help when he gets back to me."

Verne grunted in response, mimicking Ethan's actions and returning to his own lists. Ethan spent the next few hours across from Verne as they worked through their lists. Verne was slightly ahead in progress, having already looked up who was still alive before he called. Ethan checked who was alive as he went, and they both made it through their lists.

After several hours straight, an ache in his neck from poor posture, and a growling stomach because he'd worked straight through lunch, Ethan called it a day. He stood up, prompting Verne to look up from his work.

"Are we done?"

"I am, but—" Before Ethan could finish, Verne stood up too.

"Perfect. My brain was starting to hurt a little anyway." Verne grabbed his tie off the floor and shoved it in his desk drawer.

"Tomorrow morning, I'll fill you in on my talk with Mrs. Griffin." Ethan grabbed his phone only. The case material could wait to be continued tomorrow.

They walked out to the parking lot, Ethan reminding Verne to send the evidence for testing sooner rather than later. It would likely take months for them to get results, and Camilleri was still excited for this case to be solved and would approve the expenses, so they needed to take advantage of it while they could.

Once in the car, Ethan remembered the boxes in the trunk he meant to bring inside the office today. He considered for a moment carrying them back in, but decided it wasn't worth the extra time right now. He'd already collected anything of significance from them anyway. The rest was random scraps of memories and baseless theories.

CHAPTER SEVEN

TUESDAY, OCTOBER 9TH

Verne shot rubber bands off his pointer finger across their office, hitting the wall behind Ethan. Ethan barely flinched; after two years of exposure to Verne, he was nearly immune.

"How seriously are we considering the possibility of anyone other than Watt? All the original investigations considered everyone else just persons of interest, at best, since there was never overlap."

"That's assuming all four are connected." Ethan scrolled through emails, killing time until four thirty. They had come in to see a calendar invite from Camilleri for a meeting in his office for a progress update. They'd spent the morning into the afternoon calling people from their lists, returning missed calls to set up meetings with families and other people involved in the original case. In between calls, Verne had also started paperwork to get the forensic testing done.

"Aren't they?" Verne asked, putting the rubber band ball balanced back on top of the mug Ethan had gotten him last Christmas that read, "World's Okayest Partner."

"The responsible, and reasonable, thing for us to do is be open-minded to the possibility they may not be. The original investigators previously tried to pin Watt for other cases that were all unrelated to Watt and each other. If there is evidence suggesting someone other than Watt as a prime suspect, even just in one case, then we will investigate that lead. However," Ethan said, before Verne could cut him off, "I know we can't go chasing after phantom leads. If we continue to review the case and things don't seem to be adding up, then I will consider the possibility Mrs. Griffin's suspicions are correct."

"She didn't bribe you too, did she?" Verne asked, winking at him.

"You think I'd be drinking this if she had?" Ethan motioned at his third sludgy coffee from the break room.

He suffered through the cheap stuff so Vanessa could enjoy her expensive local café coffee each morning. He had of course considered the option of just brewing some at home each morning, but he'd have to carve an extra five minutes out of his sleep to get up and make it.

"Let's just hope every family we speak to isn't convinced someone other than Watt did it. One criminal, four cases, is one thing. Four criminals with a case each is a whole other headache," Verne said, as he checked his watch, a digital one made to look like a designer analog watch. He sighed before standing up.

Ethan followed suit. It was time to face whatever judgment Camilleri had in store for them. They'd only had the cases for six days, two of which were the weekend. While Ethan had worked on the boxes during that time, according to timesheets, they'd only had four days to work on it so far. It didn't bode well for them if Camilleri was going to check on them this frequently.

"Keep this short and sweet," Ethan instructed as they walked down the corridor, frequently stopped by Verne's need to say hello to everyone. It was like trying to walk with an untrained golden retriever.

Camilleri was on the phone when they arrived, but he waved for them to take a seat before turning his back to them in his chair. It only took Ethan a minute of listening to realize he was on the phone with Mayor Chippley. Verne hadn't seemed to notice, too enthralled with a game on his phone. Ethan's leg started bouncing as he listened to Camilleri reassuring the other end of the line that his detectives were quickly chasing leads and finding evidence that could break open the cases. He had his back to them as he spoke, so at least he couldn't see Ethan's reaction to him lying through his teeth.

When he hung up the phone, he spun around to face them. "What've you got for me boys?" he asked, rubbing his hands together like a fly about to dig into a pile of crap.

"Testable evidence," Verne answered, holding up his handwritten list he'd made this morning.

"That's it?" Camilleri asked, his smile disappearing.

Probably shouldn't have been so overzealous with the mayor, Ethan thought. He considered offering up that they'd begun arranging meetings with family members, but since that hadn't resulted in anything yet, it didn't seem pertinent.

"Fiona Griffin, the mom of one of the vics, doesn't believe Watt is responsible, and she's done some P.I. kind of thing and thinks there are other leads that weren't followed," Verne blurted after the three sat in a weird silence.

Ethan shifted in his seat a little, glancing over at Verne, who seemed to be purposefully avoiding eye contact. Short and sweet had apparently gone over his head, because mentioning Fiona's ideas didn't fit into Ethan's definition.

"That's absurd," Camilleri scoffed. "Since when do we let civilians do the investigating? Your focus should be finding more than just some evidence to test, not wasting the department's time and money."

"No, sir. She disclosed this during the family meeting we are doing with each of the victims' families. I have not put any weight into it. Just something she offered in passing," Ethan jumped in, trying to smother it before Camilleri made a big deal of it.

"Good. I meant it when I said this needs to be wrapped up as soon as possible if there is nothing to be done."

"Understood," Verne said, and Ethan stood up, wanting to take advantage of an exit point. He didn't wait for Camilleri to say he was done and headed out, Verne on his heels. They made it out of earshot, and Verne exhaled.

"I really thought he was going to like that we had evidence to test."

"He likes when we solve cases. Anything before that, we haven't done our jobs yet," Ethan said, deciding to let the Griffin thing go for now. No point getting upset with Verne for sharing information about the case, even if he wouldn't have shared it himself.

"The evidence isn't going to be quick, even if he's pushing us."

"No, but he was a detective before. He knows how it goes. He just has someone breathing down his neck, so he's going to breathe down ours."

Ethan gave a defeated shrug and swung their office door open before he headed for his desk, where the list of people related to the cases sat open. He dropped into his chair and decided to let Camilleri and his pressure go for now. He didn't have the energy or focus to care about that right now. He'd worked under Camilleri, first in homicide, now in cold cases. Long enough to know, even if he was doing well, he'd still get the same reaction from him. There was no point in losing sleep or time over it.

The blinking red light on his desk phone caught his attention at the same time Verne's desk chair tipped backward, Verne in it, with a rattling thud. Ethan stood up and looked at Verne over their desks, who, despite being sprawled out on the floor tangled in his desk chair, was still trying to see into the hall.

"Do I want to know?" Ethan asked, not making a move to help Verne up.

Verne rolled himself out of his tipped-over chair before he scrambled up and brushed himself off.

"I saw Dani talking to someone, and I was just trying to see who it was because she was laughing."

Ethan rolled his eyes and dropped back into his own chair. Ethan never asked, but still knew a lot about Verne's dating life. Verne was mildly obsessed with Dani, a uniformed officer in homicide, although he tried to play it cool around her. As a result, when Dani happened to walk by their door, Verne turned into a creep.

"Maybe I should go talk to her," Verne said, his head still stuck out into the hall.

"Please do." Ethan picked up the receiver to listen to the voicemail on his desk phone.

"Really?" Verne asked, oblivious to the fact Ethan had moved on from whatever romantic drama Verne was creating for himself.

Ethan watched Verne brush himself off before not so casually strolling into the hall after Dani. He was mentally coming up with a way to tease him about this later when the message started playing.

"This is Sarah Ferges, um well, Sarah Smith, returning a call for Detective Dumas. I... I wanted to thank you for taking the time to reinvestigate Rebecca's case, but I don't want to be a part of the investigation again. I don't want to sound like an awful person, uh but I'm her only family left and I don't even remember her. I can't remember anything from that day, and I spent years in therapy trying for my parents. So... please just don't call again. Thank you."

Ethan put the receiver back down. Well, there went the one eyewitness for Rebecca Smith's case. He knew it was a long shot given that Sarah Smith—now Sarah Ferges, he noted, adjusting her name on his list—was four when Rebecca had been taken from their front yard. Even back then, she'd only been able to give a vague description and said it was a man who took Rebecca. It wasn't unusual for a witness to block out traumatic events they witnessed, let alone for a four-year-old child to do so, but he'd still hoped naively he might get lucky with Sarah.

He flipped the notepad closed and checked the time, not wanting to be late to dinner with Vanessa and his in-laws. She was telling them she was pregnant tonight. He'd done well to not think about it all day, but now, he could feel the growing ball of nerves in his stomach, worrying how they'd react in case they said the wrong thing or brought up past pregnancies. He tidied up his desk for the day and headed out, leaving the office door unlocked for Verne, after he was done looking like a fool for a woman.

CHAPTER EIGHT

TUESDAY, OCTOBER 9TH

Ethan carried the dishes from the island to their dinner table, doing his best to avoid joining in on the conversation with Vanessa and his in-laws. Vanessa was set on telling her parents about the baby tonight. She acted like it was now or never. Ethan didn't think it was the right time, in part because he feared she might miscarry again. Even more so, he didn't want her parents reminding her she might lose this one too.

Having delayed joining them as long as possible, Ethan took a seat beside Vanessa, who was listening to her mom's one-person debate on her and Howard's next vacation destination. "The giraffe hotel is a unique experience. Imagine waking up and having a giraffe right at your window! But the Moroccan resort is quite the experience itself. The richest of the rich have been said to stay nearby at this ridiculously lavish resort—but Howie and I don't need that crazy of a trip."

Nor could you two afford it, Ethan thought as he passed the bowl of vegetables to Vanessa. She winked at him, and he knew she was going to go for it. He braced himself, more than willing and ready to kick his in-laws out if they weren't wise enough to keep their negative thoughts to themselves.

"Mom," Vanessa said, interrupting Lisa's comparison of the two resorts she was still rambling about.

Lisa blinked, as if broken from a trance. "What? What's wrong?" she asked, reaching across the table with her hands.

"Nothing is wrong," she said hesitantly as she reached to grab Ethan's hand, which had been holding his fork. She knocked it from his hand onto his plate and splattered him with gravy. "We're expecting!"

Lisa smiled but pulled her hand back from the table. Howard, who was busy eyeing the gravy on Ethan's shirt as if he hadn't just seen how it got there, made a throaty noise into the rim of his glass. Ethan felt Vanessa's grip tighten a little on his hand.

"We're excited!" Ethan said, determined to channel Verne's upbeat energy no matter the circumstance. He could see Lisa resist the urge to look at Howard. He imagined they wondered if he and Vanessa were genuinely excited. A small part of him wondered the same thing. He suspected his enthusiasm wasn't entirely convincing.

"Let's toast! Water for you, Ness." He raised his glass and waited for the other three to join him. "To the newest Dumas," he said, making a point of tapping his glass with everyone. He grinned long enough that Lisa's and Howard's smiles didn't look like he was holding them at gunpoint, just knifepoint.

He felt slightly guilty for it, but the rest of the dinner he monopolized the conversation, interrogating Lisa on safaris, giraffe hotels, and Moroccan spas. If Vanessa did break through his questioning, he made it a point of not letting the conversation get onto her pregnancy or babies. Her parents had already come close to disappointing her tonight, and he wasn't going to let them succeed.

The same relief he felt after a successful interrogation flooded his body as he shut the door behind Lisa and Howard, securing the lock and ensuring they couldn't spring back on them. He leaned his forehead against the front door and gave himself a few seconds. It was mentally exhausting talking to Lisa for that long during the best of circumstances, but to do so while trying to eat, keep Howard from saying something rude or insensitive, and surreptitiously prevent Vanessa from bringing up a topic that might evoke the wrong response; he felt like he'd just run a marathon.

"You didn't have to do that," Vanessa said, drawing his attention from the door to where she leaned against the kitchen doorframe.

"I don't know what you're talking about." He pretended to be fiddling with his work backpack, despite the fact she had clearly seen him leaning on the door.

She closed the distance between them, pushing her arms under his and wrapping herself around his torso. "I love you," she mumbled into his chest.

He gave up the act and wrapped his arms around her shoulders and rested his head on top of hers. He wanted to offer her comfort, tell her to ignore her parents, that they were just worried and they'd get over it. His own fear caught the words in his throat. It wasn't just that she could lose the baby. Her strength in adverse situations always amazed him. He knew she would handle it as she had every single time before, with poise and grace. Ethan, though unwilling to ever voice it, was almost as terrified that the baby would survive. How was he going to protect their baby if he had to be out working on cases to lock one guy up when there were a dozen more just like him that he hadn't caught yet?

Vanessa pulled away, trying to stifle a yawn. Despite the fact she wasn't showing yet, she already stood with her arms around her middle, as if to protect the baby. Ethan fought the urge to pull her back in.

"You head to bed. I'll finish cleaning up and be in right after you," he said, turning her away from the kitchen toward their room. She gave him a sleepy smile, clearly more exhausted than she was letting on. He watched her disappear into their room before double-checking the door was securely locked. He finished cleaning up from dinner, wiped down the counters and table, and switched off lights as he made his way from the kitchen to their room. He checked the front door again, just in case. Never knew who would try to get in.

CHAPTER NINE

FRIDAY, OCTOBER 12TH

Ethan spun his car keys around his finger as he waited outside the restroom for Verne first thing Friday morning. They had a lot of driving ahead of them today, as they were visiting victims' families all over the state, and Verne hated having to use public bathrooms he hadn't previously vetted as clean enough. Still, he accommodated Verne's behavior otherwise he'd have to listen to Verne complaining about his full bladder while refusing to let Ethan stop so he could do something about it.

They were meeting with Melody Dawson's mother first. Based on how she handled the phone call with Verne to set it up, Ethan was worried it might be too much for her, but they needed to be thorough.

They had attempted to set up meetings with all the families. Along with Melody's mother, Kelly McLane's father agreed to speak with them too. He hadn't had luck with Rebecca Smith's only surviving family, Sarah, who'd left the voicemail. For now, he'd respect her wishes, but if he had questions later on, he ultimately would have to call her. While he'd love to take her word that she remembered nothing and leave it at that, if he had a specific question about the day, Camilleri wouldn't take kindly to him saying, "Well, Sarah said she remembers nothing."

"Okay, I'm ready," Verne said, as he came out of the bathroom.

"You've got toilet paper stuck to your shoe," Ethan said, turning and heading for the exit to the parking lot. He couldn't help the faint smile as Verne swore and made a little gagging noise at having to touch the toilet paper.

* * *

The drive to Mrs. Dawson's retirement home in Bethel took a little under an hour. During the drive, Verne reviewed Melody Dawson's case again. While the original detectives weren't even close to thorough with Anne Griffin's case, they had at least been bothered to check out Vincent Watt's connection to Melody Dawson enough to know he worked on the janitorial staff at the mall Melody was taken from. Of course, they didn't include whether he was working the day Melody was taken. They left that piece of information for them to work out, which Verne was finding near impossible.

On top of not finding out, no employer contact information was taken and the mall had since been torn down and replaced with luxury condominiums, which weren't remotely luxurious in Ethan's opinion. Verne had added tracking down the mall management company, hoping they still had records, to his growing list of things to do.

When they arrived at the retirement home, a staff member led the way to Mrs. Dawson's room. She'd told the front desk to expect them. Ethan resisted the urge to shiver as he passed an open door and saw an elderly man staring blankly at the empty wall in front of him. Ethan didn't want to think about getting to that point in life.

Verne leaned close, away from the staff member. "I think I'd rather take myself out than end up in here."

Ethan eyed their guide to make sure he hadn't heard before turning to Verne and nodding in agreement. He ignored the thought that popped into his mind, that he'd never see his parents grow old.

Their guide stopped in front of an already open door, knocking as he motioned them forward. "Got two detectives here to see you, Betsy."

Betsy Dawson, a frail-looking woman who relied heavily on her walker to close the distance from her bed to the door, held out a shaking hand. Ethan barely touched her in fear of hurting her, and Verne followed suit with the lightest touch of her hand.

"Would you like me to close the door for some privacy?" Verne asked, hovering near it with a hand already out.

"Oh yes. Marjorie next door is a terrible gossip. She'll probably have the whole place believing I've gone and killed someone before you two have even left." She started laughing at herself before it turned into a lung-rattling cough that had Ethan concerned if he should call for assistance.

Verne closed the door, but the look on his face told Ethan he may have been having the same thought. Verne leaned himself against the wall by the door, the room too small for much more than a bed, nightstand, dresser, armoire, and well-worn armchair.

Mrs. Dawson had positioned herself on the edge of her bed, so Ethan helped himself to the armchair. He tried to hide the momentary alarm that he was sure crossed his face when he sat down and felt like he was about to fall through. He settled for balancing himself on the edge of the seat.

"We appreciate you taking the time to see us. You spoke with Detective Verne here on the phone. I'm Detective Dumas. As Detective Verne explained a little over the phone, we are reopening Melody's case."

Mrs. Dawson leaned toward her walker, wringing her hands. He couldn't tell if she was anxious or upset, though both reactions were understandable. Most families felt an array of emotions when a cold case was reopened, even when it was something they wanted.

"We want to give you an opportunity to ask any questions you may have and for you to hopefully help us by answering some questions we have."

"Have you found something new?" Her voice came out hushed, yet firm.

Verne answered. "We think that forensic advancements might help us nail whoever did this."

Mrs. Dawson didn't look at either of them. Her head was bowed, and they had a clear view of her wiry gray hair pinned up in a bun on top of her head. Ethan and Verne exchanged a quick glance. It was normal for the family to have questions, want clarification, to demand why it had taken them so long. A handful of times, they were silent like this, most likely trying to process. It made him hesitate to push his questions in case they completely shut down though.

"Do you still think Vincent Watt is responsible?" she asked, her head still bowed.

"We are investigating all persons of interest, but Vincent Watt is still a suspect." Ethan had a moment of worry that Mrs. Dawson may be of the same frame of mind as Fiona Griffin, but his answer gained a small nod from her.

She looked up to meet his eyes, tears gleamed on the verge of falling. Verne stirred behind him and came into view with a box of tissues extended toward Mrs. Dawson. She took them, muttering thanks under her breath, and buried her face into a handful.

After the sniffles had subdued, Ethan pulled out a small notepad from his breast pocket. "If it's alright, I'd like to ask you a few questions."

"Of course, I'm so sorry," she mumbled into the wadded-up tissues.

"Please don't apologize. We can't imagine how difficult this must be for you, especially after all these years," Ethan assured her.

Mrs. Dawson pulled the tissues away from her face, rubbing at her nose and making it bright red. "It is all so much at my age. Mel was my miracle baby, my sweet baby girl." She dabbed at her eyes, though the tears continued to fall. "I only had sons before her, and I had her so late—forty-seven! My Jerry, God rest his soul, and I couldn't believe it when I found out I was pregnant. We'd thought I was past my time." She blew her nose, mumbling another apology.

"If it's not too much, would you be able—" Verne was cut off as Mrs. Dawson let out a sharp sob.

She buried her face in the snot-covered tissues again. Ethan and Verne looked at each other; Verne looked slightly disgusted. Ethan hoped she'd change out her tissues before she rubbed at her eyes again. That was a case of pink eye waiting to happen.

"My poor Jerry, he never got to see justice for Mel. Our little miracle Mel," she got out between body-rattling sobs.

In between sobs, she continued to apologize, and Ethan continued to tell her there was no need. Ethan handed her fresh tissues until her sobs quieted to soft hiccups, and Ethan worked in their chance.

"I hope this isn't too difficult of a request, but do you mind telling us about the day Melody was taken?"

He knew it was a tough request given her current state, but if she remembered anything that the original detectives had not recorded, it could help their investigation.

"The mall," Mrs. Dawson said between hiccups. "We were at the mall."

She repeated herself several more times, only adding a word or two each time before the tears began again. Ethan extended a hand to touch Mrs. Dawson's. He wanted to offer some sort of comfort, but she seemed oblivious to his touch.

"Take your time." He wasn't confident she could even hear him over the noise she made.

It took several more minutes, and a declined offer from Verne to retrieve a glass of water on account of a weak bladder to calm her down to a state of talking once more.

"We know you, your husband, and Melody were at the mall when she went missing," Ethan summarized the little she had managed to tell them so far.

"Yes, yes, we were there shopping. I liked to buy Christmas presents early. Too much hustle and bustle at the mall when Christmas is around the corner. It was still busy for a Thursday night though. I remember it was a Thursday night because it was a week before Thanksgiving. Mel loved Thanksgiving because of the food. Though all she'd eat was the cranberry jelly and the green beans because she was a picky eater."

Verne coughed, then mumbled an apology. Ethan couldn't tell if it was truly an accident, but it was enough to startle Mrs. Dawson out of the Thanksgiving rabbit hole she was falling down.

"I needed to buy a gift for Mel, and I told Jerry, I said, 'Jerry, take Mel,' and I swear he said he would. I swear it, he said, 'Okay, Betsy.' But then—" Her hiccups cut her off, and Ethan feared they may never hear the end of her story if he didn't start pushing her.

"He didn't take Melody with him where he went?" Ethan asked.

Mrs. Dawson shook her head.

"Where did Jerry go when you had gone to buy her gift?"

"I—oh, I don't know. I don't remember. It was another store for something." She looked confused now and stared hard at the carpet, as if it held the answer she was looking for in its speckled pattern.

"That's alright, we can always come back to that if it comes to you. Do you remember what happened next? Did one of you go find the other?" Ethan asked. He knew what the case said. Mrs. Dawson found Mr. Dawson alone and then full-blown panic ensued.

"Well, after I bought Mel's gift, I walked out the store, and I remember I looked around because I hadn't known which store they'd gone to, but then I saw Jerry in the store across from me. He wasn't holding Mel's hand. We always made sure to hold Mel's hand. She liked to go play hide-and-seek if we let go."

"What'd your husband say when he realized you thought he had Melody?" Verne asked. "Did either of you remember when you last had her?"

Mrs. Dawson looked at Verne like he'd slapped her across the face. She went to speak a few times, and he could hear Verne shift uncomfortably.

"I—we. Oh well. I can't remember. I think it was outside the store. I think Jerry had her hand."

"If Jerry had her hand, how come you asked him to take her?" Verne pushed. Ethan was ready to tell him to stop. Mrs. Dawson's mental state was already fragile from this meeting, and he risked pushing her to silence if he didn't let up a little.

"I don't know," she whispered.

"That's okay, it's not important," Ethan interjected. "Do you remember anyone standing around you before you and Jerry parted ways? Other shoppers, or maybe someone who worked at the mall?"

Mrs. Dawson seemed to pause at this question. She looked puzzled as she stared at Ethan, and he let himself hope for a moment she did remember seeing Watt around. In her initial statement, she hadn't mentioned it, but maybe they hadn't jogged her memory. His momentary hope shattered though, as Mrs. Dawson slipped back into her guilt.

"We couldn't find her."

"It's alright. Do you recall what happened once you and Jerry realized Melody was missing?" Ethan asked, desperate not to lose her before she'd given them anything useful.

Mrs. Dawson shook her head. She wouldn't look at Ethan or Verne. Ethan urged her to take her time, but the minutes stretched on, and she couldn't come up with anything beyond the police being called. She had hit her limit. If they wanted to get anything else out of her, it would have to be another time, and after this meeting, he wasn't sure Mrs. Dawson would agree to another. He tried not to let his frustration show. He couldn't fault her for being torn up about Melody after all these years. He felt pain from losing a baby he hadn't even met yet. He couldn't bring himself to imagine how that pain amplified after knowing and loving the child for years. On top of that, the guilt she had from that day clearly lingered.

"I appreciate you taking the time to talk to us, Mrs. Dawson. We're going to do everything we can to solve Melody's case. We'll reach out if there are any developments in her case, and of course, if you think of anything, don't hesitate to give us a call."

Ethan pulled a business card from his shirt pocket and placed it on her nightstand. He stood up and followed Verne out of Mrs. Dawson's room. He shut the door gently behind him, and they retraced their steps back to the entrance. The same staff member that had showed them in was seated at the desk. Ethan stopped briefly to give him a business card as well and suggested someone check up on her soon.

"That wasn't great," Verne said, as they reached the car.

Ethan grunted in response as he put the next address on their list into the car's GPS. Ethan knew that the majority of the questions they'd prepared for Mrs. Dawson had gone unanswered. They could always circle back to her once she had time to process it all. The remainder of the questions helped to establish if Melody Dawson's family had a predictable routine her killer could have followed. Even without answers though, Ethan suspected it was random. Not unless the killer waited an entire year to kidnap Melody when Mrs. Dawson liked to do her holiday shopping. It was an accident he imagined hundreds of parents made every year, both unknowingly leaving their child unattended in the middle of a shopping center where everyone had somewhere to be. It was the perfect opportunity for someone like Vincent Watt.

Ethan made himself let go of the conversation with Mrs. Dawson for now. Next up was Kelly McLane's father, who Verne had said was pushy on the phone. He'd pestered Verne on whether his ex-wife, Kelly's mother, would also be speaking with them. Ethan had heard Verne's end of the conversation and his insistence that he could not discuss the coming and goings of Mr. McLane's ex-wife with him. After he hung up, Verne complained that he felt like he'd just relived part of his childhood growing up with divorced parents.

"I'll let you take the lead with Mr. McLane, since you two are already buddies," Ethan said, suppressing a smile at the snort Verne let out.

"Ten bucks says he's going to bitch about his ex-wife more than he's going to talk about the case."

"No thanks. I'm not in the mood for losing."

Verne snorted and pulled out his own notepad, where Ethan knew he had his own copy of the questions they were hoping to ask Mr. McLane. They'd agreed to try and get the same basics from all the family. They were aware that Watt was an opportunistic kidnapper based on the cases he was already serving life in prison for. However, if they could determine any predictable routines in the cold cases, it could help them get a clearer picture to determine if Watt was even a plausible suspect.

They knew now, at least, that Melody Dawson and Anne Griffin were crimes of opportunity.

After a two-hour drive, retracing their path past Rothbury ending up close to Hebron, Ethan pulled up in front of the address Mr. McLane had provided. He didn't bother to hide the doubt in his expression as he looked at the overgrown lawn littered with random pieces of junk. The house itself at least matched the yard, with cracked windows, missing siding, and a fraying blue tarp barely hanging on as it exposed the hole in the roof it had once covered.

"You're sure this is the address he gave you?" Ethan asked.

Verne flipped through his notebook and held up the page with a scribbled address that matched the one Ethan had plugged into the GPS.

"If I see a snake before we get to the door, I'm out," Verne said, as they climbed out of the car.

Ethan snorted, though he'd probably be right behind Verne. He could handle a body, but something about the way snakes slithered made his skin crawl. He did a quick surveillance of the neighborhood and noted that all the houses in sight had manicured lawns and exteriors that looked maintained.

"If I hadn't spoken to him recently, I'd have thought someone died in there and no one had bothered to check in months," Verne muttered as they trampled through the knee-high grass.

"Still a fair chance something might be dead in there."

They both stepped onto the rotting porch. Ethan took mindful steps so as not to go through a rotting board. Verne gave Ethan a sideways glance before knocking on the peeling front door through the screen door that was missing its screen.

It took two more knocks before muffled shouting reached them from the other side. The distinct unlatching of multiple chains gave them warning before the door flew open, much against the protest of the hinges. The overwhelming stench of stale beer, warm piss, and sweet rot hit Ethan before he had a chance to school his expression into indifference. He could have sworn Verne gagged a little as they both retrieved their badges from pockets.

The man who answered the door was presumably in his sixties if he was Mr. McLane. He looked like they had woken him up. His few remaining white hairs stuck out in all different directions. He had a few days' worth of stubble scaling his neck up to his cheeks. His clothes looked like he may not have changed them in weeks based on the crusted and dried content that covered the potentially once white tank he wore, and the foul odor that was coming off him.

"Mr. McLane?" Ethan asked, though he couldn't imagine there could be more than one person living in this condition.

"Who's asking?"

"We're detectives Dumas and Verne. You spoke to my partner here on the phone about us reopening your daughter's case." Ethan did his best to take shallow breaths and only inhale the outside air.

A curt nod was all they got in confirmation that he was Mr. McLane, but Ethan took it. He didn't feel like inhaling more than necessary. He gave Verne a look telling him he could take the lead. Ethan was going to keep his mouth shut as much as possible.

"We had a few questions for you about Kelly's disappearance, as we like to start at the beginning and work our way through everything again," Verne said in a slightly strangled tone. Ethan could tell he was trying to speak without breathing, and Ethan had to glance down at his shoes to stop himself from laughing. It would mean breathing in more than necessary.

"I didn't do nothing though." Mr. McLane crossed his arms over his chest, resting them on his protruding gut.

"No one is accusing you of anything. Routine questions we are asking all the victims' families, like we talked about on the phone." Verne sounded a little flustered by Mr. McLane's tone.

Ethan, letting guilt get the better of him for trying to push all this on Verne, posed the next question. "Can you walk us through what happened on September 8th, 1984?"

"How am I supposed to remember that?" he scoffed, looking between Ethan and Verne like they were crazy.

Verne's mouth gaped open a little when Ethan looked at him. He couldn't blame him. The stench mostly kept Ethan from expressing his thoughts similarly. Ethan rephrased his question: "Can you tell us what you remember from September 8th, 1984—the day Kelly was taken?"

Mr. McLane didn't even have the decency to look ashamed for not remembering the date his daughter was kidnapped. He sneered at Ethan, which Ethan met with a neutral expression. He'd dealt with enough men like McLane when he was a uniformed officer. It would take more than a mean face to get a reaction out of him.

"My bitch of an ex let her get snatched up. I was working that day."

Ethan didn't bother to even pull out his notepad. It seemed Mr. McLane was showing them just how helpful he was going to be.

"We have multiple statements, including from the babysitter, Helen, saying that Kelly was with her at the park when she was taken. Is that not what happened?" Verne asked. His tone was biting, and Ethan was prepared to cut in if he let his temper get the better of him.

"I don't know what she paid that girl to say! She's a liar."

"Your ex or the babysitter?" Verne tried to clarify.

"I want a lawyer."

"You're not under arrest or even being accused of anything, Mr. McLane. We just are trying to establish a clear timeline surrounding Kelly's kidnapping," Ethan said.

"Well, I don't like how he's looking at me." Mr. McLane jutted his chin in Verne's direction.

Ethan suppressed a sigh and looked at Verne, who was openly glaring at Mr. McLane now. "He can't help it, it's the face God gave him."

Mr. McLane turned his sour expression on Ethan as Ethan pulled out his card. "We'll let you get on with your day. Sorry for the disturbance, and don't hesitate to reach out if you think of anything you'd like to share."

As soon as the card was grasped between two of Mr. McLane's tobacco-stained fingers, Ethan had Verne by the arm and was steering him away.

"Bet she was trying to sleep with him!"

Ethan stopped and looked back at Mr. McLane over his shoulder. "Excuse me?"

"The ex. I could never prove it, but she would spread them for anyone. Bet that's how he found Kelly." Mr. McLane didn't elaborate more. He stepped clear of his door and slammed it shut, rattling more than a few windows on his house.

Ethan and Verne cleared the yard, Ethan not feeling at ease until he was back in the driver's seat.

"That man needs therapy," Ethan said at the same time Verne said, "There is nothing wrong with my face."

They looked at each other in silence until Ethan cracked, biting his lip to contain his laughter while Verne sat beside him with a forced pout. Once Ethan could collect himself, he gave Verne a pity pat on the shoulder before beginning their drive to Hartford.

"You think there is any truth behind his claim?" Verne asked, as they turned off McLane's street.

"What, about his ex-wife and Watt?" Ethan couldn't keep the incredulousness from his voice. "I think it's a drunk man's accusation. There's no merit to it. He probably just wanted to get a dig in at his wife."

Verne nodded from the passenger seat but didn't say anything else until they got on the highway. "I'd be ten bucks richer if you'd taken my bet."

CHAPTER TEN

FRIDAY, OCTOBER 12ᵀᴴ

Ethan and Verne sat in the parking garage a block from Gregory Griffin's office in the heart of Hartford, entertained by watching people attempt to park in tight spaces and then give up before moving on to another. His secretary had told Ethan he was booked for the next month. Ethan had a hard time believing that, so he reached out to Fiona Griffin, who said he usually had an hour on Fridays where he'd go through prospective clients' messages.

"Time to go meet Fiona's other half," Verne said, five minutes until the hour break. They left the parking garage, heading to the tower they needed. "Should I even bother to hope this goes better than McLane? I'm sure it could get worse, but two in one day for a Friday is too much."

"Just follow my lead. It's not an interrogation, we don't need to push anyone into silence when we're just trying to get clarity."

Verne grinned as he held the lobby door open for Ethan.

"Behave," Ethan mumbled, as he walked to security. They flashed their badges and got visitor passes to access the elevators. Eleven floors later, the doors opened on a mahogany explosion.

"Looks like Ed's office on crack," Verne whispered, as they stepped toward the receptionist.

She didn't look up from her laptop when they stopped in front of her. Ethan cleared his throat but still failed to get a reaction from her.

He glanced around for a bell to see if this was a petty way of getting him to use some system she had set up, but there was nothing but a ridiculous amount of mahogany between the two of them.

"Excuse me, I'm Detective Dumas, and this is Detective Verne. We're from Rothbury PD to see Mr. Griffin."

"Name?" she said, remaining absorbed by her laptop.

"Still Detective Dumas," he repeated. Verne arched his eyebrow with a smirk.

"Did you have an appointment?" she asked, looking up for the first time. She seemed entirely disinterested in their being there.

"We're detectives working a case. Does Mr. Griffin want us to bring him down to the station or just let us talk to him here?" Verne interjected, holding up his badge, before Ethan had a chance to remind her of their conversation earlier this week when he had tried to set up an appointment.

Her face remained expressionless, but her eyes flickered from Verne to Ethan before she picked up her desk phone. She spun slightly in her chair to angle away from them and spoke softly into the receiver. He caught the word detectives and pushy before she replaced the receiver in the cradle.

"He'll see you now." As she spoke, one of the panels of the mahogany wall to her right swung back to reveal itself as a door.

"Man, that's wicked cool," Verne whispered, smacking his hand against Ethan's forearm as they moved to head in. Ethan nodded at the receptionist, but she had already returned to staring at her laptop.

Gregory Griffin was seated in the center of the room as excessively mahogany-detailed as the reception area. He didn't speak, his eyes on his monitor as he waved a hand at the two unwelcoming chairs in front of his desk. Ethan took the left, unobstructed by his monitor, and Verne took the right.

"We appreciate you taking the time to speak with us," Ethan said, balancing his notepad on his thigh. He didn't think Gregory would take too kindly to him leaning on his desk. Despite the fact his desk had the room, as it was void of anything besides his computer and an orderly stack of paperwork. There wasn't a single photograph on its surface, or any surface in the office, Ethan realized, as he did a quick sweep of the room.

Ethan looked back at him to see he'd shifted his gaze from his monitor to stare at Ethan. "As I told my wife, I think it's a waste of our time to be dragged into this investigation."

Verne inhaled, making a slight whistling with the gap in his teeth. Ethan ignored Gregory's statement.

"We wanted to go over some facts about the original investigation, as well as make sure you were aware of what reopening a case entails for the families and the direction we're currently going with this investigation. Your wife expressed concern that the original investigation didn't take into consideration all leads. I wanted to assure you, as I did her, that we are thoroughly investigating all evidence and leads."

Gregory threw his head back and laughed. Ethan was taken aback. Verne and Ethan exchanged a glance for a moment before Ethan cleared his throat to draw Mr. Griffin's attention back to him.

"My partner and I seem to be missing something," Ethan said.

"Backbones, maybe?" Gregory suggested, still laughing.

"Excuse me?" Verne asked, the anger in his voice apparent to Gregory too, as he sat up straight in his chair, no longer laughing at them.

"Is the Rothbury PD so tightly wrapped around the mayor's finger that you can't just ignore him when he pointlessly asks you to reopen a case that was solved decades ago? Seriously, boys. Is this how taxpayers' dollars are spent?" He waved his hand at the two of them.

"The cases we're investigating, not just your daughter's, were reopened because there is the chance with forensic advancements that—"

"You can save the speech," Gregory said, cutting Ethan off. "I don't mean to sound callous, but detectives spent years trying to solve the case. They may not have convicted him in a court of law, but as far as I'm concerned, Vincent Watt is guilty."

"Your wife doesn't think so," Verne interjected.

"And my wife is a grief-stricken fool. You're making our lives a hundred times harder by entertaining this obsession of hers, only for you to break her all over again when nothing new turns up and you come to the same conclusion as the last detectives." His face was turning red as he spoke. His voice remained even, but he was visibly getting angrier as the seconds ticked by.

"Mrs. Griffin has expressed fair concern that there was mishandling of leads and witnesses during the original investigation. It is not unheard of for cases to be reopened and mistakes to be discovered that can ultimately allow us to solve cases," Ethan said, pushing back on Mr. Griffin's dismissiveness.

They had barely scratched the surface when it came to investigating persons of interest in Anne Griffin's case. Ethan wasn't putting much stock into Fiona's claims, but Gregory's stark defiance of them doing their jobs bothered him. It seemed the fathers were not going to be as receptive to progress as the mothers in these cases.

"The detectives did their job," Gregory said, leaning back in his chair. He seemed to be disengaging, and Ethan knew they were getting close to being kicked out.

"Detectives never even took a statement from her."

"Detective Hadeon didn't think it was necessary, and I agreed with him."

"And why was that?" Ethan asked, hearing the edge in his own voice. He realized he sounded ridiculous, getting riled up by Gregory on Fiona's behalf, but the callousness he had regarding justice for his daughter hit a nerve for Ethan. Parents were meant to care; they were never supposed to stop caring.

Gregory didn't say anything right away. He returned his focus to his computer, and Ethan wasn't sure if he was ending the conversation. Verne cleared his throat, and Gregory finally gave them an answer.

"I believed Fiona was under a lot of stress, understandably, as our daughter had been kidnapped, and she started having these…fantasies. I didn't need her sending detectives on pointless hunts to satisfy her delusions when they could be focused on doing their jobs. Which they did. So, I took care of dealing with the police."

"What did you tell them?" Verne asked.

"The truth. I saved them from a wild goose chase following up on her leads."

"By telling them she was crazy." Ethan didn't have to phrase it as a question. Fiona's explanation of how she was treated and Gregory's callousness painted a clear image of the way he sidelined his wife. Maybe he had done it with the true intention of keeping detectives focused on finding their daughter, but to Ethan, it seemed more likely he was worried about his wife embarrassing him.

Gregory's lips seemed to disappear as he pressed them together, not denying Ethan's accusation.

"You're satisfied with the fact your daughter's case was never closed properly?"

"I think you boys got what you came for, yes?" Gregory reached for something under his desk, and the door they'd entered through reopened behind them.

"Actually—" Verne started, but Gregory cut him off.

"Any further questions can be directed through my secretary."

His dismissal was clear, and pushing more would get them nowhere but in trouble.

Verne and Ethan stood up, creating a draft that blew a few pieces of paper off the desk onto the floor. Ethan felt like knocking the whole pile over, but he didn't need to give Gregory a reason to call Camilleri and report him for improper conduct.

Ethan stopped at the receptionist's desk as Verne headed to the elevator. He pulled a business card from his breast pocket and held it out to her. "Please tell Mr. Griffin to call me if he thinks of anything pertinent to the case that he'd like to discuss."

She looked up at him, ignoring his extended hand. "Mr. Griffin doesn't accept cards."

He stood there for a moment longer, until he was freed from his pointless stance by the ding of the elevator. He shoved his card back in his breast pocket and joined Verne, watching the elevator doors until the reception was out of view. He could feel the vein in the side of his neck pulsing. He didn't know why Gregory Griffin got under his skin so much. Fiona had said he hadn't shared the same sentiment about Anne's case, but he hadn't expected so much antagonism.

"I think it's fair to say Mr. Griffin and McLane aren't winning any best dad awards," Verne said, as the elevator doors opened, dumping them back into the lobby.

Ethan scoffed, Verne's declaration an understatement. "I want to look into Gregory Griffin a little more. Fiona Griffin might say her husband didn't do anything, but I'd like to verify that for myself."

CHAPTER ELEVEN

THURSDAY, NOVEMBER 8TH

Verne groaned as Ethan's phone rang with the distinctive blaring ringtone he'd set for Fiona Griffin's personalized alert. As the weeks bled into November, progress had felt virtually nonexistent. With Camilleri breathing down their necks, they were trying to find any thread they could pull for a lead, but it was becoming less likely they'd find anything. They were still working on other cold cases, and they could only go over the same information so many times.

They had investigated Gregory Griffin after their meeting with him and learned nothing pertinent to the case, but a lot more to solidify his character. It turned out he was living a double life. He kept a second home in Rothbury, nothing lavish or much different from his home in Southbury with Fiona Griffin. However, it appeared to be where his mistress lived, a woman named Sheila Waterford, and Gregory visited often. A quick records search also revealed that Gregory was listed as the father on the birth certificates of Sheila's two sons. The eldest was born July 1983, a year after Anne Griffin went missing, and thirteen months later in August 1984, their second son was born. Ethan toyed with the possibility it could be motive for Gregory to play a role in Anne's disappearance, but he'd have expected him to have left Fiona too, if it were about being with Sheila and their family. He decided Gregory was likely not guilty of foul play in Anne's case; however, it was safe to say Gregory Griffin wouldn't be winning any husband of the year awards either.

Ethan had made it clear to Verne that it was not relevant to their case and they were not going to mention it to Fiona Griffin.

Despite the dwindling faith Ethan had, they still were reading every piece of information they could get ahold of from the cold case files, the solved case files, and every single file on Watt.

Unsurprisingly, the results weren't back on the lab work they'd sent out. They'd gleaned nothing of substance from family members so far, and they were playing phone tag with potential witnesses.

Verne had started a tally and was up to fourteen voicemails left for Kelly McLane's mother, who had moved to Florida, and was proving to be a difficult woman to get ahold of. Equally elusive was Coppin, who had yet to return Ethan's calls. Ethan was beginning to suspect he'd have to track him down at home, but kept delaying every time something else came up.

Verne had been unsuccessful in tracking down Kelly McLane's babysitter. Apparently, the original detectives felt "Babysitter Helen" was sufficient identification. They hadn't even taken an address of residence, leaving Kelly McLane's mother as their only hope for locating Helen.

Ethan felt like they were waiting for a break to fall into their lap at this point.

"I'm going to take a hammer to your phone if she calls you one more time," Verne said with a dramatic huff as he tossed down the file he'd been reading.

Ethan hit the silence button, letting Fiona's call once again go to voicemail. The first few times she had called, he had answered and patiently explained he would make contact as soon as there was any news to update her. Ethan doubted there was a miscommunication on his part. She was persistent, or a borderline stalker, as Verne had repeatedly claimed.

"I've told her I'll get back to her. She's just eager for progress after so many years." He understood where she was coming from, at least her anxiety for answers. He didn't ever want to understand what she'd been through, but his patience was wearing thin. He was trying to do his job, and her incessant calling to check in on him only wasted precious time.

"One time, I had an ex-fling who was obsessed with me. Called me multiple times a day and kept driving by my apartment at all hours of the night," Verne said.

"How'd you get her to stop?" Ethan asked, only half listening to him.

"I slept with her again."

Ethan looked over at Verne, once again amazed at the fact no one had ever stabbed him. "I don't think that will work in this case."

Verne snorted. "God, yeah. Don't sleep with her, she's old enough to be your mom. I just meant you could pay her attention, and she'd stop at least for a little bit."

Ethan, wanting this conversation over, chose not to point out that Fiona's age wouldn't factor in his top five reasons why sleeping with her would be an issue. He looked down at his phone as a voicemail notification popped up. He considered, for a few fleeting moments, Verne's advice to acknowledge her, but decided against it. If he gave her constant access to him now, it would only make her feel even more entitled if any actual progress was made.

"I'll just call her when we have something," he decided out loud.

"If you don't, I'm stealing your phone and blocking her."

* * *

Five weeks to the day that they'd gotten the boxes from Coppin, Ethan felt Camilleri's patience running thin. The forensic reports still hadn't come in and probably wouldn't until the New Year, if they were being realistic. They'd found no new leads outside of Watt, but they also hadn't found any incriminating evidence that would close the cases.

"Do you think I should start leaving funny messages at this point? Clearly this woman isn't listening to them," Verne said, as they listened to the ringing as he tried to call Kelly McLane's mother.

"We could always contact someone in Orlando's PD—" Ethan cut himself off when she picked up.

"Hello?"

Verne stared open mouthed at his desk phone, doing a great impression of a fish out of water. Ethan urgently waved at him to speak, instead of speaking up himself.

"Hello?" she repeated, the irritation coming through the phone clearly.

"Hi, yes, this is Detective Verne with the Rothbury PD. I'm calling for Whitney McLane," Verne said, snapped out of his panic.

Ethan dropped back in his seat, letting out a breath. Apparently neither of them had had any faith that she was going to pick up. Though in fairness to them both, Ethan thought, she hadn't picked up the other nearly two dozen times Verne had called, so their expectations were low.

"It's Whitney White, now," Kelly McLane's mother sneered. Verne still looked panicked when he looked up at Ethan.

Ethan stepped in before Verne fumbled the call. "We're sorry about that mix-up, Ms. White. This is Detective Dumas, speaking. My partner and I were calling because we wanted to talk to you about your daughter's case, as it's been reopened."

There was no answer, but the call hadn't dropped. Ethan heard rustling on the other line and then the distinct sound of a can being popped open. Given the hour, Ethan was going to hope it was a soda.

"What do you need to talk about?" she asked, after a prolonged sip of her drink.

Verne held up his hand, seemingly having regained his composure, and took over the call again. "We wanted to ask you about the time leading up to Kelly's death, as well as her babysitter, Helen, that was with her that day at the park."

Whitney gave a grunt in acknowledgment. Ethan turned to a fresh page on his notepad and poised himself to take notes while Verne asked his questions.

"Did Helen take Kelly to the park often, or have a regular routine with her?" Verne asked.

"I worked late at the salon Tuesdays and Saturdays, so Helen watched her those nights since Earl was useless." Whitney took another sip of her drink right near the phone.

"Do you know if it was always the park on Saturdays, or was that unusual?"

"Don't know. She usually did whatever with Kelly. Sometimes, I'd leave a little extra money for her to take Kelly to do things, but otherwise, it was whatever Helen decided to do with her."

Ethan jotted down a note reading *Ask for Helen's info* and held it up for Verne, pointing at it with his finger to draw attention. Verne nodded as he asked his next question.

"We were looking through Kelly's case file and noticed police didn't get contact information from Helen. Do you happen to know how we might contact her, or even her last name?"

"For Helen? She's Earl's niece. She lived two doors down from where we lived in Rothbury. Last thing I knew, she still lived there and took care of her ma—Earl's sister."

"She's related to Earl? He didn't say," Ethan said, unable to hold back the anger boiling up as he jotted the information down. If the original investigation had noted any of that information, or Earl McLane hadn't been such a useless father, they'd have been able to reach out to Helen a lot sooner.

Whitney laughed dryly. "Helen's name is Helen Nguyen. Earl stopped speaking to his sister when she married a Vietnamese immigrant, and so he doesn't acknowledge Helen as family. He'd probably tell you his sister was dead if you asked."

"What an ass," Verne mumbled.

"Among other things," Whitney replied.

"I did have another question for you Ms. White," Ethan spoke up. "Did you or Earl have a regular routine with Kelly that someone might have been able to notice?"

Verne shot Ethan a questioning glance across their desks, but Ethan waved him off. He'd explain later, but a thought had crossed his mind, and he didn't have time to run it by Verne while Whitney was on the phone.

"I didn't, and Earl sure as hell wouldn't have bothered to do something with Kelly."

Ethan nodded, the inkling of an idea forming in his mind. He motioned for Verne to continue with the call as he got on his computer, requesting all case files on the three cases that had put Watt away for life.

Verne wrapped up the call, answering the few questions Whitney had. Verne turned to Ethan as he disconnected the call.

"What idea did you get? I could practically see it oozing out of your ears."

Ethan ignored the weird part of Verne's statement. "Whitney said she didn't know if Helen had a routine with Kelly, but that her and Earl didn't. We'll need to track down Helen, but I want to call Mrs. Dawson and ask about Melody's routine. It's something that's been bugging me about these cases and the ones that Watt's serving life for already. A serial killer targeting sex workers might pick victims by opportunity, but kidnapping children supposedly seven times without being caught in the act? It seems implausible. What is plausible is that Watt knew something about these families, and specifically these kids, routines that made it easier for him to take them in such public places."

He'd been floating this idea in his mind. The original detectives hadn't asked any questions of Helen, and even if they had, they likely wouldn't have considered asking about a routine. They'd made it clear early on when building the case against Watt that they believed they were random acts.

Verne rubbed at the stubble on his chin, giving Ethan a squinty-eyed look, which Ethan knew was Verne's thinking face—a rarity to see in action. "I don't know if I can believe it though. What about Rebecca Smith and Anne Griffin? And the three cases he was found guilty for? I mean one, maybe two out of seven isn't really solid."

"We'll need to go back over the cases. Ask more questions, or in some cases ask literally any questions." Ethan knew it was a very shaky theory, but that was how it would be until they investigated it and checked if it had any foundation.

"Fine, I trust you. What do you need from me?"

Ethan began dividing up the research, calls, and visits they were going to have to make to see just how random Watt could be.

CHAPTER TWELVE

FRIDAY, NOVEMBER 9TH

Helen Nguyen still lived with her mother, two doors down from the McLanes' former home. Verne had tracked down a number for Helen the day before, after they got off the phone with Whitney White. Helen, unlike her ex-aunt, had picked up Verne's call immediately and agreed to come down to the station to speak with them first thing Friday morning.

Verne was brimming with energy, the energy drink in his hand seemingly unnecessary. Verne had warmed to Ethan's theory as yesterday had progressed, and now was eager for Ethan to be right and this be their groundbreaking information that closed the cases and got them promotions.

"You're going to scare her," Ethan said from his desk chair, as he read through the files of the closed cases.

Penelope Wilks, Jacquelyn Battistelli, and Emily Harp were the three victims Watt had been tried and found guilty of kidnapping, assaulting, and murdering. He didn't know what exactly he was looking for besides a hint that might suggest Watt didn't pick his victims by chance. Based on the files, the original detectives hadn't looked for a connection. Ethan's hope was they included information that would unintentionally be a lead.

Verne's desk phone rang, and he practically pounced on it. He barely acknowledged the person on the other line before he hung up. "Helen is waiting in the lobby for us."

Ethan closed the file from Jacquelyn Battistelli's case and grabbed the one from Kelly McLane's that included Helen's original statement. Ethan had already gone over with Verne that they needed to tread carefully. Given that Helen was with Kelly when she was taken, there was a high possibility Helen could become defensive if she felt they were accusing her of anything. Even if Ethan personally believed she was partially responsible.

When they got to the lobby, Helen was standing by the waiting area, arms crossed, and brows furrowed. She stepped forward to meet them. "You're the detectives who called me?"

"Yes, I'm Detective Dumas, this is Detective Verne," Ethan said, motioning toward Verne next to him. "We wanted to talk to you about your cousin. You can follow us; we're just going to go somewhere more private."

Helen didn't respond but followed close behind Ethan as he led them to an empty interrogation room. It wasn't like the cold, sterile rooms seen on TV. They had a few like that, but not everyone needed the same level of questioning. This room was small, but the walls were painted a pale blue. There was a wooden table pushed against one wall with two semi-padded chairs on each side and a box of tissues. A water cooler sat in the corner with paper cups balanced on top.

Ethan motioned for Helen to take a seat. Verne sat opposite of her.

"Water, anyone?" Ethan asked, tucking the file he had under his arm before he poured himself one.

"I'll take one," Verne responded.

"Helen?"

"I'm all set. Thank you." She added the second part after a brief pause.

Ethan brought two waters to the table and set one in front of Verne before setting his own water and the file down in front of him.

"I just wanted to ease any concerns you may have before we start. You're not under arrest or suspicion. Rothbury PD has reopened Kelly McLane's case, and we want to talk to you about Kelly's routine as her babysitter," Ethan explained. He leaned back a little, easing a smile onto his face to try and relax Helen.

She sat stick straight, hands firmly clasped together where they rested on the edge of the table. She stared intently at the file in front of Ethan like it might attack her.

"I don't know if I'll remember," Helen said softly.

"That's okay, we're just going to ask a few questions. Let us know what you remember, okay?" Ethan asked.

Helen didn't respond for a few seconds but then gave them a terse nod. Ethan glanced at Verne and repeated the motion to Verne to signal for him to start asking the questions they'd come up with.

"Did you babysit Kelly regularly?" Verne asked. They had what Whitney White had told them already, but hearing everything from Helen would help establish the foundation of Ethan's theory.

"I usually watched her twice a week when my aunt was working." Her eyes remained trained on the file in front of Ethan.

"Was it set days or just twice a week?" Verne asked.

"Set."

"Do you remember which days?"

"Tuesdays and Saturdays." Helen looked up at Ethan as she answered Verne's question.

Helen was thankfully giving them the answers they'd been hoping for when they came up with their questions, but she looked distressed. Ethan gave her an encouraging nod and smile, but it didn't ease the creases lining her face.

"Do you remember what you'd do with Kelly on Tuesdays and Saturdays?" Verne asked.

"Can I have some water?" Helen asked, looking over her shoulder at the water cooler in the opposite corner.

Ethan stood up and grabbed a cup, filling it up with the chilled water before he brought it over and handed it to her with a smile. "Feel free to help yourself to more if you need it at any point."

She didn't look up at him when she took it but nodded and mumbled, "Thank you," as she brought the cup to her lips. Ethan took his seat, and they sat in silence as Helen emptied her cup.

"Alright, let's get back to it," Ethan said, keeping his voice soft. He couldn't tell if it was the environment or their conversation that had Helen on edge, perhaps a combination of both, but he needed to make sure they got their answers before she'd reached her limit. She was free to leave whenever she wanted, so Ethan needed to make sure she didn't leave before they were done.

"Can you repeat the question?" she asked, looking at Verne finally.

"Yeah, sure. Do you remember what you and Kelly did on Tuesdays and Saturdays?"

Helen only nodded at first, looking from Verne to Ethan and back. She dropped her hands into her lap, and Ethan could hear her picking at her nails. Ethan wondered who in her family had openly voiced their blame. He imagined Whitney White had, and if Earl had bothered to acknowledge Helen in the first place, Ethan was sure he'd have made his blame known.

"Well, Tuesdays were the library and then my house until Whitney got home. Saturdays were the park unless the weather wasn't nice enough," Helen answered.

Verne jotted her answer down as he asked his next question. "And if the weather wasn't nice?"

"I'd take her to Rothbury Mall."

Ethan sat up a little straighter, and he felt Verne tense a little beside him.

"Can you tell us about what you would do when you went to the mall instead of the park?" Ethan asked, trying not to sound too eager about the potential lead.

"I'm just going to get more water," Helen said, standing up so abruptly her chair jerked back from under her.

With a shaky hand, she grabbed her used cup and walked to the water cooler. Ethan watched her back as she bent to fill the cup and then raised the cup with her shaking hand to her lips. Rebecca Smith's sister, Sarah, said the trauma of the experience was all too much, and she'd been four and unable to remember the events now. Helen had been sixteen. Her original statement said she'd been distracted, and when she'd looked for Kelly, she couldn't find her. There was no mention as to what had distracted Helen.

"We need to ask about the day Kelly was taken. We can circle back to the mall," Ethan whispered to Verne, while Helen refilled her cup again.

"You think she can handle that?"

"My priority is the case. She'll have to deal." Ethan cleared his throat and drew Helen's attention to him. "Can we continue?"

Helen took another long sip of water before walking back to the table. Her hands had stopped shaking, but the fear in her eyes remained.

"I'd like you to walk us through September 8th, 1984, and anything you remember from that day," Ethan said.

"It was a Saturday, so my aunt dropped Kelly off at my house in the morning. I can't remember the time." She looked from one to the other as she spoke, as if she were afraid one of them was going to lash out. "We walked to the park from my house. Then Kelly played until…"

Ethan grabbed the box of tissues that was pushed against the wall and gently put them in front of Helen as she broke down. Her shoulders hunched forward as the sobs rattled her body. They needed more details about the events of the day, but Ethan knew until Helen had collected herself, they weren't going to have any more luck than they'd had when Betsy Dawson had broken down talking about her daughter's kidnapping.

Verne took Helen's cup and filled it up with more water, gently encouraging her to take some sips to help.

"Sorry, I just haven't talked about it much."

"You've never done therapy or anything?" Verne asked.

Helen let out a soft snort, but her eyes were still sad when she looked up at them. "No. My family doesn't support that. My mom isn't close to her brother, but she'd been best friends with my aunt. When I let Kelly get taken, my aunt blamed me, and when my mom defended me, she lost her friend. But my aunt was right. It was my fault."

Verne sat up straight again and picked up his pen, ready to continue taking notes. When Helen met Ethan's eyes, he gave her a small nod.

"I—I've never really told anyone about this." She paused and looked around the room, as if searching for something before her eyes landed back on the file in front of Ethan. "I was seeing someone."

"When you were sixteen?" Verne asked, clearly confused.

Ethan had a gut feeling he knew where this was going. "The day at the park, was someone there with you?"

Helen didn't say anything, but then slowly began to nod. Verne inhaled sharply beside him. That definitely wasn't in the original police report. Everything clearly indicated that Helen had taken Kelly to the park alone, had been alone, and she'd simply lost track of her because of how busy it was on that Saturday. There had been no mention of Helen being at the park with someone else when Kelly was taken.

"Who was it?" Ethan asked softly.

"His—his name was Stephen."

"Do you remember his last name?" Verne asked, taking over the questioning again.

"Amos."

"How did you know Stephen?"

Helen swallowed hard, and she looked on the verge of crying again, but she answered Verne with a shaky voice. "We both worked at the mall. I worked in the food court, and he was one of the janitors."

"Was that Rothbury Mall?" Ethan interjected, unable to help himself.

"Yeah, the one that's gone now."

Ethan felt his heart rate increase. Another janitor from Rothbury Mall. The mall Melody Dawson was taken from four years after Kelly McLane was taken. He tried to keep his reaction minimal.

"Was Stephen alone when he met you at the park?" Ethan asked.

Verne gave him a sideways look, but Ethan ignored it. He needed to ask specific questions. Helen had waited over thirty years to tell the truth, he couldn't leave it up to her how much of the truth she chose to share now.

"I—I don't know."

"You don't know, or you don't want to say?" Ethan pressed.

"I can't remember."

"A second ago, it was you didn't know, but now, it's you don't remember? I think you do, Helen. Was Stephen alone that day, or did he come with someone else?"

Helen's eyes got big, and she looked from Ethan to Verne before they fell to her lap where she had her hands clasped. She didn't say anything, but she shook her head, a small whimper coming from her.

"Helen, Kelly deserves justice. We need to know what really happened that day at the park," Ethan said softly again. He couldn't scare her silent now. Not when she was clearly hiding something.

"I didn't know!" she shouted, suddenly pounding her fists on the table in front of her as she fell back into body-shaking sobs.

"You're not in trouble, Helen. You were just a kid yourself, but we need to know what really happened that day."

"I only saw Stephen that day."

"Would Stephen join you at the park often?" Ethan asked.

Helen wouldn't meet his eyes, but she slowly nodded.

"Would Stephen always come alone?" Ethan felt himself holding his breath.

At first, Helen gave them nothing, but slowly she shook her head.

"Who used to come with Stephen?"

"His cousin."

"Did you know this cousin?"

Helen's body began to shake again as she mumbled a name between sobs.

A tiny alarm went off in his mind as he leaned closer. "Can you say it again, Helen?"

She finally looked up at him, her eyes swollen and red from crying, the guilt clearly visible. Still, when the words passed her lips, he felt like he'd been sucker punched.

"His cousin's name was Vincent Watt."

Verne jerked in his seat, causing the feet to screech against the floor, and Helen to jump from the sudden noise. Ethan did his best to school his expression, but the anger that clawed to get out was fighting him. She had known this entire time the connection Watt had to her cousin. Any ounce of sympathy he had begun to feel for her evaporated instantly. Kelly McLane was believed to be the second of Watt's seven victims, counting the three he was convicted for and their four cold cases. All but Rebecca Smith came after Kelly. Helen had known Vincent Watt. Had known he sometimes came to the park. Had known for decades and never once said something to the police. Sure, she'd been a kid at the time, but what was her excuse since then?

"Did you ever give the police this information?" Ethan asked, already knowing the answer. There were some signs of incompetence, sure, but he didn't believe they were that bad.

Helen shook her head.

"Did Vincent Watt work at the mall too?" Verne interjected. His words came out clipped, and Ethan spared him a sideways glance. Verne had his jaw clenched so tight it looked ready to pop out of his face.

Helen, who had been reduced to tears again, simply nodded as confirmation.

"Had Vincent Watt ever interacted with Kelly prior to the day she was taken from the park?" Ethan asked.

Helen nodded again.

He ran a hand down his face, shaking his head. He looked over at Verne, who had glanced his way too, and he shook his head not bothering to hide the disgust on his face now. "We'll need a new witness statement from you, as well as a recorded confession of what you just told us."

Helen opened her mouth, likely to object, but Ethan cut her off as he stood up, slamming both palms on the table. "You're lucky we're not arresting you on the spot for obstruction of justice. Five other girls died after Kelly. Five. And those are the ones we know of. I can't begin to understand why you would lie to the police about this unless you had some part in it—and trust me, if you did, I will find out, and I'll make sure they throw the book at you."

Ethan stood up and grabbed the file off the table before walking out. He heard Verne instruct Helen to remain seated and that officers would come in to take her statement. Ethan kept moving, headed back to their office. He threw the case file on his desk and pulled up everything they had on Watt. They'd hardly spent time diving into his past beyond his record, but with Helen's confession, it seemed the next logical step.

Verne eventually joined Ethan in their office. He dropped into his desk chair and let out a long sigh before he leaned forward into Ethan's line of sight. "That was wild."

"Did you assign officers to take her statement?" Ethan asked, not looking away from his monitor.

"They're in with her now. They wanted to know if we're going to arrest her."

Ethan stopped what he was doing and released a drawn-out exhale, running a hand through his hair. They had a case if they wanted to, but he had bigger fish to fry than Helen Nguyen. Still, if the other parents got wind that someone could have connected Vincent Watt sooner to these murders, preventing even one of the subsequent five murders after Kelly McLane, then they very easily could have a PR nightmare for Rothbury.

"Take it to Camilleri. If he wants us to, I'll charge her before she steps foot outside of the station today."

Ethan didn't want to deal with the blowback from Camilleri if he made the "wrong" decision. Now, if they did face backlash from families or the media, it was on Camilleri, and he couldn't put it all on Ethan and Verne.

Verne left to talk to Camilleri without another word. Ethan got up from his desk and looked at the board of victim profiles along with the basic profile on Watt. Beyond his name and age, they had included a list of his record, a timeline of his arrest and trial, and the facts on his current sentencing.

They didn't have room to add another board in their office, so Ethan grabbed a stack of sticky notes and thumb tacks. He began by adding sections for Penelope Wilks, Jacquelyn Battistelli, and Emily Harp. Now that they had two connections to Rothbury Mall and Vincent Watt, Ethan planned to meticulously comb through every piece of information he could get his hands on to see if that connection was a fluke or carried through to the other cases too.

After adding the new sections, he went back to the blank space under Watt. Ethan wrote "Stephen Amos: cousin" on a note before tacking it to the wall. He grabbed a dry erase marker from Verne's desk and added the name under Kelly McLane's section, as well as a note that Helen Nguyen and Stephen Amos were connected.

"Okay, madman. I leave for twenty minutes, and you go all crazed conspirator on me," Verne said, as he squeezed through the door to avoid Ethan, who was currently behind it to add more notes to the wall.

"What'd Camilleri decide?" Ethan asked, pausing to look back at Verne after tacking another note under Watt.

Verne dropped in his desk chair and turned to face their wall of information. "Told me to just use the threat of it to our advantage. They're going to milk her for every ounce of information, and I told them to get everything recorded and signed."

Ethan nodded, turning back to the wall again. If they pressed charges, Helen may just lawyer up and refuse to give them any more information, so using it to incentivize her was a logical call, but it blurred the lines.

"Where do you need me?" Verne asked.

"I want to get as much information in front of us as possible to see what else we might be missing. We've now got two cases with a connection to Rothbury Mall. Kelly McLane has a connection to Watt through Helen via Stephen, and I'd wager if we dig further, there are others out of the five with a clearer connection."

"You want to look at the closed cases too? He's already in jail for them."

"I'm not missing a potential connection because we don't look at all the pieces. Something in one of these," he said, motioning to the three newly added closed cases, "might hold the clue to solving one of these." He pointed at the four cold cases they had originally started with a month ago.

"Okay, fair enough," Verne said, throwing his hands up in surrender. "Where should I start looking?"

"Let's build up Watt's section first. Now that we know Watt met Kelly McLane through his cousin and Helen, I want to know every person in Watt's life he could have used as a connection to our victims, starting with Anthony Watt. We already know he was in the ER the same night Anne Griffin was taken."

Verne got on his computer, turning his monitor so Ethan could see it too. "What do you want to know?"

"What was Anthony Watt picked up for, what was he charged with, when did it start, and did he ever have gaps in his record?" He stood, his hand hovering over the sticky notes, ready for something to add to the wall.

Verne hummed as he scanned with his finger. "So, his first arrest was when he was fourteen for petty theft, and the theft kept racking up and escalating until he was thrown in jail for a couple years when he was seventeen. He got out on good behavior—guess nothing he could steal in there—at nineteen. The following year, our guy Vincent Watt was born to Mary Amos."

Ethan jotted down the information and stuck it to the wall, starting a new note. "Okay, I'm assuming becoming a father didn't magically make him a better person."

"Not even close. A bunch of domestic abuse arrests but never any charges that stuck, I guess. Aggravated assault, interesting. Multiple arrests for that, too, but no charges. I think the other party was Watt's maternal uncle, Henry Amos, if we go based on the last name being the same as Vincent's mother. I'm guessing Henry Amos might be Stephen

Amos's dad then." Verne pointed to the two spots where the last name matched. Ethan copied each name onto a separate note and added them to the wall.

"Damn," Verne mumbled.

"What?" Ethan asked, moving back to look over his shoulder.

"Anthony Watt killed Henry Amos. He was charged and sentenced for second degree murder after a drunken gun mishap. He was released for good behavior—no way this guy kept getting early parole."

"Verne."

"Sorry, okay, released on good behavior in May 1981."

"1981," he repeated, pausing mid-writing to turn back to their board. His eyes landed on Rebecca Smith's column. She went missing June 1st, 1981. Only weeks after Vincent Watt's father was released from prison. "When was his father arrested for the murder?"

"August of 1963. Why, what are you thinking?" Verne stood up to join Ethan.

"Okay, so his father was arrested when Watt was barely a year old for killing Watt's uncle." He added a note with the arrest date. "He's convicted and is in jail until Watt is nineteen. That's a long time to not have a father in the picture, and it's not like he had a father figure because his father killed his uncle," Ethan said, pointing to the note he'd already put on the wall with Anthony's release date. He moved to point at the date Rebecca Smith was taken. "Then weeks after his father is released, Watt's first suspected victim is kidnapped, sloppily too. He left a witness, and her mom had just gone inside and could have easily spotted him."

"You think his father's release triggered Watt to kidnap Rebecca?"

"It would be a strange coincidence his violent, alcoholic father is released from prison and less than a month later Watt escalates to murder." Ethan looked at the other dates of victims being kidnapped. "Let's cross-reference what other kidnappings coincide with his father's arrest and release record," Ethan added.

Verne sat back down and started reading off parole violations, arrests, and charges Watt's father faced after his 1981 release. Three more dates lined up with victims' kidnappings: Kelly McLane, Melody Dawson, and Penelope Wilks.

"Anthony Watt died at the end of May 1989," Verne read out as Ethan added a note to Kelly McLane's column.

Ethan checked, and that covered Watt's last known victim, Emily Harp, who was taken the following month. He'd have imagined his father's death was a good day for Watt, but by that point, he probably took any emotionally charged event as an excuse to kill.

"So, what was his trigger for Jacquelyn Battistelli? 1988 was the only year he struck twice, which seems strange. His timeline otherwise seemed to revolve around his father, but there's nothing on his record for early that year," Ethan spoke more to himself than Verne as his eyes jumped from date to date.

There was the possibility they were missing victims, ones that hadn't been found or were never connected. A few times, Watt got close to town lines. He could have killed in an entirely different county. It seemed like a plausible explanation for Rebecca Smith in 1981, Anne Griffin in '82, Kelly McLane in '84, and then a nearly three-year gap before picking up again in '87.

"Jacquelyn was April 1988, right?" Verne asked, snapping Ethan from his thoughts.

Before Ethan could confirm, Verne stood up and snatched the sticky notes from Ethan, wrote his own note, and slapped it to the wall.

"Mary Amos overdosed January 1988. Watt was serving a few months of jail time for assaulting a guy at a bar and was released that March." Verne had a triumphant grin. "Mary had her own lengthy rap sheet. She probably lost custody at some point. She had some heavy drug charges."

Ethan took a few steps back from the wall until he bumped into their desks. Seemingly, Watt's parents were his trigger. Parental neglect and abuse were well-known factors in a criminal's making.

"Did he have any family he'd have gone to? I don't remember seeing in his file that he was ever in foster care."

"I didn't see anything specifically from what I just looked through. I know that Henry Amos had a wife. From my understanding, neither parent had much family," Verne said, as Ethan noted this on the wall.

"He could have ended up with his widowed aunt. I could be wrong, but I'm going to guess his aunt wouldn't have been great at separating son from father. He was the spitting image of his father. I want you to see what else you can find on his family. His record suggests he stayed local his entire life, so it shouldn't be too difficult to find out where he was when he wasn't in juvie or jail."

Ethan let Verne start on that while he printed out an aerial view of the city, drawing red circles around the locations of the six known dumpsites and blue circles around the seven abduction sites. This had been done before, on a larger scale, by the original detectives, but he thought it might be insightful to do it himself. After he finished, he stared at it for a while. All it told him was that Watt never strayed far from the abduction sites, which meant Anne should have been found close to the hospital. That was the only downtown abduction site, so his options would have been limited to a dumpster rather than the wooded areas he favored. Ethan added a red-dashed half-mile radius around the hospital. Realistically, if her body was going to be recovered, it would have been by now.

The hours slipped away until Verne's stomach growled around six forty, and they agreed they'd accomplished as much as they could for today. Verne had confirmed Stephen Amos was one of Henry and Rita Amos's children and had tracked down a few family members to reach out to next week.

Ethan knew they were approaching the pivotal point in their investigation, where they were going to have to reach out to Watt's lawyer and set up a time to question him. He dreaded the possibility since Watt had notoriously refused to speak to anyone since his initial arrest. They'd never got an admission of guilt from him for the three cases he'd been convicted of back in the '90s. Ethan knew the chance Watt would speak to them, let alone admit guilt for any of their cold cases, was practically zero.

He didn't bother concerning Verne with that thought, telling him they'd pick up on Monday. He just wanted to go home and hide away with Vanessa for the weekend.

CHAPTER THIRTEEN

THURSDAY, NOVEMBER 15TH

Ethan was exhausted.

Monday, they got forensic results back on another cold case they'd shelved a few months ago while waiting for the labs. With the results in, Camilleri pulled some strings and rushed a warrant through. When they'd gotten to the suspect's home, Ethan hadn't planned on running two miles or getting hit over the head with a two-by-four. They did tack on a few extra charges, and the photographs of the goose egg on the back of his head would secure the assault charges.

Tuesday, after being cleared to return to work, they focused on the four cold cases and Watt. Verne created an in-depth timeline of Watt's movements from the day he was born to the last time he was arrested.

He discovered Rita Amos died over a decade ago. They'd had four other kids, besides Stephen, who weren't too happy Verne reached out to ask about their cousin. He learned Stephen had passed away from an accidental overdose three years ago. Of the four surviving Amos children, only one was somewhat willing to fill in the gaps for Verne. She made sure to emphasize that Rita had done everything she could for Watt, and he'd made the four years he lived with them hell. She added to the building blocks for their understanding of Watt. He'd found pleasure in tormenting the neighborhood cats, even killing a few before his aunt had enough and kicked him out. His cousin didn't know where he went after that and hadn't taken too kindly to Verne mentioning her brother's friendship with Watt. It left them with a two-year gap in the timeline, but it was safe to say he only escalated from cats. Immediately after the timeline gap, his father was released and Rebecca Smith murdered.

Ethan once again tried to reach Detective Coppin. This time, he didn't bother to leave a message. Clearly, Coppin had no intention of offering insight on the boxes.

Yesterday, Ethan spent most of his day trying to track down anyone that was connected to the management of the long since closed Rothbury Mall in hopes of finding record of Watt's employment. From Helen Nguyen's recent statement, they knew Watt was a janitor at Rothbury Mall in 1984 along with his cousin, Stephen Amos. His employment was confirmed in December 1988, when he was suspected in Melody Dawson's case. Beyond those dates, his employment was unknown, which left Ethan with nothing but a headache.

Today, the headache still lingered as he walked into their office, hoping to have a "fly under the radar" day. Verne's expression told him that particular wish wasn't going to be granted.

"Can I have coffee first, or do I need to address whatever this is now?" Ethan asked, waving his hand at Verne seated at his desk.

"Ed, or the mayor—someone—has connections because our lab results are back for Melody Dawson and Kelly McLane." Verne waved a stack of papers.

Ethan tossed his bag next to his desk as he leaned over Verne's shoulder to look at the lab results. When it was clear Verne wasn't going to do more than stare at the cover page, Ethan grabbed the report and flipped through to the first page they cared about.

He skimmed the pages a few times, adrenaline helping to clear his morning brain as he processed the words jumping from the pages.

"Well?" Verne asked, still seated and looking up at Ethan.

"We've got him again with DNA."

"Should I call Ed? He'll want to know. Do you think the DA will press charges right away, or do you think they'll want to build a case with all four cold cases at once?"

Ethan tuned Verne out as he kept going, listing all the different possibilities and avenues the positive DNA match could create in the cases. Ethan went to his own desk and added the report to the appropriate case file. It took several minutes, but Verne finally let Ethan get a word in.

"I think our next step is to talk with Watt," Ethan said.

"You think so?"

"He's now our only primary suspect in all four cases, two of which we've connected to him with DNA evidence. It's a logical next step."

Verne's silence drew Ethan's full attention. When they'd first been assigned the cases, he'd been eager for the chance to talk to Watt face-to-face. He even wanted to lead the questioning, so this apparent change of heart was perplexing.

"Are you going to tell me, or do we need to play twenty questions so I can figure out why you no longer seem thrilled at the prospect of questioning Watt?" Ethan asked, as Verne avoided eye contact by sorting through the random paperwork on his desk.

"Well, okay," Verne said, as he tossed down the paper in his hands. He leaned forward, a serious expression dragging down his face into hard lines. "I went out for drinks the other day with some college buddies."

Ethan quirked an eyebrow but stayed silent, wondering how this story was going to become relevant.

"One of them is a New Haven County ADA. Kyle, that's his name, said that he heard the DA and the mayor talking, because I guess they're friends and golf together—"

"Verne," Ethan warned before he strayed entirely off topic.

"Right, well, Kyle heard them saying Watt won't talk."

Ethan shrugged.

"Like he refuses to speak to police, the DA, his own lawyer even. He didn't testify at his own trial, he never confessed or even tried to claim innocence. Apparently, in the beginning, he used to say, "No comment," but later on, he just wouldn't even acknowledge them. Kyle said that some of the detectives tried…a more physical approach."

Ethan grimaced at the implication. He had never seen it himself, but he knew enough about Hadeon to believe he would use physical force as an interrogation tactic.

"So, you're concerned it will be a waste of time?" Ethan clarified.

"Yeah."

"Guess we'll have to hope for the best." Ethan grabbed his notepad and flipped to the list of people connected to the cases. He was still working to figure out if Rebecca Smith had any connection to Watt and the mall. He'd almost made his way through everyone again besides the sister, and he knew he was approaching the decision of whether to respect her wishes to be left alone.

"You don't care if he doesn't talk?" Verne asked, sounding surprised.

"It's our job to explore every crumb of evidence, and our primary suspect who is now linked by DNA to two of our four cases is a whole-ass cake."

"Kyle says it's a waste of time."

"Oh, well, if Kyle says we shouldn't do our jobs, we should just hand in our badges now."

Verne's concerned expression morphed into embarrassment as he shrugged and dropped back in his chair.

"I was just sharing."

Ethan knew Watt had done exactly as Verne described, having read through prior interrogation transcripts. He'd begun with, "No comment," before switching to absolute silence.

Even if they were met with silence, Ethan wanted to get in front of Watt and look him in the eyes when he told him about the progress on the cases. The connections they'd found to Kelly McLane's case. The fact that they knew he used the mall to find at least two of his victims and now had DNA evidence connecting him to both. Even if Watt didn't say a word, there was still a lot to be gleaned from body language.

He could say zero words but still speak volumes. Ethan was no expert, but he wouldn't be above asking if someone could be brought in to analyze footage. If Camilleri and the mayor wanted these cases closed, they could determine the value of it.

The remainder of the morning was spent working on their caseloads. Ethan hit another wall with Rebecca Smith's case and reluctantly called her sister, Sarah Ferges. He was sent straight to voicemail.

After leaving a message, Ethan tried Detective Coppin again, just in case. It rang out before going to voicemail. He kept his message brief; Coppin knew why he was calling.

Ethan was in the middle of holding for the New Haven County probation office when Vanessa texted. He glanced down at the message and swore, hanging up on the obnoxious hold message. He grabbed at his phone, patting his pockets for his wallet and keys before looking over to see Verne watching him, an eyebrow arched in question. It had completely slipped his mind that Vanessa had an appointment for the baby today, and he was supposed to be meeting her.

"I forgot I have an—uh, appointment. I have to run, but I'll be back. While I'm out, can you contact the prison and let them know we want to come in to question Watt? And find his lawyer's information. I want to know who is currently representing him."

Verne shouted after Ethan, but he was already running down the hall. He couldn't be late for Vanessa's first appointment. She might read into it, and he didn't want her thinking he didn't care or wasn't excited. He was excited, he kept chanting to himself all the way there. He was excited.

CHAPTER FOURTEEN

THURSDAY, NOVEMBER 15TH

The appointment took longer than Ethan had anticipated, and by the time he was walking back through the office door, it had been almost two hours since he ran out. Verne was seated in his desk chair, facing the door like he'd been waiting for Ethan.

Verne looked overly pleased with himself, which gave Ethan pause. There were moments, this being one of them, Ethan was genuinely afraid of what words were about to come out of Verne's mouth.

Instead of speaking, Verne held out a torn corner of what Ethan hoped was an insignificant form. Scribbled in Verne's handwriting was "11/26 at 9am" and nothing else. Ethan flipped over the small scrap just to be sure, but that was all Verne had written.

"Is this supposed to mean something to me?" Ethan knew, thanks to the doctor's office, that today was November 15th.

"That," Verne said, grabbing the scrap piece back from Ethan, "is our lawyer-free interrogation with Watt. His lawyer called and—"

"His lawyer called you?" Ethan asked. He walked past Verne and took a seat at his desk.

"Yeah." Verne's tone was annoyed, probably because Ethan interrupted his story, as he spun around to face Ethan again.

"Had you called the prison yet?"

"No," Verne answered, drawing out the word.

"And why did he say he was calling?"

"Because Watt wanted to talk to us." Verne's voice had softened, and it seemed the strangeness of the situation had only begun to dawn on him as Ethan questioned it.

"Did he give any indication as to why Watt wanted to talk now? I'm assuming they're aware we've reopened the cases. Did his lawyer mention them specifically?" Ethan hated that, for a moment, he resented the fact he'd had to leave work for the doctor's appointment. He'd wanted to be there, but missing that call firsthand made him feel like Watt and his lawyer had the upper hand.

Verne just shook his head, still looking slightly puzzled. "No, actually, it was weird because he called and said Watt was ready to talk, but it was on his terms."

Ethan thought it over for a minute, wondering how it could have got back to Watt. He supposed if Watt's lawyer knew someone in the DA's office, he may have been tipped off.

"Did the lawyer call for you specifically, or did someone transfer him to you?" Ethan asked, before he fully processed the end of Verne's statement. When it clicked seconds later, he lurched forward in his seat. "Wait, what terms?"

"Well, the first was he didn't want any recording—"

"Obviously, that's a no."

Verne didn't say anything, but his unwillingness to meet Ethan's eyes said enough.

"You told him no, right?"

"Ed might be willing to—"

"No."

It was moments like these he worried the kind of shit Verne might try to pull off if he wasn't here to keep him honest. He could guess the thought process for Verne—it wouldn't hurt anyone to not record. Not until Watt confessed something they had no evidence of him confessing, or he gave them vital information they couldn't later use against him because all they had was their claim he said it.

"What were his other terms?" Ethan asked, when Verne hadn't continued to share.

"He doesn't want his lawyer present, he's done when he says he's done, and he'll decide what we talk about," Verne listed off.

"Those were his only conditions? What did you tell his lawyer?" Ethan asked, afraid Verne had agreed to breaking the law just to get Watt to talk.

"I told him he's a lawyer, he knows how this works."

Ethan let out a breath that was somewhere between a sigh and a laugh. He felt a little guilty for doubting Verne's competence.

"I'm sorry," Ethan said, throwing his hands in the air.

"His lawyer said Watt wants the meeting and is aware that he will be recorded."

"So, Watt's lawyer was trying to see if we'd risk him going back on his word for a chance to talk to him?" Ethan asked.

Verne shrugged. Ethan let it sink in that in eleven days they'd be seated in the same room with Vincent Watt, who seemed willing to talk for the first time ever. Part of him wondered if it was a game to waste their time.

"The lawyer asked for you, by the way."

"What?"

"You asked if he called the station or me specifically. He called for you."

Ethan nodded, trying to ignore the hairs on the back of his neck that stood up. It didn't necessarily mean anything. There could be a whole list of reasonable explanations as to how Watt's lawyer, and presumably Watt, knew Ethan was one of the detectives looking into the cases, but it still made Ethan a little wary.

"Okay," Ethan said, and clapped his hands together, determined not to go down a rabbit hole of assuming the worst-case scenario. "We have eleven days to prepare ourselves to talk with Watt. It's not just the first time for us, but also for any detective if he actually talks, so we can't screw this up, or Camilleri will probably threaten to make us beat cops."

Verne snorted but didn't disagree. Ethan stood up and placed himself in front of their board, arms crossed over his chest as he tried to take it all in again. The new information they'd uncovered already about Melody Dawson and Kelly McLane gave him hope there was more to the cases than the original detectives had bothered to find out. He just needed to figure out which was the right loose thread to pull to unravel the entire mystery.

"Let's push this mall connection more. I want to look at all the cases, not just the cold cases. I really think Rothbury Mall played a bigger role than just Melody and Kelly." Ethan glanced back at Verne, who nodded and turned to his computer to start pulling up relevant files again.

His eyes trailed to the top of the board, where they'd added a photo of each of the seven little girls. Rebecca Smith. Anne Griffin. Kelly McLane. Penelope Wilks. Jacquelyn Battistelli. Melody Dawson. Emily Harp. Every one of them was smiling down at him, but he felt like their eyes were begging for him to do better. He couldn't save them, but he refused to let them be forgotten.

CHAPTER FIFTEEN

THURSDAY, NOVEMBER 22ND

There were only four days before Ethan would be sitting face-to-face with Vincent Watt, and instead of preparing, he had spent his day chopping vegetables, stuffing a turkey, preparing casseroles, and making Vanessa peppermint tea to battle the constant nausea. He'd given Verne strict instructions to keep him updated via texts since Verne opted to work Thanksgiving instead of dealing with his own family's get-together, which he promised Ethan would have ended with someone threatening to stab someone else with the carving knife.

Through some miracle, Ethan managed not to burn anything and get the food on the table as Howard and Lisa pulled into the driveway. Vanessa shuffled into the kitchen, finally drawn from her fetal position on the couch by the smell of food.

"Thank you," she groaned into Ethan's chest as her parents knocked on the door.

Ethan rubbed her back, prolonging the moment before he'd have to open the door and switch into host mode. He felt his phone vibrate twice from his back pocket and cursed himself for not having checked the last few texts Verne had sent before his in-laws arrived.

Vanessa broke away, making her way to her spot at the table. Ethan took a deep breath and forced a smile before he closed the distance between himself and the front door. He threw it open, doing his best to look thrilled to see them. Lisa stopped in the entry long enough to take off her coat, not bothering to acknowledge Ethan as she blew right by him, dessert in hand, to get to Vanessa in the kitchen.

"Took you long enough, it's freezing," Howard said in way of greeting. He shrugged off his own coat and tossed both his and Lisa's toward Ethan, who caught them, despite the momentary desire to just let them fall to the floor. Howard made his way to the kitchen, and Ethan, not so carefully, tossed their discarded coats onto the bench next to the door.

He could see everyone was occupied for a moment, so he took the chance to glance at his phone before he got sucked into a family dinner that might leave him unable to look for hours.

> What makes someone jump from cats to kids??

> these r the most boring transcripts ever. he says nothing.

> if watt left the hospital w anthony did he take anne at the same time?

> or like did he go back? feel like it would b 2 obvs 2 go back

> Potentially we're missing something in his escalation. Maybe attacks that weren't murders? Also, you already knew he said nothing in the transcripts, hence your excitement that HE wanted to talk to US.

> That is something that bothers me about Anne's case too. The timeline is obviously strange and we're missing the key part of it. Maybe we'll get lucky and he'll feel like sharing.

> Sitting down for dinner, won't respond for a few hours.

👍 ok

Ethan slipped his phone back into his pocket and made his way into the kitchen. Howard was opening a bottle of wine, which wasn't surprising, though Ethan wasn't sure if that had already been in the house or if he'd missed Howard carrying it in. Neither option would have surprised him; he'd learned two years ago that Howard would drop off wine while Ethan was at work to have his own stash here. He didn't like Ethan's wine-picking skills.

Lisa's homemade apple pie was already in the oven, which was good because Ethan had bought a frozen one. He could pass as a good enough cook, but baking was where he drew the line. Lisa was finishing up what he'd expected was one of her backhanded comments as he caught something about frozen desserts cutting corners. He and Vanessa made eye contact across the kitchen, and she mouthed, "Sorry." He shrugged. They'd been married long enough for him to expect all of this by now.

"Let's eat," he said, drawing everyone into a seat around the table.

"I'll carve the turkey, as the head of this family," Howard said, snatching up the carving knife. He looked at Ethan like he expected a fight, and when Ethan graciously waved at him to go ahead, Howard responded with a smug sneer like he'd won one over Ethan.

Ethan ended up tuning out much of the dinner conversation as his mind toyed with the question Verne had posed about Watt taking Anne. Without witnesses, without security footage, and without a way to get either of those things, Ethan knew that they were at the mercy of Watt. He was their only feasible suspect—what were the chances he would be at the hospital the same night as Anne and miraculously have nothing to do with it? Fiona Griffin was of that mindset, but Ethan and Verne couldn't get behind that. Which reminded him he needed to call Fiona and ask her about Rothbury Mall. Maybe there was another missing link there.

"Ethan?" Vanessa nudged him.

"What's up?" Ethan asked, suddenly aware of the three sets of eyes on him.

"Mom's talking to you," Vanessa said, hushed.

Ethan looked from Vanessa to Lisa; the latter sat with her head tilted and eyes wide, making him think of an owl. He caught Howard's scowl out of the corner of his eye and the shaking of his head as he returned to looking at his plate. Yet again, Ethan managed to do something Howard didn't approve of—nothing new.

"Sorry, Lisa, I'm tired, I guess. What had you said?"

Lisa nodded sympathetically at him, but Ethan didn't miss the concerned glance she spared Vanessa before repeating herself. "Ness was telling me work's been keeping you busy again."

"Yeah, the cases my partner and I are working on had some breakthroughs." He pushed the food around his plate as he spoke, trying to keep it vague.

"He's always so hard on himself. He's going to help families get closure. Ones who lost all hope before he started investigating."

Vanessa took his free hand and squeezed it. He looked over, and she was smiling at him with so much pride in her expression.

Howard grunted into the rim of his wine glass, but Ethan didn't bother to acknowledge him. He only broke eye contact with Vanessa when Lisa spoke up again.

"Are any of these cases I would know?"

"You know I can't get into details while investigations are ongoing," Ethan said.

He felt conflicted whenever Lisa asked him to share. He really couldn't share most things. Though it was different than when he was on homicide and there was a greater risk of jeopardizing the case if significant information got out. He knew he probably overshared with Vanessa. She'd become accustomed to his sharing, and if he didn't tell her anything, then it would just create a disconnect between them, so he carefully filtered the facts. Ethan was even less willing to divulge anything where Howard and Lisa were concerned. Especially when Howard's main goal was to always find fault with Ethan. Ethan had heard it all too. How he seemed to make his job more difficult than it was, or how he spent a lot of time at work for a case that didn't seem that complicated or urgent. Easy enough for him to say when Ethan had left out all the pertinent details.

"When we moved here, it was a dangerous time. I was absolutely petrified. We had moved to this new city from our quiet little Pennsylvania town—"

"Mom, we moved from a suburb of Philly," Vanessa cut in.

"We didn't have those kinds of crimes!" Lisa insisted.

Ethan didn't bother to argue with Lisa that Philly was a much larger city with significantly higher crime rates than Rothbury.

Vanessa nudged his knee under the table. "You told me some stuff."

Ethan met her eyes, silently begging her to stop talking before he turned back to Lisa, who was looking from Vanessa to Ethan expectantly. Ethan held back his "Yes, but that was different" comment that he suspected wouldn't go over well. He'd always given abridged versions, and he'd shared even less since learning she was pregnant. However, with Anne Griffin in the forefront of his mind, he found himself talking before he could reason himself out of it.

"You probably don't remember this, but in 1982, you took Vanessa to the Rothbury ER, and that same night, a little girl was abducted from there."

"I didn't know that."

Vanessa sounded upset. Ethan looked to Lisa and Howard for their reactions. If they remembered anything about that day, even something they may deem insignificant, they could be witnesses for the case. Considering how few there were, Ethan could use all the help he could get.

Howard glowered disapprovingly. Lisa sat shaking her head, as if lost in thought and unaware of the movement.

"Yeah, July 10, 1982." Ethan defaulted to interrogation tactics, knowingly giving the wrong date to see if the Ashbys remembered the details to be useful witnesses.

"No," Howard said at the same time Lisa replied, "It was July 8th."

"That's right. I'm so tired I'm mixing up dates now," he lied. "So, you do remember it?"

"Yes! Oh, it was horrible! I remember the news and that poor mother's pleas on the TV and radio. I held my baby girl extra tight those months after when they were constantly talking about searching for her." Lisa reached out a hand across the table, and Vanessa met her halfway. Lisa squeezed and smiled at Vanessa, back to her eager-to-know self. "Are you going to find out what happened to her? I think I remember they chalked it up to a murderer."

"Yeah, there is a primary suspect. I know it's been a while, but do you think you'd be able to give an official statement? Just anything you might remember from that night." He knew Lisa loved to talk, and maybe if she got going, she'd remember something useful.

"That's enough nonsense," Howard cut in before Lisa could answer. "You're upsetting my daughter."

Ethan glanced over at Vanessa, who he'd failed to notice had withdrawn her hand from Lisa's and sat with both protectively wrapped around her stomach. His own stomach dropped at the sight. This was why he kept the case talk to a minimum and filtered what he shared. The prospect of witnesses, when he had so few, had distracted him. He put his arm around Vanessa's shoulder.

"I'm sorry," he whispered.

"It's okay," she said, but when she looked up, he could see the tears in her eyes.

The remainder of dinner, Ethan sat quietly, allowing Lisa, and occasionally Vanessa, to dominate the conversation. When dinner was finally winding down, Vanessa cleared her throat and placed her hand on his leg under the table.

"I had my twelve-week OBGYN appointment last week, and the nurse was able to determine the gender. I had her put it in an envelope so Ethan and I could look at it later, but I was thinking maybe we could open it now while we're all together."

Vanessa looked at Ethan, her eyes searching his, but it was too late to object. Though surely, there was very little he could do to fall lower in Howard's esteem.

"Oh, yes, yes!" Lisa cried, clapping her hands.

Ethan nodded and gave her a reassuring smile, placing his hand on top of hers where it still rested on his leg. She smiled back and leaned forward giving him a quick kiss before standing up.

"I'll be right back," Vanessa said, before she disappeared down the hall.

He felt a tightness in his chest that he willed to go away. He'd never admit it to Vanessa, or anyone else for that matter, but finding out the gender terrified him. It felt like it had jinxed every other pregnancy. He knew there were medical explanations for why they'd lost the others, but it always came right on the heels of finding out the gender, so he couldn't help but connect the two.

"I hope it's a boy," Lisa shared in hushed excitement.

"I'd have to teach him how to play sports. Ethan works too late to be playing ball," Howard said, determined to criticize Ethan at every opportunity.

Ethan brushed aside Howard's comment, for Vanessa's sake.

"Oh, what if they have a cute little outie belly button like Vanessa! I wonder if that's genetic?" Lisa continued.

"She doesn't—" Ethan started to correct Lisa, but he dropped it as Vanessa came back in. She had an envelope gripped in her hand, a nervous giggle escaping her as she sat down.

"You do it," she whispered and handed him the envelope.

He took it and gave her a questioning glance, one last opportunity to back out before it was too late. Lisa urged him to read it with claims that the anticipation was killing her. Vanessa didn't give him the signal he'd hoped for, so he slowly broke the seal on the envelope and removed the card the nurse had put inside.

Girl!

Ethan tried to keep his hands from shaking as he turned it around so Vanessa could see it clearly.

"A girl," she said with such awe in her voice Ethan forgot about his fear of jinxing her. "We're having a girl."

She beamed as she turned to face her parents. Lisa started crying, of course, and even Howard managed a smile. Lisa got up from the table to hug them both, practically smothering Ethan before releasing him and going back to hugging Vanessa. Ethan decided now was a good enough moment to excuse himself, heading to the bathroom so he could check his phone and give Howard and Lisa the chance to gush over Vanessa.

He skimmed through the thirty-three texts Verne had sent, nothing relevant and all of them some level of absurdity that Verne should never voice to anyone else unless he wanted people to believe him unhinged. The fact Verne wasn't making any progress in the cases made Ethan feel slightly better about being home on Thanksgiving instead of at the station helping. After washing his hands, he braced himself to make it through the remainder of the evening.

He could hear their conversation as he got closer and paused, just out of view in the darkened hallway.

"I know it's an awful thing to say, but I am a little happy Ethan's parents aren't in the picture. It means I don't have to compete with another grandma," Lisa said from somewhere in the kitchen where Ethan couldn't see her.

"Mom! That's horrible."

"I know, but it is true. I mean, obviously it would be better for the baby if it had two sets of grandparents, but you married an orphan. At least your dad and I are close so we can help you with the baby."

Ethan clenched his jaw and resisted the urge to burst into the kitchen. He wanted to hear more before he interrupted and inevitably halted the conversation.

"You know he won't work any less just because you give him a kid," Howard scoffed from his seat at the table. Ethan could see the smug look on his face.

"Ethan's excited to be a dad, and I know he'll work less once the baby arrives because he doesn't want to miss anything." Her voice cracked at the end.

He flinched a little, as if she'd slapped him. He wasn't sure he'd realistically be able to cut back. Cases and developments didn't work around a detective's schedule. He was happy for her confidence, as misguided as it was.

"Are you worried he'll struggle to adjust to the role? He won't have parents to rely on like you do," Lisa said, circling back to his dead parents.

"You're not going to be there for Ethan then? I know you guys have always been hard on him and so critical—don't interrupt me, Dad—but he's done nothing but make sure I'm happy and been there for me when I wasn't. He was nineteen when his parents died, not a little kid. His mom and dad did a great job raising him, and I know he'll have their example to go on with our baby."

He saw her push her chair back, and before he had time to retreat or make himself known, she came storming through into the hall. She stopped when she saw him there, and he could see now that she was crying. She let out a soft "oh" and looked back into the kitchen.

"It's okay," he whispered, as he pulled her into a hug.

She tried to whisper an apology, but her silent tears had become hiccupped sobs. He didn't think what Howard and Lisa had said would get to her that much, but he supposed the pregnancy hormones may have amplified her reaction.

He kissed the top of her head and pulled away. "It's okay, Ness. Really."

Lisa came into the hall and stopped in her place when she saw them. "Is everything okay?" She asked. He couldn't tell if she knew he'd overheard, but he didn't care either way.

"I think we just need to call it a night. Ness isn't feeling well, and I have to work tomorrow," Ethan said, one arm wrapped around Vanessa's shoulder protectively.

Howard appeared behind Lisa. "What's going on?"

"Ethan has work tomorrow, so we need to leave," Lisa said, the annoyance clear in her voice. "Before we've even had the pie I made."

"Don't be silly. We're having dessert." Howard turned back to the kitchen.

"Leave!" Vanessa yelled.

Ethan jumped a little, Lisa made a strange squeak, and even Howard turned with clear shock in his expression.

"I don't feel good. Please, just go home," she said softly when all three of them looked at her. "I need to rest."

Lisa reached out and took her hand. "Of course, darling. Is there anything you need? Your dad and I can run to the store and bring you back anything."

"I'm okay, thank you."

Ethan watched her pull her hand back, clearly angry with her mom. Ethan would have felt bad for Lisa if he hadn't just overheard what she said. He was just grateful Vanessa had no problems setting boundaries.

Ethan quickly packaged up leftovers for them and made sure they took everything they needed so they wouldn't have an excuse to come back tonight. He even made a show of helping Lisa into her coat and said goodnight to them both like he hadn't heard anything.

When he came back in from walking them out, Vanessa nearly knocked him over tackling him in a hug.

"I'm so sorry. That was horrible. I don't know why they'd say those things, but I don't feel that way. I wish I could've met your parents and that they could've been there for all our big moments. And I know you're going to be a great dad and that your work won't stop you," she rambled, half her words spoken into his shirt. He hugged her back until her squeezing got to the point of restricting his breath, and he wiggled to loosen her grip.

"Thank you for standing up for me, but I really am okay. I know I'm not their favorite person, and I no longer lose sleep over it," he said, only half joking. He cared when they dated, were engaged, and even the first few years they were married. Now, he was just glad Vanessa didn't seem to resent him and his career nearly as much as her parents. He knew she would still prefer he didn't work so much, but that came with the job.

They stood in the hallway until Ethan's feet started to go numb from standing in one place for so long. He pulled away and held her at arm's length. Vanessa sniffled, wiping at her face with the back of her hands. He rubbed her arms, planting a kiss on her forehead and reassuring her that he was okay.

"What's that smell?" Vanessa pulled a face.

Ethan hadn't noticed that there was a strange smell, but now that she pointed it out, he realized something burning. He looked around for a source before it dawned on him.

He gently shoved past Vanessa and grabbed a towel, cursing as he burned his hand through it pulling out the pie Lisa had left in the oven. The crust was far past the golden perfection she always strove for and was now a charred black mess.

"Oh, appetizing," Vanessa said beside him as they stared at the pie on the stove top.

"Least it didn't burn the house down. That would have really made this Thanksgiving dinner perfect," he teased.

Vanessa produced a fork from the silverware drawer and poked at the crust. She broke a chunk free and flung it off the pie, revealing the extremely caramelized apples underneath. She stabbed one and blew on it before popping it in her mouth as Ethan watched slightly horrified.

"It only tastes slightly burnt, though very hot," she said with the apple balanced on her tongue as she tried to cool it down.

Ethan took the fork from her and did the same, not blowing on it nearly enough before he put the apple in his mouth. They took turns burning their tongues and freeing the apples from the burnt crust, laughing at each other every time they huffed and fanned their mouths.

CHAPTER SIXTEEN

FRIDAY, NOVEMBER 23RD

Ethan let out the deep, shoulder-slouching sigh he had been suppressing all day as he pulled up outside the Griffins' home. When he'd tried to call Fiona Griffin this morning to have this conversation over the phone, she barely let him get two words in before she cut him off saying she couldn't talk on the phone, and he'd have to come see her in person. He'd tried to persist, on a time crunch to prepare for the Watt interrogation Monday, but she hung up while he was explaining why driving to Southbury was inconvenient.

Verne had offered to come along, but he needed Verne at the station more than he needed him as a buffer. Their workload had increased now that they were reaching out to witnesses and families to clarify if anyone could connect the victims to Rothbury Mall.

To avoid wasting time, Ethan had left the visit till the end of the day, reasoning with himself he'd just grab takeout for dinner from Vanessa's favorite restaurant in Southbury to make the trip worthwhile.

Ethan let out one more sigh before he climbed out of his car and made his way up to the front door, ignoring the cold bite in the air. Verne's fancy wool coat didn't seem so ridiculous to Ethan now as he rang the doorbell and stood there rubbing his hands together.

Fiona swung the door open fast, much like the first time he stopped by, and he couldn't help wondering if there was a hole in the drywall from the erratic way she opened it.

"Ethan! So good of you to stop by, come in!" Her chirpiness threw him, especially since his call this morning had been the first he'd made in weeks since he'd started dodging her calls. For a moment, he wished he'd brought Verne.

Ethan found himself ushered through the door and down the same hall to the kitchen as before, not even given the chance to take off his shoes by the door. Fiona was right behind him, as she veered off to the island while Ethan stood by the table he'd sat at previously. He contemplated having a seat, but he wanted this conversation brief.

"It was so nice of you to return my call, I was beginning to worry. Is all going well?" There was no bite to her tone, but Ethan met Fiona's blank gaze. If he were closer, he might have been able to read more into her words, but from where he stood, it seemed like she was making conversation.

"Verne and I have a heavy workload," Ethan said, leaning against the back of a chair around the Griffins' kitchen table. "I called earlier because we're following a new lead, and I had a few questions for you."

Fiona began chopping vegetables, and Ethan noticed a pot already on the stove behind her. He'd obviously interrupted her and hoped he could use it for a quick exit.

"Do you finally have a different primary suspect than Vincent Watt?" Fiona asked.

"I had some questions about yours, and Mr. Griffin's, routine with Anne leading up to her disappearance," Ethan said, avoiding her question. He couldn't give her the answer she wanted to hear.

Ethan waited for Fiona to acknowledge him, but when it seemed like she wasn't going to say anything, he pulled out the pocket-sized notepad from his pocket along with a pen, flipping to a blank page.

"Who was Anne's primary caregiver during the day?"

"When I got pregnant, I left my secretary position. When Anne was born, I stayed home."

"Did you have a routine you liked to follow? Places you'd go regularly, people you'd see?"

Fiona paused, though she remained looking down at the vegetables on her chopping board. Ethan stood up straight, curious if she'd recalled something. Slowly, she began chopping again before she answered tersely. "Not particularly."

"Maybe you'd take Anne out to meet up with other moms? Or to unwind with a shopping trip?" Ethan pushed, not ready to reveal his hand just yet. If Fiona mentioned the mall, he felt like it would strengthen the lead potential.

"While my husband seems well to-do now, back in the eighties, he was still new in his career, and the financial benefits of being married to a lawyer had yet to materialize."

Ethan nodded, knowing he had to tread carefully now as he ventured into being more direct with Fiona.

"In the months, or even weeks, leading up to Anne's disappearance, did you or Mr. Griffin take her to Rothbury Mall?"

This time, Fiona's head lifted, her eyes narrowing slightly as she seemed to be assessing Ethan. While she hadn't stopped chopping, she had significantly slowed her pace, but Ethan couldn't help but continue to glance down at the knife.

"Does this have to do with Vincent Watt?" she asked.

"We are following a lead that may connect the cases further," he replied. He didn't want to give her too much, but he knew if he was too evasive, she'd only push back.

"I don't believe I ever took her to the mall," Fiona answered, her eyes dropping back to her task.

"And Mr. Griffin?"

Fiona scoffed in response, but it was answer enough for him given what he'd seen of Gregory Griffin. He didn't seem like the type to take his daughter, or wife, anywhere.

Ethan couldn't help the sense of disappointment. Early today, they'd confirmed another connection to Rothbury Mall. Emily Harp, one of Watt's original three victims, now had ties to the mall. While she'd been taken from a park, like Kelly McLane, they learned every weekend her father had custody, he would take her to the Toys-R-Us in the mall. Her 1989 case expanded their timeline for Watt's employment. He and Verne were still trying to confirm if the same could be said for the other cases, but if Anne's wasn't connected to the mall, then it could potentially weaken the theory.

Lost in his own head, Ethan realized Fiona had been speaking. Sheepishly, Ethan met her gaze.

"I'm sorry, what was that?"

For a moment, annoyance flashed across Fiona's face before morphing into a disingenuous smile. "Was there anything else? No updates to share?"

"Not yet, but I'll let you know." He flipped the unaltered notepad closed and slid it back into his pocket. "I should get going, it's getting close to dinnertime."

Fiona came from where she'd been in the kitchen and ushered him back the way he'd come in. "Yes, don't want to keep a pregnant wife waiting. And hopefully, you had a lovely Thanksgiving yesterday. It was just me home; Greg had to work to get ahead on some cases."

"Yeah, I'm stopping to pick up food," he replied, as they made it to the front door. He spared a glance to the side and saw the drywall was pristine behind the door, not even the tiniest crack or dent to show just once she'd lost her grip.

"Don't hesitate to keep me updated."

"Have a good night, Fiona," he replied, as he stepped onto the front step into near darkness. She didn't wait, and the door closed firmly behind him with the faintest sound of the lock sliding in place.

He half jogged to his car, nearly dropping his keys only once, before he slid into the driver's seat. He pulled out his phone to call the restaurant, mentally chanting to himself what he'd need to order. His thumb hovered over the call button, when a light seemed to go off in his mind, and his head snapped back toward the Griffins' house. He'd never mentioned the pregnancy.

CHAPTER SEVENTEEN

MONDAY, NOVEMBER 26TH

Verne was behind the wheel as they headed an hour and a half east to talk to Watt. Ethan absentmindedly tapped his phone against his thigh, ready to reply should Vanessa text. She'd taken a sick day because the nausea was still too much, but he'd been unable to stay home with her. He felt guilty, but he couldn't miss interrogating Watt. She'd last updated him on her plan to take a nap, and he hadn't heard from her since. The rational part of his brain told him she was probably doing exactly that, but he was still on edge, concerned something might happen while he was so far away.

"If it's a boy, you should name him Jason," Verne said, which stopped Ethan mid-tap. He'd caved and told Verne, though he didn't go into detail about the significance. Verne hadn't been his partner during Vanessa's past pregnancies.

Ethan snorted and returned to staring out the passenger window. "I'm not naming my kid after you."

"What if I died valiantly before he was born? Would you name him Jason then?"

"Highly unlikely."

Verne gasped, and Ethan heard a thump and knew Verne had slapped his hand over his heart. Ethan didn't want to think of baby names. During her first pregnancy, they'd picked out names, but he wasn't sure Vanessa would want to use them. He hadn't worked up the nerve to mention it and, the more he thought about it, he decided it best to let her initiate that particular conversation.

After he'd spent the weekend mulling over Fiona Griffin's comment about his pregnant wife, he'd needed a second opinion on the matter, but he was beginning to think Verne hadn't been the best choice.

"You know, you probably just mentioned it to her and don't remember," Verne said, after a few minutes in silence.

Ethan nodded as he recalled the handful of times he'd spoken to Fiona, but he knew he hadn't mentioned Vanessa. Lost in his thoughts, Verne seemed to take his silence as a cue to change the subject.

"Are you ready for today?" he asked, pulling Ethan out of his head.

Verne's nerves had increased as the day got closer, and Ethan could tell. He was worse than a cop going into his first interrogation.

"Dealt with worse."

Which wasn't a lie but didn't answer Verne's question either. It was rare he ever felt ready for an interrogation, but that wouldn't help Verne. There was a degree of unpredictability Ethan didn't enjoy. He grabbed one of the many files currently jammed into his bag. Among those files were some of the crime scene photographs from Kelly McLane's, Melody Dawson's, and Rebecca Smith's cases.

Ethan flipped open the file he had pulled out to a scribbled page of notes he and Verne had compiled. Since Watt's lawyer called, they dug up as much as they could about Watt and any further Rothbury Mall connections so they could spend the interrogation gleaning new information on the cases, preferably confessions. With their three confirmed connections, Ethan was holding on to hope that his gut feeling wasn't misleading him.

"Ideally, he'll do most of the talking. I'll take the lead on this to make it easier." Ethan had considered explaining that he didn't want Watt to play off Verne's nerves, but thought better of it, as he didn't want to exacerbate them.

"Are we going to talk about the forensic evidence at all?"

"I have those files, but at this point, it's not top priority to wave them in his face. He can deny it if he wants, but it doesn't make the science less true." Ethan didn't plan to waste their time on the forensic evidence. He was interested in what the evidence didn't tell them.

Verne nodded twice in confirmation and then sat silently. Ethan eventually turned on the radio, letting the noise do its best to drown out both their thoughts.

* * *

"All weapons, cellphones, pens, keys——" The guard rambled the list off in the most monotonous tone, clearly bored with the rehearsed dialogue and with Verne, who seemed to carry every item he owned in his pockets. Verne shrugged sheepishly when he threw a condom and some unwrapped mints into the holding bin from his coat pocket.

"Damn, I feel naked," Verne muttered to Ethan under his breath as they moved through the metal detectors.

They were instructed their prohibited items would be kept in a locker while they spoke to Watt and could be retrieved when they turned in their visitor badges. Ethan retrieved his backpack, emptied of all possible weapons, and returned his detective badge to his side. He clipped the visitor's badge to his shirt before falling in line behind Verne and the guard designated to be their chaperone.

The room they were shown into was lit by two bare fluorescent tubes that hummed over their heads. It was warm. The surface of the table was sticky and left a film on Ethan's hand when he pulled it away. Verne's main complaint was the pungent urine odor, even after he touched gum on the underside of the table.

Ethan got as comfortable as he could in the metal chair. He pulled the files out of his backpack and set them off to the side so Watt would see just how much they had on him. He did a mental assessment of the room, noting the camera in the corner behind him. He arranged their recording device in the center of the table, making sure it was pointed at where Watt would be seated.

They waited twelve minutes for Watt to be brought in. Enough time that Ethan had begun to worry that Watt had backed out and would refuse to see them. Verne may have shared that concern, but he remained silent on the subject. Instead, he helpfully announced every minute's passing, which made Ethan even more grateful to hear the buzz of the door that alerted them to Watt's arrival.

He had seen Watt's mugshots. He knew what he'd looked like when he was arrested and on trial. He'd even seen the updated photograph of Watt in the prison's records. In person, Watt looked less sinister than Ethan had expected. He had chiseled features, a little gaunt, but Ethan supposed time and prison food would do that. His thick, wavy hair made Ethan self-conscious of where he thought his own had started to thin and recede.

Watt shuffled to his chair and allowed the guard to properly secure him to the table. He was short, shorter than Verne, which, under different circumstances, Ethan was sure Verne would have mentioned. As Watt was situated, Verne started to roll up his shirt sleeves.

As soon as Watt had sat down, he'd locked eyes with Ethan and hadn't broken contact since. His unfaltering gaze unsettled Ethan, but he couldn't let Watt have the upper hand, so he maintained the contact.

"I'll begin the recording," Ethan said, leaning forward and pressing the red button on the recorder. He spared a glance over his shoulder and confirmed the camera light was on as well. "Today's date is November 26th, 2018. The time is 10:21 am. I am Detective Ethan Dumas, and present is also Detective Jason Verne. We're with Rothbury PD. Please state your full name and spell it for the record," Ethan stated.

"Vincent Anthony Watt. V-I-N-C-E-N-T. A-N-T-H-O-N-Y. W-A-T-T."

His voice was softer than Ethan imagined. Even knowing that Watt and his lawyer requested this meeting hadn't stopped him from fearing that they'd be met with an immediate wall of "No comment." He appeared unaffected by his surroundings and managed to look relaxed even with all the chains hanging off his limbs.

"Lou told me about you two," Watt said, before Ethan had a chance to dive in.

Ethan glanced at Verne.

"His lawyer," Verne replied to Ethan's silent question.

Ethan turned his attention back to Watt, choosing to ignore Watt's attempt at mind games.

"We work with cold cases and recently reopened four that had been linked to you," Ethan explained, taking control of the conversation. "You may be familiar with their names. Kelly McLane, Melody Dawson, Rebecca Smith, and Anne Griffin."

Watt stared at him as he spoke, but there was no physical reaction. If Watt recognized the names, it wasn't obvious. Ethan paused, just in case Watt had something to say, even just to deny knowing them. They sat in silence; the echoed shouts and bangs of the prison filled the space.

"Did your aunt blame you for your Uncle Henry's death?"

Verne shifted in his seat. This hadn't been something they discussed ahead of time. Watt tilted his head to the side, and his gaze narrowed on Ethan.

"She didn't blame me. Why would she? I didn't kill him."

"But your father did."

"It was an accident," Watt said, his voice even. Ethan wondered if he believed that.

"I'm going to be honest with you Vincent, Vinny? Do you mind if I call you Vinny?"

"Not at all," he said with a slight sneer in his voice that made Ethan think he did.

"I don't believe your aunt shared your opinion. Your uncle and father had quite the violent history. Your father had a few arrests for aggravated assault against Henry."

Watt shrugged. "I didn't kill him, so how could I be to blame?"

"Has anyone ever told you that you share a strong resemblance to your father? I'm sure your aunt noticed it too. I'd go so far as to say you look like a carbon copy of him."

Watt's left eye twitched.

"Maybe blame is the wrong word," Verne chimed in. "I think you mean to ask, did his aunt take out her anger and hatred of his father on him because he looked like him?"

They waited for Watt's response but were met with silence. Ethan was beginning to think this was how the interrogation would go. The only way it could be worse is if Watt resorted to "No comment."

"She did," Watt answered. He broke eye contact with Ethan and seemed to look beyond him at the wall over his shoulder. "Vile woman, vile temper."

"Did she hurt you?" Ethan asked.

Watt sneered. "Of course not. Did you ever see a picture of Rita? Tiny woman. Couldn't hurt a fly, though not for lack of trying. No, she preferred mind games and neglect."

"I can't imagine it was easy for you having to live with her. Were you and your mother close?"

Watt had collected himself again and reestablished eye contact with Ethan. He moved his hands to clasp one another, and the cuffs rattled against the table. He took a deep breath like he was about to give a monologue. "No."

"You weren't close?"

"Not particularly. She didn't possess a strong maternal instinct. I'd go so far as to say she probably would have liked it better if I hadn't existed."

"That must have been hard growing up knowing she would've been happier without you."

"I had my ways of coping."

Ever so slightly, the side of Watt's mouth curved up in a smirk. If Ethan hadn't been looking for it, he might've missed it.

"Ways to cope with your father's arrests and slip-ups or just your mother?" Ethan asked.

He was itching to pull out the timeline that showed the victims' deaths lining up with potential triggering events in Watt's life, but didn't want to risk spooking Watt into silence.

"Everyone needs coping mechanisms, detective. It's unhealthy to keep it bottled up."

"I can't imagine how difficult it was to have your father come back into your life when you were nineteen. You were a man at that point, and I'm sure he didn't treat you as such since you were a baby when he went away."

"We didn't have a relationship like that. He moved back in with my mother and me, which was difficult. But like I said, I found ways to cope."

"Do you remember approximately when your father got out of prison in 1981? February, was it?" Ethan flipped open a file that he had tucked under his arm and pretended that he was referencing dates.

"May...I believe," Watt answered faster than he had previous questions. Almost forty years later and Watt remembered the correct month.

"You're right, it was May. And then only a couple weeks later, Rebecca Smith was kidnapped from her front yard before she was found assaulted and murdered less than a mile from her home."

Watt didn't flinch, twitch, smirk or show any sign that Ethan had connected the dots. He didn't seem to have anything to say either. They once again sat in silence.

"I'm curious to hear how the DNA evidence my lawyer heard about concerns me." Watt had looked away from Ethan and started staring at his hands.

Ethan and Verne exchanged a glance. Neither of them had mentioned new evidence, which confirmed their suspicion. Watt's lawyer must have someone who tipped him off.

"In both Melody Dawson's and Kelly McLane's cases, viable DNA was recovered from previously collected evidence. The collected DNA came back as a match for you from the clothing that had been found on or with the victims," Ethan explained.

Watt didn't look up.

"The only time in my life that I can remember my mother not using drugs were the first two weeks he was out. It was an awful, impulsive decision on her part. She had extreme withdrawals, all while pretending to be a doting housewife. And then she'd make me do everything when he wasn't paying attention. She was pathetic."

Watt kept his eyes lowered on his hands. Meticulously manicured cuticles, short and clean nails, slender fingers with thick, knobby joints. Ethan had never imagined evil hands, but Watt's would stick with him.

"He was worse than her. First thing he did was start drinking again, and then naturally he started hitting her again. The worst part was he thought he could come into my home and start knocking me around like he had the right to just because I had the misfortune of sharing his DNA."

The story felt rehearsed. Ethan wondered who he'd told the story to before. Just his lawyer? Obviously not detectives. Had he practiced just for them?

"He'd been nothing to me my entire childhood. My mother never took me to visit him because she did blame him for her brother's death. She was adamant that he wasn't drunk when he pulled the trigger, even though her brother was. He was a functioning alcoholic, so even if he'd had a few drinks, he would've been clear headed enough to know what he was doing. Still, as soon as he got out, she was there to pick him up and bring him to our home. A home I was paying for at the time. She was always too high to hold down a job, and the money she did make with her...methods, all went on drugs."

Verne chimed in before Ethan had a chance to decide where to direct their conversation. "If you were the one with money, why didn't you leave when she brought him back into your lives?"

"I couldn't leave her in that house with him. She'd have ended up dead within a few months. She didn't know how to tell him no. If she had, I'd never have been born."

All the girls you killed would still be alive, Ethan thought. The world would have been a much better place had Mary Amos been able to tell

Anthony Watt no from the beginning. Instead, Ethan had to listen to Watt's lamenting.

"Did you ever have to play referee between your parents?" Watt asked.

Ethan didn't make it a habit of discussing his parents with strangers, regardless of caliber, but especially convicted felons. Luckily, Verne was less reserved than him about most things.

"My parents always fought. Most of my childhood was them going through a divorce. My dad was rarely home because of work, but when he was around, it was awful. Both are New Yorkers too, so you can imagine the lungs on them. Sometimes, it'd get so bad I'd have to get between them and just yell for them to shut up until one of them gave up yelling over two other people."

Watt was watching Verne with a slight smirk on his face. Ethan had met Verne's father, and the stark image Verne created fit the loud-mouthed ex-detective he'd met. He felt a little bit of pity for Verne, imagining him as a kid, short and whistly gap-toothed, trying to break up a marital spat. Verne finished his overshare, and Watt turned to Ethan.

Ethan ignored the tightness in his chest as he remembered his parents. Grotesquely in love, he once explained to Vanessa. Highschool sweethearts, they had managed to grow stronger instead of apart. Ethan used to make gag noises whenever they kissed or even hugged around him. Watt stared at him with expectation, and Ethan weighed his options and knew he'd be better off playing along if he wanted to steer the conversation back to the cases.

"Yeah, often. My parents didn't get along and they were always fighting." Ethan swallowed the bad taste it left in his mouth to betray their memories. He couldn't recall a single time they'd fought, but it wouldn't help to keep Watt talking if he admitted as much. Still, despite Ethan and Verne's sharing, Watt's smirk slipped back to a blank stare.

"You both still seem fortunate enough to never have wanted to see your father die, particularly by your own hands." Watt didn't sound angry or even resentful, just matter of fact. He leaned forward in his chair, so his chains clanked as he moved.

Verne made a humming noise that Ethan knew to be his stalling tactic when he didn't know the appropriate response. Verne spared a sideways glance at Ethan that he ignored. Verne knew Ethan's parents were dead, but Ethan wasn't about to dredge those emotions up now even for the benefit of Watt talking.

"Why didn't you?" Ethan asked, since it seemed the question Watt wanted them to ask.

"He wasn't worth the jail time."

"You're not confident you're capable of getting away with murder?"

Watt's left eye twitched at the question, and Ethan knew he hit a nerve.

"I'd say you've managed to evade being caught for some time on several cases, like the ones we've been investigating. The oldest one is over thirty-seven years old. That's a long time to get away with murder."

Ethan knew he walked a very thin line between getting a reaction and a complete shutdown.

"He was in and out of jail the remainder of his life. It was easier to distance myself than try to be involved in one another's lives," Watt explained without addressing Ethan's comments.

"You two didn't stay out of each other's lives though. In fact, it seems that whenever he needed bail posted or someone to pick him up from the ER, you were the one that would do it."

Ethan needed to build his way up to Anne Griffin's case. They had the evidence for Melody Dawson and Kelly McLane, along with the connection to the mall. Then they'd circle back to Rebecca Smith to emphasize that they'd figured out his triggers. There was still the unknown on whether Rebecca Smith's case could be linked to the mall, and he remained hopeful, even if Anne Griffin's couldn't be linked.

"He'd call my mother when he needed something, and since she was always too high to be of any use to anyone, I'd go and do it to get her to quit whining. Don't confuse my unfortunate position for caring. I'd have much rather left him to rot."

Verne started to tap his foot, antsy to speak, so Ethan leaned back to allow Verne to take the lead. "Maybe I'm dumb, but I just don't get it.

You didn't really like your mom, you sure as hell didn't like your dad, so why'd you bother? I mean, if it were me and I thought that two people were so worthless, I'd have been out of there."

Watt's face cracked a little and a slight frown pressed his brows down. He shook his head ever so slightly.

"An honorable man doesn't just leave his mother with an abusive man. What kind of person would I have been if I'd just walked away from a situation because it wasn't desirable? I stayed and found ways to survive. I didn't run like a coward." He spoke passionately and made Ethan's stomach twist in disgust.

"Honorable? What do you know about honor? An honorable man couldn't do this to a child!" The anger in Ethan's voice was barely contained, but his hands remained steady as he yanked photograph after photograph from the file and slapped them down on the table in front of Watt. "Nothing but a monster could do this to another person, let alone to an innocent child," he said through clenched teeth.

Over a dozen photographs of Melody Dawson's, Kelly McLane's, and Rebecca Smith's bodies were splayed out in front of them. Ethan, even with his decades of experience, couldn't bear to see children abused and mutilated. He could taste bile. Verne didn't even pretend that he could handle it and had turned his gaze to some point beyond Watt's head. Under different circumstances, Ethan would have been annoyed at his lack of control, but this was one of those times he wouldn't fault him.

Watt's eyes devoured the photographs. He didn't look away, after realizing what they were, or show disgust at the girls' conditions. He almost seemed lost in the photographs and unaware that Ethan watched him, with such contempt, as he saw his crime scenes again. He wanted to reach across the table and get his hands around Watt's throat. For every girl he touched, for every family he destroyed, and for every parent and soon-to-be parent, like himself, who feared people like Watt. Just as violently as he'd put them out, Ethan swiped them up and gathered them back into the folder.

Watt looked up at him like a child whose favorite toy had been snatched from his hands. "Quite the gruesome scenes you're carrying around."

"And yet you didn't seem to mind looking."

"I've been told I have a strong stomach."

"We have DNA evidence connecting you to two of these girls, Vinny." Ethan would get his jabs in where he could, though he'd much rather choke the arrogant bastard.

Watt let loose a single cackle. The joy he derived from this sickened Ethan.

"Have I amused you?"

"Why bother with this charade if you know it's me? If you're seeking remorse, keep on seeking. I had none thirty years ago, why would I have any now? Did you think I found Jesus or that I've become so forlorn in my cell that I'll just tell you everything? You can show me your pretty pictures and bore me with your evidence. I have nothing to gain from this except..." He paused, a wide smile splitting his lips apart to show smoke-stained teeth.

"I do get an element of pleasure knowing you want what's in here." He motioned at his head, the cuffs rattling in protest.

Ethan balled his fist in his lap as he decided his next move. Watt had the upper hand, and they all knew it. They had the evidence on him for Melody Dawson and Kelly McLane whether he denied it or not. That didn't help Rebecca Smith or Anne Griffin. Without his cooperation, there was hardly a chance for them. All it took was Watt to change his mind about talking and they'd have lost their window of opportunity.

"The argument could be made that you have nothing to lose either," Ethan said.

Watt awkwardly clapped his hands. "Touché, detective. I suppose I don't since some lawmakers thought it would be helpful to get rid of the death penalty. I'd been looking forward to that final cocktail."

"I hear you're healthy too. Many more years to become forlorn, as you say." Ethan didn't know anything about Watt's medical record, but he was grasping at straws to gain the upper hand.

"There are plenty of people who wish I wasn't. I get hate letters from people promising to end my life when they get their hands on me. There are lots of ignorant people who don't understand how life without parole works."

"Can you blame them?" Verne mumbled.

"Of course not. I did kill those girls; the ones I'm in here for and those two you have the evidence for."

Verne made a strange sputtering sound like his thoughts and mouth had gotten out of sync. Ethan clenched his jaw to fight his disbelief from escaping. He wanted to physically lash out at Watt to wipe the smug look off his face.

"You're admitting that you were responsible for the kidnapping and murders of Melody Dawson and Kelly McLane?" Ethan clarified. They had the DNA evidence, but if, down the line, Watt tried to plead not guilty to the murders, a video recording of his self-proclaimed guilt would be much harder to refute.

"I can tell you more about them if you'd like. I can remember every detail of every girl. Each one is like a precious gem in my mind."

Ethan wanted to break his nose and call it a day. He caught Verne's head nod in his periphery, but Watt's eyes were on Ethan. It seemed Watt had deemed him in charge. Ethan leaned back and did his best to look calm.

"Yes, we'd like to hear it."

Watt was a storyteller, horrifically captivating, and seemed to love to hear himself talk. For two hours, he made sure to go over every detail from the moment he decided Melody Dawson and Kelly McLane were his victims to the moment he left their bodies where they were found. Ethan had to stare at his hands more than once to blink away tears when Watt made sure to drag out recounting the abuse. He spoke about them like they were grown women and not children. He laughed about how they screamed, how Melody Dawson cried for her mom and Kelly McLane begged to go home.

Verne was noticeably pale, and Ethan worried this might be where they learned Verne's limits. Verne stayed as tense as Ethan the entirety of Watt's confession. At one point, when Ethan's survival instincts tried to kick in, he worried if either of them relaxed, they might physically lash out at Watt. He didn't know how they made it through, and more than once, he silently questioned if Watt was ever going to stop. It helped that Watt didn't need them to speak because neither seemed capable.

"And when I was done, I'd snap their necks. It was the easiest way because there was no clean up and I could just leave." He smiled and sat back.

"You mentioned with Melody Dawson that your job at the mall, as a janitor, helped you. But it helped you with Kelly McLane too, that and your cousin, Stephen."

"Did you have a question for me detective, or just thinking out loud?"

"Did you find all your victims at the mall?"

"Isn't that your job to figure out? Surely, Rothbury PD hasn't gone so downhill they need me to do the investigative work too." Watt smirked, clearly pleased with his mocking return.

Ethan held his gaze for several moments before he decided to let that line of inquiry go for now. Watt's avoidance was answer enough. He wasn't going to confess so easily to everything. They'd gotten lucky that he so freely gave them a confession for Melody Dawson and Kelly McLane. Of course, there was the distrust in the back of Ethan's mind as to why he did that, but Ethan wasn't about to look a gift horse in the mouth, as his mom would've said.

"Did you take anything from them?" Ethan asked, shifting gears.

"Of course not! Why would I risk such a reckless connection to them when I have a photographic memory?"

There had been nothing in Watt's file about a photographic memory, but Ethan supposed it made sense, given the detail of his recall. "What about Rebecca Smith, the third victim in those photos? The abuse and killing is almost identical to all your other victims."

"You said you had four cases." Watt had relaxed back in his chair and returned to his stoic state. "But you've only shown me three girls."

Ethan flipped open the file and moved past the crime scene photographs to the last photograph in it. When Anne Griffin had first gone missing, the detectives had obtained a photograph from her family for the missing persons file. Ethan placed it in the center of the table, just out of Watt's reach.

"This is Anne Griffin, but I'm sure you know that," Ethan said, as he closed the file again so Watt couldn't get another look at the crime scene photographs.

"I assume she's the fourth girl." Watt barely even glanced at the photograph. Ethan wanted to wave it in his face and make him look at her, but instead, he remained still.

"Anne was taken from Rothbury ER the same night that your father was admitted after sustaining injuries from a brawl."

Watt tilted his head and shrugged but didn't challenge Ethan on his point. Ethan was past the point of tiptoeing around him in fear he'd shut down, so he took Watt's bait and kept talking. "That very same night, you were called on your father's behalf to pick him up so the hospital could release him to someone. How did you do it so easily, and without anyone noticing?"

There was the slightest furrow of Watt's brow that gave Ethan hope he'd touched on something. "Was part of the thrill taking her while her parents were right beside her asleep? I suppose your father didn't notice either since he was still intoxicated."

"He was rarely sober, so I'm sure he was unable to comment on much of my activity."

Ethan looked at Verne. "Well, that explains how he was able to do it with his father there. I guess we were wrong to assume he would have had to make two trips."

"I think the hospital staff would've remembered if he came back after taking his dad," Verne said, following along with Ethan.

"I'm still confused on whether he would have taken his father home and then gone somewhere else with Anne, or if he just left him in the car while he did his thing."

"Seems like a lot of work to take him home. I mean, if the guy was such a drunk, I'm sure he'd have stayed in the car. Couldn't have taken that long, his kind usually has issues, so they end up being the quickie type." Verne motioned with his pinkie. He was laying it on thick, and it had gotten to Watt. He hadn't interrupted them, but Ethan could see Watt had shifted several times as the two of them talked like he wasn't there.

"You're right. He'd have probably stayed close to the hospital too. He probably freaked out after. She was only his second victim, and so he panicked and was sloppy. Had to get it over with before his father sobered up enough and realized his son was a freak."

Watt slammed his fists, a sharp ring of metal on metal as the cuffs and chains smashed against the table. "I will not sit here and be mocked."

Ethan arched an eyebrow and feigned confusion. "Mocked? No, we simply need to talk through the events to figure out what happened since you don't want to share details. Leaves Verne and me in a tough spot of filling in the blanks."

"Not the ideal way of doing it, but it gets the job done eventually. It's like a real-life game of Clue. Alternatively," Verne said to Watt, leaning in as if to tell him a secret, "you could tell us about Anne Griffin and Rebecca Smith. It'd save us a lot of time pestering you about it. Or we could continue to take guesses. Every time we have a new one, we could drive over here, have them pull you out of your cell, and sit you down so you can hear about it."

Watt held eye contact, but he didn't move a muscle on his face. He seemed unfazed by Verne's apparent threat. Ethan supposed when someone was serving life without parole, more of your crimes being solved wasn't much of a concern. Ethan hoped the disturbance of his peace might sway him though. Watt seemed to have enjoyed the attention these last few hours, but only when he was in control. Verne's threat could just as easily push him into silence.

"The cliff trails in Rothbury are secluded. Have you ever been?" Watt asked. "There's lots of places you can go down into and no one will pass by for hours. I imagine you could dig a grave before someone passes by."

Ethan gave Verne a quick look. He believed he knew which trails Watt was referencing, but they'd never connected him to them. The Naugatuck River ran by them, which did match Watt's MO, but his known dumping sites tended to be on the other side of Rothbury.

"Did you use the trails?" Verne asked, clearly not sharing Ethan's concern that if they pushed him, Watt would shut them out before he was done.

"She was such a tiny thing, wasn't she?" Watt nodded at Anne's photograph still on the table between them.

Ethan slid it back toward himself and tucked it away in the file. "Was there a trail you favored?"

"I once climbed one of the trees on a trail. No reason for it, I just wondered if I could, so I started climbing and climbing. It was one of those old ones that was taller than the rest but with only a few branches low down. It took me a while to get up. I had to use some of the rocks to climb up and then jump into the tree. Took a few tries, but once I got high enough, I could see for miles around. I imagine if I'd fallen from up there, I'd have died. Splat."

"Vinny—Vincent," Ethan corrected himself, too desperate to push his buttons now. "Did you bury Anne Griffin?"

"I must amend my statement earlier, that my mother lacked maternal instinct. I recall she used to sing me a lullaby, even when I was too old to want her to. She'd come into my room high as a kite and try to rock me, though usually she'd just push my head to her chest and sing slurred words."

"Vincent, let's focus on the trails," Ethan interrupted. He was afraid they were losing him on his tangent, and he had little hope he'd be able to do much to refocus him once they had.

Watt began to hum a tune. Ethan's stomach dropped, and he knew they'd lost him.

"Rock-a-bye baby, on the treetop. When the wind blows, the cradle will rock. When the bough breaks, the cradle will fall, and down will come baby, cradle, and all." The humming soon turned to a full rendition of the lullaby, and Watt sang it over and over. By his fourth or fifth round, he started to get louder.

"I think he's done with us," Ethan said. He turned off the recording device. They stood up and gathered their material. Watt did not falter in his singing or react in any way to them getting up from the table. He kept his eyes trained straight ahead of him.

"We're done!" Ethan shouted, as he pounded on the door a few times to get the guards' attention. Watt had continued to raise his voice to the point that he now screamed the lullaby.

"For fuck's sake, can they let us out of here?" Verne shouted to Ethan as the door mechanism unlatched and they stood back to let the guards in. Their deadpan expressions made Ethan wonder if this was a normal stunt of Watt's. They didn't seem at all fazed to hear him scream a lullaby.

* * *

Verne napped the entire way back, which gave Ethan too much time to mull over the meeting. By the time they got back to the station, he felt like his mind was spinning and pulsing, ready to explode. He'd tried to analyze Watt's motives, from wanting to talk to them after decades of silence to providing a location and then shutting them out. He'd held his tongue until they'd made it to their office. The door was barely closed when he began.

"I think he's playing games," Ethan said.

"It may be a new victim if it's not Anne Griffin," Verne said at the same time.

"Why would he lie?" Verne stopped mid-stride, looking a bit comical, like he was playing a game of freeze tag. He straightened up and planted his hands on his hips.

"Why wouldn't he lie? What does he gain from telling us the truth?" Ethan asked. "He's got more to gain by lying. He'd waste our time, which I'm sure he'd find pleasure in. If it were a victim we hadn't found, why would he willingly surrender that information to us?"

"But he confessed to Melody Dawson and Kelly McLane. He didn't lie then," Verne countered.

"He didn't really have much room to deny it either. We had the DNA evidence, which he and his lawyer somehow knew about. We're lucky he's already in jail because it would appear we have a mole." Ethan dropped himself in his seat and unpacked the files they'd brought with them to the prison.

"Okay, but what if it's Anne Griffin? Why do you think he's playing games and not just giving us information? Maybe he just knows we're figuring it out. He probably learned we were investigating all the cases he was the primary suspect for and decided it was easier to cooperate than have us bother him."

Verne tapped his foot, hands still on his hips, clearly stumped. Ethan had already spent the whole drive attacking this from different angles. He understood Verne's wishful thinking, but experience told him something was not right. Verne threw his hands up in the air and finished the last steps to his desk, dropping down and facing Ethan.

"So what? You want to pretend he didn't say anything?"

"No." He held a finger up as Verne went to protest. "I'm not saying we don't investigate it. However, before we send a team to search miles of trails with no clear direction of where to focus or what they're looking for, I want to try and corroborate his claim."

Ethan waited for Verne to decide if he approved of the plan. It required Verne to smack his rubber band ball from palm to palm, occasionally giving Ethan a quizzical narrow-eyed look.

"Fine," Verne said, as he slammed the ball down. "But did you really consider the chance it's Anne Griffin out there?"

"I did, and while there's always the chance that I'm wrong, I don't think I am. I don't honestly believe there is a victim buried out there. You heard him. He didn't stop to bury them. He even chose a method that was quick and didn't require clean-up."

Verne nodded, seeming to follow Ethan's logic at least.

"Even if there is somebody buried out there, I don't believe it's Watt's victim," Ethan added.

Verne didn't challenge Ethan. He understood Verne's thought process; Anne's body had never been found. However, his gut instinct told him it wasn't her. The same instinct fueled the voice in the back of his mind questioning if her case fit at all.

CHAPTER EIGHTEEN

FRIDAY, NOVEMBER 30TH

Camilleri kept looking from one to the other. Ethan had found a ceiling tile to study, so Camilleri was in his peripheral. Verne had managed to turn the simple question of how long they had known about the potential lead into a long-winded explanation.

"Since Monday?" Camilleri cut off Verne when he got to the part in his story that answered his question.

"Yes, but—"

"No, but! Dumas?" Camilleri turned on Ethan and forced him to make eye contact.

Ethan contemplated playing dumb, forcing Camilleri to ask the questions, but he knew what he wanted to know, and pretending otherwise would just dig them into an even deeper hole. "We felt it necessary to look into his confession further before briefing you on the matter, sir."

"Don't bullshit me. You're worse at it than Verne."

Ethan could see Verne beside him trying not to giggle at the comment. Ethan sat up a little straighter in his seat. "Honestly, I thought he was bluffing. He's never once mentioned to detectives, inmates, or even journalists that he buried any victims. It didn't seem plausible, so I wanted to investigate further before we wasted resources on a potential bogus tip."

"I think he just wanted us to go scrambling after a lead so he could brag that he made us look like idiots," Verne added. Ethan was grateful for the backup.

"And this was sufficient reason to fail to do your jobs?" Camilleri asked, no longer seated behind his desk but perched on the corner closest to Verne. Ethan swore Verne shrank back just the tiniest bit when Camilleri spoke.

Ethan resisted looking at Verne. When he'd proposed not rushing the lead, he hadn't anticipated that Verne's big mouth would cause him to blurt out everything to Camilleri.

"No, sir," Ethan answered, turning to hold Camilleri's gaze.

Ethan knew the answer didn't satisfy Camilleri, but it was an honest answer, and it ended his line of questioning. Camilleri got up and walked back to his seat. He took a minute to push some papers around and straightened a few files. Ethan thought of Gregory Griffin and his air of superiority.

"If the media were to catch wind of the fact two of my detectives ignored an important lead," Camilleri said while looking between them with his "I dare you to challenge me" look, "it wouldn't just be your asses on the line. So, as soon as we can get a team out there, you two are following this lead."

Verne began to respond, which Ethan knew was a poor choice, but Camilleri interrupted before much more than a sound passed Verne's lips. "And one of you will be there at all times during active search hours. Am I understood?"

Ethan nodded, and a few seconds later, probably after deciding his point wasn't that important, Verne nodded too.

"Right. Go!" Camilleri said. He looked at his laptop, effectively dismissing them. Ethan and Verne filed out of his office. Neither said anything until they were several corridors away and nowhere within earshot of Camilleri.

"No fucking way," Verne said first.

Ethan shrugged, Verne summarizing how he felt about Camilleri's decision. They had no reason to trust Watt. However, Ethan knew to choose his battles with Camilleri. He had a valid point. If the media found out about this, there would be hell to pay. The public rarely understood the behind-the-scenes.

"You know what will really be awful?" Verne asked.

"If Watt isn't lying?" Ethan responded. He'd already begun a mental list of how Camilleri could get angrier about this situation. Top of that list was Watt had, in fact, not lied. Second was he had.

"I probably just jinxed us," Verne said.

Ethan remembered Verne had said that to him on the first cold case they'd worked together when they'd had to go door-to-door to try and find potential eyewitnesses. Verne had commented how they'd managed to not get any weirdos and then said what would become his bad luck phrase: "I probably just jinxed us." The next house, they were greeted by a very chatty gentleman in his seventies, who happened to be completely naked. Verne claimed this phrase controlled their fate.

"Let's just hope we don't come out of this looking like fools," Ethan muttered.

CHAPTER NINETEEN

MONDAY, DECEMBER 17TH

Ethan shuffled from foot to foot, hands shoved in his pockets to keep himself from fidgeting too much. He'd rather have been at the office doing paperwork than in the middle of the woods, in the freezing rain. Verne had already retreated to the car, announcing on his way he planned to crank the heat and break the chill in his bones until Ethan wanted to switch.

The following Monday, Camilleri had sent them out to the woods, and they'd been there every day since. They were now on day fifteen, and Watt's vague description of the location had led them to absolutely nothing thus far. Cadaver dogs had picked up a scent in one of the many areas that dropped down off the path and gave lots of privacy. It was all they had to go on, so they settled on that spot, which was about half the size of a football field. The dogs hadn't been much help narrowing it down further than that, as they kept signaling all over the clearing. Camilleri had grumbled a few times already about pulling the plug to prevent draining more of their budget.

Ethan was still skeptical there would be anything to dig up, despite the cadaver dogs. He'd spent sleepless nights, after Watt's interrogation, questioning his motives. There was no reason to believe him. Even before his conviction, he hadn't given a crumb of information regarding a case, and now, supposedly, he'd just handed over a burial site with seemingly nothing to gain. Still, Camilleri had a forensic anthropologist on stand-by.

Ethan's phone vibrated, and he snaked it out of his pocket.

> Anything yet?

Ethan looked over his shoulder to where the car was just barely visible on the dirt road up the hill, surrounded by forensic vans.

> Yeah we uncovered a ton of bodies and some buried treasure. Did I forget to tell you?

> Asshole 👍

Ethan chuckled and slid his phone back in his pocket. He turned his attention to the forensics team, not that there was much to see. They were just a group of very muddy figures, mostly knee deep in holes they'd carefully dug to not destroy any evidence they might uncover.

Though they'd been switching off so one could stay at the station and try to figure out who might be buried here if it wasn't Anne Griffin, both Ethan and Verne had decided to come out to the dig today. It was close enough to the hospital to be a feasible dumping spot, but not as close to the abduction sites as Watt's other victims. It was a consistent factor in his murders that no victim was found very far from where they went missing. Verne and Ethan had narrowed it down to four missing persons cases that could be connected to Watt based on his MO.

Ethan moved around the inner perimeter of the tents, glancing at the never-ending dirt and mud the unfortunate CSIs had to contend with, as well as the steady stream of water trickling in as they worked. So far, the most exciting thing someone turned up was a matchbox car that the CSI said he had as a kid. He walked laps around the perimeter of the tents in an attempt to stay warm for another couple hours before the monotony was shattered.

"Detective!" a CSI shouted, gloved hand shooting up to identify which suited figure spoke.

He squelched his way over. Despite the PPE he had on, the mud had managed to seep through the shoe protectors and made each step treacherous as he navigated his way between holes. He would have to remind himself to leave these shoes in the garage, so he didn't trail dried mud into the house.

"Is it a body?" he asked, as he approached, unable to see into the hole she still stood in.

Her impatient glare was answer enough. A man could hope, he thought, especially when he was freezing and the ache in his joints was painful to the point of distraction. He was into his forties now; it would take his body days of coddling to recover. Ethan stood at the edge of where the CSI had halted her digging. He wasn't entirely sure what he was looking at.

"This," she said, slowly smoothing out what he now realized was fabric, "appears to be a towel."

He crouched down to get a better look, momentarily forgetting the ache in his knees and hips. With her gloved hand, she carefully loosened more dirt from the fabric and lifted it with care. It was hard to say what color the towel had been before it had spent time in the ground, but Ethan could make out a faint striped pattern.

"Is that staining from being in the ground?" Ethan asked, motioning at a darker spot along one of the long edges of the towel.

"Difficult to say, though given the color, it is possible it's blood. Until we get it to the lab, I can only speculate."

"Verne!" Ethan shouted, before he'd pushed himself back into the standing position. He turned toward the entrance of the tent and saw Verne had already made his way from the car and donned PPE.

"I saw you head in and figured I shouldn't miss the excitement," Verne explained as he weaved his way around the other dig sites to join Ethan.

Ethan motioned toward the CSI, realizing he couldn't remember her name.

"What'd you find, TJ?" Verne asked.

He crouched down as Ethan had been a minute before. She repeated the process and held up the towel so Verne could get a good look. Other CSIs had taken notice of TJ's find, and one brought over an evidence bag for her to properly process it. Ethan and Verne retreated to the edge of the tent, the rain pouring down beyond the cover and running under the flaps where they stood.

"It could mean nothing," Verne said, breaking the silence between the two of them.

Ethan nodded, looking around at the large amount of unprocessed area in the clearing.

"A towel doesn't give us much of a lead. After all, it could have been left by a hiker at some point and over time just got buried." There was an unhealthy part of him that didn't want Watt to have been helpful, but his desire to give a family closure outweighed that.

Verne nodded, rocking back and forth, his shoes making a suction-cup popping.

"Don't suppose we got lucky and one of the missing persons cases we've found was reported missing with a striped towel?"

"No, though that would have been nice."

Ethan watched as TJ and another CSI worked on properly logging the towel into evidence. They talked in hushed, almost reverent, tones. He couldn't hear exactly what was being said, but he caught the odd word and recognized the forensics jargon.

"I'm going to have them narrow their focus in that direction," Verne said, waving his hand toward the patch of woods TJ had been digging toward. Ethan nodded and caught the attention of the closest CSI to reiterate Verne's plan.

CHAPTER TWENTY

TUESDAY, DECEMBER 18ᵀᴴ

Harassing Sarah Ferges was not something Ethan enjoyed in the slightest, but it paid off. When he got into the office the morning after finding the towel, he had a message on his office phone from her saying she'd call back at eleven to answer his questions. He'd planned on heading out to the trails again, but, after sending Verne a quick text with the change in plans, he spent his morning doing paperwork to be by the phone when Sarah's call came in.

At eleven on the dot, his desk phone started ringing, and he practically pounced on the phone.

"Detective Dumas," he answered, reminding himself to tread carefully. Getting Sarah to agree to call hadn't been easy. The last thing he wanted was to scare her off before he had a chance to get the answers he needed.

"This is Sarah Ferges, Rebecca Smith's sister." She sounded annoyed.

"Sarah, thank you for returning my calls," he said and continued before she could tell him to leave her alone again. "We're following a new lead in your sister's case, and I needed to know if you and your family shopped at Rothbury Mall prior to Rebecca's death."

"The mall?"

"Yes, specifically Rothbury Mall," he reiterated.

"I'm not sure. I don't really remember."

"I know you were young, but it's important you try to remember anything," he said, trying to keep the plea out of his voice. He knew it was a long shot. Sarah had only been four at the time, but he was clinging onto the hope she'd remember something.

"I do have a vague memory, but I don't know how accurate it is," she said slowly after a few seconds of silence.

"That's okay."

"It's—it's not a certainty, and my mom's obviously not around to confirm it, but I think she used to take us when she got her hair done every other week at a salon in the mall. She was still going to the same place until she passed away. But I think I remember a little play area by the window Becca and I would play in, and it looked out into the mall." Her voice trailed off at the end.

Ethan felt like he could run a mile with the adrenaline coursing through him. He knew there was a chance Sarah could be misremembering; after all, the memories from when someone was a preschooler weren't exactly reliable. It felt too close to what he needed to be a mistake on her part. Two little girls sitting in the window of a mall salon were in the perfect position for a mall janitor to walk by and see them.

"Was that all, detective?" Sarah asked, pulling Ethan out of his mental celebration.

"Yes, thank you so much, Sarah. This has been a great help."

"Okay." She paused, and he heard her take a deep breath. "Now please, never call me again."

The line disconnected, and Ethan held the phone for a few more seconds, not sure why he was so surprised by Sarah's request. It was the same request she'd made roughly two months ago that he'd ignored for the sake of the case. He put the phone back on the cradle, shoving aside the guilt he felt for having harassed her. It was for the good of the case. It was for justice for her own sister. He told himself once they closed Rebecca Smith's case, maybe Sarah would feel differently about how persistent Ethan was in order to get answers.

He jotted down the new lead Sarah provided and set to work following it. For the rest of the day, he used an old mall directory he'd found online to track down salons still open that had been in the mall and relocated after it was closed. There had been four salons in the mall, according to an archived 2001 directory—two of which closed shop when the mall closed. He knew from Sarah that her mom had been going to the same salon until she passed away only a few years ago, so it had to be one of the ones on this directory. After tracking down the two still open, it was the second that confirmed in their mall location they had a play area that was by the windows. They weren't willing to confirm if Joan Smith, Sarah and Rebecca's mother, had been a client, but given they were the only salon who had that setup for kids, he'd wager Sarah's memory wasn't false.

Ethan updated their wall, adding a new note under Rebecca Smith with the connection to Rothbury Mall that would get them one step closer to closing her case. Now, Rebecca Smith along with Melody Dawson, Kelly McLane, and Emily Harp were all connected to Rothbury Mall, which was quickly becoming the clear hunting ground for Vincent Watt. He'd focus on the closed cases next, see if Jacquelyn Battistelli and Penelope Wilks had ties to the mall. His eyes drifted to the column for Anne Griffin, with the note that he'd added to say no connection to the mall. It bothered him how many differences existed between the other six cases and Anne's, but Watt had been there in the ER. He shook his head, snapping out of the mental spiral he would dive down if he tried picking apart the perplexity of her case at this hour.

He checked the time and shot Verne a text with the promise to update him tomorrow. He wanted to get home at a reasonable time to see Vanessa before he had an early morning at the trail. He could already feel the ache in his bones just thinking about tomorrow.

CHAPTER TWENTY-ONE

SATURDAY, DECEMBER 22ND

After Tuesday, their week progressed slower than Ethan would have liked. The only promising aspect of the week was Ethan had found a connection between Rothbury Mall and a second of the three closed cases. Penelope Wilks, who'd been taken from her backyard while playing with her twin brother August 10th, 1987, had gone to the mall every Tuesday with her mom and brother for an indoor walking group her mom did with her friends. Mrs. Wilks had broken down when Ethan shared the reason for wanting to know about Rothbury Mall, and he felt guilty for opening an old wound, but it had brought him one step closer to closure for all the families.

However, there had been no more progress at the trail site. It was a nightmare with the snow piling up around the tents and the frozen ground making the CSI's efforts that much more strenuous.

Verne had offered to take the weekend shifts, which Ethan gladly accepted, as it gave him the chance to spend time with Vanessa. Naturally, Saturday afternoon, they discovered skeletal remains.

The bones were uncovered five yards from where TJ had discovered the towel. Shepard and Pereira were digging, Verne recounted. Ethan was only catching pieces of what he said, thanks to his reception in the woods. Vanessa leaned into Ethan's phone, as if getting closer to it would make Verne's words less choppy.

"Can't he text you?" she whispered, sitting back as he cut out again mid-sentence.

"Verne, just call me when you've got better service," he repeated himself three times.

Ethan couldn't understand Verne's response before Verne hung up. Vanessa was reclined beside him, hands absentmindedly rubbing her growing bump, watching him expectantly.

"Ness, I don't know anything yet," he said, putting his phone back on the coffee table.

"Why couldn't he just text you now?"

"It's probably too much to fill in over text."

She'd become invested in getting answers once the digging had begun. She'd promised not to search Watt's name, but she'd been searching for missing persons in the area near the woods during Ethan's late evenings at the site. Ethan had come home to find her crashed on the couch with a pile of printed news articles. When he'd woken her up to have her move to the bed for the night, she insisted on going over them right then and there in case he had another late night the following day. He would give her credit where credit was due. Two of the articles were cases Verne had also found.

He resisted the urge to check his phone anyway, desperate to know what was happening and if they knew anything beyond that they found remains. He supposed it was good Camilleri found a forensic anthropologist after all. Tests would need to be run for definitive answers, but he assumed Verne would at least be able to tell if it was a child's remains. He considered texting him to make sure he paid attention but decided not to underestimate him.

He still had his doubts about Watt's motivation for sharing the location. Verne believed it could have been Watt trying out different disposal methods, but Ethan wasn't convinced. If that were the case, there could be countless more victims out there.

To make matters worse, Ethan had been so focused on the Rothbury Mall connection, he found himself lying awake at night mentally going over the cases to see if he'd missed a clue. For five of the seven cases, it had now been confirmed that Rothbury Mall was a key location. He had arranged times to speak to Jacquelyn Battistelli's family after Christmas.

"Ethan," Vanessa said, nudging his leg with her foot. "Just remember, you're helping a family get closure."

He forced a smile, not at all relaxed by her efforts, but he still appreciated them nonetheless. He tried to silence the constant whirling of thoughts in his mind as he stood up, clapping his hands together.

"How about some hot chocolate and we put on *The Holiday*?" he asked.

Vanessa's mind seemed to have moved on from the trail, the body, and her theories, which was more than Ethan could say for himself, but he drank the warm sugar and laughed on cue with the movie, doing his best to ignore it all, at least for the night.

CHAPTER TWENTY-TWO

MONDAY, DECEMBER 24TH

Verne didn't call back on Saturday or Sunday, and by the time Ethan walked into the office Monday morning, he was ready to strangle him for ignoring his calls and texts. Vanessa said she'd be right behind him since she now had to wait until Monday night for an update.

Verne sat hunched with his face down toward a report flipped open on his desk. Ethan was greeted with the stench of onions and wet dog.

"So you're not dead, even if you sure smell like it," he said, as he settled in at his desk. He looked over at Verne, but he got no reaction out of him. He was still hunched, his head propped up with his arm resting on his desk.

"Verne."

Nothing.

"Jason?"

Not even a twitch to show he was messing with Ethan. Ethan stood up and leaned over the short divider, holding his breath, and poked Verne's head. He half expected it to go rolling.

Verne looked up at him with a blank stare and puffy eyes.

"The remains found at the dig. Were they human? Did they belong to a kid? Did you lose your phone?" Ethan snapped, frustrated to be out of the loop and not in the mood for Verne's weird games.

It seemed to take him a few too many seconds to process. "They're off being examined, but they looked pretty tiny, and they were definitely human."

Ethan sat down, watching Verne as he did. He seemed off, tired, and not his usual energetic self.

"Do you smell that?" Ethan asked. He tried again, "Has food gone bad in your trash?"

He was almost certain the source was Verne, given his current state and the fact he was in a sweatshirt and sweatpants. An outfit Ethan had never seen him wear to work before.

Ethan felt like he was talking to a brick wall. "What are you reading?"

"Transcripts from Watt's past interrogations," Verne finally answered. "I'm seeing if he ever slipped up and gave us a hint we missed."

Verne looked at Ethan properly. His eyes were bloodshot, and the bags under his eyes had reached a new level.

"How long have you been reading them?" he asked.

Verne looked at the clock on the wall. "Like five."

"Five this morning?" He looked a lot worse than an early morning.

"Five p.m....on Saturday."

That confirmed that Verne was the source of the smell. Ethan wondered if the smell would linger after Verne had left. He could always work in the break room.

"Go home. Shower. Please." He held his breath as he got up and took the transcripts from Verne, making sure not to lose his spot as he did.

As if he'd been switched into slow motion, Verne tried and failed to snatch the transcript.

"Go," Ethan said sternly, pointing at the door like he was giving a dog a command. "And ask an officer downstairs to give you a ride home. You're worse off than if you were drunk," Ethan added, scanning Verne's desk for his keys, which he promptly snatched up too.

Verne's bottom lip stuck out a little, but he didn't seem energized enough to commit to it. He pushed himself out of his chair and brushed past Ethan without any protest.

Ethan watched him go down the corridor and wait for the elevator. The last thing he needed was Verne hurting himself, or someone else. When the elevator arrived, Ethan felt bad for the officer already in there. Verne's stench could ruin a morning.

Once he was out of sight, Ethan cautiously stepped back in the office, smelling if Verne's stench lingered. It wasn't too bad, not enough for Ethan to justify the annoyance of sitting in the break room all day. He left the office door open to help air it out.

He tossed Verne's keys into his desk drawer for him to find tomorrow before taking a seat at his own desk with the transcripts Verne had been reading. It was all the same material they had gone through before they'd interrogated Watt. He wasn't sure why Verne had put the energy into going through it all again, but he'd read through an alarming amount of the textbook-thick stack. It was a little strange he was reading printed transcripts, but he figured it would've been more difficult to read as much as he had if he'd been staring at a computer screen.

Ethan skimmed a few pages, which turned into twenty pages. It was easy enough to do when it consisted of detectives, including Hadeon, asking questions and Watt answering, "No comment." It could still be telling if the suspect had a poor poker face, but more often than not, if they were cocky enough to do that for hours, they also knew how to keep a straight face.

Out of consideration for Verne's efforts, he dog-eared where he got fed up reading "No comment" and set it back on Verne's desk. Verne could continue to kill himself with that tomorrow.

Ethan turned his attention to figuring out the potential identity of their Doe. The towel was the best lead they had. They'd narrowed it down to four cases that might work for the location, but Verne had recalled correctly. A towel had not been mentioned in any of the four missing person reports.

He returned to Anne Griffin's case and considered that Watt had given them her crime scene. Where they found the remains was within a five-mile radius of the hospital, but to physically drive to an access road would have taken him well outside of the perimeter he stuck to. He had the towel to consider too. It wasn't the kind a hospital would use, but Ethan supposed Watt could've had it in his car and used it to conceal Anne while carrying her through the woods. There was also the fact it hadn't been found on or near the remains, which raised the question if it was relevant.

"Congrats on the break."

Ethan looked up; Tom Robinson stood in the doorway smiling. They met at the academy, worked their way up from officers to detectives, landed spots in homicide, and took their lieutenant exams together. They split up four years ago when Ethan was unexpectedly transferred to the cold case unit, and Robinson was made lieutenant in homicide.

"Mr. Big Shot came to congratulate the little guy?" Ethan smiled back, temporarily abandoning his search.

"The real congratulations come from Riley, who found out through Vanessa that you two have a little one on the way. Now, what the hell is that about?" Robinson threw his arms up.

Ethan chuckled, not sure what to say. He hadn't told anyone besides Verne that Vanessa was pregnant. He figured it would look bad if he asked Robinson not to make a big deal about it. Especially if Robinson told Riley, who'd, inevitably, tell Vanessa, who'd think he didn't want the baby.

Robinson walked in and took Verne's empty chair. Ethan resisted the urge to tell him not to sit there because of the smell, but if he could survive walking into the office, then he was probably safe.

"How far along is she? Too soon to know the gender?"

"It's a girl," Ethan said, swallowing the lump in his throat.

"Congrats! She'll have you wrapped around her finger the moment she's born. Riley says Tiana can do no wrong where I'm concerned, and she's right." His words trailed off into a laugh as he shook his head. Robinson knew about the other miscarriages, but they never spoke about them. He was sure Vanessa and Riley had cried together, and he imagined the Robinsons had discussed it.

"How's lieutenant life treating you?" Ethan asked, needing to change the subject.

"It's exhausting. The paperwork. The managing. I swear we weren't as helpless as some of these guys." If Robinson had sensed the edge in Ethan's voice, he didn't react. "I heard whispers of a Lieutenant Dumas."

Part of him wanted to get up and close the door. That was subject number two he hadn't shared at work. Camilleri hinted at it after the chief had been happy with the close rate on cases. He hadn't told Verne. Part of him felt guilty at the idea of abandoning him for a promotion now.

"It's just a whisper right now. You know how political it all gets. I took the exam when you did and then switched units, so it all kind of got pushed back. It would mean another transfer too, if I were to make lieutenant."

Ethan hadn't spoken to Camilleri about it in nearly four months. When they had, Camilleri had danced around it with questions about transferring units and hinted that the size of the cold case unit stunted his career growth. Since then, the baby had taken front and center in his mind along with the cases they were working.

"Maybe if you crack some more of Watt's secrets, it'll push you into that new title."

"I almost hope that he doesn't have that much impact on my life. He's even worse in person than I'd imagined."

Robinson laughed as he pushed himself back out of Verne's chair. "Before I forget, Riley says we need to get together. Plus, I think she wants an excuse to get a babysitter and have a proper night out. Give Vanessa my best, and Merry Christmas!" He didn't wait for Ethan's response as he gave Verne's desk a slap on his way out.

He skimmed through cases for several more hours and concluded he needed to talk to Fiona Griffin. He couldn't explain it, he'd brush it off as detective's intuition again, but he found himself questioning if Fiona might have been right about Watt. It felt like the more he looked at the other cases, the less Anne Griffin fit the mold. Still, he felt admitting as much to Fiona could be a mistake, opening a door he may not be able to shut again.

CHAPTER TWENTY-THREE

MONDAY, DECEMBER 24TH

There was a small part of Ethan that wondered if he hated himself. Stopping by the Griffins' on his way home Christmas Eve rather than leaving it for later in the week, or even into the new year, would suggest as much.

Fiona answered the door within moments of Ethan knocking. She looked entirely unsurprised by his unannounced visit, despite it being a month since they last spoke. She waved him in without a word and promptly shut the door on the snowy gust that followed him.

"I hope this isn't a bad time," Ethan said, listening to see if Gregory was also home.

"I'm alone, if that's what you're asking."

She didn't wait for Ethan or offer her normal ushered hospitality. She took off back down the hall. Ethan kicked off his snow-covered shoes and made his way after her to the kitchen where they'd spent the last couple meetings. When he got to the doorway, he realized she wasn't in there.

"In here," she called from the second hallway that led off the kitchen.

He'd never gone that far before, and he found himself cautiously walking down it, like he expected a perp to jump out at him. The first door he came to was ajar, but the few inches of the room he could see made him pause. He looked down the length of the hall, light pouring into the hallway from a doorway a little farther down, Fiona still out of sight. He reached out and pushed the first door open. It was a nursery, a pink explosion really. Pale-pink floral wallpaper, faded magenta carpet, baby-pink frilly curtains, an armoire, and a wood crib with floral sheets that matched the wallpaper. It was a room stuck in time.

A shadow broke the pool of light ahead, and he quickly pulled the door back and closed the distance between himself and the next doorway. He found Fiona, in what had to be the master bedroom, perched on the side of the bed holding a framed photograph. He stopped at the door, not comfortable with the notion of entering Fiona and Greg's bedroom.

"He's with them tonight."

"Sorry?" Ethan, still thinking about the nursery and the sadness of keeping the room as it was, didn't process what Fiona had said right away. "Oh, Gregory?"

"Her name is Sheila. They have two boys."

Ethan swallowed, resisting the urge to fidget. He knew this, but he hadn't imagined Fiona was aware of Gregory's second family. He and Verne had agreed it was not their place to get in the Griffins' marital issues, and for all they knew, maybe it was an agreed-upon arrangement.

Ethan's silence didn't seem to even register to Fiona. She set down the picture frame, and Ethan could see it was of her and Gregory on their wedding day.

"He's going to be a grandpa. I saw on Facebook today. I have a fake account so I could be friends with his sons and daughters-in-law. People will add anyone these days."

Ethan let out a small sound that was close to "oh," not sure how else to respond. Surely, she was hurt, but she seemed too calm.

"His eldest son was born a year after Anne disappeared. Sheila used to be his secretary. He didn't even try to deny it when I found out or ask how I knew. Do you want to know how I knew?"

She looked at him, and he was surprised to see she looked collected. There wasn't even the shine of tears in her eyes. He found himself nodding as he stood in the doorway, hands in his pockets, all his intentions of talking about Watt and Anne pushed aside.

"Sheila had the audacity to show up one night with her baby, pregnant with the second, and begged me to let him go." She let out a single dry cackle before standing up and walking toward Ethan. He found himself backing up to clear the doorway, but she stopped before getting close enough to leave the room. "I told that stupid whore I wasn't stopping him, he just didn't love her enough to leave."

Ethan clenched his jaw to stop his mouth from hanging open in shock. Whatever he had prepared himself for driving over did not even come close to the conversation that they were having now. He was still trying to figure out what he should say when she decided to leave the room and march the few steps to the door he'd stopped at before. She pushed the door open and went in, leaving Ethan no choice but to follow her.

"I'm assuming you saw Anne's room already," she said from the rocking chair Ethan hadn't seen during his initial peek.

"I did, briefly."

"I got to keep it as long as I didn't ask Gregory any questions about what he did outside our marriage."

Ethan arched an eyebrow, but given what he knew about Fiona, it sounded exactly like the sort of deal she'd make for herself.

"I'm guessing you didn't stop by to chit-chat," Fiona said, after a prolonged silence had fallen over them.

Ethan rubbed the back of his neck, really wishing he'd left this for another day now. Despite it only being just past four p.m., it was nearly dark outside, and he really wished he was settling in for his Christmas Eve traditions with Vanessa. He only had himself to blame for being unable to let work wait for a few days.

"I've been looking over all the cases we have—the closed and the re-opened cold cases that Watt is the primary suspect in," he explained.

Fiona continued to watch him calmly from the rocking chair with her hands folded in her lap. It gave him pause to see her looking so out of place in the nursery. She was dressed like she was hosting a fancy dinner party, not ready to rock a baby to sleep.

"I think you might be right." His voice trailed off a little at the end, knowing once he said it, Fiona Griffin would never let him backpedal from this confession.

"About?"

"Anne's case has too many inconsistencies with the others. I know some of them can be reasoned with circumstance, but too many differences being reasoned away becomes sloppy police work."

The words tumbled out of him, the confession freeing after the slow build of realization that had begun over the last month of looking further into all seven cases.

"I don't know if Watt should still be our primary suspect in Anne's case."

Fiona was grinning at him, and it gave the faintest impression of the Cheshire cat from *Alice in Wonderland*. Despite her unnerving look, it felt right to have told her.

"What does your partner think?"

"I haven't brought it up much with him yet." Ethan shuffled his feet a bit, feeling caught.

"It's just a hunch I have really, but I found a connection for most of the other cases except Anne's. I still have a couple to confirm, but chances are, they're going to align with my theory."

"The mall."

"How'd—"

"I'm not slow, Ethan. You don't answer calls, return messages, then you stop by and ask me about Rothbury Mall. Another month of nothing, and now, you've got a lead and connection that Anne doesn't fit into."

Ethan felt his ears warm in embarrassment for thinking he'd been subtle. He carried on, not wanting to waste time denying the truth. It wasn't an active homicide case where secrecy was key.

"Watt was at the hospital, we know that much. He was there for his father, who he had a very complicated relationship with, and I don't truly believe he'd have taken Anne while with him. Watt wouldn't have committed a crime of that scale around his father."

Fiona nodded along as he spoke, but didn't interrupt him as he continued through the theories and doubts in the original detectives that had been festering in his mind.

"And while he did take kids that weren't far from parents or those watching them, he never took a child from right beside their parents. There was too much risk. He took them from busy shopping areas, from open yards, from noisy playgrounds, where he could get away quickly and relatively unnoticed. But from the bed between you and Gregory and in the ER..." His words trailed off as he thought of all the holes in the case against Watt.

"I see why Graftner made you a cold case detective."

Ethan stopped pacing and looked at Fiona, slightly puzzled at the change of subject. It threw him to hear the name of his former captain. Stranger was the fact Fiona knew Graftner had screwed him out of the promotion to lieutenant in homicide when he'd moved him to cold cases.

"I wasn't aware you knew Graftner." He heard his clipped tone, his suspicion unbridled.

"Yes, well, when you run in the same circles, you end up discussing work." She paused before explaining herself. "I knew his wife from book club. Sometimes, the men would join us for dinner, and he'd mention when things happened at work every now and then."

Ethan stared at Fiona for what felt like five minutes, but was likely no more than one, before he gave her a curt nod. He couldn't imagine why she'd remember something like that from four years ago, or why Graftner would have bothered to mention a rather insignificant transfer from homicide to cold cases, but his phone started ringing and any further suspicion was halted.

He pulled it out of his pocket, angling it for privacy, to see Vanessa's name light up the screen along with her contact photo. He glanced at Fiona before answering. "Hey, I'm almost done at work and then I'll be home."

"Oh, Mr. Serious voice right now. Well, I was just calling to tell you it started snowing heavily and you should come home sooner rather than later."

"Okay, I'm in Southbury, so I'll be a bit, but I'll head out now," he said, softening his tone.

"Drive safe. I love you."

"I love you too," he said, before hanging up.

"I should head out."

She led the way back to the front door and stood there watching Ethan put on his shoes.

"Sorry for the puddle," he mumbled, as he avoided the melted snow that had pooled around where his shoes had been. He opened the door and stepped out into the lashing snow. The visibility was already alarmingly low; it was going to take forever to get home.

"I hope you get home safe. Have a Merry Christmas with Vanessa." She shut the door as the last syllable left her mouth.

CHAPTER TWENTY-FOUR

MONDAY, DECEMBER 31ST

"Please tell me this is great news," Ethan said, as he joined Verne in their office.

Ethan had managed to have shorter days the week since Christmas, which Vanessa had appreciated. He'd even managed to remain disconnected while home, to give Vanessa his undivided attention, but told Verne to text him if any case progress occurred. Ethan hadn't anticipated Verne would call him at four thirty in the morning, telling him to meet him at the station as soon as possible. Ethan had had genuine fear when waking Vanessa, on her day off, to say he was going into work early.

"It's news," Verne said, holding the file against his chest before surrendering it.

Ethan flipped it open, skimming the report of the forensic findings from the dig site. Camilleri's forensic anthropologist believed their victim was female, between the age of two and three based on dental development, backed up by expert opinion. That information was followed with the medical examiner's determination that cause of death was most likely blunt force trauma. It had caused extensive fractures on the back and left side of the skull, and part of the skull was missing. Both had noted multiple partially healed bone fractures that were consistent with wounds found on abuse victims.

Ethan looked up at Verne. "Keep reading."

He kept skimming, catching that they worked out the bones were from around the eighties. Due to soil composition, like pH levels, and other natural factors that Ethan didn't care about, they couldn't narrow it down more than that, and it could still be off by a few years, give or take. He trailed his finger farther down the page, skipping the jargon-filled explanation. Then it popped out at him: partial DNA profile. He flipped to the next page, skipping over how they collected the samples, to the explanation of who.

"There is no match in the system," Verne said, before Ethan finished reading.

Ethan tossed the file on the desk, pacing in the little amount of space he had.

"The age is off for Anne Griffin."

"Yeah, she's definitely eliminated," Verne agreed.

"We've got an age range to work with, but it doesn't match Watt's MO." Ethan stopped pacing and turned to face Verne.

Verne had perched himself on the edge of his desk. "A broken neck versus a crushed skull is a strange jump."

"He made it clear himself he didn't like mess or effort."

"What if it was an early victim? He was testing out his ways, seeing what worked best for him? It's not unheard of for serial killers to evolve, and if he realized that it was too much for him, he could have switched things up to the broken neck and no grave," Verne offered.

"It doesn't seem like a kill where someone was figuring out their methodology. It could be believable that he lost control of the situation, maybe the cause of death was accidental? But how he did it, taking her into the woods, clearly wasn't an accident."

"And you don't accidentally bring a shovel into the woods," Verne added.

Ethan took a seat behind his desk and pulled up the cases they'd considered so far. Two fell into the approximate age range when they went missing. They had been going off the assumption that Watt stuck to dumping his victims relatively close to where he kidnapped them. One girl went missing shortly after Anne Griffin was taken in 1982 and the other was late 1985, in between Kelly McLane's and Penelope Wilks's murders.

"Say we went with the theory that it was an early victim. We don't know for sure if he killed prior to Rebecca Smith, so potentially, prior to snapping his victims' necks, he killed his victims with blunt force trauma. It is not unreasonable for us to believe there are more victims than the ones we have confirmed and suspect," Ethan said, working through his doubts aloud.

"To counter that, how many victims would we think it'd take to go from one to the other? That's a big jump, even for a guy like him."

Ethan couldn't pretend to have an answer to that. "Let's consider what we've got." He started counting on his fingers as he listed them. "One, Watt knew about the victim and where they were buried. Two, the victim's age falls within the age range of his other victims. Three, the victim was found in a wooded area just like his other dump sites—"

"To be fair, it's pretty hard to have a dump site that isn't a wooded area around here, unless you just leave a victim in the street," Verne interrupted.

Ethan ignored him. "Four, our victim's cause of death is blunt force trauma to the head. Five, our victim was likely killed and buried in the eighties. And six, if we go off Watt's trigger, then the victim must have been kidnapped around a significant date relating to one of his parents."

"Don't forget they found a girl's swimsuit with the victim."

Ethan looked up from his hands, thrown off by Verne's casualness. "I missed that in the report. Why didn't you say sooner?"

"It was in there. I hadn't paid that much attention Saturday. Kind of focused on the bones and less on what clothing was in the grave too," Verne said, his voice taking on a hint of defensiveness.

Ethan turned back to his computer, his mind turning over this new piece of information. The combination of a towel and a swimsuit made more sense now. Neither of their potential victims went missing in a swimsuit, or in the summer. He knew there might be extenuating circumstances to explain a swimsuit outside of summer months, but it was the best lead they had for now. "If we base our search around the swimsuit, we could start by guessing our victim was taken between June to August, maybe as early as May. We can then narrow it down to at least that decade."

"Safe guess." Verne moved to stand behind Ethan. He could feel his breath on his neck and gave him a warning glance. Verne took a step back.

Ethan added in the age range they wanted to consider, giving a year extra on each side just in case. Since the site was in Rothbury, he did the initial database search for Rothbury only. There were a dozen cases of missing children, but they all quickly became unlikely matches.

"Broaden the search, maybe do the county. Or add more years; they did say science with soil or something could affect their estimate," Verne suggested.

"I'll try county first," Ethan said, as he broadened their search to New Haven County. The results more than quadrupled when the page refreshed.

"Well, shit," Verne sighed.

"I'll print it out. I'll work my way from the top, you go from the bottom."

Verne went back to his desk, and Ethan handed him the printed list. Several hours later, they had managed to skim all the files and eliminate most of the missing persons cases. Ethan had found two cases in his half of the list, and Verne had found one.

Two of the three cases reported the missing girls in two-piece swimsuits. Based on the evidence photos of the found swimsuit, which was a solid-colored one-piece, Ethan decided to start with one of the girls from his half of the list. Just shy of three years old, Naomi Beavis went missing from her front yard in July 1983; it was almost a year to the day that Anne Griffin was taken from the hospital. She'd last been seen in a blue one-piece swimsuit, which matched the one found with their Jane Doe.

"She would fit," Verne whispered, after they silently read through the case on Ethan's monitor.

He printed out information on her family that was in the file and held it out to Verne. Her family was still listed as living in Seymour, several towns south, in the same house she had been taken from in 1983.

"You up for a solo visit to gently," Ethan emphasized, "request DNA samples from her closest living relatives to run against our victim?"

Verne took the sheet. "'Course I am."

Ethan was about to warn Verne to tread carefully, given the file's mention of potential abuse, when his office phone interrupted him. "Detective Dumas."

"You and Verne, my office," Camilleri said, followed by the click of the receiver.

"Did you do something to tick Camilleri off?" Ethan asked, still holding his phone.

Verne gasped. "Me? Piss off Ed? Never have I ever."

Ethan gave him a warning glance as he grabbed the report on the victim. If he was mad, it was wise to have some progress on the case to wave in front of him.

They took their time to get to his office, mainly so Verne could recall every interaction he had with Camilleri the last week to make sure he hadn't done something to put them in Camilleri's bad book. They concluded Verne may be innocent as they reached Camilleri's door. Ethan paused halfway through the door when he saw there were two detectives waiting in Camilleri's office with him. Verne pushed into the back of him, forcing him to finish entering the office. He couldn't get much of a look at either, as they stayed angled toward Camilleri.

"How's the case going?" Camilleri asked. He didn't acknowledge the elephant in the room. Ethan could see the Rothbury badge of one of the detectives, so they hadn't stepped on any toes to piss off a neighboring department.

Ethan glanced at Verne to see if he was surprised too, but he was too busy blatantly staring at them. Camilleri obviously had a plan.

"They obtained a partial DNA profile from the victim, and we have a potential lead from a missing persons case that matches with what we know so far," Ethan answered.

"I'm going to go ask the family if I can collect DNA samples to see if our partial could be a familial match," Verne said, finishing the brief.

"When are you interrogating Watt again?" Camilleri asked.

"We were planning to see where this lead takes us. He hasn't given us anything to close the Griffin or Smith case, so we can work on—"

"Or other cases. Closing any case is good for the department."

Ethan didn't have a response that wouldn't express his distaste for Camilleri's callous take. Fortunately, Camilleri moved on, standing up from his desk, which caused the other two detectives to rise.

"You may remember Detectives Barnett and Soto, Dumas. They were new to homicide a few months before you took on cold cases."

Ethan smiled and gave both a nod of acknowledgment, not recognizing either detective beyond the smallest nag that he might have crossed paths with them at the station. He rarely took the time to look at people's faces here unless they spoke directly to him.

"Detective Verne." Verne shook both detectives' hands. Ethan realized he probably should have done the same, but it seemed too late now, and supposedly, he already knew them.

"Camilleri has brought us up to speed on the cases, so we can jump in where you need us," the taller one with the blonde bun explained.

Ethan was leaning toward it being Barnett who spoke up, having the vaguest memory of her having helped on one of his last homicide cases before his transfer, but Camilleri hadn't clarified which detective was which, so she just as easily could've been Soto.

"You're adding them to our cases?" Verne asked, the displeasure dripping from his words.

Ethan wanted to elbow him in the ribs. It was uncomfortably silent, and Ethan knew he wasn't the only one feeling it. Camilleri brushed Verne off with a wave of the hand.

"Appreciate the gift, Jay. Some detectives beg for extra hands on their cases, and these two are a couple of the best up-and-coming detectives we've got."

Verne scoffed and mumbled something that sounded like "My ass" to Ethan. He didn't react to Verne and just offered their new case partners a silent plea not to hate them because Verne was a toddler when it came to sharing.

"Happy for the help," Ethan said to Barnett and Soto. Neither detective looked like they cared about Ethan's attempt to play nice.

Camilleri dropped himself back into his seat, and he looked pleased with himself. "Off you all go. Make us look good."

No one moved until Ethan, closest to the door, led the way out. Barnett, or Soto, pulled Camilleri's door closed behind her.

"You two grab a conference room while we grab what we've got so far," Ethan said, as he turned and walked away without waiting for a response. He felt Verne follow close behind and was somewhat relieved when he demonstrated uncharacteristic sense to wait until they were a few corridors away from Barnett and Soto before he started complaining.

"We don't need extra hands. Extra hands mean more people I have to explain myself to, and when it's you, I can just apologize after I do the thing."

Ethan stopped walking, and Verne walked into him. "Is that how we work?"

"It's worked so far." Verne grinned.

"Watt may give us another location, which could mean another case, and we don't want to lose sight of closing Anne Griffin's and Rebecca Smith's cases." Ethan started walking again. "We still get to make the calls. We're still the leads. We'll tell them where we need help."

Verne grunted but didn't complain, so Ethan accepted that as he was satisfied. They shoved the case material and the excess they'd collected over the past few months into boxes. Ethan took photos of their boards before pulling the notes and printouts off the wall to reconstruct in the new base they'd set up in the conference room. Once they'd gathered everything they needed, they hauled it down to the conference rooms, spotting the one Barnett and Soto had snagged.

"Verne," Ethan said, as they got close.

"Yeah," Verne grunted. He had offered to carry three boxes, Ethan could only assume, to show off.

"Don't even think about trying to sleep with either of them," he said, before pushing open the conference room door.

CHAPTER TWENTY-FIVE
WEDNESDAY, JANUARY 2nd, 2019

Soto had taken an interest in Watt's recent interrogation with them, so Ethan decided to have her accompany him on the second trip. They'd spent the drive talking about homicide, the two years Soto tried out a degree in mathematics before switching to psychology, and her childhood adventures as an Air Force brat.

"You sure about this?" she asked, as she emptied her keys, phone, and Swiss Army knife into the cupholder of the car. He and Verne never thought to leave their stuff in the car when they visited prisons.

"Yes."

By habit, Ethan preferred to be the lead. After their group catch-up, Ethan combed through all the interrogation records again to brainstorm tactics. Watt had never been interrogated by a female detective, and Ethan thought it might throw him off, even briefly. It didn't take a psychologist to determine that Watt had an issue with females, between his mother, his aunt, and his choice in victims.

Soto hadn't seemed fazed, either, when he pitched the idea. There was always a risk bringing new detectives in mid-investigation. He'd worked cases before where the focus derailed when too many approaches were added at once. Luckily, Barnett and Soto were willing to run with their plans, "as long as they weren't stupid," per the conditions set by Soto.

They moved through security swiftly and settled into the same interrogation room Ethan and Verne had been in before. The stench of urine was worse than Ethan remembered.

"Smells like my brother's house. He's got three dogs, and I swear he just lets them piss on his carpet when his girlfriend isn't home," Soto said, not looking up from her notes.

The alarm sounded that Watt was being brought in. Ethan watched his expression for when he saw Soto, but if Watt was startled, he didn't let on for even a split second. He smiled a tight-lipped smile as the guards secured him. They gave their instructions for when they were done with him and left. The door slammed shut with a vibrating thud, and silence settled between them.

Ethan began the recording, stating the necessary information and having Watt do the same. As soon as they'd finished the formalities, Watt spoke up.

"Where's the short one?" Watt asked, his eyes trained on Ethan. Maybe it did bother him that Soto was there.

"We recovered a body from the location you provided to detectives the last time they came to speak with you," Soto answered. Ethan remained facing forward, but he could see Soto repositioning herself. She clasped her hands together on the table and sat up straighter with her body angled toward Watt who, in turn, had angled himself toward Ethan.

Watt leaned back in his chair, his emotionless mask back. Had this been the first meeting, Ethan might not have noticed the slight unease in Watt's demeanor, but, in comparison to his mood the last time, he was practically antsy. He fidgeted and turned his wrists in the cuffs so there was a continuous faint clink of the chains.

Soto was good at the waiting game. Ethan had shifted his attention to the clock on the wall to force Watt to waste time in some other way than staring into his eyes. Six minutes they sat in silence.

"Why are you focusing on me? Are you too inept to catch someone who isn't already locked up?" Watt asked, lifting his shackled wrists for emphasis.

Ethan looked back and met Watt's gaze again. From Watt's expression, he seemed detached from their conversation, but he couldn't mask the twitch in his eye or the clear annoyance in his words.

"What do you mean?" Soto asked, jamming it together so it only sounded like two words.

Watt's jaw tightened when Soto responded, but he seemed to have picked up on how this visit was being run.

"You're clutching at straws. Even with forensic advancements, after this long, there's very little that'll be testable. So, why even bother?" he asked, directed at Ethan again.

Soto let out a whistling exhale. "You've got a funny way of thinking about police work. The thing is," Soto leaned in even more as she spoke, "somewhere out there is another victim who hasn't been brought home to her family, who has been wanting her home since the day you snatched her. So, we bother for them. Really has nothing to do with you. In the grand scheme of things, you're just another obstacle in our way."

Ethan didn't know what to expect from Watt, but when Watt let loose a cackle, the tension between his shoulder blades released. If Watt felt humored, then he may not refuse to talk and there was a chance to get more out of him.

"So serious, detective. Did you ever consider a career on the big screen?" Watt finally acknowledged Soto and even turned to look at her as he spoke.

Ethan dared a glance away from Watt to Soto and watched her shrug off his insult. "Took theater for a year, didn't really work for me."

"You'd be better off in the kitchen with a house full of kids anyway."

Soto ignored him. "Returning to what you chatted about last time, let's start with the disappearance of Anne Griffin on July 9th, 1982."

"Your friend here, and the short one, did mention that. Sad, but probably a little late to be worrying about now. I'd wager she's been dead a while. Just speculation, of course. I can't speak on something I know nothing about."

Ethan felt his jaw pop from how tightly he was clenching his teeth. Now, Watt wanted to pretend he had no clue, when last time he spoke to him and Verne, he'd never denied knowing about her. He'd come in expecting Watt to dance around the topic of Anne Griffin, but he had still foolishly hoped Watt would help him decide whether his gut instincts about Anne's case were on point. Singing a completely different tune from last time only confused matters.

"If that's the case, you can tell us more about Jane Doe. You led detectives right to a body from the eighties. Right during your prime," Soto sneered at Watt.

"I did wonder if you'd find anything. Lots of woods and places to be undisturbed out there. But you found someone?" he asked, as if he were surprised by the information.

"We did, but I don't think that surprises you, or it shouldn't, since you lead our people right to her. I've got to say, it's quite the different MO from your other victims."

Ethan watched as Watt appeared to reflect on Soto's words. Watt was scheming, and it unsettled Ethan.

"Even I'm not perfect." He avoided eye contact with both of them, staring off between their heads.

"No, I suppose not. Why'd it happen like that?" she asked.

"The situation called for it."

"Personally, I can't imagine a situation that would. Can you, Dumas?"

"No, but then again, I don't kill people."

"Right. That would make it hard to relate. Perhaps you can enlighten us," she said to Watt, who had slipped enough to show annoyance with the direction their conversation had turned. "Or you could give us another location."

Ethan sat up straighter. That wasn't something they'd discussed. If he told them something, Soto handed Watt the option to skip over the victim buried in the woods. Soto must have sensed he was going to interrupt because she kicked him, hard. He inhaled sharply and sat back, balling his fist under the table to resist the urge to rub his ankle.

"Are you familiar with Rothbury geography?" he asked Ethan.

Ethan nodded.

"The old train depot, if you can even qualify it as one, with the tracks that head west? Just a quarter of a mile or so south of that, there's a rundown tree fort, or there was, at the time. Popular hangout for high schoolers in my day."

"What about it?" Soto asked, when he was clearly done describing the location.

Watt shrugged. His face stretched wide in a grin; his eyes refocused on the space between their heads.

"What are we going to find there?" Ethan asked.

"Oh, guards!" Watt sing-song screamed at the top of his lungs. Soto flinched, and Ethan ground his teeth against the pitch of Watt's voice.

It could have gone worse, Ethan reminded himself as he shut off the recording and watched the guards uncuff Watt from the table and escort him out. Ethan followed Soto out of the prison to the parking lot.

"We've got another one!" Soto grinned as she looked back at Ethan.

"We blew past Griffin, didn't get a chance to mention Smith, and got nothing on our Jane Doe," Ethan said, as he counted off his fingers to emphasize the ways that went wrong. "And you kicked me."

"I'm sure it'll barely bruise."

"Soto."

Ethan stopped dead in the middle of the parking lot. He wasn't in the mood to joke about this. He'd wanted to put more pressure on Watt about the original cold cases and see what he'd give in terms of Anne Griffin. He'd needed to push Rebecca Smith's case now that they knew she was connected to Rothbury Mall and at least get something on their Jane Doe. If there was another victim, he wanted to know, but he didn't want to become Watt's puppet or end up with a stack of cases he couldn't close because they were a bunch of Does.

Soto planted herself in front of him, arms crossed over her chest. "I'm not going to apologize. I know there was a plan, but I saw an opportunity and took it. Yeah, I probably shouldn't have kicked you, but you were going to open your mouth and steamroll me, so I made sure you let me do my job. Sometimes, you don't get the answers you want. You're not a rookie detective; you know that just as well as I do."

Ethan didn't know if he should reprimand her further or be impressed by her conviction. After a few more seconds of staring each other down in the prison parking lot, the bite of January making his joints ache, he chose the latter. They couldn't change how it went, and his eyes started to water from the wind.

"Just pray his lead was worth it."

He dialed Verne as soon as they were on the road.

"Hit me, baby," Verne answered.

"You're on speaker," Ethan warned. "Watt gave us—well, Soto, another location. We think?"

"Loving the confidence. Where are we sending our guys now?"

Soto had pulled up the coordinates for the approximate location Watt had given them as Ethan started driving back to the station.

"The best access point is off a service road," she said, as she zoomed out on the map. "It looks like it's in the middle of nowhere. From what I could see on the satellite images, what used to be the train depot is now just a pile of rotting lumber."

"Any chance he was more specific about what we are looking for this time?" Verne asked. Ethan could hear Barnett in the background repeating the location to whoever she was speaking with.

His screen lit up with an incoming call: Fiona Griffin. He hit decline.

"A quarter of a mile south, near a tree fort. See if we can get a team out today or tomorrow, at the latest."

"Got it, I'll update CSI. See you back at the station." Verne hung up.

"Does she call often?" Soto asked.

"Sometimes."

"During the debriefing, I got the impression Fiona Griffin is pushy," Soto said.

"She's involved."

Soto snorted, clearly not fooled by Ethan's tactful description. Eager to move away from the topic of Fiona, he switched the conversation back to the present.

"What did you make of Watt?"

"He's cocky, which I'd expected. Clearly didn't love that I'm not a dude, but, given his obvious disdain for females, that's also not surprising."

"I was curious how he'd handle that. You're the first female detective to have interrogated him."

"I'll be getting that on a plaque." He heard her text and then her phone went into the cupholder. "I want to know why he got all dodgy and weird when we started on the new vic. Something about him—he didn't like the prying."

Ethan recalled Watt's hastiness to breeze past the topic. He'd been willing to give them the location last time, but today he offered up a second location to avoid talking about the Jane Doe.

"What if it wasn't his crime?" Ethan said, more to himself than to Soto. He kept going before she even had a chance to answer. "He was evasive as soon as the victim was mentioned, and you brought up the difference in MO."

Ethan had already been toying with the idea, questioning the MO when he and Verne had been looking through missing persons cases. He knew it complicated things more if that were the case, but ever since he'd read the cause of death, he found it difficult to fully get behind the idea it was another of Watt's victims. One deviation from the pattern was plausible, but essentially a complete 180 was a lot harder to explain.

"I don't know if that's it. More like he didn't want to give us too much, or then we'd know it was him for sure. I never said how they were different, so if he'd elaborated, he'd have been admitting he knew something else."

Ethan nodded along, but he still wasn't convinced. He wanted to discuss it with Verne, privately, and see if he thought Watt's reaction was strange. He remained lost in thought, going over the interrogation in his head in case there were any clues he'd missed. After a couple minutes Soto put headphones on, and they drove back to the station in silence.

CHAPTER TWENTY-SIX

WEDNESDAY, JANUARY 2nd

Ethan texted Vanessa to let her know he was working late before driving over to Fiona Griffin's alone. He knew he should have told Verne about his Christmas Eve visit and his growing suspicions as soon as he and Soto got back to the station, but there was the logical part of him that believed he needed more evidence first. If he could show Verne and the others his gut feeling was right, then they would have to consider it as more than Fiona's delusions.

Fiona answered the door so quickly, Ethan would have believed she'd been standing there waiting for him, despite the fact he hadn't called to say he would stop by.

"Ethan, what a pleasant surprise," she said, as she stepped back to make room for him in the entryway.

"Sorry for the unannounced visit. Hopefully, I'm not interrupting yours and Mr. Griffin's dinner."

Fiona's lips pressed into a thin line before she turned her back to Ethan and shut the door. "Greg is working late."

Ethan nodded, though she wasn't looking at him. He assumed that meant Gregory Griffin was with his other family. He felt a pang of sympathy for Fiona, but it worked in his favor that Gregory wasn't around.

When Fiona turned back to face him, she had a smile worthy of a place among the Stepford Wives plastered on her face.

"I've been going over the information I remembered from the hospital, and doing research of my own," Fiona explained, as she led him to her living room. "It took some digging, but I vaguely remembered a name. I combed through records and online databases, and I located a nurse who worked at the hospital. I believe she was there when Anne was taken."

Spread out on the coffee table were webpage printouts, thoroughly annotated, and an open phonebook that had to be at least two decades old. He got closer and checked the cover to confirm; it was a 2002 phonebook. Only seventeen years old then.

He put the phonebook back as he found it and perched on the edge of the couch to scan over the other items on the table more closely. There was a lot of information here, and the way she had it methodically laid out didn't give him the impression she cleaned it up every day. He spared a glance at Fiona, who was standing above him with an air of expectation. He turned back to the table, wondering how rarely Greg Griffin came home if she could keep her work out in the open.

In the phonebook, Ethan saw that there were at least two dozen tabs in the residential sections. He quickly flipped through to the various tabs and saw that there were names highlighted and then crossed out in red.

"Did you call all these people? And how did you remember her name? You'd never given detectives a name before."

He knew Fiona wanted to get answers about what happened to Anne. He didn't think she'd be so desperate for him to believe her that she'd fabricate information, but he couldn't help the skepticism in his voice.

Fiona seemed indifferent to the accusation, instead moving to sit beside Ethan on the couch. She took the phonebook into her lap, as well as printouts that Ethan could see were from online white pages websites.

"I mentioned her name to the original investigators, but they never did anything with the information. And I didn't even bother telling you because you seemed to be another adversary until you saw sense." She spoke so matter-of-factly, Ethan wasn't sure if she was even intending to offend him or just saw that to be the truth. "When you came to me last week and said you had your doubts, I recalled that it was something detectives, and I, failed to follow up on, so I've spent the time since following up. That's what I was going to tell you when I called today."

Ethan gave her a sideways glance as he picked up more of the printouts off the table. He couldn't help but feel like it was a little too convenient. Fiona hadn't seemed like the type to forget a piece of information she felt might help her find out what happened to Anne, but he didn't want to get into it with her over a feeling. Even if a feeling was what landed him here in the first place.

"Right, so who do you believe the nurse from that night was?" Ethan asked, realizing the pattern in the names was they were all a variation of Katherine. She had printouts with both "k" and "c" spellings, variations with a "y" and without, but all had a last name starting with "Man."

"I recalled another nurse calling her Katherine, but all I could remember from her name badge was the beginning of her last name. I found a phonebook and narrowed down my options and then got on the computer and did a little detective work to find out if any of these women were nurses. Once I had a list, I started calling them, and I found the one."

Fiona reached out and plucked a printout from the table, tapping her slender finger to the name at the top: Kathryn Manson.

Ethan accepted the printout from her. He read Fiona's notes on the sheet, which included that she was a nurse at Rothbury Hospital from 1969 until she retired in 2011. Scribbled farther down was the name of a retirement home and presumably the address.

"You spoke to her?"

"This morning, yes."

"You spoke about the case, and July 9th, 1982?" he clarified.

"I called, confirmed she was a nurse at Rothbury Hospital at the time, and told her a detective would be reaching out about a cold case."

Ethan set down the printout and ran a hand down his face. He shouldn't be surprised by Fiona's behavior. In fact, it would have been stranger if she hadn't reached out and essentially scheduled an interview. It didn't change the fact he couldn't let this get out of control.

"I'll follow up with her soon and see if she remembers anything, but from now on, I need you not to call and tell people that I'll go talk to them before I've even had a chance to look over the information."

Her lips were pursed, and he half expected a fight from her, but she settled with a small nod of acknowledgment. She handed him the printout again before she collected the other sheets that had been the dead ends and neatly stacked them on top of the phonebook.

"Into the recycling?" he asked, as he stood up and folded the printout into a small rectangle before he tucked it into his shirt pocket.

"No, just a banker box. Greg doesn't bother to look at what I've kept over the years, so he won't notice a new box."

Ethan nodded, not sure what he could really say to the depressing truth of her statement. He led the way back to the front door but turned around before opening it.

"You didn't tell me before because you didn't think I believed you, but now that I'm not sure Watt did, it is there anything else you suspect, or know, that you haven't told me?"

She held his gaze, her green eyes seeming to search his face before she held eye contact.

"I've told you everything you need to know."

Ethan in turn studied her face, not pointing out that that wasn't exactly the definitive answer he wanted from her, but he suspected she knew that. Still, she only hurt her chances for answers by not being upfront with him, and she didn't seem to need his reminder to know that.

"I'll get in touch with Kathryn, and if I have any news, I'll let you know."

He let himself out the front door, his mind working to figure out how much further down this path he should venture alone before he'd crossed a line by not telling Verne. There was a small voice in the back of his mind that said he'd already crossed that line, but he ignored it.

CHAPTER TWENTY-SEVEN

THURSDAY, JANUARY 3RD

The following morning, Ethan and the gang, as Vanessa had dubbed them, made the trip out with CSI to canvas for Watt's tree fort. Verne had tried to get a team searching the day before, but no one wanted to spend a New England evening traipsing through the woods. They claimed to be tied up with a more pressing, time-is-of-the-essence, case. Ethan hadn't particularly wanted to do it the next morning either. He had his hands shoved as deep in his pockets as he could while still being able to navigate the underbrush with some grace.

Barnett looked as miserable as Ethan felt, her jaw clenched, her body so hunched, one nudge from behind would send her rolling forward. Soto and Verne were elated. They'd taken the lead, shared stories about local hiking trails they loved. Ethan had never known Verne to hike.

"We've brought more cadaver dogs to speed up our search a bit," TJ said, coming up beside Ethan. He didn't turn to look at her but kept his eyes on the ground so he wouldn't trip on the rough terrain.

"Are they staying in the truck until we get a better idea of location?"

"No, they got here before, us so they're a quarter mile or so out."

Ethan gave the slightest nod. He wasn't willing to expose his face too much from behind his coat collar. He should have skipped shaving this morning. He tried to listen out for them, but he knew they only alerted their handlers if they found something.

What felt like an hour later, though Soto informed him it was only fifteen minutes, the four detectives and several CSIs reached the crumbled remnants of a tree fort that matched Watt's description. The dogs had already canvassed the area directly under it and had moved on to work the perimeter moving out from the fort.

"Any indication of what we're looking for?" Pereira asked; his CSI windbreaker looked useless in this weather. The group of them had formed a circle, partially shielding one another.

"Presumably another victim," Soto answered.

"We did find other evidence last time too, so anything could be related," Verne added.

"Good thing he came out here to tell us that," Shepard mumbled under his breath to TJ.

Ethan cleared his throat, giving Shepard a look that dared him to continue. Shepard held Ethan's gaze, but he didn't say anything else while in earshot of Ethan. He wanted to be out here as much as the CSIs wanted to hear Verne remind them how to do their job. He still hadn't talked to Verne alone about the interrogation with Watt. Nor had he had a chance to look further into Naomi Beavis, potentially their Jane Doe. They'd put the DNA collection on the back burner.

"Anything else, Dumas?" Verne asked, snapping Ethan out of his thoughts.

"No, you covered it." He'd missed the rest of what Verne had said to the group.

The CSIs disbursed and left the four of them standing there. Ethan looked up at the tree that had a few boards clinging on where the trunk had split. He tried to picture a young Watt coming out here with friends, but he could neither imagine Watt young nor anyone wanting to befriend him.

"Do any of us have to stick around?" Barnett asked.

"Yes. We all do." He looked at Verne as he said this to emphasize he couldn't "lead detective" himself out of this responsibility. "The more of us helping canvas the area means the greater chance of finding whatever it is that may be out here and, hopefully, soon."

"I have work to do back at the station," Verne tried through chattering teeth.

"It'll still be there when we're done here, bud." Soto gave Verne's arm a slap. "Plus, you're an outdoorsy guy. I'm sure you're more than accustomed to a little chill like this with all your hiking experience."

Soto hadn't seemed to buy Verne's act after all. Ethan didn't push the point further. The look of determination was clear on Verne's face, and Ethan didn't expect he'd hear a single complaint out of him for the rest of the time they were out there.

"We can split up. Verne, you and I will head this way. Soto and Barnett, you can go that way." Ethan pulled out his phone to check he still had a signal. It wasn't great, but he'd still be reachable. "Call if you find something."

With nothing left to discuss, they split up. Ethan found a long enough stick to prod the undergrowth with as they walked. Verne had decided it was just as effective to swipe through it with his foot. Verne recounted his date from the night before, who, Ethan was shocked and somewhat relieved to learn, didn't work at the station. There was always a first time for everything. He only half listened and only entertained the matter long enough for them to be out of earshot so he could discuss Watt.

"Let me guess. After dinner, you convinced her to come back to your place, you hooked up, you'll never call her back. If she reacts like a normal human being, you'll be shocked and probably sleep with her again because she'll be emotionally vulnerable and that's how you prefer your ladies," Ethan said when they were alone, and he'd heard enough of Verne's playboy story.

"Okay, uncalled for," Verne huffed as he gave another patch of undergrowth a sweep through with his shoe.

"I wanted to talk about Watt's interrogation yesterday. Soto went rogue." He jabbed at some dense bush around a tree and tried not to be too obvious as he jumped when a bird flew out. "I guess rogue is too harsh. We hadn't scripted the interrogation, but she gave him a pass on Jane Doe for the new location."

"Was he talking about Jane Doe?"

"Not exactly, but she hardly took the time to get it out of him." Ethan tried to think how to explain Watt's behavior.

"Are you mad we got another lead?"

"I'm not mad. I just think there's more to uncover about Jane Doe, and we didn't get a chance. He questioned if we found someone, and then Soto brought up the difference in MO between Jane Doe and his other victims. She didn't specify what that difference was, but he didn't brag like before. He just, I don't know, got standoffish. And then when she had the chance to push, she gave him the choice to tell us more about Jane Doe or give us another lead."

Verne stopped and leaned against the tree he'd been searching around. "I don't see the problem. Ideally, we'd have got both, but he gave us another lead. A lead that might get us closer to closing Anne Griffin's case."

Ethan opened his mouth to mention Fiona Griffin, Christmas Eve, last night, and the growing gut feeling that Anne Griffin's case wasn't related to Watt, but he found himself holding back.

"You should've been there. It was too vague. He was boastful when we spoke to him. This was different. Something was off. You just have to listen to it when we're back at the station."

"Maybe he didn't want to give us details. He doesn't get anything if he does, and we can't do much more to make his life worse, despite what he's given us. We're in a weird standoff." Verne pushed himself off the tree and walked on.

Before he had a chance to try and convince Verne further, his phone rang. When he checked, it was an unknown number. Verne had continued without him, so he didn't bother to shout out for him to wait.

"Detective Dumas," he answered. He could hear someone, but the signal was poor. He could only catch every other word, and what he could make out sounded like the other person saying they couldn't hear him.

"Hold on." He jogged back to a clearing he and Verne had passed on their way out from the start point. "Can you hear me now?"

"Hi, yes, much better. This is John. John Coppin Jr., I was calling you back on behalf of my dad. You'd left a message for him."

"Yes, thank you for getting back to me." Ethan left off the fact it was about three months since his first message for Detective Coppin, and that it had been far more than one message.

"I know you said it was urgent in your message, is there anything I can help with?"

"I was hoping to speak with your father, it's about a case he previously worked."

There was a long pause on the other end. "I'm not much help then. My dad had a heart attack a few months ago. It took a toll on him, and long story short, he's been in a coma ever since." John's voice began to waiver, and Ethan guessed he was a few seconds away from crying.

"I'm very sorry to hear that and hope he makes a speedy recovery." There was silence on both sides, and Ethan wasn't sure if John expected Ethan to say more. "When he wakes and has recovered, please have him give me a call."

John's sob came as a response, and Ethan thought it best to hang up. He wasn't confident he would ever get a call back from either John, but at least he knew Detective Coppin hadn't just snubbed his request for help.

He tucked his phone away and jogged back to where he'd left Verne. He couldn't see him ahead and wondered just how far back he'd gone to get a proper signal. He slowed down as he got to a decline and used the trees along the path to keep himself upright.

"DUMAS!"

Ethan's heart leapt in fear and excitement to hear Verne shout like that. It had to be good. He gave up on his effort to not fall and ungracefully descended the slope, only ending up on his ass once.

"Verne, where are you?"

"Over here!"

"That is completely unhelpful!" Ethan shouted back as he spun in circles to see him.

"Here!" Verne came into view from behind a dense patch of trees. "I think I found something."

Ethan jogged after him as he disappeared around the trees. On the other side was a small clearing, smaller than their office. There was nothing there. He stopped hard in his tracks, confused why Verne shouted about this.

"Do you see it?" Verne asked.

"There is absolutely nothing here."

"In the undergrowth right there." Verne pointed to the far side of the clearing.

Ethan had to get closer and squat down to see what Verne saw. Underneath one of the leafy plants was a rusty knife with a dried substance on the blade. It would have to be tested for them to be sure, but it looked like blood to him. There was enough contrast between the rust and the substance for him to know it wasn't just more rust. He took out his phone and snapped a few pictures and sent them to TJ. He had to hold his phone up above his head for them to send, but a few minutes later, he heard his and Verne's names.

"We're over here." Verne had stepped back into the path to direct the two CSIs that had come to collect the knife.

Ethan backed out of their way so they could process. They did a quick swab to confirm it was blood on the blade, but it didn't tell them more than that. Ethan wasn't sure there would be much else they could do with the knife. He imagined, from the amount of rust on it, that it had been exposed to elements that were not DNA friendly.

"Good chance it's just a lost knife from a hunter," one of the CSIs said, as she dropped it into an evidence bag.

Ethan and Verne walked out of the clearing to give them room to process the surrounding area and make sure there wasn't anything else of significance.

"I feel like I've done my part. Potentially found a murder weapon," Verne said, as he tried to hide the fact he was shivering. "Can we head back now?"

Ethan gave in, mostly because he couldn't feel his hands or feet anymore and wanted a hot cup of sludgy coffee from the break room to warm him up. He texted Barnett and Soto to keep them updated and stay on site until someone relieved them.

* * *

The conference room where they relocated their investigation material had more board space, which was necessary as their victim list had grown. Jane Doe was listed next to Melody Dawson now. Naomi Beavis's name was listed under Jane Doe with a question mark.

He'd had a chance to speak with Jacquelyn Battistelli's family and learned her grandmother often took her to Senior Discount Tuesdays at Rothbury Mall. She had been the last victim he'd needed to confirm his theory. Now, they had a connection with Rothbury Mall and six of the victims: Penelope Wilks, Jacquelyn Battistelli, Emily Harp, Melody Dawson, Kelly McLane, and Rebecca Smith. Just another reason Ethan's belief Anne Griffin was not connected felt justified.

Verne had numerous documents spread out in front of him, his brows furrowed in concentration as his eyes darted from document to document. Ethan sat with Anne Griffin's file open in front of him, but he wasn't going through it. He knew now was the perfect opportunity to bring up to Verne his visits with Fiona Griffin.

"I've been thinking," Ethan started, before pausing for Verne to acknowledge him.

"Should I be scared? I really don't want to go back out to the site, if that's what you're going to say," Verne said, looking up at Ethan.

"I think we need to consider the possibility Anne Griffin's case isn't connected to the other cold cases."

Verne tilted his head to the side, reminding Ethan faintly of a dog waiting for a command.

"I stopped by Fiona Griffin's home on Christmas Eve, and again last night," Ethan explained. "I don't think Watt took Anne. We've confirmed now that every other known victim had a connection to Rothbury Mall while Watt was a janitor there, except Anne."

"Yeah, according to Fiona Griffin though," Verne interjected.

"You think she's lying?"

"From the start, she seemed determined for us not to think it's Watt, so if it would help her get her way, why wouldn't she lie?"

Ethan couldn't hide the frustration from his expression as he glared across the conference table at Verne. He knew Fiona kept things from them, and now, he didn't want to tell Verne about the nurse, as it would only give his argument ammunition. It seemed clear to Ethan that she just wanted her daughter's case closed, not to derail the investigation.

"Why would she potentially stop her daughter's case from being closed? It's not like she's loyal to Watt and is trying to protect him. She just doesn't want lazy police work, which is what she'll get if we lump Anne Griffin in with the rest just because Watt was at the hospital."

Verne shook his head slowly. "That's not what I'm saying. It's just, why do you believe she's right now? Just because Anne didn't fit into your one theory doesn't change that Watt was at the hospital around the same time she was taken."

Before Ethan could respond, Barnett and Soto practically stormed the conference room. The former's teeth still chattered, and the latter's jaw was so tight Ethan could see it from his seat.

"We'll discuss later," Ethan mumbled under his breath to Verne, who didn't bother to acknowledge he'd heard him.

"Did you find a potential murder weapon?" Verne gloated.

"No. Just a frozen deer carcass," Soto said, grabbing the closest chair to her and taking a seat. Barnett moved to the other side of the room to sit opposite. Ethan looked from one to the other, waiting for an explanation as to why they were both here.

"We got some uniformed officers to remain on site," Soto said, after she'd taken her time to remove her coat, gloves, and hat. "And don't worry, Camilleri approved it," she added before Ethan could ask if she had bothered to consult anyone.

"It was so cold, and I swear I saw something moving inside the deer," Barnett added.

"Did CSI find anything else before you guys headed back?" Ethan asked.

"No, they just kept giving us updates on nothing. We kept trying to stay in the car and another group of them would want us to come over so they could brief us on the absolute nothingness that they and the dogs had found." Soto grabbed one of Verne's documents, scanning it over before tossing it back down.

"Did one of you guys sleep with one of them too?" Verne asked, as he nodded the way he did when he tried to sympathize with a victim's family.

"No," Barnett and Soto said in disgusted unity.

Verne arched his eyebrows and looked at his papers with newfound interest. It was a miracle Verne hadn't had HR complaints made against him by now.

"So, nothing to report then?" Ethan asked, reverting the conversation back to the case.

"Nothing," Barnett repeated.

"The officers know to call me as soon as CSI gives them anything worth knowing about," Soto added.

"Fine. In the meantime, we can work on finding out more about our Jane Doe. We have our suspected victim, Naomi Beavis. Since you two are back, you can go over to her family's home in Seymour and see if anyone is willing to provide a DNA sample to help identify her," Ethan said.

"Do you think if we figure out who she is, Watt will 'fess up?" Verne asked.

"Why would he? He's got nothing to gain." Soto had stood up and started to put her layers back on.

"Regardless of what he confesses to, we need to do whatever we can, and right now, that's figure out who Jane Doe is—so go." He waved his hand at Barnett, who hadn't moved from her seat.

"Text me the address," Soto said on her way out of the conference room, with Barnett grumbling right behind her.

CHAPTER TWENTY-EIGHT

FRIDAY, JANUARY 11TH

Ethan felt slightly ridiculous that he and Verne had been having the same dispute for over a week now. Ethan hadn't even told him about Kathryn Manson. Verne had made it clear he did not believe Fiona Griffin, and he didn't like that Ethan was willing to believe her.

Verne's opposition to Fiona had forced Ethan to feign an urgent matter involving Vanessa's pregnancy cravings, giving him the opportunity to leave earlier than normal. He then headed to Kathryn Manson's retirement home in Hartford. It was fortunate that she'd never moved out of state, and he wondered if that had crossed Fiona's mind when she'd been searching for her. It was so long ago. Kathryn could have moved, passed away, or changed her name.

None of those things had happened, so rather than spending his Friday evening at the station with Verne where he was expected to be, or at home with his pregnant wife where he wanted to be, he was at the retirement home to talk to a retiree about a disappearance she might not remember.

* * *

The fluorescent lights had him blinking rapidly a few times after coming in from the dark. The lobby didn't appear to have been updated

since the nineties but was well maintained with a slight odor of
disinfectant. He walked up to the reception desk, where a staff member
sat writing notes in a log.

He waited patiently for her to notice him, and after a minute or so,
she looked up with a start.

"Oh! I'm so sorry, how can I help you?" She closed the log and gave
him her full attention.

"Sorry, didn't mean to scare you," he said with an apologetic smile.
"I'm here to see Kathryn Manson. I called yesterday and spoke with her
about stopping by to visit."

Ethan pulled out his badge to identify himself, and the woman
behind the desk conferred with her computer before nodding and
handing him a visitor pass.

"She lives in building D, number 308. If you walk toward the end of
the hall to the right," she pointed toward the hall, "and go out the doors,
you'll take the path around the courtyard and see the entrance for her
building. Just buzz her, and she can let you in."

Ethan stuck the visitor pass to his jacket and followed the directions.
He buzzed on number 308 outside building D as instructed, and the
mechanical click of the door unlocking was his only confirmation that
Kathryn was still willing to see him.

He took the stairs up to the third floor, too energized for the elevator.
The stairs dropped him off right outside number 308. Several of the
other doors nearby had welcome mats on the carpeted hallway. The door
opposite 308 even had an all-white tinsel wreath hung on the door. He
knocked, taking note of the lack of anything decorative on 308 in
comparison to every other door in sight.

Ethan was about to knock again when he heard the unlocking of a
deadbolt. The door cracked open slightly, and Ethan angled himself so
he was visible through the opening.

"Kathryn Manson," Ethan said with the hint of a question in his tone.
"I'm Detective Dumas."

He held out his badge toward the crack in the door, not seeing much beside a shadowed figure. The door came toward him, as if she meant to shut it in his face, but he heard the rattle of a chain and then the door opened wider, and he got a proper glimpse of the woman inside.

Kathryn Manson stood wringing her boney hands, sunken eyes darting every which way, as if she expected someone to jump out and attack. She wore an oversized cardigan that hung limply from her small frame, making her look especially frail. Her tongue darted out and licked at her lips nervously as she stepped back, eyes still searching the space behind Ethan.

Silently, he cursed Fiona Griffin and whatever strange situation he was walking into because of her. A nagging voice in the back of his mind, that sounded suspiciously like Verne, reminded him he could've stuck to the investigation and not strayed off course to follow Fiona's leads, but it was too late now.

The door slammed closed behind him, and Ethan couldn't help the slight shiver in his spine as he heard the chain and deadbolt slide back into place. Realistically, he knew Kathryn posed no physical threat, but when he walked a few steps farther into the small apartment, he wished there was more light in the space.

He stopped in the middle of the small living area, not sure where to sit, as Kathryn only had a single armchair. She came in right behind him, but rather than take her seat, she just stood a few feet away, still wringing her hands.

"Thank you for agreeing to speak with me in person. I believe you spoke with Fiona Griffin, the woman who told you a detective would be reaching out."

Kathryn nodded, her tongue darting out of her mouth again, but she didn't say anything to indicate whether she understood the purpose of his visit.

"Right," he said, and fished his small notepad and pen out of his jacket pocket. "I wanted to speak to you about a cold case from July

1982. It's my understanding you worked at Rothbury Hospital in the ER at the time."

All she gave him was another nod.

"What did you do exactly?" he asked, pen poised over his notepad.

Kathryn finally spoke, her voice raspier and deeper than he'd expected. "I was a nurse."

"Do you know what cold case I'm referring to, Ms. Manson?"

She still hadn't looked directly at him, her eyes refusing to settle on one point. When he asked his question, he noticed her gaze seemed to settle on a point behind him and her hands stopped moving.

"Ms. Manson?" he asked, prepared to repeat himself.

"I know." Her voice seemed softer. She didn't continue until he cleared his throat. "The little girl. The one taken when her parents brought her in and fell asleep."

"Yes, Anne Griffin. Were you working that night?"

Kathryn had resumed wringing her hands. Slowly, she dipped her chin, so imperceptibly that Ethan wasn't sure it was an answer until she nodded again, more force in the motion.

"I was in the ER that night. I remember."

Ethan's stomach dropped. His mind felt torn in so many directions. Why hadn't she been listed on witness lists? Why did Fiona wait so long to mention her? Why had Kathryn Manson never come forward?

"What do you remember? Start from the beginning."

Her eyes suddenly darted to him, widening as she seemed to take him in. "Who are you?"

His brows furrowed, his hands holding his notepad and pen dropping to his sides. "Ms. Manson, I'm Detective Dumas. You were telling me about July 1982 when you worked in Rothbury's ER."

Kathryn backed up, shaking her head as she did. The back of her legs hit her chair, and she practically crumbled into her seat.

"I don't know you." It came out more of a question than a statement.

Ethan swallowed down his frustration. He should have known it was too good to be true.

"I'm going to show myself out, Ms. Manson. Make sure you lock up behind me," he said, as he put his notepad and pen away.

She didn't acknowledge him. It wasn't until his hand grasped the doorknob that she spoke.

"The baby died."

Ethan froze. He didn't turn around, afraid the movement might draw attention to him and confuse her again.

"The baby died, and then she was gone."

Unable to leave it at that, Ethan turned around to face Kathryn again. "Anne Griffin is dead? Did you see something that night?"

Kathryn stared at him, confusion written all over her face. "Who are you?"

Ethan physically deflated. Could he trust any information he got out of Kathryn? It was clear she was suffering from mental decline, and not surprising given her age.

"I'm leaving now. Take care, Ms. Manson."

He let himself out of her apartment. He retraced his steps back to the front desk and asked that they check on her and make sure she locked her door. Once in his car, he considered calling Fiona. He knew she'd want an update, but he couldn't bring himself to have that conversation right now. Instead, he called Vanessa, smiling as she picked up and immediately began to list all her pregnancy cravings from the day.

CHAPTER TWENTY-NINE

TUESDAY, JANUARY 15TH

"We've got bodies!" Verne shouted, as he burst through the conference room doors.

Verne had interrupted Barnett, Soto, and Ethan's planning meeting. The DNA collected from the Beavis family hadn't been a match. It set them back to square one identifying their Jane Doe, so Ethan assigned Barnett to head up that investigation.

"In the woods?" Barnett asked.

"There are multiple victims?" Ethan followed up at the same time Soto asked if he said bodies, as in plural.

"TJ just called." Verne was out of breath. "So far, they've got two almost complete skeletal remains and potentially two others they haven't all the way dug up. They've just got random bones, but it's looking like a mass grave site."

Ethan snatched his phone off the table and yanked his jacket off the back of his chair. Soto had already put hers on between Verne bursting in and Ethan getting ready to go.

"I'll come with you," she said behind Ethan as he headed for the door.

He looked back at her and Barnett, who hadn't made a move to put on her coat.

"No," he said with more bite than he intended. "I want Barnett focused on our trail site Jane Doe. Soto, I need you to go through records and find out if we had any other mass graves recovered in the surrounding areas. From here on out, we consider Watt a person of interest, but he's not our primary suspect," Ethan instructed, as he edged out the door Verne held open for him.

Soto and Barnett exchanged a look, but neither protested. Verne stood silently waiting, and when Ethan looked at him, he couldn't gauge if Verne agreed with his call or not.

"Keep us updated," Soto said, as she yanked her coat back off.

* * *

As soon as they were in the car, Verne behind the wheel, Verne picked up the conversation they'd been having for nearly two weeks. It wasn't quite an argument, but each day, it seemed to be edging in that direction.

"Made any progress finding a primary suspect in Anne's case?" Verne asked, in a tone that Ethan knew meant he wasn't genuinely asking.

"No. I've been going back over the case files, but so far, I haven't found anything to point to another person of interest. The whole hospital might be guilty at this rate."

Ethan stared out the window. He couldn't tell Verne he had felt like there was something in Anne's case he'd forgotten that was slowly driving him crazy trying to recall. To make it worse, Kathryn Manson's haunting statement played on repeat in his mind. *The baby died, and then she was gone.* When he'd updated Fiona yesterday that Kathryn Manson had no useful information, Fiona's only response was she'd search other avenues. He hadn't mentioned Kathryn's statement. Fiona would have written her off. It didn't fit with her belief that Anne was still alive. He needed to be able to talk everything through with someone other than Fiona, but Verne had made it clear he was not on Ethan's side in this.

"You can't make something appear," Verne mumbled, after a few minutes of silence.

"And you can't pin a case on—"

"An innocent man?"

"That's not what I was going to say. If Watt didn't do it, then you should want to find the right guy as much as I do. You can't choose when to care about justice."

Verne slammed on the brakes, haphazardly veering the car off to the shoulder as the car that had been driving behind them laid on their horn and flipped Ethan and Verne off as they flew by.

"Jesus, Verne!"

"I'm not a corrupt cop." Verne had twisted to face Ethan, his face flushed.

"I'm aware. We wouldn't be partners if you were."

"Watt should be the primary suspect, and you haven't found anything that says otherwise. You might pity Fiona, but that doesn't mean you can just go all—" Verne cut himself off and waved his hands in the air to seemingly emphasize what he thought Ethan was doing to the investigation.

Ethan arched an eyebrow but nodded slowly. He couldn't ask Verne to put faith in Ethan's gut feeling when Ethan couldn't explain what made him so sure his gut was right. He'd wanted to be able to turn to Verne for help in this, but clearly, he'd pushed Verne too far.

"I'm sorry. I'll drop it."

"Dumas! Seriously you—wait, what? You'll drop it?" Verne's mouth fell open a bit, as he'd been prepared to fight Ethan on the matter.

"You're right. Watt should be the primary suspect. Fiona Griffin is just a grieving mother."

Verne's eyes narrowed, but Ethan stayed calm and unaffected by the scrutinization. Slowly, Verne started to nod and turn back toward the wheel. Ethan let himself relax a bit into his seat.

"Okay, then we're good?" Verne asked.

"We're good," Ethan confirmed.

Verne nodded again before he shifted the car back to drive and pulled back on the road. Ethan didn't try to make conversation and let them fall into a comfortable silence the rest of the ride. The silence gave him time to go over everything he remembered since meeting Fiona Griffin. Retracing every conversation and interaction he could remember to find the source of the nagging feeling he missed something.

CHAPTER THIRTY

FRIDAY, JANUARY 18TH

Ethan white-knuckled Howard's favorite pinot noir as Vanessa let them into her parents' house. Ethan cared about them, from afar, but too much face time with Howard when he had the weight of cases on his mind left him vulnerable to Howard's criticism. Ethan gave their car one last longing look before he shut the door behind himself. He should have canceled.

"Mom! Dad! We're here!" Vanessa shed her coat, gloves, hat, and scarf into Ethan's arms, which he promptly dumped on the Ashbys' staircase banister. He added his own coat on top and kicked off his dress shoes next to her boots. She was off to find her mom.

"Good, you brought something this time," Howard said, as he came out of his office off the entry.

Ethan held out the wine, label showing, so Howard could see he wasted his money to buy the top-shelf label instead of the perfectly delicious nine-dollar alternative. Howard accepted it and read the label, like it wasn't the exact one he always ordered when they went out for dinner. "I'll put this in the wine locker. It won't pair well with what's for dinner."

Ethan held his tongue and looked past Howard to the kitchen, where he could hear Vanessa's and Lisa's laughter. Vanessa's came out in short nasally bursts that would soon turn to snorting. That at least brought a smile to his face and reminded him why he bothered to try with Howard after so many years.

Howard led the way, and Ethan followed, finding their wives hunched over bags. "Ethan, come here!" Vanessa said, holding out her hand for him to come over.

"What've you got?" he asked. As he got closer, he realized the bags were overflowing with baby clothes.

"Mom went wild at the store." Vanessa pulled onesies, hats, and sweaters out of the bag that looked too small for even a newborn to wear. Her tone had changed, and he thought her excitement sounded forced. He placed a hand on her lower back, trying to angle her toward him.

"Do you want to go through this later?" he asked, in a hushed tone.

Vanessa was holding up two vibrantly pink onesies; one read *Mommy's Mini Me* and the other *Daddy's Princess*. She just stared at them. He took them from her without a word and placed them back in the bag.

Ethan was saved from further intervention by Howard's announcement dinner was ready. Ethan ushered Vanessa away from the clothes. He pulled out her chair for her to sit and then took his own seat just as Lisa plopped a generous spoonful of steamed carrots and peas on his plate. He tried not to pull a face as she added a pork chop and mashed potatoes. He'd tried countless times to make it known, in his almost nine years of marriage to Vanessa, that he hated only two vegetables: carrots and peas. Clearly, he still hadn't got through to Lisa, and he was too concerned about upsetting her to say it outright.

"How is the Anne Griffin investigation going?" Howard asked, as Lisa finished serving.

Ethan, who'd been about to shove a mouthful of mashed potato-covered peas and carrots in his mouth, couldn't mask the surprise at Howard asking him about work. Let alone that he remembered a case Ethan had mentioned to them on Thanksgiving, nearly two months ago.

"It's going," he replied, before realizing he sounded as inept as Howard believed him to be. "Truthfully, it has us stumped and has been pushed aside for new developments, but my partner and I are still working to close it. We've been in contact with the primary suspect, and there's hope he may confess."

Ethan pushed back the doubt in his mind as he repeated the version of the truth he'd been feeding to his team.

Howard studied Ethan. He could tell Howard he solved every cold case and got closure for everyone, and Howard would still find a reason to be dissatisfied.

Howard picked up his wine glass and took a sip. Ethan ate his forkful of food, chewing slowly as Kathryn Manson's words filled the silence in his mind. Eager to not think about work for once, he turned to ask Lisa a question, but Howard spoke up.

"Does that mean the case will be closed soon?"

Ethan looked back at Howard, taking in the furrowed brows and his darting eyes. Ethan picked up his own wine glass and took a long sip, holding Howard's searching gaze. Lisa and Vanessa paused their eating and turned their attention to Ethan, waiting for a response.

"Hopefully."

Lisa gave a soft laugh, usually her way of dispelling any awkwardness when it arose between Ethan and Howard, but Ethan wasn't done.

"It's funny you'd bring it up. You don't usually remember cases I mention."

"Ethan," Vanessa said in a hushed, but stern tone.

Howard sat back in his chair, the need for answers gone from his face. He picked up his own wine glass, mirroring Ethan's move from moments before as he took his time to swig the wine. After a prolonged sip, he set the glass back down, the ghost of a sneer on his face.

"I was just trying to be nice, Ethan. For my daughter's sake. Or is it an issue now that I feign interest in your job when before it was an issue I didn't?"

Ethan felt his ears flush, despite his best efforts to appear unaffected by Howard's words. He felt Vanessa stiffen slightly beside him and the defeated sigh of Lisa across the table from her. He picked up his silverware and dropped Howard's gaze to start eating again. He heard the huff from Howard, which he refused to acknowledge with even a glance up.

Vanessa, always eager to keep the peace, brought up school and funny things that had happened this week with students and other teachers.

When the torturous night was finally over and they'd made it to the car, Ethan had hoped Vanessa wasn't going to say anything about dinner. However, as soon as he'd reversed the car out of the driveway and started home, she released a drawn-out sigh.

"He was just trying to be nice; I'd asked him to put in more of an effort," Vanessa said.

Ethan glanced over, but she was looking out the passenger window. He reached his hand out and found one of hers resting in her lap. He gave it a squeeze before bringing it to his lips.

"I'm sorry. I'm just on edge with the cases."

Vanessa didn't say anything right away, but she let him continue to hold her hand.

"I worry about how your work is going to affect us when the baby comes."

Her words came out so softly, barely more than a whisper, but it didn't make them hurt any less. He knew Howard and Lisa had their doubts, but hearing Vanessa say it was so much worse. Ethan still had her hand in his, but the other holding the wheel clenched it tighter to expel the anger and hurt he felt hearing her admit that.

He couldn't offer her more than platitudes because he had the same concerns. He was a cold case detective for now, but he hoped to transfer back to homicide. His workload was an issue now; it would only get worse if he was promoted as Robinson and Camilleri had hinted.

"You and our baby are my number one priority. I promise." The words almost tasted bitter with the fear he was making a promise he couldn't keep.

Vanessa squeezed his hand before freeing hers from his grasp, her hands resting on her stomach. He stopped at a red light and glanced over at her. This time, Vanessa met his gaze. Her eyes were watery, and her lips trembled in her efforts to smile through the tears threatening to fall.

"I love you, but you and I both know your duty and badge have always come first."

His lips parted, but he couldn't find the words to argue that she was wrong. A single tear rolled down her cheek as the car behind them honked. Ethan tore his eyes away, seeing the light had turned green. He gripped the wheel tightly with both hands and drove home in silence, not wanting to make Vanessa more promises she wouldn't believe.

CHAPTER THIRTY-ONE

WEDNESDAY, JANUARY 30TH

The days were slipping away from Ethan, but nothing new had surfaced in the Anne Griffin case to point them in a different direction, away from Watt. To add to his stress, Fiona's calls remained incessant, and with nothing new to report, no time to follow more false leads, and not in a mood to be chastised by her, he'd resorted to dodging her calls.

The team was gathered around the conference table. As they settled in, Verne made an offhand comment about grabbing drinks the night before with his ADA buddy, Kyle. Kyle had let slip that the DA's office had a game plan for Watt and were waiting on them to "make a move." Ethan coerced Verne to call Kyle, with an audience, so they could all hear Kyle's insight. He was eager to share and told them the DA planned to offer Watt a plea deal. With the recorded interrogation from Ethan and Verne's visit, the DA's office was willing to negotiate the charges in exchange for full confessions for all four cold cases. All off the record, of course. As soon as Kyle hung up, the uproar began.

"They absolutely cannot," Soto scoffed. "Offering him a deal because he admitted to being a bigger psycho than we thought?"

"He's in on multiple life sentences without parole. Adding more would have been nice, but unnecessary. If a deal gets us answers, we should be happy," Ethan said. He had to play the voice of reason, despite his own frustration with the entire thing.

Soto threw herself back in her chair, Barnett huffed, and Verne looked almost embarrassed.

"A plea deal is just dumb," Barnett said.

"Fucking dumb," Soto mumbled.

"We'd be better off just throwing the book at him, and if he shuts up, he shuts up," Verne added.

Everyone fell silent and looked to Ethan, as though expecting him to make it all better.

"I say we press on. Until we get shut down, we keep going," Ethan said.

"Maybe, if we find more, the DA will feel prosecuting him would be a solid win rather than settling for a plea deal," Soto said with a definitive nod.

"And so, what if they give him a plea deal? We'll get cases closed either way," Barnett added.

Barnett sounded far more upbeat than Ethan could muster for a plea deal. Sure, if they closed their cases and got closure for families with Watt's confessions, then it was a good thing. He'd repeat that to himself until he believed it, and eventually, he'd drown out Kathryn Manson's words and the nagging forgotten piece that lingered as the weeks dragged on.

"Verne, I'm going to pay the Griffins a visit, if you want to tag along. You two can work on the reports. I want to get those to Camilleri as soon as possible."

"Great, I always enjoy a pushy mother who thinks I'm inept at my job," Verne mumbled.

Soto and Barnett both made sounds of acknowledgment, though neither looked enthused to be put on paperwork. Ethan hadn't ever met a detective that was—no one went into this job because they enjoyed pushing paper.

"Give us a call if you need anything," Ethan said on the way out the door.

"But don't need anything!" Verne added.

* * *

Ethan knew he had to get ahead of the news about Watt when it came to Fiona Griffin. For a fleeting moment, he considered sending Barnett and Soto; however, he didn't trust Fiona not to expose his extracurricular investigation. Even taking Verne was a risk, but he hoped having him there would temper Fiona's reaction.

Verne hadn't known the plan, to tell Fiona about the potential plea deal, until they were walking up the Griffins' front path, but he managed to make his feelings clear in the thirty odd seconds he had to process.

"She's going to murder us and then hide us in her basement and—" Verne cut himself off when Gregory Griffin answered the door.

Ethan did his best to school his expression to hide the surprise at Gregory being home during the day midweek—or him being home at all. He'd seen him so infrequently over the last few months, it seemed wrong for him to be in his own home now.

"Good afternoon, Detective Dumas and Detective Verne," Ethan said, recovering from his shock as he motioned between the two of them. "We met a couple months back."

Gregory looked between the two of them with thinly veiled disdain. "I recall."

"Is Mrs. Griffin home? We'd like to speak with you both about your daughter's case," Ethan said, moving on. He didn't want to linger on the memory of their last interaction; it seemed Gregory remembered it as fondly as Ethan.

"She is," he said, though he remained rooted in place.

He stared them both down, before finally relenting. Ethan liked to think it was because they didn't falter under his gaze, but he suspected it was more to do with the wind beginning to blow snow into the house. Gregory stepped aside and gave them an uncomfortably narrow gap to walk through into the entryway.

"Shoes." It came out as a barked command from Gregory.

Ethan was already half out of his first shoe anyway. Verne mumbled an apology for his smelly feet as he kicked off one of his dress shoes. Ethan swallowed down the gag as the sour smell wafted toward him.

"It smells like a crime scene," Ethan whispered, as he did his best to distance himself from Verne and his feet.

Verne shrugged but flashed Ethan a grin when Gregory turned away from them, his disgust clear in his frown lines and flared nostrils.

They followed him into what seemed to be a second living room; at least it wasn't the same space he'd been in only a couple weeks earlier when he and Fiona had discussed Kathryn Manson. The hallway of photos had seemed sad enough. This room took it to a new level. Shadow boxes of baby items filled the shelves on one wall. More photos hung on seemingly every free space in the room, and a photo album labeled "Anne" sat in the middle of the coffee table.

"Wow, this is intense," Verne said, looking around the room.

Ethan was grateful Gregory had stepped out of the room, hopefully to get Fiona so they could get this over with and get out of there.

"Just let me do the talking. You know she hasn't let go of the idea Anne is alive," Ethan whispered. He perched himself on the edge of one of the two couches that faced each other.

"Not that you've done much to help convince her otherwise." Verne dropped down next to Ethan, bringing them back to eye level.

Verne and Ethan exchanged looks, silently challenging one another. Before Ethan could give anymore instructions, Fiona walked in the room, Gregory right behind her.

"Ethan, what a surprise," Fiona said, though from her tone she didn't seem to appreciate the surprise. She turned to Verne before Ethan could respond. "I'm sorry, I don't recall your name."

"Detective Verne."

"Oh, don't be silly. We're on first-name terms here," she said, waving off Verne's formal introduction as she took a seat across from them on the second couch.

"Jay," Verne answered, shifting in his seat. Ethan cocked an eyebrow at him, amused he gave in. Verne hated when families or anyone related to an investigation called him anything other than Verne, but he clearly didn't want to tell Fiona that.

"Nice to see you again, Jay. Greg says you wanted to speak about Anne's case?"

"We wanted to let you know what is likely coming next in Anne's case, so you hear it from us before it's in the news." Ethan couldn't bring himself to meet Fiona's gaze, instead focusing on a photo he could see over her shoulder. "I know you're somewhat aware of the happenings in the case. Within the last couple of weeks, there have been substantial developments, and there's a strong possibility the DA will offer a plea deal."

Gregory scoffed, but Ethan continued. Wanting to get everything out before Fiona inevitably interrupted.

"We also believe, due to forensic evidence from some of the cases and similarities between them, that it is most likely that Watt is responsible for Anne's disappearance. With this information, the DA will likely choose to offer Watt a plea deal in exchange for him pleading guilty and providing information needed to close all involved cases, including the location of Anne's remains."

Fiona's immediate keening caused Ethan to flinch as she flew from her seat. Verne inhaled sharply, and even Gregory took a step away from her. He half expected her to attack, but instead, she remained on the other side of the coffee table, her calm composure gone as her chest rose and fell rapidly.

"She is not dead," she got out between gritted teeth, though her voice was chillingly calm in comparison to her reaction. "You have done exactly what the original detectives did: absolutely nothing. You've ignored the leads I gave you. Failed to produce your own, despite saying you believed me. Did you even follow through or just say you did? Did you bother to do your job?"

"Mrs. Griffin," Verne interrupted, holding out his hands as if he were approaching a wild animal. "I assure you we have done every—"

"Don't assure me," she bit back, cutting Verne off. "If you had done everything, then you wouldn't be stuck on this ridiculous notion that *he* had anything to do with Anne's kidnapping."

Ethan remained silent. In an ideal world, he would have loved to have followed her leads, solved Anne's case, and brought her home to Fiona. However, this world was far from ideal, and he'd only made it worse for Fiona.

Fiona ran her hands down her clothing, smoothing out creases that weren't there. Ethan finally made eye contact. He'd expected to see anger, frustration, even resentment, but she looked concerned and anxious. Her eyes darted to the corner of the room, behind him. Without another word, she turned and left.

The air in the room stilled. Verne seemed to be in the same state of shock as Ethan. He'd never had someone react so poorly to the chance of closure. Though he shouldn't be surprised; the only closure Fiona would have accepted was finding Anne alive.

Gregory, who hadn't said a word since Fiona had come in and had remained standing by the doorway, laughed. Ethan and Verne looked at each other, and Verne's face reflected Ethan's own disbelief.

"After all this time, she gets a damn answer and she's still not happy. Women," he said, his laugh dying down to a chuckle. "You boys seem to have upset her enough for one day. I'll show you out."

Gregory walked into the hall with Verne close behind. It was a split-second decision, but as Ethan had stood up, he'd noticed a small side table with a single deep drawer in the corner where Fiona had glanced. He quickly pulled out his phone and started recording as he quietly opened the drawer. On top were the papers and printouts he'd seen weeks earlier when Fiona had been searching for Kathryn Manson. He rifled through them, prepared to end the recording when he caught a glimpse of a brochure he'd never seen before. He lifted the papers off it long enough to record its seven-letter acronym before he shut the drawer.

He barely had time to press his phone to his ear when Gregory reappeared in the doorway.

"What are you doing?" Gregory asked.

"Yeah, I'll pick up dinner. I love you too. Bye." Ethan turned to face him. He pretended to hang up and slid it back in his pocket. "Sorry, pregnant wife with cravings."

Gregory looked him up and down but didn't say anything. He stepped back and motioned for Ethan to leave. Ethan complied, quickly shoving his feet into his shoes to join Verne, who had already stepped outside. Without a word Gregory slammed the door behind Ethan and latched the deadbolt.

"He's really just a ray of sunshine, isn't he?" Verne said, as they stomped through the gathering snow.

On the drive back to the station, Ethan zoned Verne out. He had gone back to the recording and screenshot a still of the brochure. Now, with the time to read it, Ethan saw it was for a private laboratory's DNA testing sector. He considered sharing what he'd found with Verne, but decided he'd look into it first. He didn't want Verne to think he was falling down another rabbit hole of Fiona's making.

* * *

The following day, while Verne, Soto, and Barnett dealt with the paperwork, Ethan feigned a need to follow up on another cold case in their never shrinking pile. Verne was in the conference room, so Ethan had their office to himself.

He had the website pulled up for the private DNA laboratory. Their frequently asked questions section explained how they could create various types of DNA profiles from collected samples. None of it was new information, he knew how DNA testing worked, but he'd never put much weight into the private sector.

The website boasted claims of being able to close cold cases for police by offering expedited forensic testing that could help solve murders, rapes, and other crimes. He couldn't help the dejected scoff that escaped him. Forensic testing took time, especially with the never-ending backlog, and active investigations always had priority over cold cases. Yet they were promising results in as little as a week after receiving the DNA sample.

Ethan continued skimming questions until he reached the end of the page. While he could understand why Fiona might choose to use a private laboratory, given her clear distrust in police, he couldn't figure out what she'd need tested. After how things were left yesterday, she probably wouldn't answer any questions he had.

He closed out the browser window and attempted actual case work, but he couldn't get the nagging question of what she could possibly have tested off his mind. He decided it must be her contingency plan if they claimed to have found Anne's body so she could verify herself. That was the only logical explanation.

CHAPTER THIRTY-TWO

TUESDAY, FEBRUARY 26TH

It took a few weeks after the reports were filed for the team to get the news they'd been expecting. The DA went with a plea deal. Watt gave an official written statement, as required by the terms of the plea, as well as a recorded statement. They were still working with Soto and Barnett on the victims found at the two locations Watt had given them. Those cases weren't included in the plea deal, which only encompassed Melody Dawson, Kelly McLane, Rebecca Smith, and Anne Griffin. He pleaded guilty to all four with an explanation for each.

"We should probably wait for Soto and Barnett to get back," Verne said. Just a minute earlier, he'd barged into their office announcing he had a copy of Watt's recorded statement.

"Or we could watch it now, and then we'll just watch it again once they're back. It's not like it's pay-per-view," Ethan countered. Soto and Barnett hadn't been on the case long enough to be nearly as invested as they were.

Verne shut their office door and dragged his chair over as Ethan pulled it up on his computer. He turned the volume up and braced himself. He always felt a rush of adrenaline before he watched a confession tape, and he had to will himself to sit still.

They listened in silence as Watt walked his audience through each victim's kidnapping and murder in detail. Ethan had his fists balled in his lap as he listened to Watt recount each child's abuse as if he'd been wooing them. After the second victim, Ethan had to pause it for a minute. It was just as difficult to stomach as it was the first time Watt told them.

"Need the trash?" Verne asked.

Ethan waved him off and took a few deep breaths before he hit play again. He couldn't form the words to explain the fear that gripped his insides. He'd worked too many cases related to children, and Watt wasn't even his first case that involved pedophilia, but hearing what Watt did to those girls had Ethan forcing bile back down his throat. As he listened to Watt brag, he couldn't get the fact that he was going to have a baby girl in a few months out of his mind.

He'd zoned out the recording, his mind spinning out over his unborn daughter, when Watt's voice drew him back to the present with the mention of a name. He had moved on to Anne Griffin. Ethan sat up straighter and forced himself to pay attention. He wanted to hear every word of the explanation that Watt had been unwilling to give them when they visited.

The details of the kidnapping were in line with what they'd already known from the initial investigation. He was there because his father had been admitted into the emergency room. Anne, like his other victims, had been a victim of opportunity. He grabbed her while her parents slept. He had his car, and his father wasn't discharged right away, so he left with Anne. His accounts of her abuse sounded exactly like the others down to the secluded wooded area. However, when Watt answered the question as to where he disposed of her body, Ethan hit pause.

"What are you doing?" Verne asked, a hint of annoyance in his voice that Ethan chose to ignore. He hit rewind, going back a minute, before he started the video again.

"After I finished with her, I put her in one of those black trash bags in my car and threw some rocks in there with her. Then I dropped the bag into the river." The DA clarified, which river, and Watt confirmed, the Naugatuck River.

Ethan hit pause again. He sat back and absentmindedly rubbed his hand across the days-old stubble that covered his chin as he processed. "I don't believe him."

"About which river?" Verne asked.

"No, about where he dumped her body. All of it—how he did it, if he did it." He stood up and scooted past Verne's chair. He needed to pace to process. "How did he dispose of his other victims?"

"He just kind of left them where he'd killed them."

"And how do we know that?"

"Because of evidence, the general disruption to the debris, and his confession?"

"Exactly! Evidence. Even though it took a while for Watt to confirm for us, we already had a good general idea of what happened and where because the evidence had shown us. We just needed either his confirmation it was him or his DNA to confirm the evidence."

The look on Verne's face told Ethan he wasn't quite following Ethan's thought process. Ethan pointed at the monitor. "He never disposed of the bodies."

"What about the victims he's been giving us the last few months? Those victims were all buried."

"He knew where they were, but that's the only connection we have that links him to those cases. The first victim's head was bashed in, which couldn't be more different from his MO. Then, at this second site, the victims are significantly older than the girls who have already been linked to him. Plus, their remains all suggested they were killed with a knife. All of them had cuts in their vertebrae."

Ethan fought to keep his voice even and not shout at Verne. He was mad at himself that he'd allowed it to go this far now. He should have gone to Camilleri with his belief that Anne Griffin might not be Watt's victim. He should have insisted the connection was shaky at best and that he may be coerced to confess if it was the only way to get his plea deal.

"Okay, so the new cases are weak right now. Maybe he switched up his MO. Doesn't mean the motivation behind the kills aren't the same.

We haven't found out everything on all the new victims yet. Maybe they were later kills, and he escalated," Verne deflected.

"So, you're suggesting that in the roughly six months between Emily Harp's murder and his arrest, he changed his victim profile, the rate at which he killed, how he killed, and his disposal method?" Ethan asked, unable to hold back the bite and volume of his voice.

Verne frowned and crossed his arms over his chest. "So what? We're completely wrong and just let him plead guilty to murders he didn't commit?"

"Not murders, just Anne Griffin's. He didn't just change how he disposed of the body once when there was no reason to warrant a switch."

Verne scoffed and threw his hands up as he got exasperated with Ethan. He ran a hand over his head, disheveling his already unkempt hair before he shook his head and stared Ethan down with more determination than Ethan was used to seeing from Verne.

"What if there was?"

"Was what?" Ethan snapped.

"A reason that warranted it. It's not like anyone asked him during his statement why he dumped her body. Maybe he had one, but no one asked."

Ethan stared Verne down, undecided if he accepted that logic. Verne did have a point that they hadn't asked why because it probably seemed irrelevant in comparison to the where. He realized it was the fact Watt was only willing to discuss Anne once he got a plea deal and never before then that got to Ethan.

"I don't buy it." He returned to pacing their office. "I think we need to get face time with him again. Push this."

"No."

Ethan stopped, his back still to Verne. He hadn't expected that. He turned to see Verne had sat up a little straighter in the chair.

"No?"

"We can't backtrack now; they just signed the plea deal! What evidence do you have that he's lying? Why would he take responsibility for a crime that he didn't commit? Just to avoid a few more life sentences being added to the ones he already has?"

Ethan opened his mouth to answer, but Verne wasn't done and cut him off, sticking his hand in the air to silence Ethan.

"I don't know what kind of spiraling shit you're going through, or if Fiona Griffin really got in your head, but Watt's good for this." Verne stood up and wheeled his chair back to his side of the desk. He sat down and got on his computer, not looking at Ethan.

"If we're wrong, then we've failed to do our jobs," Ethan snapped.

"What are you going to do? Run to Ed and tell him Watt pleaded guilty to a crime he didn't commit?" Verne shouted, slamming his hands down on his desk. His cup of pens rattled near the edge, tipping as it sent pens bouncing in every direction.

"I don't run to Camilleri for things. I'm not you."

Ethan regretted that dig as soon as the words passed his lips. The hurt in Verne's eyes was apparent. Verne could sulk and let his temper get the best of him at times, but he rarely let something genuinely upset him. Verne didn't argue or storm out, which Ethan would have expected. He simply turned back to his computer and didn't say another word, which made Ethan feel much worse.

He sat down, the tension thick in the air. He considered picking up the pens that had fallen off Verne's desk, but it felt silly to crawl around the floor right now. Plus, he wouldn't put it past Verne to knock them back off as soon as Ethan picked them up.

A few times, Ethan opened his mouth to speak, but he couldn't form even the feeblest of apologies. He couldn't even muster the words to admit Verne had a valid point. He wanted to argue that Watt had nothing to lose by lying to them, even if Verne could counter that Watt also had nothing to gain.

He minimized Watt's recording and pulled up the trail and tree fort cases. He read through what CSI, the anthropologist, and the pathologist had told them so far and came to the same conclusion he had for weeks. Watt wasn't responsible for all these murders. There were too many inconsistencies between the murders they knew he committed, the young victim from the trails, and the mass grave at the tree fort. To Ethan, it seemed like Watt had tried to have them run in three different directions at once.

Soto believed that Watt must have overheard someone brag in prison and turned to that when pressure was on him. It was a possibility Ethan found far more believable than the theory Verne and Barnett leaned into that Watt varied so drastically in his killings. Barnett argued that Watt had been in solitary confinement almost as soon as he went to prison in the nineties, but guards talk, and depending on his cell location, who knew what conversations he overheard?

Whatever the case may be, Ethan didn't believe Watt was responsible for them all.

* * *

Neither Ethan nor Verne spoke to the other for several hours. A few times, someone popped into their office to talk to one of them. Soto stopped by, scolded them for leaving pens on the floor, which she picked up, and let them know she and Barnett were going out to the mass grave location. A couple hours after she'd stopped by their office, Soto called to let them know that she and Barnett had just left the crime scene— CSI believed they'd uncovered everything there was to find. Even with this update, neither spoke directly to the other. Ethan reached a point where he'd scrolled through case information too many times for him to even consider it productive anymore. He looked across at Verne, who stared at his screen with the same determination he'd had since he'd started ignoring Ethan.

"What are you working on?" Ethan asked, in his attempt at an olive branch.

"I'm playing solitaire," Verne mumbled.

Ethan chuckled before Verne shot him a glare that made him pretend it had just been a tickle in his throat. They held eye contact until Verne cracked a sheepish smile that Ethan couldn't help but return. Ethan didn't comment on the solitaire, his silence a form of apology.

"I want to get in to talk to Watt again—not about Anne Griffin or any of those cases," Ethan added before Verne had a chance to get defensive. "Soto had mentioned that she thought Watt may have shared other prisoners' disposal sites. If we go in and push this point, he might crack or slip up."

"I don't ever tell you what to do in our investigations, but you need to step back and let one of us handle this. I think you're too close and invested for anything good to happen now. All you risk doing is pissing off Ed, or Watt, or his lawyer." The pleading looks in Verne's eyes gave Ethan pause.

He couldn't let this go when his instincts were telling him to dig in, despite Verne making a valid argument. He'd have to prove Watt's confession was a lie some other way, since paying him a visit was off the table.

"Okay, I'll step back from Watt," he conceded. He checked the time, knowing he had more to do but no energy left with which to do it.

"Vanessa's cooking dinner tonight, do you want to come over? She misses you."

Verne grinned standing up, "I'm in. I love the chance for free food and to bully you with Vanessa."

"You know what," Ethan said, as he gathered his stuff to leave.

"Kidding, kidding!" Verne shouted, as he headed out the office door.

CHAPTER THIRTY-THREE

TUESDAY, FEBRUARY 26TH

"Surprise!" Verne shouted, as he practically plowed Ethan down to get in the house first.

Vanessa peaked around the corner in the kitchen, smiling when she saw the two of them unceremoniously dump coats and bags by the door.

"Aw, Jay! Ethan didn't tell me you were coming over tonight. How are you?" She walked up to Ethan and gave him a quick hug and peck on the mouth before she moved on to hug Verne.

"I'm fine, but holy shit…wait, sorry, can I swear in front of it? Not it, shit sorry, the baby. But damn, you're getting big! I mean, not like fat, just like your belly is so big because of the baby. I mean, not because—"

Vanessa held up a hand; the other covered her mouth while she tried to cover the snort laugh. "Please, stop before you hurt yourself."

Ethan gave Verne a wide-eyed look, shaking his head. Ethan made a mental note to never let Verne around another pregnant woman again.

"Sorry," Verne mumbled, his entire face and neck a deep shade of pink.

Vanessa, who had recovered from Verne's verbal word vomit, waved them to follow as she headed back to the kitchen.

"Dinner is almost ready. It's nothing fancy, Jay. Though probably to your childlike palette," she teased with a wink. Turning to Ethan, she said, "And you're giving up your portion of leftovers for him to eat. I get to keep mine."

Ethan threw his hands up in mock surrender before he leaned over to Verne and slapped his arm. "That's fine, he'll just buy me lunch tomorrow."

"The dollar menu at McDonald's is a thing for a reason," Verne quipped.

"I see my worth to you." Ethan put a hand on his heart.

Ethan made himself useful setting the table for the three of them. He grabbed beers for him and Verne and a bottled smoothie for Vanessa, her current pregnancy fix. Once dinner was ready, he carried it over as Vanessa and Verne took their seats.

"So, how's it going?" Verne asked, waving at Vanessa's belly with his empty fork.

"Oh, it's going." Vanessa laughed, but Ethan noticed the tightness in her smile and the way it didn't quite meet her eyes. This was supposed to be an exciting and happy time for them, but it was impossible to brush aside the fear and anxiety laced through every moment with the past pregnancies looming over them.

"She's getting bigger and stronger every day though," she added, a hand falling to her growing bump.

It still surprised Ethan a bit to see her this pregnant. It made him want to tuck her in bed and not let her leave until their little girl was born. Even then, he could only imagine the new fears he'd have for Vanessa and the baby once she was with them.

"And when are you popping?" Verne asked, through a mouthful of food. He at least had the decency to look embarrassed when he met Ethan's disgusted gaze across the table.

"June 14th is my estimated due date." Vanessa flashed Ethan another strained smile before she turned back to Verne. "Enough about me, how are the cases? Tell me everything because Ethan thinks I might get nightmares or something if he tells me any of the details."

Verne laughed, though he glanced to Ethan, hopefully recalling the conversation they'd had before walking inside. Ethan hadn't shared the details of the cold cases or any of the subsequent finds off the trail or at the tree fort with Vanessa, and he'd rather Verne not either. He knew Vanessa was an adult, fully capable of knowing her limits, but she was already stressed with her pregnancy. Something so close to home, given the circumstances of the cases, would be unnecessary stress.

"Well, did he tell you he became BFFs with one of the moms from the case?"

Ethan glared at Verne across the table. Somehow, bringing up Fiona Griffin was worse than if he started listing all the believed causes of deaths for their victims.

"Oh, is this the over-involved mother?"

"Yes! She had my partner here convinced we had the wrong guy, and he got all side quest-y on me." Verne spoke with a lighthearted tone, but when Ethan looked up from his plate to meet his eyes, there was a hardness in his gaze. The olive branch of dinner and Ethan's word to back down didn't erase Verne's dislike of the situation Ethan had put them in.

"What can I say? I'm a man after the truth," Ethan answered with a forced laugh to move on from the awkwardness.

"She must be happy the case is closed now?" Vanessa asked, seemingly oblivious to the tension or at least choosing to ignore it.

Verne snorted as Ethan scoffed; at least they were on the same page there. Ethan didn't speak up and let Verne answer for them.

"She is not happy about it." Verne punctuated his sentence with a stab of his fork in the air. "She kind of went off on us...well, mainly him. I think she believed he was more under her thumb than he was. She didn't like when we told her last month that the guy was getting a plea deal."

"It's not that serious though," Ethan cut in. "Everyone grieves and handles news differently."

"Yeah, Mrs. Griffin handled it very differently," Verne said pointedly.

Ethan glanced sideways at Vanessa, her brows were slightly furrowed as she looked between him and Verne. Ethan picked up his beer and took a swig, trying to seem more relaxed than he felt.

"Maybe you had a soft spot for her because she's a bit feisty like Vanessa," Verne said.

Ethan, who had just taken another sip of his beer, choked as he tried not to spray beer all over the table. He managed to swallow before a cough erupted from him, and Vanessa leaned over, patting his arm like it would help.

"Don't put that in my head, that's so weird," Ethan groaned. He rubbed at his eyes, choosing to ignore the fact his reaction had Verne laughing so hard he had to hold his side.

"God, your face! I wish I'd taken a picture!" Verne wheezed out the words between laughs.

Ethan leveled him with an unamused expression, unable to help the glance toward Vanessa, who looked mildly confused but equally amused by what was happening between Verne and Ethan.

"I'm not sure if I should be offended or flattered," Vanessa said when she caught Ethan staring at her. She swatted at Ethan but smiled.

"I don't see it," Ethan said, unwilling to let his mind go there. He looked over at Verne, and Verne winked. Asshole was just trying to get in his head.

The conversation moved on as they all finished eating. Eventually, Vanessa got up, starting to clear the table. Ethan stood to follow and grabbed as much as he could balance. Verne gathered the rest and then dumped it all by the sink.

"I'm gonna head out. Thank you for a delicious meal," Verne said. He gave Vanessa a hug before he turned to Ethan and slapped him on the back. "I'll see you tomorrow."

Vanessa walked Verne to the door while Ethan started on dishes. She came back once Verne was gone, but Ethan shooed her off to bed, assuring her he could handle cleaning up. He tried to let his mind be blank while he worked, but he'd never been great at it. His thoughts drifted to the cold cases, the hiking trail, and the tree fort, unable to give himself a moment of peace.

CHAPTER THIRTY-FOUR

FRIDAY, MARCH 22ND

The mass grave at the second site had required longer days for the four of them. A new report from the labs and anthropologists seemed to come in every day, and each day, the evidence moved them further away from Watt. Multiple victims, identified through DNA, had gone missing and were likely killed when Watt was less than ten years old. While Ethan suspected his mental instability may have already been prevalent by that age, he didn't believe Watt had made his first kill so young, let alone murdering grown women, which all their victims from the second site turned out to be.

More than seven weeks had passed since Ethan and Verne told the Griffins about the plea deal. Camilleri was on them to either solidify Watt as a suspect or rule him out completely for the trail and tree fort, so that he and Mayor Chippley could hold their press conference.

They were all exhausted and needed a break. Barnett wanted to get home to her family, Soto wanted to cook herself dinner, Verne wanted to see the uniformed officer he hooked up with, and Ethan wanted to see Vanessa while she was actually awake. With a mutual agreement to get out early, they worked through as many lab reports and Jane Doe cases as they could before four p.m. and then made a run for it before someone pulled them into a conversation they couldn't escape.

Ethan had to park behind Vanessa's car when he got home and found his spot taken. He'd wanted to surprise Vanessa with his early day but hadn't anticipated she'd have anyone over. He let himself inside and noticed a pair of heels in the spot where he normally kicked off his shoes. He placed his bag on the floor and quietly took off his shoes. He could hear voices but couldn't make out what was being said. Two voices, but he could only place Vanessa's. The second one, though familiar, felt out of context and escaped him.

He followed the voices through the kitchen to the family room doorway. It clicked in his mind just before the family room came into view how he knew the voice. He stopped when he saw her, a gripping feeling in his chest and a warmth flooding his neck and face.

"Fiona."

"Ethan, you're home!" Vanessa said, as she got up from her seat. She was already six months pregnant and had started to struggle to get out of her favorite chair. She wrapped her arms around him and buried her face in his chest, seemingly oblivious to the rage he fought to keep out of his expression. He wrapped his arms around her and stared down at Fiona, who remained seated on his couch.

"This is a surprise," he got out in the most even tone he could muster in the moment.

"Mrs. Griffin stopped by to thank you personally for what you've done to help her get closure and brought flowers as an apology," Vanessa said, as she pulled away from his hug. He kept an arm around her.

He glanced away from Fiona long enough to notice Vanessa had a bandage on her hand. He momentarily forgot his issue with Fiona and pulled away enough to take Vanessa's hand in his.

"What happened?"

"Oh, it was stupid," Vanessa said and pulled her hand back, her cheeks flushed. "The flowers were in a lovely glass vase, and when Fiona handed them to me, it slipped, and I dropped them. I cut it cleaning up the glass, but it didn't even hurt. Fiona offered to help bandage my hand, so I invited her in for tea."

Fiona smiled up at Ethan and Vanessa, but only Vanessa returned the smile as Ethan looked warily between the two.

"I am embarrassed for how I behaved when you and your partner stopped by. I wanted to leave the flowers and say I have truly appreciated everything you have done for Anne. It means the world how hard you worked to get answers," Fiona said.

She sounded so sincere that Ethan might have believed her had he not been witness to, and the recipient of, her tirade. This crossed too many lines. He wanted to shout at her to get out of his house. It was one thing for her to show up at his work unannounced or call his phone whenever she felt she deserved updates, but his home with his wife and daughter was overstepping.

"You should have stopped by the station, not my house."

"Ethan, don't be rude," Vanessa whispered. He looked down at her, and she frowned up at him. He regretted now that he hadn't shared in detail Fiona's behavior. He'd tried to spare her unnecessary stress, but now, he realized he'd left her open to this kind of manipulation.

"Sorry, I'm just tired. It really was a team effort though, and I'm sure they'd have loved to hear that too," Ethan said.

She didn't seem bothered by him, or at all guilty for being caught in a clearly inappropriate situation. She stood up, smoothed out her dress, and plucked her purse from the couch. "I should head home and start dinner for my husband."

Ethan narrowed his eyes. Probably another lie. He'd wager Gregory Griffin was with his other family tonight, like she'd led him to believe was the case most nights.

Vanessa pulled away from Ethan. "Of course, it was lovely to meet you. Thank you for staying and helping me clean up the mess."

"I hate to be a bother, but is it alright if I use your bathroom before I leave? It's just a bit of a drive home if I hit traffic."

Vanessa showed her to their bathroom while Ethan waited in the family room. He felt rooted in place. Ethan regretted more than ever that he hadn't completed the main bathroom renovation he'd started when they first bought the house. Fiona seeing their bedroom was a whole new layer to the violation of her being in his home.

Vanessa came back, and he pulled her back into the family room so Fiona wouldn't have any chance of overhearing.

"Why did you invite her in?" he whispered.

"I didn't know what to do. She was waiting for me when I got home from school, and she seemed sweet. We talked for a bit outside, but it's cold, and then the whole mess with the flowers happened in the entryway. She helped me clean up the glass and bandage my hand, and at that point, she was already in the house. I felt rude asking her to leave before you got home after she did all that." Her voice had the edge of defensiveness, but Ethan didn't care. He felt like he was having to scold a child about stranger danger, and his wife should know better.

"You know it's weird she showed up here, right? I never gave her our address."

"It's not like you can't Google these things now. It is a little weird, but she's a harmless old woman."

"What if she was some lying psycho who wanted to cut our baby out of you!" Ethan hissed.

Vanessa took a step back, immediately wrapping her arms around her belly.

"That's an awful thing to say." Her eyes had started to get teary, and he realized that was too harsh and twisted to have said.

"Ness, I'm sorry. I just—"

Ethan heard Fiona coming back toward them. Vanessa quickly swiped at her eyes with the back of her unbandaged hand as Ethan and she both stepped out of the family room to meet Fiona halfway. He couldn't help himself when he stepped slightly in front of Vanessa to shield her from Fiona.

"Thank you again for the tea, dear. It was lovely to meet the strong woman behind such a fine detective."

She was laying it on thick, and he didn't see what she could possibly gain from unnerving him. He walked toward her and fought the urge to clench his fists. He didn't want to upset Vanessa even more or let Fiona see just how much her presence in his home affected him.

"Let me walk you out."

He followed her outside in his socks and no coat. He slammed the front door behind them, following Fiona to her car. He waited until he knew Vanessa wouldn't be able to hear him from the house.

"What are you playing at?"

"Excuse me?" she asked, without even bothering to look at him as she dug her car keys out of her purse.

"I don't know what you said to her or what you think you've accomplished showing up at my home, but it won't change what happened in Anne's case. Watt pleaded guilty and confessed to murdering her. You need to move on and stay away from my family."

Fiona didn't react to his words. She acted like he hadn't even spoken when she reached for her car door. He slammed his hand against the door so she couldn't open it.

"Am I understood?"

"It must have been very hard for you to work these cases the last few months. I hope you keep them safe and hug them tight. You never know when you'll lose the ones you love." She tipped her head as if she were offering him words of comfort, not the strange passive-aggressive threat it sounded like to him.

"Stay away from us, or there will be consequences," he said, as he took his hand off her car.

He felt like his insides were quivering. She may not have made a direct threat against Vanessa and their baby, but it was enough for Ethan. He watched her get in her car and drive away. He stood on the driveway, the cold air stinging his lungs as he regained his composure. She was crazy. He wondered if it would be too much to get a restraining order. He knew a judge who would probably be willing to if he explained the situation. Verne and Soto could back him up; they'd picked up on her off behavior too.

When he couldn't stand the cold any longer, he went back inside. Vanessa had curled back up in her chair with her tea.

"Ness, I'm so sorry I said that," Ethan said, squatting down in front of her. "Please forgive me. I just got scared when I got home and found her here with you."

Vanessa stared at him over her mug as she took a long sip. He could see she was thinking hard about something. Her eyes always gave her away like that. She'd be easy to crack during an interrogation.

"Why did it bother you so much that she was here?" Vanessa asked.

"Because she was angry with Verne and me. She doesn't think her daughter was kidnapped and murdered by the guy that confessed."

"Maybe she had a change of heart and wanted to apologize."

Ethan snorted. Vanessa always saw the best in people.

"I don't think that's the case."

"Why would she come over here then?"

"I don't know. I just don't like it. No one related to cases should know where we live, let alone be stopping by our house," he said, his voice rising again as his anger reignited.

The act felt malicious. Her words hinted at a threat, but nothing that could be substantiated. She could have just wanted to get under his skin. Get back at him for upsetting her in her own home. He didn't know the answer, but the why was less important to him right now. It was more critical to ensure it didn't happen again.

"I think you're getting too upset over this. She was sweet and just seemed like a lonely woman. She told me how her husband works a lot, and after losing their daughter, she's felt like there's a giant hole in her life and I can understand that." She had her hand on her belly again.

Ethan couldn't imagine the pain Vanessa felt from the miscarriages. He reached out and placed a hand over hers. "I love you."

"I love you too," she whispered.

She took another sip of her tea before she looked at him with a small smile spreading across her face. "You know, we were talking and realized we had a mutual friend. You remember the lady I worked with that set us up, right?"

Vanessa looked at him expectantly. He nodded and reached out, kissing the top of her good hand. He remembered a senior detective's wife being nosey, and one of the times she stopped by the station, she insisted he let her set him up on a date with a young teacher that had started at the school. Ethan couldn't tell you whose wife she'd been, but he was glad he'd been too scared of upsetting a superior to tell his wife to mind her own business. He'd have missed meeting Vanessa if he had.

"Well, funnily enough, Polly Graftner and Fiona were in a book club together for years! We actually knew Polly at the same time. Small world, huh?"

Polly's name rang a bell; he couldn't remember the context, but he'd talked to someone about Graftner recently. He wasn't sure he'd ever connected the fact that was who Polly was married to. Bringing up Polly had Vanessa wandering down memory lane, and Ethan didn't have the heart to go back to the issue he had with Fiona being at their house.

Vanessa had done nothing wrong, and he couldn't fault her for seeing the good in Fiona. That was just who she was and part of why he loved her so much. Vanessa and the baby were safe, he reminded himself, and Fiona had just wanted to play on the fear she expected him to have as a husband and soon-to-be father. He would deal with her when he was at work and not put more stress on Vanessa.

CHAPTER THIRTY-FIVE

MONDAY, MARCH 25TH

The moment Ethan saw Verne in the conference room Monday morning, he was heated all over again. Verne came in ready to tell Ethan all about his weekend, but Ethan didn't have the patience to wait. He needed to vent before he bit someone's head off.

"Fiona Griffin was at my house when I got home Friday."

"Wait, what?" Verne froze where he was, mouth gaping.

"I got home, and there was an unfamiliar car in my driveway—"

"Did you think Vanessa was cheating on you?"

"Why would I think that?"

"Who's cheating on who?" Soto asked, as she walked in on their conversation. Despite asking her question, her deadpan expression suggested she wasn't remotely interested in the answer.

"Fiona Griffin was at my house when I got home Friday," Ethan repeated.

That caught Soto's attention. She stopped her efforts to collect case files from their pile and sat down in the chair next to Ethan. "She was at your house? Like 'creepy stalker sitting across the street style'?"

"No, that would have been preferable. I pulled in, and there was a car I didn't recognize in my driveway."

"The cheating makes sense. I would've gone there too."

"Right? Who doesn't see a car they don't know at their house and think their partner is cheating?"

"Someone who trusts their partner."

"He's clearly never been cheated on," Soto said to Verne.

"Can I continue?" Ethan asked. They nodded in unison. "I get inside, and she was with Vanessa. She lied to her and told her she was there to thank me for everything we did for Anne."

"She should apologize after how she flipped on us," Verne said.

"She shouldn't have been there regardless of whether she owed me or anyone else an apology." Ethan was going over the way she left in his mind. She excused herself almost as soon as he was home. It seemed like she just wanted to get under his skin by him seeing her there. "And then, when I followed her out to her car—"

"Were you trying to be intimidating because I've told you, you're really not scary," Verne said.

"I think it's the dad persona. It's hard to take him too seriously when he looks like he should be wearing a punny t-shirt, jean shorts, and beat-up white sneakers," Soto added on.

Ethan looked between the two of them and then down at his white button-up and black dress pants. He'd had plenty of suspects crack during interrogations he'd led. He could be intimidating.

"Anyway, when I followed her outside, she made a threat about keeping our daughter close because you never know when you'll lose the ones you love. She really had the audacity to lie her way into my home and then threaten my family. If she tries to come around Vanessa and the baby again, I'm going to get a restraining order."

Soto and Verne exchanged a look, but neither said anything. Ethan let the silence hang between them until he couldn't take it any longer.

"What?" he snapped.

"I may not understand the full scope of the situation, but a restraining order seems a bit much. You really think a judge is going to give you a restraining order against a grieving old woman who lost her daughter and then told a soon-to-be-dad not to take his family for granted?"

"She showed up at my house."

"That's creepy, but not actually a crime," Verne said. He'd picked up files and started to flick through them, not making eye contact with Ethan.

"She found my address and lied her way into my home." Ethan felt like his argument was weakening each time he reiterated a point. The more he said it out loud, the more absurd his reaction sounded, even to him.

"No one is arguing that it isn't messed up, but it's not illegal. It's just weird. Maybe she'd had time to reassess and really did have a change of heart and genuinely wanted to thank you," Soto said. She stood up from the table and moved over to the whiteboard, turning her back to Ethan and Verne.

Ethan looked at Verne to back him up, but he was nodding along with Soto. He knew his reaction had been a lot. He ran a hand down his face and groaned.

"I guess maybe I overreacted," Ethan sighed, as he grabbed the files he had worked on the week before.

He hated to admit as much, especially after Fiona had made it clear that she didn't approve of his detective work, but he couldn't go around threatening grieving mothers, even if they crossed a line. He told himself once Camilleri was off their backs, he'd apologize. He wasn't in a rush to admit he'd been in the wrong—the greater wrong.

To get Camilleri off their backs, he had to stay focused on the remaining cases. Four cold cases closed seemed like glory enough for the department, but if Watt was connected to any other cases, Camilleri and Mayor Chippley wanted those closed too, to bolster their success in the public eye.

Piling on to Ethan's stress was Camilleri's invitation for a meeting to discuss Ethan's promotion. He'd made excuses pushing off the meeting for now. He already felt guilty knowing he'd end up working longer hours when Vanessa would want him home more once the baby arrived. He hadn't mentioned to Verne yet either, that he'd be leaving him.

And maybe it was too prideful of him, but he knew it took Watt and his cases to get him up for promotion. It all could've played out differently if Watt hadn't accepted a plea deal. Watt's influence on his career trajectory bothered Ethan, especially when Ethan didn't buy Watt's confession about Anne Griffin. He had once again spent the weekend thinking about the confession and the timeline Watt gave. He knew Kathryn Manson wouldn't hold up as a reliable witness, but her claim didn't align with Watt's story. *The baby died, and then she was gone.* According to Kathryn, Anne died before Watt left the hospital with her, not after.

Ethan looked around the room at all the boards with tacked-up victim profiles, lab reports, crime scene photos. He ran his hand down his face, feeling exhausted. He needed to focus on the cases in front of him. He'd given a lot of time and energy to Anne's case, and he knew these victims deserved the same. He shoved aside the questions still lingering about Anne and forced himself to focus on the present.

CHAPTER THIRTY-SIX

TUESDAY, APRIL 9TH

Despite solving the cases, Ethan, Verne, Barnett, and Soto weren't visible on-screen for the press conference. They stood to the side while the multiple cameras were panned on Camilleri and Mayor Chippley, as Chippley rambled on about community safety, quality police work, and families getting the closure they deserved. If the public had seen how that closure was received, they wouldn't be clapping so fervently.

Rebecca Smith's sister, Sarah Ferges, had a brief phone call with Verne to receive the news. Melody Dawson's mother, Betsy Dawson, wouldn't stop crying when Barnett and Soto went to deliver the news in person. Kelly McLane's mother, Whitney White, seemed satisfied, though she also didn't seem that torn up about it. Ethan didn't bother to have anyone tell Kelly McLane's father, Earl McLane.

Guiltily, Ethan was relieved that they could move on now that Watt had been ruled out as a suspect for their additional cases. However, Camilleri had also given them the news that Barnett and Soto would be going back to homicide now that the Watt cases were closed. Despite Verne's initial reaction to them joining the cases, he seemed more upset than any of them that they'd be returning to their usual routine.

Ethan didn't mean to zone out Mayor Chippley's political spiel, but he could only listen to the self-righteousness for so long. He ran through takeout dinner options for tonight, and which ones he thought wouldn't completely gross Vanessa out with her pregnancy aversions.

"Dumas, your phone," Soto whispered and nudged Ethan with her elbow.

He hadn't registered the noise until Soto said something. A few reporters had started to look his way. He fought it out of his pocket and hit silence before he shuffled his way past the milling group on the outskirts of the camera view to get out into the corridor.

"Detective Dumas." There was a sense of relief, followed by a sense of dread at the unknown number. It wasn't Fiona Griffin, not that he'd heard from her since he'd found her in his home a few weeks back.

"Hi, it's Detective Coppin."

The voice on the other line sounded strained. Ethan was momentarily confused. It seemed like years ago, instead of months, since he'd tried making contact and heard back from Coppin's son. He felt bad he hadn't reached out to check on Coppin's state, or at least let his son know he no longer needed a call back since the cases were closed. Chances were, anything Coppin had to offer now would be redundant.

"I'm glad to hear you're awake. Your son told me about your heart attack. How are you doing?"

"About as great as when I was shot in the lung in ninety-eight," he laughed, but it turned into a coughing fit. He mumbled an apology as he recovered. "Just been taking it one day at a time. I'm still fighting, but at least I'm alive."

"I'll let everyone here at Rothbury know you're making a recovery."

No one had asked him about Coppin, not even Verne, but he felt like he deserved to think people cared. He had once been a Rothbury cop after all.

"I'm guessing you hadn't reached out before to exchange niceties. You're working a case that I worked? I can't remember the details. Junior said you'd left a message about it being urgent."

"It was urgent at the time, but we've closed the cases now."

Ethan nodded at the uniformed officers that passed to get into the press conference. He moved farther down the corridor, so he didn't risk being overheard. Last thing he wanted was a reporter eavesdropping on his conversation.

"Entertain an old man, won't you? What cases of mine were you working?"

Ethan hesitated, not sure it was even worth getting into, but he couldn't deny a part of him still wondered why Coppin had stuck it out so long with Fiona.

"We'd reopened several cases, but the main one I'd wanted to ask you about was Anne Griffin's. Her mother was very open about the fact you two didn't give up on the cold cases that couldn't be definitively linked to Vincent Watt. I guess I wondered why you spent so much time on them, but never pushed for evidence to be tested as the science progressed? I know jurisdiction would be tricky, but you could have reached out to a Rothbury detective if you really believed there was something there."

As the investigation had diverged and the connection with the mall panned out for three of the cases, he'd pushed Coppin to the back of his mind. However, now that Ethan had him on the phone, it opened the floodgates. He didn't understand why Coppin and Fiona had put so much time and energy into their investigation if Coppin never used his influence to get anywhere with the cases. Why had Fiona never told Coppin about Kathryn Manson, or why hadn't Coppin found her himself if he'd been working that hard to find answers?

"Anne Griffin," Coppin repeated softly. "That's a name I haven't heard in nearly thirty years."

Ethan's brows furrowed. "I'm not sure if your memory was impacted by your current health issue, but Fiona Griffin had given me the impression you were still occasionally working the cases, unofficially, for years after the initial investigation. It was only a few months ago, too, your boxes of notes and documents were dropped off. They ended up beating the official case files to the office."

There was silence from the other line. Ethan could hear Coppin's labored breath come through, at least letting him know he hadn't ended the call. When it had reached an uncomfortable length of time, Ethan cleared his throat and seemed to snap Coppin out of his thoughts.

"I don't know. You've lost me, son," Coppin whispered.

"You don't know?" Ethan asked, now as confused as Coppin sounded.

"I don't remember boxes, or the last time I heard about Anne Griffin. I worked that case decades ago. It was before I transferred to Southbury."

"There were three boxes. You had them delivered to my office back in October. You attached a note that said you wanted me to have everything for the cases. You mentioned my wife." Ethan's voice rose slightly as his emotions got the better of him. He didn't know what the medical toll a heart attack and coma would cause on the brain, but he couldn't believe Coppin just completely lost the memories of his time with Fiona or the boxes he'd sent.

Detective Coppin mumbled, "Oh," before the silence was back. Ethan wracked his brain for what he could say to jog Coppin's memory.

"When did you receive the boxes?" Coppin asked.

"I don't remember the exact date, but it was around the first week of October, last year."

"I didn't send you any boxes," Coppin said with conviction.

"You're sure?"

"I know I didn't send you those boxes because I had my heart attack September 27th."

Ethan's mind felt like it was spinning as he tried to piece this new information into the narrative. If Coppin had his heart attack September 27th, he would not have known the cases were being reopened. Verne had only found out a day before Ethan from Camilleri.

"Did you talk to Ed Camilleri?" Ethan asked, the frantic note in his own voice made him want to cringe in shame.

"Rothbury's major crimes captain? Not since we both were lower-ranked guys in Rothbury."

"They were full of your notes, copies of documents, and newspaper clippings," Ethan said, as if that would make it all fit together now.

"You mentioned Anne Griffin's mother, right?"

"Yes. She's the one who said you'd been working with her since the original detectives essentially shelved Anne's case."

"That was the baby from the emergency room?"

"Yes," Ethan said, the hope practically oozing off the word.

"She must have got me confused with someone else. I haven't seen her since the eighties when her daughter went missing."

Ethan had a sinking feeling in his gut.

"So, you didn't even know I was going to be reopening these cases?" Ethan asked, just to hear Coppin shoot him down once more.

Coppin answered a resounding no. Ethan thanked him for returning his call and wished him a quick recovery before he hung up. He considered if he should go back in for the remainder of the press conference, but he didn't trust he'd be able to keep a straight face for the photographs and questions. He turned in the opposite direction and headed for his office. He needed space to think.

It had never crossed his mind that the boxes weren't from Coppin, or that Fiona would lie about Coppin's involvement. It was a lie he could have easily found out, but only if he'd been able to speak with Coppin. When he'd reached out, he hadn't been able to confirm it because of Coppin's state. Almost as if Fiona lied with the certainty Coppin wouldn't immediately contradict her.

As soon as he thought it, he tried to dislodge the seed of doubt from his mind. Fiona was certainly a determined person, but causing a heart attack had to be too far-fetched even for her. He didn't know how someone would even go about causing someone else to have a heart attack, but he imagined it ran a high risk of killing the person, and he didn't want to believe Fiona would take such drastic measures to cover a lie. As Ethan approached his office, it raised a new question as to why she lied and involved Coppin if she hadn't seen him since the original investigation.

He unlocked the office and almost slipped on an envelope that had been slid under the door. He swore under his breath, bending over to grab it before he shut the door behind him. He wasn't in the mood for someone to pop in for a pointless chat.

The outside of the orange envelope had "DUMAS—PRIVATE" scribbled across it. There was nothing else indicating who it was from. A small part of him hesitated to open the anonymous mail, their old training against anthrax attacks echoed in the back of his mind, but he doubted he'd be deemed significant enough for anyone to target. Regardless, he bent the envelope back and forth to get an idea of what was inside.

When he'd convinced himself it was likely fine, he tore it open and slid the bound stack of paper on his desk. The cover of the packet had a logo and acronym he immediately recognized as that of the private laboratory he'd seen the brochure for in Fiona's living room. He picked up the packet and quickly flipped through for a note but found nothing. The envelope was empty too.

Ethan didn't need a note to tell him it was from her.

He tossed the envelope in the trash before he dropped into his seat and started at the beginning of the packet. The first page explained that the following pages were the results from the requested DNA testing. Individual A, whose DNA had been tested for a familial match to Individual B, was a match. He skimmed along to where it explained how Individual A was a maternal relative of Individual B. Ethan flipped through the packet, but it was mainly charts showing DNA markers and explanations of accuracy.

He flipped to the end, still half expecting to find a note from Fiona scribbled among the pages. Once he'd finished skimming, his mind scrambled to piece it all together. Fiona presumably was one of the tested individuals. Otherwise, why would she have sent the results? Which raised the next question as to what she hoped to accomplish. It didn't seem likely that she would have gone to the trouble and expense of having Anne's DNA tested using an old sample. That left Ethan with several options to consider: Fiona had a second child she never told Ethan about, she knew something about Anne she hadn't told him, or it was unrelated to Fiona. The latter was unlikely, though he was banking on his gut instinct to make that call. Given the level of devotion Fiona had shown finding Anne, he couldn't imagine she'd have another child. That left his last option, and a likely one considering how things seemed to be coming to light; she knew something about Anne she hadn't told him.

Before he could decide his next move, he heard voices approaching, and then the office door opened. Ethan didn't know why, but his first instinct was to hide the report. He put it in an open file on his desk before he flipped it closed.

Barnett was in the middle of making fun of something the mayor said as she led the way, with Verne and Soto behind her. Barnett locked eyes with Ethan as he rearranged the files on his desk but turned back to Verne and Soto to finish off whatever she'd been saying.

"There you are! I didn't realize all we needed was to get a phone call to get out of that torture," Verne said, as he dropped into his desk chair. "Who called you anyway? Fiona?"

"No. It was Detective Coppin. He woke up from his coma and was doing well enough to return calls."

He kept the newly discovered truth about the boxes and Coppin's involvement to himself. Another secret he was keeping from Verne, which was becoming an unfortunate pattern where the Anne Griffin investigation was concerned.

"Not much use now," Soto said. She perched on the edge of Verne's desk and grabbed his rubber band ball, plucking the top few off and shooting them across the office into the trash can. Ethan could hear a few ping the discarded envelope on top.

"Yeah, not much use but still considerate of him," Ethan said, distracted by the report and weighing the benefits of showing up at Fiona's house to demand an explanation.

"You know, now that Watt is officially out of our lives and the captain isn't on our asses for the other cases, we should go grab drinks," Verne said. He was already standing up and collecting his stuff.

Barnett and Soto agreed, all three of them turning to Ethan for his answer. He was torn. He could use a beer and a chance to unwind before he went home so he didn't unintentionally unload his stress on Vanessa. He also knew he wouldn't be able to drink away the questions that whirled around his mind at the moment.

"Rain check. I should get home and see Vanessa if I'm leaving early."

Barnett and Soto nodded, already heading out the door. Verne lingered behind and seemed to size him up.

"Everything good?" Verne asked.

"Yeah, Ness is just far along now. Trying to make the most of our time before there's a little one there." Ethan waved him off, doing his best to offer Verne a reassuring smile.

"Right, and the call with Coppin, nothing to share?"

"Say what you actually want to say," Ethan snapped.

Verne's eyes widened just a bit, and his lips pressed together in a thin line. "Nothing, just checking. See you tomorrow."

Verne jogged out of the office. He could have told Verne the truth right then and there. He'd even asked, and yet Ethan still held back. He wanted to be able to look into the report and confront Fiona on why she lied about Coppin, but if he told Verne about either thing, he might try to stop him. He'd gone this long without telling Verne everything; he'd just have to hope Verne forgave him when he told him everything one day.

CHAPTER THIRTY-SEVEN

WEDNESDAY, APRIL 10TH

Ethan barely slept, but it gave him plenty of time to think. Too much time even. He'd mentally gone over the contents of the three boxes delivered to his office back in October, trying to think about it with the understanding it was only compiled presumably by Fiona Griffin. It at least made more sense why the majority of the content pertained only to Anne Griffin.

At one point in the middle of the night, he'd sat up when a new thought had occurred to him. Whoever had sent the boxes had also written the note. A note that, at face value, didn't tell him much, at least gave him a handwriting sample of the impersonator. When he settled enough to lie back down, he assured himself that first thing tomorrow he'd find the note.

Luckily, he recalled shoving the note that had been taped to the boxes into one of them after he'd finished sorting through them originally. He also knew the boxes were still in the corner of his and Verne's office.

The next morning, when he got to the office, he dug through the boxes to find the note. Naturally, the note had ended up in the bottom of the last box he checked.

Hope your wife and you are well. Had these still and wanted you to have everything from the cases.—Det. John Coppin

The hairs on the back of his neck stood up rereading the note. If Fiona had written it, as he suspected, she knew about Vanessa before she'd ever met Ethan. Which meant she'd likely stalked Ethan. The idea cast a sinister light over every interaction, every strange comment he'd brushed off at the time as a slip in his own memory.

He swallowed the lump forming in his throat as he placed the note on his desk. He wished he'd kept the envelope the lab results had been dropped off in as further proof the same person was behind all of it, so when he eventually confronted Fiona, he could show her everything he had. Unfortunately, the cleaner had already been by to empty the trash, which lost him that piece of comparison.

He turned back toward the boxes. He might not have the envelope, but he had boxes of handwriting samples on the sticky notes. A half hour later, Ethan had compiled over thirty pieces of evidence that the person who impersonated Coppin was also the person to write the sticky notes about the case. Ethan was no expert on handwriting analysis, but it appeared everything had been written by the same person.

Ethan knew it still didn't prove with certainty it was Fiona, even if his gut said it was her handwriting. He could only say that they'd all been written by the same person, but without a sample of writing he knew to be Fiona's, he couldn't pin it on her. He dropped into his seat and swore under his breath.

He needed to come up with something. He wasn't sure how long he sat there scheming how to get a handwritten note from Fiona, preferably signed by her, when it finally dawned on him that the morning he found the boxes, he'd received two handwritten notes.

He tore his desk apart to find it, dumping the contents of every drawer onto the floor until he saw it in the mess from his designated junk drawer. Fiona had given him a card, which she'd written her information on, the morning she'd come to introduce herself.

Ethan laid it next to the letter and the sticky notes. He studied all his evidence, needing to be confident he was not jumping to conclusions.

Her ornate f's gave her away. They were identical across every piece of writing he had.

Ethan didn't understand why Fiona had lied about Coppin. She had nothing to gain from the lie. They were going to do their best to get answers regardless. They'd been assigned the cases by the mayor's request. If anything, she had slowed down their investigation. He supposed he would have found her even more overbearing to begin with if he'd known she'd spent decades collecting newspaper clippings and trying to investigate on her own, but it wouldn't have changed the results.

He checked the time on his phone and wagered Verne wasn't coming in. Chances were, Verne had a pitcher or two, which he was known to do on nights out celebrating. He was probably passed out on his couch, or whoever's house he managed to make it to, sleeping it off. It was for the best. He still wanted to hold off telling Verne anything until he knew everything himself.

Ethan grabbed all the handwriting evidence and the DNA results. He needed answers.

* * *

"Ethan, what a surprise," Fiona said, as she answered the door.

Ethan brushed past her, leaving on his shoes, and showed himself to the kitchen. She didn't seem surprised, nor did she protest as she followed behind him. He laid all the handwriting samples out on the table, slapping them down aggressively and hurting his palm a little as he did.

"Do you notice something about all of these?" Ethan's arms were crossed over his chest, still gripping the DNA test results, as he tried to keep his breathing normal. He could feel his heart racing from the adrenaline.

Fiona gave him a disapproving frown but seemed willing to entertain him as she leaned over to look at all the papers. Her chestnut hair fell in her face, preventing him from gauging her reaction from her expression, but she hummed as she looked and took her time to study each one, which only frustrated Ethan more since he knew they were all written by her.

"They all appear to be handwritten?" she offered when she had finished and straightened up to face him again.

"A gold star for you. Anything else?"

"You seem to want me to have noticed something specific, so why don't you just enlighten me on what that is?"

"They were all written by you. Even the ones supposedly written by Detective Coppin." Ethan managed to get out without gritting his teeth. He was angrier than he expected he'd be confronting her. He'd wanted to stay calm and levelheaded about the situation, but on the drive over, he started remembering all the little comments Fiona had made throughout the investigation about him getting home to his wife and to not keep his pregnant wife waiting. By the time he made it to the Griffins' house, he had wound himself up over it.

"That's quite the bold accusation, Ethan."

"Yet you don't deny it."

She moved from the table to the stove. "Coffee? Tea?"

"No."

She shrugged and busied herself preparing a cup of tea. Ethan stayed quiet. He'd figured she was playing games now that he'd caught her.

"It took you a while to notice," she said, once her back was to him.

"I had no reason to believe you were lying. Not until Detective Coppin called me yesterday and had no idea what I was talking about."

"I'm glad to hear he's okay. His health problems did come at a convenient time for me, I will admit."

Ethan studied her back, trying to decide if it was just convenient. Even with all her deceiving, he couldn't bring himself to honestly believe she could harm Coppin. She took advantage of his situation though, to make the most of the cases being reopened.

"You haven't mentioned the envelope." Fiona brought her tea over to the table, brushing his papers aside. "I thought that would be what brought you over."

"What if Verne had found it?" He slapped the packet down on top of all the papers. A few fluttered farther onto the table from the draft the packet created, but he didn't bother retrieving them.

"He's smart enough to read and know Dumas isn't his name, isn't he?"

Ethan didn't justify her mockery with an answer.

"I am assuming you took the time to read it."

"Yes, it seems A and B are related."

"Anne is alive."

"Watt confessed to murdering Anne."

"And I pretended to be Detective Coppin."

Ethan stared at her but remained silent. If she believed Anne was still alive, he knew she'd want to convince him. She'd been trying to do as much for months, and now, she supposedly had DNA evidence that proved it. She held his eye contact in silence as she sipped at her tea.

"I'm sure you're curious how I got her DNA."

"I assumed you were just baiting me. Maybe used some old, preserved DNA or faked a test since you impersonate cops now," he pushed back.

"No. I just followed the evidence trail you seemed to have ignored during your investigation. You didn't even try to find her. You just accepted she was dead, despite there being no proof. I had to figure it out myself. I shouldn't have had to do your job," she snapped.

"Fine, I'll bite. Where did you get the DNA, Fiona?"

"I collected a blood sample from Anne."

"So, it was old DNA you had tested?"

Fiona threw up her hands, her impatience twisting her face into a scowl.

"I truly believed you were more intelligent than this. It wasn't old DNA. In fact, I collected it only days before I sent it off to the lab." She drummed her nails against the mug, and when he didn't speak up, she sighed. "I know you found it strange to come home and find me in your house that day."

She waved a hand vaguely at the lab results and tipped her head, watching him. He tipped his own head in confusion, wondering how they had gone from the lab report to her visit to his home.

"My house?" Ethan managed to get out.

He had known from the moment he got home and had found her there she never would have stopped by without an ulterior motive, but he'd thought he had figured that out. She'd wanted to get under his skin, get into his head. He'd spent so much time focused on her being there, he'd neglected to consider what she did while there.

"An oil-slicked vase can be very difficult to hold onto," Fiona said, before she took a long sip of her tea.

Ethan's brows furrowed, and he remembered now why Vanessa had even invited Fiona in. She'd dropped the vase and then managed to cut herself...and Fiona had helped her bandage up her hand. His jaw went slack as he realized the implications.

"No. No, Ness is—no." He fumbled the words, his mind scrambling with the delusional and rather frightening claim Fiona was attempting to make.

"Vanessa is Vanessa. I know her parents. I've seen papers and stuff." He couldn't form coherent sentences or remember how to explain her birth certificate, medical files, and other paperwork he knew were locked in their fire safe at the back of their bedroom closet.

"Whatever sick game you're playing, leave my wife out of it."

"You can't deny the truth, Ethan. You may have tried to ignore it in the investigation, but now, I have evidence. You can't be a blind fool forever!"

Her words seemed to snap him out of his panic. He straightened up and stared her down.

"This," he picked up the lab report, "means nothing. You haven't proven anything besides that you're sick in the head with this report. Telling anyone about it won't help since you didn't collect the supposed DNA sample in any admissible capacity."

He gathered up the evidence he'd brought over when he'd naively thought this would be a conversation about her pretending to have worked with Coppin.

"You know I'm telling the truth," Fiona sneered.

He spun back around to face her, so he could make sure she heard his words loud and clear.

"I didn't tell you because it wouldn't have changed anything at the time, but Kathryn Manson did remember something. She told me she saw Anne die and be taken from the hospital. Watt confessed; you need help."

He didn't wait to hear her response. With his papers crushed against his chest, he stormed out, leaving the door wide open behind him. He didn't look back until he was in his car driving away. For a moment his eyes deceived him, and he saw Vanessa's reflection in the rearview mirror watching him. He blinked rapidly, dislodging the seed of delusion planted in his mind, Fiona's face shrinking from view.

CHAPTER THIRTY-EIGHT

WEDNESDAY, APRIL 10TH

Ethan knew there were a lot of things he should do in response to Fiona's outlandish claim. He should go to the station and tell Camilleri everything he'd failed to tell him in reports about the investigation and Fiona. He should show up at Verne's doorstep and confess everything he'd kept from his partner ever since he started following his gut over the logical process of things. Hell, even finding Soto and Barnett and telling them would be better than what he found himself doing: going home.

He needed to have eyes on Vanessa. Fiona was unstable, that he had no doubts about now. He wasn't sure how exactly she came up with a fake DNA test, but he was sure if he looked online, he'd find whatever bogus report she'd printed. She probably knew he'd looked in her drawer and was doing this as a last desperate cry for attention because she couldn't accept Anne's case being closed.

Tomorrow, he'd do something, but right now, he just wanted to be with his wife and his baby and make sure they were safe.

When he pulled in the driveway, he was relieved to see only Vanessa's car. He took a few deep breaths to calm the anger inside of him that had his whole body feeling jittery. He shoved everything into his glove box. He paused at the front door to take a few deep breaths to relax, before he let himself in.

"Did you get my text?" Vanessa shouted from somewhere in the house as soon as he'd shut the front door. She waddled into the hall and immediately groaned. It still caught him by surprise when he saw her now. She'd never made it this far before.

"No, I hadn't checked my phone," he confessed. A quick glance at his phone confirmed Vanessa had sent him a list of different takeout foods she was currently craving.

"I thought you were home early because you got my text. Your daughter is hungry."

He looked up at her with a smile and a cocked eyebrow to counter her arms folded over her belly and her pouty bottom lip.

"How about a takeout buffet?" he offered.

Vanessa's pout turned into a grin.

Ethan's smile dropped for a moment. His mind was playing tricks on him, and he'd seen a trace of Fiona in Vanessa's smile. He knew he only saw it now because the idea had been planted in his head.

Still, despite his mental conviction, Ethan spent dinner trying to see Lisa and Howard in her, instead of Fiona and Gregory. The harder he looked, the more confused he became.

After they'd stuffed themselves with their takeout buffet, they moved to the family room to sprawl out. He lay the length of the couch, and Vanessa squashed into her armchair, channel surfing. Every time he looked at her, he started studying her profile until he couldn't take it anymore. He stood up so abruptly, Vanessa jumped a little in her armchair.

"Are you okay?" she asked, staring up at him with a frown.

"Yeah, I think I just need to sleep. It's been a day." He wanted more than anything to be able to vent to her right now, but she was the very last person he could turn to with all of this.

"Okay, well, I'll go to bed now too."

She turned off the TV, then reached out her hands expectantly. Ethan stepped forward to help pull her up. She came up on her tiptoes, her hands cupped either side of his face, her belly pressed against his as she gave him a kiss.

"Whatever has you stressed out, it'll be okay. Okay?" Her voice was soothing, but her words stabbed and twisted an imaginary knife into his gut.

He swallowed the lump forming in his throat as he nodded and pulled her into a hug. It all had to be okay, he reminded himself; he'd make sure of it.

CHAPTER THIRTY-NINE

THURSDAY, APRIL 11TH

It wasn't easy, but Ethan managed to get Verne out of the office all day on other case errands. He'd tossed and turned all night, mostly brainstorming what to do but occasionally weighing the choice of sharing everything with Verne. Fiona Griffin's newest stunt added to a large heap of secrets he'd kept from Verne already. However, Ethan decided to find out more on his own first. If something came of it, then he'd bring Verne up to speed.

He locked himself in their office, the boxes he now knew were from Fiona unloaded on every surface he could cover. He decided the first logical move was to disprove her claim that Vanessa was Anne Griffin, so if she tried going public, he could immediately shut her down.

He'd already sent the report to a friend he could trust to check it out without anyone knowing. Ethan needed to know if it was even authentic. He had also gone in the fire safe that morning and taken Vanessa's birth certificate and social security card. To his untrained eye, neither seemed like forgeries, but he knew a guy who was also looking into those for him too.

Over the last six months, he had looked through Anne's case so many times from the moment the Griffins arrived at the hospital to years later when Vincent Watt was arrested. Now, he needed to look through the case to trace the Ashbys' movements at the same time. It was easier said than done since the Ashbys had never been a part of the investigation. Police had never tracked them down to ask if they'd seen something suspicious or remembered anyone that could help the investigation. He only had the hospital logs to go off, which quickly reconfirmed the Ashbys' and Griffins' times at the hospital didn't overlap. He had no surveillance footage to study, and he couldn't just go to his in-laws and ask them if they kidnapped Anne.

When he'd seemed to exhaust all the answers from the boxes, Ethan started brainstorming. Once he knew the birth certificate was authentic, that should be proof enough to make Fiona back off. In case it wasn't enough, he could gather all of Vanessa's medical files from birth, show Fiona what she claimed was impossible.

As he sat at his desk, rifling through all the case files, he considered Lisa and Howard. It was no secret to him he wouldn't have been his in-laws' first choice, and he wasn't particularly fond of spending time with them, but they weren't evil masterminds like Fiona's claim would make them out to be. Vanessa had extended family who Ethan had met at their wedding and a few holidays over the years. If Lisa and Howard had suddenly had a one-year-old, someone in their family would have questioned it. At the very least, they would have had to lie and say Vanessa was adopted.

He shoved himself away from the desk, roughly combing his fingers through his hair as he let out a frustrated grunt. He was not getting anywhere. He should have asked Fiona why she even thought Vanessa was Anne in the first place. He wondered if she'd seen her name on the hospital's log. Had she been looking up all the people that had visited the hospital around the same time? He cursed himself for not being more level-headed in the moment and asking the questions he should have asked as a detective. Now, he couldn't just show back up at her house and ask her why.

An idea popped in his head, and before he could talk himself out of it, he grabbed his keys. He didn't let himself question his choices as he drove from Rothbury to Southbury and parked several houses down the road from the Griffins'. He was close enough that he could see Fiona's car in the driveway. He reclined his seat a bit so he wasn't as visible but could still see the door and driveway clearly.

Logically, he knew what he was doing crossed a lot of lines and was definitely illegal. If he were thinking straight, he would have called Verne and told him everything or gone to Camilleri and confessed the mess he'd made of things. If he were in his right mind, he would have done anything other than start an illegal stakeout on Fiona Griffin with the intent to break into her home once she left.

* * *

By lunchtime, Fiona was still in her home, Ethan was still reclined in the driver's seat of the car down the street, and he'd heard back about Vanessa's papers; they were very much real. His contact had tracked down evidence to verify the birth certificate application and the proof of birth at the hospital in PA where Vanessa had been born. Ethan was surprised how relieved he felt, given the confidence he'd had telling himself the Ashbys couldn't have pulled off what Fiona was inadvertently accusing them of doing.

It did cross his mind that he could simply ask Lisa and Howard about their hospital visit the same night Anne was taken, but he didn't know how to explain it to them. Lisa would get anxious and flustered, and Howard took any question from Ethan as a personal attack. There was no way he could even bring it up casually at this point, and he knew he could never tell Lisa and Howard what Fiona was claiming. That was an even bigger can of worms than telling Verne and Camilleri.

Over an hour passed since he'd gotten the call about Vanessa's papers when his phone started to ring. He jumped at the sudden break in the silence, but quickly answered when he saw it was Paul, his connection for the lab report review.

"That was fast. Is it fake?" he answered, ignoring the pathetic eagerness in his voice.

"It seems legitimate. I used to work with a woman before we both went into the private sector, and now, she works for this company. I reached out, and luckily, she owed me a favor and looked at the test too. They ran a few different DNA tests there, but from what she could see, it looked like the person who ordered it was most interested in the mitochondrial DNA to confirm that Individual B is in the maternal lineage of Individual A."

"So, it's not a definite identification?"

"Well, yes and no. Individuals A and B are related, unquestionably, and the mtDNA shows that."

"Explain it to me like I'm dumb," Ethan groaned, thumping his head against the headrest.

"Basically, it's a form of DNA that traces only maternal lineage. The mother will transmit a complete set of mtDNA to their child," Paul explained it all with a made-up Jane, John, and Kate. In hindsight, Ethan wished he'd just googled for clarity. "Does that make sense?"

Ethan grunted in response before letting out a deep breath. "So, A and B are related."

"Yeah, definitely related."

"Do you have the ability to run this kind of testing at your lab?" Just because the lab results weren't false didn't mean Fiona wasn't lying. It just meant whoever's DNA she sent in were related to one another.

"Technically, I could do it," Paul sounded hesitant. "But it's not really something I should do."

"Would a hair sample work?" Ethan asked. He chose to ignore the silent no in Paul's voice.

Paul let out an exasperated breath, before his mumbled yes came through the line.

"If I could get you two different samples of hair, could you run this kind of DNA test on them and tell me if they share a maternal lineage?"

"Don't you have access to forensic testing? Unless this is something more complicated. I'm not sure getting involved would be smart."

He hadn't explained much to Paul, because reading a lab report wasn't a huge favor. Running tests was different, and he realized he shouldn't have asked so freely. It sounded suspicious that he wasn't using their forensic labs.

"We're just so swamped with cases that the lab will take too long to get this back to me and I'm on a major time crunch. If there's any way you could slip it into your schedule this week, I'd owe you big time."

There was silence on Paul's end, and Ethan was afraid he hadn't been convincing enough or had paused too long before he'd given Paul a reason.

Paul cleared his throat. "Okay, sure. If you can get me a good hair sample from each, I should be able to get mitochondrial DNA to get results for you."

"Perfect, I'll drop it off soon. I've got to run. Thanks for this." He hung up before Paul had a chance to change his mind.

Now he just needed to get a sample of Lisa's hair to test with Vanessa's. Lisa had insisted on throwing Vanessa a surprise baby shower and had asked him to help with preparations. He'd told her he was too busy, but now, it would give him the excuse he needed to stop by. If he went over prepared, he could collect some of Lisa's hair easy enough.

Ethan pulled up Lisa's contact, planning to call her and tell her he could help this weekend to plan. His thumb hovered over the call button when movement down the street caught his attention. He glanced up to see Fiona walking out the door to her car. He sank a little lower in his seat, but she didn't look around as she climbed in. She backed out of the driveway and, fortunately for him, drove off in the opposite direction.

His heart was pounding in his chest, but he waited until the clock showed five minutes had passed. When Fiona hadn't come back, he decided now was his chance. He sat up properly in the car and drove around the neighborhood before returning to outside the Griffins' home. In case anyone happened to have looked out, it would appear he had just shown up and hadn't been sitting a few houses down for a few hours now.

He parked outside their house. He reached over and opened the glove box, fishing out a pair of disposable gloves he kept in there in case he ever found himself in a crime scene. Some PPE was better than none. He shoved them into his pocket before he got out of his car and did his best to look like he should be there.

Ethan took the path up to the door and knocked, knowing no one would answer.

"Fiona, it's Detective Dumas, are you home?" he shouted, so if anyone did happen to witness the beginning of the plan he'd laid out over the last few hours, they might not suspect what he really planned to do.

After a few more knocks and fake attempts of getting Fiona to answer the door, he strolled around the side of the house to the gate. He was partially hidden from view by shrubs on the side where the neighbor might be able to see him. He pulled on the blue gloves before reaching over and wiggling the latch.

Unlocked.

He quietly let himself into the backyard, pulling the gate closed behind him. He walked to the first window on the back of the house and tried wiggling the sash, but it was locked. He went window to window to check if any were unlocked, but it seemed his luck was used up on the gate latch.

As he rounded to the other side of the house, still within the backyard perimeter, he silently thanked whoever was helping him today. There was a door into the garage that was locked, but rattling the doorknob told him it wouldn't take much to break it down. Saying a silent prayer and an apology for what he was about to do, he slammed his shoulder into the door. It groaned under the weight but didn't give. He repositioned himself and tried again; this time, the crack of dry wood splintering seemed to echo in the empty garage.

He froze, prepared for an alarm to go off. If they had a security system, it seemed the door from the yard into the garage was not connected to it. He stepped over the mess of wood he'd made and closed the door; it didn't quite latch now.

His eyes adjusted to the dimness of the space, and he could make out the door up a few steps that must lead into the house. He jogged over and tried the doorknob, suppressing the excitement when it opened. Under less illegal circumstances, he'd be concerned that an elderly couple did not lock an essential exterior door, but right now, it worked in his favor.

He stepped inside, taking only a second to get his bearings. Time was of the essence, especially since he didn't know what exactly he hoped to find. All he had to go off was the belief that Fiona must not have given him everything she had when she'd sent the boxes. There had to be something that fed the delusion Vanessa was Anne.

The house was a modest size, which at least gave him an advantage during this time crunch. He was fortunate Gregory Griffin's ego hadn't made him live in an absurdly large house, though he supposed it was the cost of maintaining his second family that prevented that.

He found his way to the kitchen, a room he could use to get his bearings, before he jogged down the hall to the living room that had the little side table. He went there first, despite the fact he'd briefly looked through the drawer's content already. He yanked it open, only to find the drawer was now empty. The discovery had him momentarily frozen as he questioned if he'd imagined seeing things in this exact drawer only a couple months earlier.

Fiona probably wouldn't have expected him to break in and search her home, but she seemed to have suspected he'd come back to the drawer at least; she got rid of the evidence that he'd found here. He looked around the room, quickly opening any decorative storage boxes on shelves and looking for more side tables just in case. None had anything that would help him.

His heart was pounding in his chest as he concluded this room had nothing. He headed to the hall, trying to think like Fiona. Ethan knew Fiona would have kept everything hidden from Gregory all these years, and while Ethan understood Gregory wasn't home much, he was home enough that Fiona wouldn't have left anything lying around somewhere he would see.

It was like a light bulb turned on in his mind. The nursery. Every second counted as he ran to the room he'd caught a glimpse of on Christmas Eve. Even in the light of day, it still made the hairs on the back of Ethan's neck stand up. He felt a wave of guilt walking into the shrine Fiona had maintained for Anne, but if there was going to be one place in this house Gregory wouldn't look, Ethan would wager on it being this room.

Ethan started with the dresser. He opened doors, doing his best not to make it too obvious he'd been here as he moved clothes aside and checked for false bottoms on drawers. Fiona didn't seem like the type to go to that length to hide something, but at this point, he wouldn't rule anything out.

He stuck his arm in each open drawer, feeling the bottom of the one above it for anything tucked away. When the four-drawer dresser turned up nothing, he went to the rocking chair. He lifted cushions, got on the floor to check the underside. The crib was next but still turned up nothing.

Beads of sweat started to run down his forehead. He froze when he heard a car seem to slow down outside the house, but then it kept going. He had no idea how long Fiona would be gone, but he needed to hurry. Last was the armoire tucked near the corner of the room. He opened it to find hanging baby clothes, a few boxes full of baby memorabilia tucked on the top shelf, and a folded quilt on the bottom shelf. He shut the doors and then dropped to the magenta carpet to check the underside.

Ethan froze; head turned sideways to look under the armoire. He could see a rough opening behind it. He quickly pushed himself up looking at the armoire. It was snug against the wall and seemed to be solid pine—he wasn't going to be able to move it easily on carpet, which meant Fiona wouldn't be able to, but there was something behind it.

He threw the door open again and parted the clothes. He pulled out his phone for a flashlight and flashed it along the backboard of the armoire. Along the left side of the back, there was a small hole, only large enough for a finger to fit in, but he tried it and gave a gentle pull. The back, which he now realized was false, pulled away to reveal a large cut out in the back of the original armoire. Beyond that was a rough opening in the wall, probably only five feet tall and two feet wide, that allowed the armoire to hide the opening.

Ethan paused to make sure he didn't hear Fiona getting home, but it was still quiet. He turned back to his find and pulled the false back out completely, leaning it against the side of the armoire. With his flashlight, he illuminated the space and inhaled sharply.

The ceiling appeared full height, but there was no window or light. On the subfloor, an old rug had been set down to fill the small space; it couldn't have been larger than a four-foot by four-foot space. None of that had been what made Ethan react. The three other walls that did not bear the rough entry were covered with newspaper clippings, photographs, printed webpages, handwritten notes. It looked like something out of a movie, even down to red string that connected different pins all over the walls.

He placed his phone in the bottom of the armoire to give him enough light as he braced his hands on either side of the opening and climbed through. He twisted awkwardly to get inside, before straightening up once through the hole. He picked his phone back up, illuminating the space again.

"Holy shit," he mumbled.

Fiona Griffin was not just a grief-stricken mother unable to give up on her daughter. Fiona Griffin was a disturbed stalker. Ethan could see the photographs clearly now that he was in front of them, and he felt like his blood froze in his veins.

They were photographs of Vanessa, of him, of Lisa, of Howard. Not just since October, when she'd shown up at Rothbury PD and introduced herself. There was a photo from last Fourth of July at the Ashby family reunion. Hanging in another spot was a photo of Vanessa having lunch with Lisa, Vanessa's hand resting on her small swell that was clearly taken during the spring, taken during a past pregnancy. Bile rose in Ethan's throat as his eyes frantically took in more and more photos of his family over the years. A photo of Vanessa in high school.

He was so shocked by it all he didn't register the new sound he could hear at first. Not until it seemed to be growing closer. Sirens. It was enough to break him from his frozen state. Frantically, he began to take pictures of the space. He couldn't risk Fiona destroying it if she suspected something. He needed proof, and later, he'd need to see the photos not only to see what else was on the walls but so he didn't convince himself it was just a strange nightmare.

Not so gracefully, he pulled himself back out of the hole in the wall, through the armoire. He frantically replaced the false back, doing his best to move the clothes back so they looked undisturbed. He closed the armoire and retraced his steps through the house to the garage, back out the garage door he'd broken. He tore off the gloves he'd worn for his crime and shoved them in his pocket. The sirens had come to a halt outside the front of the Griffins' home.

Ethan's stomach was in his throat, but he did his best to look relaxed and calm as he came around the other side of the home. He pulled his badge out and held it in hand as he opened the garden latch, seeing one officer peek into his car as the other approached the front door.

The one at his car spotted him first. The officer, a young-faced man who looked more like a boy to Ethan, hovered his hand over his gun.

"Officers, Detective Dumas, Rothbury PD," Ethan said, as he held up his badge and empty hand to show he meant no harm.

The senior officer, who had been heading toward the door, changed paths to meet Ethan. She looked far more relaxed as her hands rested on her vest, not nearly as eager to pull a gun as her partner. Still, her wary eyes took Ethan in before flickering to his badge.

"A bit out of your jurisdiction here, detective," she said, in way of greeting.

He let his hands fall to his sides as the rookie joined the senior officer. He plastered on his friendliest smile. "I work the major crimes cold case division, and Mrs. Griffin is the mother of a cold case vic I'd been working."

"We got a call from a concerned neighbor that saw a man enter the backyard after knocking on the front door and no one answered." The officer said it like a statement, but Ethan knew that really it was a question and chance to explain himself.

"I was supposed to meet her here to talk, but she didn't answer the door, so I went around back to check windows and make sure she hadn't taken a fall. She's elderly and often home alone. It just appears like she's not home. She probably forgot about the meeting."

The rookie officer was already nodding, apparently satisfied with Ethan's explanation. The senior officer still watched Ethan with a critical expression, but after a few more seconds of silence between the three of them, she gave Ethan a single nod.

"I'll just have to call her later and reschedule," Ethan added, slipping his badge back onto his belt. He didn't wait for the officers to ask more questions as he headed toward his parked car that was currently blocked in by their two cruisers.

He gave the officers one more friendly smile before he climbed in his car and watched them briefly speak to each other before getting in their cruisers. They peeled off one after the other. Ethan headed in the opposite direction, desperate to put distance between himself and the horrific truth he found buried in Anne Griffin's nursery.

CHAPTER FORTY

THURSDAY, APRIL 11TH

Ethan knew it wasn't exactly a lie when he told Vanessa he'd be up late working on a case and insisted she go to bed without him. It was for her own good that she didn't know anything about what he'd found in the hidden space at the Griffins'. Now was certainly the time bringing Verne up to speed could help, but if he did that, Verne would insist they hand everything over to Camilleri.

Instead, Ethan sat with the photos he'd taken open on his laptop as he zoomed in to thoroughly study everything Fiona Griffin had pinned to the walls. To the right of his laptop, he had a notepad where he'd begun writing out a timeline based on the evidence he'd found. He was deep diving on Facebook, looking at his, Vanessa's, Lisa's, and Howard's pages to see if the photos Fiona had were from their pages or photos they'd been tagged in. Some were online, but others were clearly taken by someone who'd followed them.

He zoomed in on another section of his photo and saw a list of names. The top two were crossed off. He wasn't certain, but he believed his name was third on the list with a star next to it. His brows furrowed as he squinted to make out all the other names, but the quality wasn't great.

Unfortunately, most of the writing in the photos was illegible because of the lighting. The photos he'd taken in the space had only his flash to illuminate them, and the writing looked too shadowy and grainy for him to be sure what he was reading.

He was going through the photos again, his third time through, when a newspaper clipping, slightly covered by a photo of Vanessa, caught his attention. It tugged at the back of his mind, sure he'd seen something like it before. He zoomed in as best as he could to see part of the headline. "LOCAL HIGH S—, WINS CHAMPI—" was all he could see of the two-line title. Underneath the headline was a grainy team photograph that made everyone look like a smudged face, though Ethan supposed it could just be the poor quality of his own photos. He stared at it, trying to figure out why it felt familiar when it finally hit him, despite the exhaustion clouding his head.

He'd seen an article in the boxes back in October that covered a local high school softball team's championship win. Vanessa's local high school softball team's win. He swallowed the bile in his throat as he leaned back in his chair. His eyes slid over to the timeline he made based off the photos pinned to the walls in that room, scanning the extent of Fiona's delusional behavior.

> *December 2018—Ness outside our house*
> *July 4 '18—Ashby family party (Lisa's Facebook)*
> *Maybe 2017 or 2018—Ness and me in grocery store parking lot*
> *Thanksgiving '15—Ashby family gathering (Howard, Lisa and Ness tagged on Facebook)*
> *early '15—Ness with students at school (school's Facebook)*
> *'15 to '10 probably—bunch of photos of Ness out in public*
> *May 2010—our wedding photos (all on Facebook)*
> *Sometime between '10 and '05—Ness and me on dates and out*
> *Maybe photos from when Ness was in college?*
> *Newspaper clipping from Ness's high school softball team*

He knew now was the time to go to Camilleri. Beyond time really, but he also knew he couldn't do it. If he handed this over, it didn't fix the fact Fiona was targeting him and Vanessa for who knew what reason beyond a delusion she'd clearly clung to for seemingly decades. Ethan's next step was to disprove Fiona's theory. Once he had the DNA evidence proving that Fiona was wrong, then he could turn it all over; he was willing to face the consequences of waiting. He just couldn't let Fiona's claim go unaddressed for too long. He didn't trust what her next move would be otherwise.

Shutting down his computer, he put everything away in his bag, not wanting Vanessa to accidentally see it in the morning. By the time he climbed into bed beside Vanessa, it was past three in the morning, and he only had a couple hours before he'd have to be up and heading to work.

CHAPTER FORTY-ONE

SATURDAY, APRIL 20TH

Ethan had gotten the samples of Vanessa's and Lisa's DNA to Paul six days ago but hadn't heard back from him yet. After fourteen unanswered texts, he worried if he sent any more, Paul would just block his number and he'd never hear back. Still, the looming anticipation for the results had him distracted, which Lisa didn't appreciate. She'd already scolded him twice for not being an attentive helper at Vanessa's shower. He bit back the remark that it was his baby too, as she handed him another plate of appetizers to carry out to the guests fawning over Vanessa's belly.

He pushed his way into the banquet hall from the back prep room and locked eyes with Vanessa, who looked less than pleased with her surprise shower. He'd cracked on the way there and told her. She hated being the center of attention and had explicitly told Lisa she didn't want a shower.

He mouthed, "Sorry," across the room as he put the appetizers on the buffet table.

"There's the dad-to-be," Tom Robinson said from the corner he'd retreated to, likely to hide from all the baby talk.

"Hard at work, thanks to Lisa," he said, joining him, so he was out of view of the little window Lisa kept poking her head through to call him back. "I thought men weren't supposed to come to these things."

"That's what I told Riley, but she said you'd want the company."

"Well, I appreciate her, because now, I have someone to hide with. Lisa has me working this like a one-man catering service."

"Yeah, Riley's mom did the same to me, even though she'd hired a caterer for Riley's. We could always sneak out and grab a few beers at the bar down the road. I've been wanting to catch up on Watt. You guys did good with that one. I mean, closing one cold case can be a headache, but four?" Robinson raised his cup to Ethan in show before downing what was likely a mocktail.

Ethan's stomach sunk a little. "Yeah, it was tough. I had a good team, which made all the difference," Ethan answered vaguely. He looked around for a reason to avoid this conversation. Paul's impeccable timing saved him as his phone started to ring. "Got to take this, work."

Robinson nodded, and Ethan started walking away before he answered. "Hey, were the samples good?"

"Yeah, I was able to pull testable DNA no problem. I ran the mitochondrial DNA tests twice just to be sure, but the two individuals don't have any maternal relation."

Ethan stopped walking.

"No, that has to be wrong," he said, and even repeated himself when Paul explained again that he ran the test twice to be certain. "No."

"I'm sorry, it doesn't mean they can't be distant relatives or related through a paternal lineage. It just means they're not from the same maternal line," Paul explained, though the more he spoke, the worse Ethan felt.

"Got it. Thanks, Paul," Ethan said and hung up. He took a deep breath and tried to calm himself. He couldn't get worked up about this now. It was Vanessa's baby shower. He was surrounded by too many people to start spiraling now.

If he thought too much about the fact Lisa and Vanessa weren't related, then he'd have to think about what that meant for Fiona Griffin's claim. Maybe there was still a reasonable explanation that didn't mean Fiona was right about Vanessa. Lisa and Howard might have used an egg donor, though he wasn't sure when that actually became a fertility option.

"Ethan!" Lisa shouted from the doors leading to the back.

He took another deep breath before he turned around, a forced smile plastered on his face. She was waving him over with another plate of food in her hand. He couldn't help when the thought snuck up on him as he approached her.

Lisa didn't even look like Vanessa. He had never considered it in depth before, but they didn't have similar features. Vanessa was daintier than Lisa in every way. Maybe he'd thought she looked like Howard, but that wasn't true either. Howard was too stout and broad featured. As he neared Lisa, he looked over at Vanessa, who looked miserable as multiple friends had their hands pressed up to her stomach.

"Ethan!"

Lisa's demanding call snapped him out of his frozen state as he closed the remaining distance between him and the window she was using to torment him today.

"What can I do?" he asked, in the chirpiest voice he could muster.

"Hun, put these out, and then can you find Howie. He's supposed to be helping you, and then, when it's time for cake, you two will have to carry it out." Lisa shoved the plate into his hands, disappearing back into the prep room.

He didn't argue and put the plate with the other appetizers that had hardly been touched. He popped one of the "babies in a blanket" in his mouth as he went on his hunt to find Howard. He wasn't in the lobby or in the parking lot. He walked around the outside of the rental hall to use the side entrance to get to the bathrooms so Lisa wouldn't rope him in to doing something else for her before he found Howard, who he hadn't even realized was supposed to be helping him. Typical that he'd let Ethan do all the work.

Ethan pushed open the men's door and saw him immediately, standing at the sink washing his hands.

"Shouldn't you be out there helping?" Howard asked, glancing up at Ethan long enough to let him know he disapproved before dropping his eyes back to his hands.

"Lisa sent me to find you, so you could help."

Howard scoffed, taking his time at the sink probably just to annoy Ethan.

"You know, I've been wondering who the baby is going to look most like," Ethan said, unable to help himself.

"Is that so?" Howard shook his hands off before yanking a wad of paper towel from the pile on the counter.

"I don't know if you've ever given it much thought, but Vanessa doesn't really look like you or Lisa."

Howard didn't turn to look at Ethan directly, but their eyes met through the reflection in the mirror. Howard's lips were pressed thin, and his eyebrows rested even lower over his eyes as he glared at Ethan.

"How interesting," Howard finally answered, as he tossed the wet paper towel into the trash can next to Ethan.

Howard stepped forward as if he intended to leave, but Ethan didn't move from his spot, which blocked Howard from reaching the door without shoving Ethan out of the way.

"If I didn't know better, I'd think Vanessa was adopted. She doesn't share any of your or Lisa's physical traits that I can see."

"Is there a point to this riveting rambling, or are you drunk at your wife's baby shower?" Howard's expression had returned to one of disinterest that he usually sported when Ethan spoke with him.

Ethan stared back, hoping if he remained silent, Howard might get antsy, or at least show some sign that Ethan had hit a nerve, but all he got was an impatient huff from his father-in-law.

"I've always said Vanessa made a mistake marrying you, and now, she's making an even bigger mistake having your child." Howard shoved past Ethan, and Ethan let him.

Howard knew exactly what words would get to Ethan, and they both knew Ethan would do nothing about it. It had always been easier for Vanessa if he didn't rock the boat.

Ethan spun around as Howard yanked open the door. "The truth always comes out eventually, Howard."

Howard seemed to pause, just for a moment, before he walked out and let the door slam behind him. Ethan wasn't sure why he'd said anything, but he felt a sense of calm as he took in the silence of the bathroom. Howard had done well not to react beyond his jabs at Ethan's worth. However, his lack of reaction was his mistake. Howard's style was to berate Ethan.

What Howard hadn't said spoke volumes. He'd underreacted, and Ethan's gut said he was hiding something. If there was one thing Ethan had realized when it came to this mess with Fiona and the case, it was that he needed to listen to his gut.

He took another minute before he rejoined the party. As he drew closer to the party hall, he decided it was time to talk to Verne. Ethan didn't know how to handle this, or how much he could reveal to Verne, but Ethan knew he had delayed it long enough. With Paul's bombshell in the wake of Fiona's, he could no longer reason with himself that he was better off handling this alone. Fiona clearly still knew more than she'd told him, and he needed to get ahead of it.

Ethan came back through the doors in the lobby, hanging back against the wall. Howard and Lisa had taken it upon themselves to give a speech and play a slideshow, which they'd managed to start before Ethan had returned. As his eyes adjusted to the now dark room with a bright projection on the far wall, his brain took a moment to process what he heard and saw.

Lisa's sharp voice rang loud through the microphone. "I've waited her whole life to see my sweet little Ness become a mommy and make me a grandma! She was the most perfect baby, and from the moment I first held her, she was my entire world."

The image behind her changed from a toddler-aged Vanessa at a park, to Vanessa on "Halloween 1982," as the slide read. Only three months after Anne Griffin went missing.

Vanessa's bright green eyes and pudgy-cheeked smile were projected on the screen. She was reaching toward the camera, and Ethan shivered. If he had put the photo side-by-side with the one in the Griffins' hallway, someone might say the little girls looked like twins—Vanessa Ashby and Anne Griffin.

Fiona was right. He had been a blind fool.

CHAPTER FORTY-TWO

MONDAY, APRIL 22ND

The moment Verne walked into their office Monday morning, Ethan handed him a coffee, told him to sit down, shut up, and listen until he was done. He paced around their office as it took him over an hour to explain almost everything. He left out breaking into the Griffins' home and finding Fiona's hidden room with her evidence of stalking, but he still suggested that he believed she was stalking them. That much was clear without admitting his own guilt since she'd known where he lived and believed Vanessa was Anne in the first place.

"I know that's a lot, but what are you thinking?" Ethan asked, when he was done, pausing in front of Verne.

"You lied to me."

Ethan let out an exasperated sigh, shaking his head a little. Of course, that would be what Verne got from everything he'd just told him.

"That's your takeaway? And I barely lied. I strategically withheld information that was not pertinent to the situation."

"You kept secrets about our case from me. That's a lie of omission." Verne put his coffee down and crossed his arms over his chest. "Plus, I think evidence that our main suspect might not be a suspect is pert— whatever that word is you just used!"

"I kept it from you because if this gets out, it will blow up my family!"

"It was our case first! And…and you didn't know that at the start!"

"I know I should have told you sooner, but you'd made it clear where you stood on Fiona, so I waited until I had enough to bring to you."

"And when you were screwed?"

"This is serious, Verne. I know I could have told you sooner, but I made an executive decision and I'm telling you now, so move on and focus," Ethan snapped. "I don't know what Fiona's next move will be, but she left that DNA report almost two weeks ago and hasn't made a move since. I don't trust her. She might try to blame us for covering up. We could end up social pariahs and lose our jobs, and right now, that's really feeling best worst-case scenario."

"Oh, so now there's an us," Verne mumbled.

"Do you understand that no matter how this comes out, Vanessa's life is blown up? My wife's life is blown up, and therefore, my child is affected. You can be as angry as you want with me, but if you care at all about Vanessa, I need you to at least temporarily let my omissions go."

Verne was silent for longer than Ethan would have liked, but eventually, he nodded as he dropped his arms to his side and sat up straighter. "We could bury the evidence you have. Technically, Anne Griffin's case is closed, and it's not easy reopening a case."

"That would work if Fiona didn't have evidence of her own."

"It's not like Vanessa willingly gave a blood sample, so Fiona can't really prove whose DNA that report actually talks about, right?"

"Yes, simply put, that's true. But even if she told people who she supposedly collected that DNA sample from, it would cause a shitshow. So, even if it doesn't hold up as enough new evidence against our closed case, it could lead to an investigation into us, and Fiona knows I know because I confronted her about it."

"True," Verne said, biting the inside of his cheek as he thought about it. "Okay, but that becomes her word against yours."

"Yes, but her word against mine is an issue if we're under investigation for mishandling a case."

Verne threw his hands up in response. Neither said anything for a few minutes.

Ethan didn't want to say it, but he knew he screwed them over. He should've listened to Verne when Verne asked him to stop. Instead, he'd decided he'd do it alone, and now, they were in this mess.

On top of it all, he was ignoring the most important and pressing part of it all; he needed to tell Vanessa the truth before someone else did. He'd spent the remainder of his weekend after the baby shower imagining how he could go about it. No version went well.

"If the papers aren't fake, wouldn't that mean there's a real Vanessa Ashby out there?" Verne asked, interrupting Ethan's thoughts.

"They must be fakes. Howard and Lisa taking Anne would work conveniently with their timeline since Anne went missing right after they moved here." Ethan rubbed his temple as he dropped into his own desk chair, slumping under the weight of it all.

"But if the Pennsylvania hospital has a copy like you said, then there had to have been a Vanessa Ashby before, well, your Vanessa Ashby. I mean, they must have had a baby with them that day they checked into the ER; otherwise, someone would have noticed a couple pretending to have a sick kid."

Ethan sat up in his chair as he processed what Verne said. He hadn't given it much thought that the only reason the Ashbys were at the ER shortly before the Griffins was because Vanessa had needed to be seen. He'd been so caught up in the fact Anne Griffin was Vanessa Ashby that he'd ignored the other glaring holes in the story.

Howard and Lisa would have had to either fake having a sick baby with them when they signed into the ER or actually had a baby with them. That in itself was one problem, but they'd signed out before the Griffins had gotten there, which didn't make sense. He couldn't imagine the Ashbys as evil mastermind types, but surely, if they left with Anne, then they must have been planning to kidnap a child when they went to the hospital. It could have been a canvassing ploy so they could get an idea of the ER layout before they came back to follow through on the kidnapping.

"Have you talked to Vanessa's parents yet? Have you talked to Vanessa yet?" Verne's voice rose on the second question, like he'd just realized Vanessa was very much in the middle of all of this.

Ethan shook his head. "I think I just need more time to figure out the best way to approach this before I make my next move."

Verne pulled a face but didn't say anything, which made Ethan nervous.

"What?"

"I just think you should go to Ed sooner rather than later. You don't want someone else getting to him first."

Ethan narrowed his eyes toward Verne, and Verne put his hands up defensively. Ethan couldn't decide if Verne was just warning him or threatening him. He knew Verne had every right to storm to Camilleri's office and spill everything, but he needed now more than ever to trust that Verne had his back.

"I just need a few more days to figure it all out."

"And probably tell Vanessa," Verne said, and Ethan shot him a look. Verne raised his hands again in surrender. "Or not? Maybe don't tell her? Hell, what do I know?"

"Can you cover for me if anyone comes looking for me? Just tell them I'm following up on something," Ethan said, as he stood up and grabbed his things.

"Yeah…are you going to tell me where you're going?"

"I have an idea. I promise I'll fill you in later."

Ethan didn't wait to hear Verne's response. It was a long shot, but he believed there was a way to confirm whether there was a Vanessa Ashby before Anne Griffin was taken. He just had to figure out how to get to it.

CHAPTER FORTY-THREE

MONDAY, APRIL 22ND

"Ethan?" Lisa opened her front door hesitantly.

She looked beyond his shoulder, probably checking if he was alone. Ethan could only recall a handful of times that he'd stopped by the Ashbys' home alone.

"Hey, sorry to bother you, I'm just coming to pick up those files Vanessa called about."

Lisa's brows furrowed, clearly confused, which was fair since Vanessa hadn't called about files. Her confusion left her guard down enough to open the door fully. Ethan didn't wait for a formal invitation and stepped in, closing the door for Lisa.

"Oh, well, Vanessa didn't call about any files," Lisa said, glancing at the front door now closed behind Ethan.

"She probably forgot, pregnancy brain."

"Howard isn't home, and he's the one that knows where everything is in the basement." She had a pair of garden gloves in her hands that she was twisting, as if nervous.

Ethan did his best to put on his most reassuring smile. He knew Howard golfed almost every day until three, which meant Ethan had several hours before Howard would be home. Given they were hiding something as dark as having kidnapped a baby, he figured they wouldn't like him snooping around. Especially now that he suspected the real reason they insisted on keeping all of Vanessa's medical files and belongings from her childhood was to limit access to the truth.

"I'm sure I can find them. You get back to what you're doing, and I'll be quick. Ness's doctor just really needs these to make sure they have an accurate medical history."

Lisa's eyes darted around, and Ethan imagined she was trying to think up an excuse to deter him.

"It's for the baby," he said.

The tension in Lisa seemed to melt away, and he knew he'd found the spot. She finally looked at him and smiled. Whatever internal war she'd been waging at the thought of him going into the basement couldn't win out over her love for the baby.

"I'm just working in the garden…are you sure you're fine to go down there?" Lisa asked, just a hint of the worry creeping back into her expression.

"I won't be long at all. You can head back out there. I'll let you know when I'm leaving." Ethan put his hand on her back, gently guiding her to the back door still open, likely from when she'd come to answer the door.

"Okay," she said, and stepped out onto the back porch.

Ethan went to the basement door, opening it and reaching in to hit the switch. The humming of the lights coming on filled the air at the bottom of the stairs. He'd only just stepped onto the first step when Lisa called his name. He turned back around to look at her where she leaned back into the house.

"Maybe don't tell Howard about this. He gets a little sensitive about people going through the basement. He has a system."

Ethan smiled and pretended to zip his lips. Lisa's secrecy was even better for him.

* * *

It took longer than Ethan would have liked to locate Vanessa's records. Part of the reason being it seemed Howard never threw anything anyway, nor did there seem to be an obvious system of organization, despite Lisa's claim. The other part being Ethan's lock-picking skills were rusty, so it took him several tries to pick the lock of the filing drawer that was locked. As soon as Ethan had tugged on the handle and met resistance, he knew he'd found the right set of drawers.

Now that he had it open, he was working fast to skim through the unmarked files to find what he was looking for, which was another layer of difficulty because he wasn't sure exactly what that was. It was the second drawer from the bottom that finally gave him hope.

At the back of the file drawer was a document-sized lockbox, which took a little more finessing and time to unlock than the drawers but proved worth the effort. The box was stuffed full of medical documents, clearly something Howard didn't want anyone finding since it took two keys, or paperclips, to access.

He spared a glance to his phone to see he still had a couple hours before Howard would be home. He could look through it here, and if it was important, he'd take it. He stood up with the lockbox and set it on top of the filing cabinet to get a better look at each document. A quick flip through the documents confirmed they were all medical documents for Vanessa Ashby, born May 17, 1981. He flipped back to the beginning of the stack, taking his time to skim them more thoroughly. It didn't take more than a few pages of reading for him to find something.

Vanessa was diagnosed at birth with a congenital heart defect and at nine months old underwent open heart surgery. Ethan knew he was no expert, but he was confident a surgery of that magnitude would have left Vanessa with some scarring, even if it had become faint over time. He knew with certainty Vanessa did not have any scars.

His own pulse quickened as he took the time to read more thoroughly. While her surgery had been a success, Vanessa was still expected to have lifelong complications and need monitoring for the rest of her life.

Ethan flipped through the rest of the pages, his hand shaking a little from the implications of the documents. He wouldn't let himself think about the reality these documents confirmed. As he flipped the last page, he saw there were a few polaroid photos in the bottom of the lockbox.

"Holy shit," he whispered, unable to help himself.

He held up the first photo from the pile. It was a photo from a first birthday, a little girl sitting in a highchair smiling with a cake in front of her. She wore a pink dress, and very clear down her chest, disappearing into the top of the dress, was a prominent scar—still healing from the looks of it.

What truly caught Ethan's attention wasn't even the scar though; it was how unlike Anne Griffin this baby looked. Where Anne had blonde hair, green eyes, and fair skin, this baby had curly black hair, dark eyes, and an olive complexion. The baby in the photo looked like she belonged to the Ashbys from coloration alone.

Ethan dropped the photo back on top of the pile, shoved the documents back in, and closed the lockbox. He tucked it under his arm and closed the filing cabinet, doing his best to return the space to the state he'd found it. He retraced his steps upstairs, making sure to turn off the lights at the top.

He tucked the box under his arm in his jacket so Lisa wouldn't notice it as he approached the still-open back door. He had to blink a few times for his eyes to adjust from the dimly lit basement to the sunshine outside. It took him a second to spot Lisa, kneeling in the back corner of the yard where she maintained her garden. She was bent over the corner dedicated to Lisa and Howard's dog that passed away when Vanessa was a toddler.

"Lisa, I'm going to head out!" Ethan shouted from the doorway, not wanting to get close enough for her to see what he was taking.

Lisa's head whipped up from where she'd been bent over. She quickly tugged on the brim of her sunhat, shading her face from view.

"Any luck?" she called back.

"No, but it'll be fine. Vanessa would know anyway if she had any defects or medical conditions."

Ethan wished he could see Lisa's expression as he said that, but all he got was a shadowed face nodding once from across the yard. She raised a gloved hand in a wave before she turned back to her work, her shoulders dropping as she leaned back over the patch she was working on.

He practically ran to his car, tossed the lockbox in the passenger seat, and got out of there as fast as possible. As he drove home, he kept throwing glances at the box. His stomach felt like it was in his throat as he let the reality of his discovery sink in.

He had another piece of the puzzle and a hundred more questions. Verne had been right; Vanessa Ashby was a real person, but Ethan wasn't married to her.

CHAPTER FORTY-FOUR

MONDAY, APRIL 22ND

Ethan made two calls. The first was to Vanessa to tell her he was going to be working late and to go ahead and eat dinner without him. The second was to Verne, telling him to order food and be prepared to work all night if that was what it took because he'd found more information, and now, they had a whole other layer of shit to dig through.

Verne was outside the station accepting the bag of Chinese takeout from the driver when Ethan arrived. They walked quickly back to their office, the lockbox tucked under Ethan's arm as Verne hurried behind with the rustling "THANK YOU" bag of food.

As soon as their office door closed, they both started talking at once.

"Me first," Ethan said, as he tossed the lockbox onto Verne's desk.

Verne motioned for him to go ahead, taking a seat at his desk and putting the takeout next to the lockbox.

"You were right. There—"

"Sorry, I didn't catch that," Verne said with a devilish grin.

Ethan sighed. "I said you were right."

"Okay, continue."

"There was a Vanessa Ashby."

Ethan moved to stand next to Verne and opened the lockbox. He moved the documents to one side, so the documents and photos were visible. He found the one that referenced the open-heart surgery and pointed at it.

"Vanessa, the real Vanessa or first Vanessa, I don't know what to call her, but the child I believe is Lisa and Howard's biological child had open-heart surgery when she was nine months old because she was born with a heart defect," Ethan explained.

He grabbed the only photo he'd looked at in the Ashbys' basement, from the first birthday, and held it up, pointing at the visible scar.

"And Vanessa, my Vanessa, doesn't have a scar."

Verne glanced between the medical document and the polaroid in Ethan's hand, his brows visibly dropping as he seemed to take in what Ethan was showing him.

"And your Vanessa has no trace of a scar? It couldn't have faded?" Verne asked, glancing up at Ethan.

Ethan shook his head and grabbed a few more of the photos at the bottom of the lockbox. They were a mix of polaroids and prints, but it was eerily similar to the Griffins' collection of photos of Anne Griffin. A few had dates inked on the back, but the oldest one was from July 4th, 1982. Anne was taken from Rothbury Hospital July 9th; just five days later.

"Vanessa, this one," Ethan said, shaking the photo in his hand, "looks more like Howard and Lisa. I mean, I never really gave it much thought that my Vanessa didn't really share her parents' coloration, but it was never that different. I knew she was blonde as a kid, but as she got older, her hair got darker and more a shade of brown. Her eyes are green, but in science, they teach that's a recessive thing anyway, so it wasn't impossible."

"I need food. This is hurting my brain." Verne grabbed at the takeout bag, removing a carton and fork before he dug into his lo mein. Even as he shoveled food into his mouth, he was staring wide-eyed at the evidence Ethan was showing him.

"You know what this means?" Verne asked, after a minute, while he had a mouthful of food.

Ethan looked at him warily, positive he already knew what Verne was about to say. Ethan still shook his head no, and let Verne tell him what he'd thought.

"We need to go to Ed."

"No."

"Dumas."

"I need more time."

"You need to go home and tell Vanessa everything. Then we need to go to Ed first thing."

Ethan shook his head and tossed the photos back into the open lockbox. He ignored Verne's stare as he reached into the bag and grabbed his own carton of General Tso's, dropping into his desk chair. He shoveled too much into his mouth at once, eager not to talk about this because he knew Verne was absolutely right, that they were far beyond the point at which Camilleri should have been told everything.

They ate in silence, Ethan avoiding Verne's searching gaze until they were both done eating, and Ethan had no buffer left to push off further discussion.

"What if there is more to this? Fiona could still be lying. What if Vanessa is just adopted and that's why her and Lisa aren't related?"

Verne didn't speak, but the arch in his eyebrow said enough.

Ethan groaned, elbows resting on his desk as he dropped his head into his hands. He was torn between his duty as a detective and his vows as a husband. He didn't want to say it out loud, but he could only have one priority. When he finally looked up, Verne's sullen expression confirmed which he'd have to choose.

"How do I tell the woman I love that her entire life is not only a lie, but entwined in all of this?"

Verne shook his head slowly. Ethan didn't expect him to know any more than he did, but it would have made things easier.

"It's going to destroy her."

"I know," Verne answered softly.

"I don't even have all the answers. We still don't know how she was taken, how Fiona found her, and now," he said, as he waved his hand at the lockbox still on Verne's desk, "we don't know what the hell Howard and Lisa have actually done."

Verne just nodded.

"Fuck!" Ethan stood up, swiping his arm across his desk and sending most of his desk contents flying against the wall.

Verne jumped up, gripping both Ethan's arms before Ethan could take another swipe at the remaining items. Verne was several inches shorter, but strong enough to keep Ethan's arms pinned when he made a feeble attempt to shove Verne away.

"Whoa." Verne's voice was stern, and Ethan had the impression Verne was speaking to him like a dog. "Vanessa is gonna need you to keep it together. You can't flip out now."

Ethan glared at Verne, desperate for an outlet but knowing Verne didn't deserve the brunt of it either. He gave Verne a terse nod, and Verne slowly let go of his arms, stepping away with his hands slightly raised, as if he expected Ethan to attack.

"I need more time," Ethan finally said. He surveyed the mess he'd made of his desk and decided he was too tired to deal with it. He left it scattered across their office floor as he slumped back into his desk chair.

"I know, but you don't have more time. This is a huge mess." Verne held up his hands as he started listing off. "One, Watt falsely confessed, and I don't know what that means for the other cases and the plea deal. Two, Fiona knows more than we know, which is scary as hell. Three, the longer you wait, the bigger chance there is that Fiona says screw it and fucks us over. Four, if anyone tells Vanessa before you do, do you think Vanessa would be able to forgive you when she finds out you knew?"

Only number four truly mattered to Ethan, and Verne was right. Vanessa loved him, but if her life was going to be blown up, and he let her be blindsided, then he didn't deserve forgiveness, even if she offered it.

"I just need another day. Tomorrow, I need to find out more, and then I'll tell her tomorrow evening. First thing Wednesday, we can go to

Camilleri. We'll bring him everything. I just need a day to tell her and let her have a day before our lives implode." Ethan hated the pleading in his own voice, but he knew if Verne said no that he'd have to do what Verne said.

Verne rolled his lips together before he gave Ethan a small nod.

"Thank you."

CHAPTER FORTY-FIVE

TUESDAY, APRIL 23RD

Ethan had one of the worst night's sleep of his life. He'd ended up on the couch in their family room, afraid his tossing and turning would wake up Vanessa and she'd know something was wrong. He made himself coffee and left before she even woke up, unable to face her.

On his drive to the station, he tried to imagine the worst-case scenario of how telling Vanessa tonight would go. Vanessa hating him, leaving him, and never letting him see their child because she blamed him was his worst case.

He mumbled greetings in return to the few officers, who said, "Good morning," as he passed on his way into the building. He made his usual beeline to the elevator to avoid getting caught in small talk in the lobby, which would let his coffee get cold and start him off in an even worse mood, given the gray cloud hanging over him.

"Detective Dumas?"

He turned to see a uniformed officer approaching him from behind reception. The guy had his phone in his hand and kept looking from it to Ethan.

"Can I help you?" They never had a good reason for stopping him in the lobby. Bad news always seemed to make it to him the quickest here.

"Captain Camilleri requested you be sent to his office as soon as you get here."

The officer was still looking from his phone to Ethan. Ethan caught a glimpse and realized he had his picture from the database pulled up. Poor guy. He was at least a decade younger in that photo, and Ethan felt like the last week alone had aged him significantly.

"Okay, thanks," Ethan said, turning to head for the stairs. No need to rush into Camilleri's office blind. He dialed Verne, but it went straight to voicemail. He tried twice more, both unsuccessful. He had run out of stairs and stood in the stairwell. He thought he might be sick. Had Verne changed his mind and gone to Camilleri behind his back? Or had Fiona Griffin gotten fed up and called Camilleri? Why else would he insist on seeing him before he could stop by his office?

He walked out into the corridor; Camilleri's door visible but shut straight ahead. He slowed down his pace even more, texting Verne.

> You better have a good reason for ignoring my calls. On the way to Camilleri's office. If you know why please text back.

Verne didn't answer, and he knew he looked crazy to anyone who saw him moving so slowly down the corridor. He stalled in the hall until he took one last long swig of his coffee and shoved the empty travel mug in his bag. Verne still hadn't texted back, and he had no other choice but to knock on Camilleri's door. Camilleri called for him to come in immediately.

Ethan felt like he'd walked into a scene from his childhood. Camilleri sat behind his desk; Barnett stood by his side. Soto and Verne were sitting in the chairs in front of Camilleri's desk. It looked like they'd recreated the time in ninth grade when he'd been caught copying off Jamie White's math test twice in one month.

"Close the door," Camilleri instructed.

Camilleri was calm, expressionless. He wasn't even bright red, which was Ethan's usual indicator that he'd blown something out of proportion. He slowly closed the door, silently questioning the point because the moment Camilleri started yelling, the entire floor would hear what he had to say.

Verne caught his eye as he moved to stand between him and Soto. They'd fucked up. He had fucked up really; Verne was just caught in the crossfire. That much was clear from how washed-out Verne looked. Verne wasn't scared of Camilleri, and Verne looked petrified.

Were they all in trouble? Had Fiona had enough of waiting on him? Why was Barnett standing with Camilleri when Soto and Verne were both seated in front of him?

"You have five seconds to explain yourselves," Camilleri said and tossed a copy of the DNA test results toward the edge of his desk. Ethan didn't have to lean forward to see what it was, but Soto grabbed it to get a better look.

"I can explain," Ethan said, before Verne opened his big mouth and messed up what he was about to do.

"I sure as hell hope so, because you three are seconds away from losing your badges."

If Ethan hadn't heard the words coming out of Camilleri's mouth, he'd have thought he was chatting to them about the weather.

"No one knows anything about that except for me. I hid it from everyone."

Verne made a noise like he was going to say something, but Camilleri looking his way was enough to make Verne stay quiet.

"Detective Barnett received this in her mail this morning, as well as a letter from Fiona Griffin. Do you care to guess what that letter said, Dumas?"

Ethan cleared his throat and glanced at Barnett. She wouldn't look at him. Under other circumstances, he would have agreed with Barnett's decision. This information undermined all the cases, not just Anne Griffin's. But this was personal. She hadn't even tried to reach out to him, to warn him. He could only imagine what Fiona had written in that letter that made Barnett go straight to Camilleri without hesitation.

"That she gave me this information some days ago. I was working—"

"How many days?" Camilleri cut him off.

"Two weeks."

Camilleri turned to Soto and Verne. "Neither of you were aware?"

Both denied knowing, and Ethan was glad that Verne hadn't done anything that could link him to this. It was Ethan's problem, and Fiona had sent it to him specifically. Verne didn't need to go down for this too.

"Everyone but Dumas, out." Camilleri waved his hand at Soto and Verne. Barnett moved out from behind Camilleri's desk to the door, refusing to meet Ethan's gaze.

When the door closed behind them, Ethan stayed standing. It didn't seem like the time to make himself comfortable. He waited for Camilleri to say something, but Camilleri had grabbed the report and started to flip through it. The clock was behind him, and he didn't dare check his watch, so he just stood there for an excruciatingly long time until Camilleri acknowledged he was still there.

"Quite the mess you've made."

"Arguably, I didn't make the mess…sir."

"This not only affects Anne Griffin's case, and the other three cases, but any case you've ever closed could be open to scrutiny. You just put your entire career on the line, for what?" Camilleri leaned back in his chair like they were discussing something less pressing than Ethan's livelihood.

"Did Fiona say who she believes Anne is?"

"She did. Taking right under your nose to a new level."

"Then you know why I risked it," Ethan said through clenched teeth.

He knew he should be pleading for his badge, for Camilleri to help him, but he would not apologize for wanting to protect his wife.

"Is she lying? Can this be dismissed?" Camilleri asked, waving the report around.

"No." It barely came out as more than a whisper. There was no turning back now.

"Now is not the time to be cute with me, Dumas. I need to know everything from the beginning, because I will throw your ass under the bus no questions asked if you keep trying to pull one over on me."

Ethan started from the morning they got the boxes, explaining Fiona's role in their existence, as well as the cases being reopened. He went through all her pushiness, anger, little comments, and her inappropriate visit to his house when she got the blood sample. He picked up the pace when he explained what he'd done to refute the claim Vanessa was Anne Griffin. He left out breaking into the Griffins' home and what he found there, skipping to the documents he stole from Lisa and Howard, though Lisa had given him permission to go look. He also left out the part that Verne knew; he owed his partner that much.

"I'm going to need your badge and gun," Camilleri said, once Ethan had gotten through everything up to this moment in his office.

Ethan had expected as much when Camilleri said Barnett received the report, but hearing Camilleri say it still felt like a blow to the stomach. He wanted to argue, shout that Fiona was crazy and manipulative, fight Camilleri for his right to fix this. He felt a lump in his throat, and he was afraid he'd lose it right there in Camilleri's office if he didn't get out immediately. He unclipped his badge and gun from his belt and placed both on Camilleri's desk.

"Until further notice, you are suspended from all investigations, pending review. You are to have no contact with individuals regarding cases, including Anne Griffin's. You are not to reach out to Verne, Soto, Barnett or any other officer or detective for any case-related matter. You are to hand over any case materials in your possession, including the evidence you collected from the Ashbys' residence. Am I clear?"

"Yes."

"I have an officer waiting outside who will escort you out. Do you need to collect any personal items from your office?"

"I know I'm in no position to ask for favors, but my wife is pregnant, and the stress this could put on her could harm the baby. I know we—you guys need to investigate, but please don't drag my wife into the middle of whatever media investigation frenzy this might cause."

"Do you need to get anything from your office?" Camilleri repeated, ignoring his plea.

"No."

"You're dismissed." Camilleri picked up his phone and started to make a call. Ethan hovered for a second longer, as if Camilleri would change his mind, but all he did was wave him away.

Officer Richards was waiting for him outside the door. She silently walked Ethan to the elevator.

"I can manage from here, thanks," he said, as she followed him to the door.

He didn't think the escort was necessary, especially with the number of officers and detectives rolling in and seeing him be tossed out. She stood by the door as he walked to his car.

He got in his car, not sure what he should do next. He could go home and wait for Vanessa to get out of work, but he didn't know if he could sit there all day and not go crazy. He also couldn't risk Camilleri making immediate moves and getting to her before he did. He had his phone open, getting up the nerve to call her, when Verne popped up on caller I.D.

"We aren't supposed to be talking," Ethan answered.

"Hello to you too. Also, thank you for not getting my ass fired with yours."

"I'm not fired, just suspended."

"Right."

"Did you call to remind me I fucked up?" Ethan asked.

"Hey, I didn't make you lie, or wait to go to Ed. And I didn't turn you in. That was all Barnett. Soto also would like me to tell you she had no part in that either, and she feels for you, but if you ever compromise any of her cases again, she will murder you."

Before Ethan had a chance to respond, there was rustling, and then Soto came on the phone. "To be specific, I said I will slit your throat in your sleep."

"Don't take my phone!" Verne's muffled voice came through before more rustling, and then Verne was back. "She's going to help me look into your Vanessa, the real Vanessa, and your kidnapper-in-laws."

Ethan let out a deep sigh. Camilleri moved quickly. He should be grateful it was Verne and Soto, at least, and not complete strangers who would lack any compassion for Vanessa, but the pit in his stomach wasn't placated by Verne still being on it.

"What's your next move? I haven't told Ness yet, and I need to be the one to tell her."

Verne made a soft humming noise, and he knew he wouldn't like his answer. "Well, Camilleri said we need to gather all the evidence we can based off the information you provided that Lisa Ashby is not Vanessa's biological mom and that there was a different Vanessa Ashby. On the bright side for us, you were smart to get the lab work done at an outside lab we're allowed to use."

"And you don't think there's a chance this is a huge misunderstanding and the Ashbys adopted Vanessa?" Ethan offered, despite knowing how ridiculous it sounded.

"They just happened to adopt a kidnapped baby right after she was kidnapped and name her the exact same name as their biological child, who seemingly vanished?" Verne didn't have to say the rest, his tone said it for him. Ethan was reaching, and it was more outlandish than the truth seemed to be.

"We've got to follow the lead," Verne said when Ethan only grunted in response.

Both were silent. Ethan tried to come up with another explanation, but he knew as well as Verne and Camilleri did that this was too much to be a coincidence.

"I'm sorry, man."

"I need to be the one to tell her, or she'll never forgive me. Can you buy me a few hours?"

"Soto and I will hold off making any moves as long as possible."

* * *

On the drive home, he called Vanessa. He knew she had a prep hour and would be able to talk. It only rang twice before she answered and sounded panicked.

"What's wrong?" she asked, before he had a chance to say anything. He hadn't considered, until he heard her voice, that calling her so early in the day when he was supposed to be at work was unusual.

"I'm okay. I can't explain over the phone, but I need you to tell the office to find you a substitute for the rest of the day and come home as soon as you can."

"Okay, now I'm worried. Why can't you tell me right now?" Her voice got stern, and he knew she was going to get defiant with him if she didn't get more from him.

"It's complicated, and I know I'm being vague, and you hate when I'm vague, but I just got suspended and this is serious. I need you to come home now. Please." He fought the urge to raise his voice. He wanted to shout at someone, but he couldn't take it out on her. She was the last person who deserved that.

"I'll be home as soon as someone can cover for me," she softened her voice. "I love you."

"I love you too."

He hung up and punched the horn of his car, angry tears prickling the corner of his eyes. He ignored the man in the car next to him who waved his finger at him, agitated by his honking. None of this was going to be okay.

CHAPTER FORTY-SIX

TUESDAY, APRIL 23RD

Ethan made it home before Vanessa. He realized he'd left this morning without his house keys, which seemed to be in line with how his day was unfolding. He paced the path, checking his phone every few minutes for a call or text from Vanessa, or Verne, or even Soto. Any distraction from the impending havoc he would be wreaking on Vanessa's life.

He started counting his steps and lost count around five hundred. He stared at the grass, only now aware he needed to start lawn work again since the false springs of New England seemed to have genuinely passed. He stood there, arms folded across his chest, when Vanessa pulled into the driveway.

"Why are you outside?" Her cheeks were flushed and her eyes wide. She grabbed his arms, taking him in. "You're sweating like you've just run miles! Ethan, what is going on with you?"

He didn't know what to say as she brushed by him, her steps cautious and slow as her hands rested on her belly. He fell in line behind her silently. She made it up to the door and let them in.

"I forgot my key."

"What?" She peeled off her jacket and slipped off her shoes. He noticed her labored breathing.

"I was outside because I forgot my key."

"You could have waited in your car with the AC on if you were hot."

"I wasn't hot. I just needed space to think," Ethan retorted lamely. He could've sat in his car. He hadn't thought of that once he'd made it to the door and realized he didn't have his house keys.

She stared at him, her eyes narrowing as she scanned his face. He tried to keep his expression neutral. He needed to be the calm one now. He couldn't blow up her life while he was preoccupied with what Fiona, Lisa, or Howard were all hiding.

"What's wrong?" she asked, just above a whisper.

He cupped her hands in his and grimaced when she shivered. "I love you."

"Are you having an affair?"

"What? No!" He dropped her hands. "Why would you even think that?"

"You work late all the time; you've been secretive lately too. Then you call me in a panic and tell me I have to come home, like maybe a mistress was going to show up at the school and expose you, so you had to tell me first. Plus, you lead with, 'I love you'!"

"I tell you I love you all the time."

"But not when you've made me leave work early!"

"I am not having an affair," he said through gritted teeth. "Nor have I ever."

"Okay, sorry," she mumbled. "I love you too."

Ethan had delivered the worst news imaginable to families regarding their loved ones, but now, he couldn't form the words to explain he'd unknowingly unraveled her entire existence.

"I need you to sit down," he said, as he took her hands again. He practically dragged her to the family room. He couldn't bring himself to look her in the eyes.

"Seriously, what—"

"Vanessa, I need you to sit there, remember you love me, and listen. It may not make sense, but I'm going to do everything I can to fix this."

"You're being weird, and it's scaring me."

She sank back into the couch, her arms resting on her stomach. A lump formed in his throat. He started to pace again to help the words flow.

"I've been working on the missing persons case that's related to the murdered girls. Anne Griffin. Except, it turns out the guy didn't kill her or even take her. It was just shitty police work, and she just got lumped in as one of his victims. Fiona Griffin, the woman that came here, she knew. Somehow, she'd figured it out, and she tried to tell me, and I didn't believe her. The evidence wasn't there, but I guess it was."

He swallowed hard and glanced in Vanessa's direction, immediately regretting it. She looked at him like he had two heads.

"What I mean to say is Anne is alive—"

"What?" Vanessa interrupted, struggling to push herself forward.

"Let me finish. She was taken from the hospital, and somehow, Fiona found her. She sent me evidence. Other stuff was discovered. We took too long. Fiona told Barnett; Barnett went to Camilleri. He suspended me. Verne and Soto are going to keep me in the loop, but I had to tell you because shit is going to hit the fan, Ness."

He stopped pacing. He was out of breath, his clothes felt too tight, and his skin felt like it was on fire. He shrugged off his suit jacket and tossed it on an open seat, fighting the top button of his shirt to get some air. He finally stole another glance at Vanessa and wasn't comforted by her wide eyes and slightly gaping mouth.

"Ethan, I—should I call Jay?" She made a move to get off the couch. "You're making no sense. Maybe you're having a panic attack?"

"No! Shit. I'm not explaining this well." He ran his hands down his face and took another deep breath, forcing himself to slow down. "Fiona found out Anne is alive and where Anne has been since she was taken."

"Okay." Vanessa looked wary, but she leaned back.

"She told me, but I didn't go to Camilleri. Yesterday, I found more evidence that complicated things further. I planned to tell you tonight, but then I got to work, and Fiona had gone around me. I got kicked off the case and suspended, because of my obstruction, but also because of my connection."

Vanessa's forehead was creased, her lips thinned as she pressed them together. "I don't understand. What were you going to tell me? And what connection? Jay was working the case too. You should fight this."

His chest tightened as he saw the anger on his behalf written all over her face. He closed the distance between them and dropped to his knees. He took her hands in his.

"Ness, I don't know how else to say it, so I'm just going to say it. Fiona has DNA evidence…that you are Anne. She got a blood sample that day she stopped by. I had the DNA test legitimized by a lab I trust and had my own tests run and—"

"No."

Vanessa's body had tensed; he felt the stiffness through her hands that felt suddenly resistant to his grasp around them. Her green eyes didn't quite meet his gaze as they scanned all over his face, as if she were waiting for the part where he took it back. He needed to get as much of the truth out as he could while he had momentum.

"I don't know how or why they did it, but Howard and Lisa aren't your biological par—"

"No."

"I can't imagine the shock you're feeling, but—"

"Shut up!"

Her words were like a slap to the face. She yanked her hands free. The tenseness that had frozen her just moments before, gone. Her face twisted into an expression of anger that Ethan hadn't expected. He pushed himself back onto his heels. He reached for her hands again, but she stood and moved beyond his reach, knocking him off balance and onto his ass.

"You cannot honestly believe that crazy woman's lies? She's manipulating you!" She threw her hands up in the air as her voice rose.

Ethan pushed himself off the ground and tried to reach for her, but she stumbled away from him. He put up his hands in surrender, remaining still as she edged farther away.

"I've seen the lab work. I confirmed its authenticity. I had tests run too. I tried to prove her wrong. I tried to find the evidence that Howard and Lisa were your parents, but they're not."

He was stumbling over his words, desperate for her to see he'd tried to fix things.

"You're wrong! My parents would never! I can't believe you'd believe that woman over my parents!"

Ethan couldn't bring himself to tell her about the real Vanessa Ashby. They didn't have all the answers, and it wouldn't make her understand any better. He stepped forward and reached out his hand again.

"You're wrong." He could hear the wobble in her voice as she fought back her own tears. She stepped back until she bumped into the doorway, her arms wrapping around her belly.

"Ness," he pleaded. He hadn't realized he'd started to cry until his own tears blurred her face into a watery portrait. "I'm going to figure it out. I just need you to trust me. Please."

"How long have you known?"

The lump in his throat felt like it was choking him. "Over a week."

"Exactly how long?"

"Twelve days." Twelve excruciatingly stressful days he wanted to say, but didn't.

She didn't say anything. She barely stayed in the doorway long enough for the word "days" to leave his lips when she turned and headed down the hall. Ethan wiped his eyes with the back of his hand as he followed her. She headed into their room. He was just a few steps behind, but far enough to give her the physical distance she clearly wanted.

"Ness, please talk to me. We'll get through this together."

He didn't see the shoe. It hit him square on the nose, and he heard a stomach-churning crunch. He doubled over, hand flying to cover the gush of blood.

"What the hell!" he shouted, as blood poured down into his mouth, spraying a little as he spoke.

He rushed to their bathroom, head tipped back, grabbing the first towel he could reach before turning to Vanessa. She hadn't even stopped to see the damage she'd inflicted. She was moving back and forth from their closet to the bed, shoving clothes into a duffle bag she'd produced from somewhere.

"What are you doing?" His voice was muffled through the towel.

"Packing."

"Why?"

"I'm going to my parents' house."

"I don't think that's a good idea. It'd be better if you stayed home. I don't know what Camilleri's going to do next."

She whirled on him then, her eyes widening at least as she took in the blood-soaked towel pressed to his face. The softness in her expression was fleeting as she quickly turned away again.

"But it was a good idea to trust a psycho woman set on destroying my family? It would be better if I were home—with my parents."

He knew that he wasn't going to win this argument. She'd made up her mind. She clearly needed time to process, but he wanted her to do that here with him.

"Can I at least drive you? You shouldn't drive when you're this upset."

"You've done enough."

He'd never seen so much rage in her eyes. He resisted the instinct to step back. She broke their stare and zipped the bag closed, huffing as she lifted it onto her shoulder. She stepped around the lone shoe on the floor and the blood drips. Ethan didn't try to reach out. Her need for space was clear.

He followed her, from a distance, into the hall. She opened the front door, careful as she positioned the bag to not unbalance herself and stepped outside.

"I love you, Ness," he said, as she started to pull the door closed.

She didn't give him a chance to say anything else as the door slammed shut behind her. Ethan wasn't sure how long he stood there staring at the front door. It was long enough the blood stopped trickling from his nose. He'd let the towel hang in his limp hand as the blood had begun to form a crusted coating where it was smeared on his face. His head started to ache, and his throat felt sore. Had he yelled? It felt like he had, but he couldn't remember now. He glanced into the bedroom doorway and saw the darkening blood stains. He knew he should clean that up. Vanessa would be upset if he let it stain the carpet.

He moved down the hall, stopping in the kitchen to fill up a glass of water. When he pulled his lips away, a watery blood mark remained on the rim. He put the glass down and continued to the family room. He dropped onto the couch where Vanessa had been sitting when he blew up her life.

The light reflecting off something outside streamed through the window, blinding him where he lay on the couch. He closed his eyes, his head pounding, as he replayed the morning. The more he thought about it, the worse it seemed. How had he lost control so fast?

* * *

Ethan didn't remember falling asleep, but back-to-back texts from Verne peeled his eyes open. He rubbed at his face and winced, reminded of his argument with Vanessa. The sun was no longer blinding him through the window, and he'd clearly been out for quite some time, as he could now see streaks of orange and pink in the sky.

He rolled himself on to his back and groaned at the stiffness in his limbs and neck. He was getting too old for sleeping on couches. He wiggled the phone free from his pocket. It took his eyes a second to adjust, but he had eleven, now twelve, texts from Verne. Nothing from Vanessa or his in-laws. Were they even his in-laws, if they weren't really Vanessa's parents?

Verne in varying degrees of urgency wanted him to turn on the news. His last text read *FUCK DUDE NOW*, which was enough to get Ethan up and frantically throwing pillows to find the remote. Why the hell did they have so many damn pillows?

He finally found it in the basket for remotes, which he probably should've looked in first. He turned on the TV and swore as he flipped through news channels searching for something so urgent he needed to see it right now.

Fiona's face filled up most of the screen. Fuck. The banner under her face read "ROTHBURY PD IGNORES FAMILY'S PLEA FOR HELP." Camilleri was going to be pissed. He caught the end of her interview, and the news station flicked from Fiona inside her home back to the newsroom, where two reporters wore their best tragic expressions.

A growl escaped his lips as they summarized Fiona's accusation of Detective Ethan Dumas' obstruction of justice for her missing daughter, who she believed she'd found after all these years. Police injustice, they called it, as they discussed his apparent narrow-minded focus on Vincent Watt. He turned off the TV, staring at his strange, deformed reflection in the screen. It seemed Fiona hadn't mentioned Vanessa, or he was sure the reporters would have jumped all over the fact he was married to Fiona's long-lost daughter.

He hated to admit, but there was a selfish part of him angry that Fiona not only brought the media into this but was compromising his entire career. Ethan opened his text conversation with Verne, composing a text to ask what, if anything, Camilleri was going to do about this.

Before he had a chance to send the text, the conversation disappeared as Howard's face filled his phone screen, cropped from a Christmas photo a few years ago. His thumb hovered over the end call button, but Vanessa was with them. What if something was wrong with the baby? He took a deep breath like he was about to plunge into icy water and hit accept.

Howard's voice filled the room.

"What did you do? You let that woman get on the news and drag our family into her delusions! Do you know what this is doing to Ness? Lisa's been trying to comfort her all day, and then we find out this is on the news, and it gets her going all over again. You need to fix this!"

Ethan couldn't get a word in. He wondered what Vanessa had told them, if they'd denied it. He wondered if they felt any remorse or were just filled with panic for themselves. She must not have told them he'd been suspended because how could he fix it at this point? Fiona had taken it to the local news, and he could only imagine the field day national news channels would have with this story. He wondered if Watt's lawyer had reached out to the DA or if he'd be next to go to the news. Mayor Chippley's press team was probably already on damage control to distance themselves from this mess.

"Am I clear?" Howard hissed before ending the call.

Ethan stared at his phone, the text he had been composing to Verne back on the screen. He locked his phone without sending it. He didn't understand how Vanessa could be over there. If he'd had the evidence at home he could've shown her the reports, the tests, the incriminating evidence against the Ashbys. He hadn't just taken Fiona's word for it.

He tossed the phone onto the couch and made his way to the kitchen. He needed a beer and a game plan. He had Verne on his side, and Soto wasn't his enemy, so he at least had those two things going for him.

He grabbed the first beer his eyes landed on in the fridge, twisting off the cap and dropping it onto the counter. He watched it spin a few times before it came to a stop. Vanessa wasn't home to sigh and sweep it into the trash can. He reached out and did it himself before he brought the beer to his lips, wincing a little as it pressed on the bruise. A swig turned into him downing the entire bottle at once. He could go for another, but a hangover tomorrow wouldn't do him any favors.

He went back to the couch and began texting Vanessa. He typed out "I'm sorry," but it felt inadequate. He added a few lines about not realizing how this would blow up so fast, but that just made it seem worse. He cleared the message and stared at their conversation. It seemed so stupidly normal and insignificant now.

He leaned back and closed his eyes. He just needed to figure out how to fix everything.

CHAPTER FORTY-SEVEN

WEDNESDAY, APRIL 24TH

The ringing sounded so distant; it didn't wake Ethan up at first. In his dream, it was a world away. Bleary-eyed, it took him a few seconds to realize he was home, on the couch, and in the dark. His phone was face down beside him, having slipped off his lap while he slept. He snatched up the phone and answered, his voice rough from sleep.

"Bad news, we've got a warrant and he's making us go now." Verne sounded hushed and out of breath.

It took Ethan a second to process. He pulled the phone away from his ear to squint at the time. 2:13 a.m.

"A warrant for where?" he whispered back, before realizing he had no reason to; he was alone.

"Your in-laws' place, or like the fake ones. The Ashbys' house."

"Right now? Ness is there."

"Ed's friends with a judge, I guess. Soto tried to argue we should wait, but he was all, 'They might get rid of evidence.' Plus, we can't risk them planning a little vacation before we question them."

"On what grounds was the warrant issued?" Ethan asked, holding his head. Despite only having one beer, he felt like he'd downed a six pack.

"The documents you took from the Ashbys'."

"Even though I broke into the filing cabinets and then the lockbox to find them?"

"I think Ed left that out, and they weren't down there with you, so it becomes your word against theirs. He told us you'd been given access by Lisa."

Ethan felt his chest tighten. He needed to get Ness out of there.

"How long do I have to get to Ness?"

Verne was quiet.

"How long until you get there?"

"Ed sent Soto and a team maybe ten minutes ago. I called you as soon as I could. He just kind of sprung it on us. I hadn't even known he was trying to expedite a warrant."

He hung up and dialed Vanessa. He didn't have time to intercept them, but he had to at least attempt to warn her. The monotonous ring gave way to her overly zealous voicemail recording. He cursed Camilleri, Howard, Lisa, Fiona, and every other person he could think to blame for this mess as he hung up and tried again.

He knew he could drive over there, but Camilleri could have him arrested for interference, and then he'd be even more useless to Vanessa. He paced the length of the family room. By now, Soto and the team were likely at the Ashbys'.

Ethan stopped trying to call in case Vanessa tried to call him. He stared at the time on his phone watching the minutes slide by. Every time the screen fell asleep, he frantically tapped it, as if a moment of the screen sleeping was enough for him to miss everything.

His eyes had begun to sting from his focus on the numbers, which required excessive blinking to fight the exhaustion. He'd been staring with such intent that his brain didn't register an incoming call for a few seconds.

"Ness!" he answered as he fumbled to get the phone against his ear, but her sobs seemed to echo through their home as soon as he accepted the call.

"Ness, breathe, honey. Just tell me what's happening." He tried to keep his voice even and calm, despite the anger that clawed at his chest hearing her distress.

"Mom—they took Mom and Dad. They took them. And—" Her hiccupped sobs worsened.

"Take deep breaths. It's going to be okay." His words had never felt so insincere.

Ethan knew he should be logical right now. He understood why Camilleri had made the call. Howard and Lisa would be exhausted, most likely shocked too, and give Verne and Soto an advantage in interrogations. However, the part of him that refused to think like a detective about this was outraged at how out of his control everything had become. Some DNA tests, a different missing child from 1982, and a pissed-off rich woman didn't warrant this urgency.

"She said—she said go home. After she asked me questions. Your friend said to go home and keep the blinds closed."

Soto must have been the one to talk with Vanessa. Standard since she was present when they got there, but still, it sent a new wave of anger through him. He'd done it himself plenty of times, but for it to be Vanessa on the receiving end made him hate the process.

"I'm coming to get you."

Her response hardly counted as words as more sobs tore through her and echoed through the phone.

CHAPTER FORTY-EIGHT

WEDNESDAY, APRIL 24TH

After Ethan collected a still-distraught Vanessa, he got her home and tucked into bed with plenty of tissues, fluids, and snacks by her bedside. Soto had already left by the time he'd gotten there, and the detective left overseeing the search wasn't inclined to tell Ethan anything.

Luckily for Ethan, Verne disregarded the risk to his own badge to keep him updated. Verne had texted him that they had Howard and Lisa in separate interrogation rooms and were making them sweat it out a bit before anyone went in to talk to them. Verne offered that if Ethan got to the station in time, he could sneak him in.

Ethan had been torn on what to do. He'd declined the offer at first, but as he scrubbed at his own blood on his bedroom floor from the day before, he felt like he had to be there. He wanted to hear what Howard and Lisa had to say for themselves. He checked on Vanessa one last time before telling Verne he was on his way.

He made it to the station in record time, leaving his car a few blocks away. He felt paranoid and a little foolish, given the early hour, but he didn't want Camilleri recognizing his car at the station and finding out he was there. When Ethan had shared his hesitation, Verne had told him to meet him at the rear stairway exit and knock three times.

He'd barely finished the third knock when he heard Verne grunt from the other side as he bodied the door open. They didn't say a word as

Verne turned and led the way down the corridor. Verne motioned him into the observatory and then firmly locked the door behind them.

Verne just nodded his head in the direction of the one-way mirror. If Ethan didn't know any better, he would have thought the glass transparent from the way Howard's eyes seemed locked in on where he stood.

"Has he said anything?" His voice came out hushed, even though Howard wouldn't be able to hear him. He turned his back to the window and faced Verne instead.

"Not much. He refused legal counsel when Soto first brought him in. We've left him in there since."

"And Soto?"

"She was getting the wife settled."

Ethan nodded.

"I'm going to grab Soto, and we'll head in. Lock the door behind me. Camilleri might stop in, and the last thing we need is him finding you hiding out in here."

"Don't try to push him too much. He'll refuse to talk if he feels pressured. He likes control."

Verne paused at the door. "I got this, don't worry."

Ethan made sure to lock the door behind Verne before returning to his spot in front of the window. He leaned back against the table that sat opposite the window.

It took Verne and Soto several minutes to head in, and when they did, it was too forceful. Ethan couldn't help but shake his head. Their body language was too assertive, and the noise they were making just to take a seat was aggressive. Howard wouldn't respond well to the threat these two clearly posed. That was the thing he understood about men like Howard and Gregory Griffin; they needed to be the biggest presence in the room.

They got themselves situated, and Soto fidgeted with the recorder before clearing her throat.

"This interview is being recorded. I am Detective Gabrielle Soto."

"I am Detective Jason Verne."

"We are with the Rothbury Police. Can you state and spell your full name for the record?"

"Howard John Ashby." He spoke each letter slowly as he spelled, dragging it out.

"Mr. Ashby, to confirm, you have waived your right to legal counsel?"

Howard didn't acknowledge Soto. They held eye contact for over a minute before Soto repeated herself.

"I waive my right." Howard's words came out monotone.

"You've been brought in for questioning regarding the kidnapping of Anne Griffin on July 9th, 1982, from Rothbury Hospital."

Their voices were coming through the speaker with a static blanket that left a soft buzz in Ethan's ear. He felt his chest tighten hearing Soto explain the connection that Fiona Griffin had found, and he had confirmed. Despite already knowing, it still felt surreal to hear it voiced by someone else. To know it couldn't be taken back.

Ethan kept his eyes trained on Howard, who remained as still as he had prior to Verne and Soto entering. Howard was sitting upright, body angled straight ahead, his fingers loosely intertwined in front of him on the table. There wasn't the slightest reaction to the accusation. No angry outbursts. Not even a move to deny it.

Ethan had seen enough interrogations to know even innocent people weren't relaxed in an interrogation room. There was no calm aura in the gray-washed rooms with the metal tables and chairs. The level of calmness Howard exuded was something he expected from the likes of Vincent Watt. It took a specific type of person to sit there, unbothered, when the conversation was about kidnapping or murder.

Ethan hadn't noticed Soto had a file under her arm when she'd walked into the room, but now, she pulled out papers that were in evidence bags. He didn't need a closer look to know it was the hospital logs from the ER, the only copy that included all of Fiona's notations.

"Does this look familiar to you, Mr. Ashby?"

Not even the slightest movement of his head.

"This is the hospital sign-in and sign-out logs from Rothbury Hospital's ER on July 8th and July 9th of 1982. You'll see here that under the 'Patient/Guardian' column the patient, Vanessa Ashby, was admitted on July 8th and discharged later that day, at 10:46 p.m. Can you confirm for me that those signatures both belong to you?"

Howard's eyes briefly swept over the documents Soto had pushed directly in front of him, but he didn't react any further. Soto didn't let his uncooperativeness slow her down.

"Farther down, you will see that Anne Griffin was also admitted to the Rothbury ER on July 8th, just minutes after you signed out of the ER."

"I am sure several patients left prior to her disappearance," Howard spoke dryly. He sounded unimpressed with the evidence.

"I suppose I should get to the point," Soto said, with the faintest trace of a smile.

From her folder, she produced more evidence. He knew it was used for the warrant; Verne had told him as much. However, seeing Soto pull out medical documents and photographs from the lockbox he'd stolen from the Ashbys' basement still surprised him.

"It is our understanding that Vanessa Ashby, born May 17th, 1981, had a heart defect that required open heart surgery. It left her with a rather noticeable scar, a significant physical marking that someone would still have today."

Howard's body stiffened, his brow furrowing. He must not have expected them to have this evidence. Maybe he hadn't thought the police would find it quickly in his home, or he was cocky enough to believe they'd miss it. Either way, it was a reaction.

Verne finally spoke up, leaning in a little. "Here's the thing. We've got DNA confirming the woman you raised as Vanessa Ashby is actually Anne Griffin. Even without the DNA, we know she's not the Vanessa Ashby who these medical records belong to," Verne said, as he tapped on the evidence on the table between them.

"So, on one hand, we know you and Lisa Ashby kidnapped and raised Anne Griffin as Vanessa Ashby," Verne said, holding up his left hand

and then his right hand. "And on the other, we have the disappearance of your biological daughter."

"I want a lawyer."

Ethan kicked the trash can, scattering random office waste across the tiled floor. The naïve part of him had hoped that, once faced with the facts, Howard would confess. He knew Howard was too proud for that.

Verne and Soto cleared out, unable to continue questioning him now that Howard had requested a lawyer. There were two knocks before Ethan heard the click of a key in the door. Verne snaked his head in the door opening.

"We're heading to talk with Lisa now. Soto's made sure the coast is clear so you can run across to the next room."

Howard's cocky mask had fallen, and he looked exhausted. The furrow of his brow was replaced by a droopiness that dragged his whole face down. His eyes, half closed, were downcast to his lap, and he had pathetically folded in on himself.

"He'll crack eventually. I'm not worried," Verne said from the doorway.

"Yeah…yeah, he can't hide from the evidence forever," Ethan responded, his mouth on autopilot. He'd said the same thing numerous times over the years about countless suspects. Often enough, it rang true.

* * *

Lisa was snotting all over herself in between sobs. While Howard was the symbol of strength in their relationship, Lisa was the one Ethan would put money on to break first.

Verne got them through the procedural introduction for the recording and stated why she had been brought in for questioning, just as they had with Howard, but this time, they didn't rush into the evidence. Instead, Soto offered Lisa a packet of tissues she pulled out of her pocket and asked Lisa how she was doing.

Between hiccupped sobs, Lisa asked when she could go home, where they had Howard, and if she could call Vanessa to check on her. Ethan's chest tightened, but he reminded himself why they were here to begin with; her concern for Vanessa was tainted.

"Mrs. Ashby, we're investigating a lead involving the disappearance of Anne Griffin," Verne said.

"But Ethan said you closed it. He told us weeks ago. He said you closed it."

"Yes, new evidence was brought to light," Soto said.

"I just want to go home," Lisa whimpered into a tissue. "I just want my family."

"Can you tell us what happened at the hospital on July 9th, 1982 when Anne Griffin was taken?" Verne asked.

Lisa's eyes dropped to her lap, and she shook her head.

"Okay, then let's talk about what happened to your biological daughter, Vanessa Ashby. She had a heart defect." Soto's voice was gentle, despite her words being firm. "What happened to your daughter?"

Lisa didn't move this time, not even to shake her head. After a few minutes of silence, Verne spoke up again.

"Do you remember what happened at the hospital when you and Howard kidnapped Anne Griffin?"

Lisa didn't react for a few seconds, and Ethan thought she was going to ignore the question again. Then there was the slightest movement of the head. He stepped closer to the glass, his breath caught in his throat. She was nodding. Slowly, barely, but nodding.

Verne sat up straighter, and the two detectives gave each other a look as Lisa still had her eyes cast downward. Verne spared a backward glance at the glass, as though to say, "We've got them."

"Could you tell us what you remember?" Verne's voice was softer as he returned his attention to Lisa.

There was no further acknowledgment she'd heard Verne except a new outburst of tears. They gave her a few minutes, and then Soto repeated Verne's question to no avail. It seemed that was all she would give them for now.

Verne and Soto tried a few more variations of their question, but Soto's words got snippier, Verne's voice got louder, and Lisa's wails got longer. It was well past seven in the morning by the time they called it on the questioning. Soto had a uniformed officer escort Lisa to a holding cell with clear instructions there was to be no communication between the Ashbys.

When they joined him in the observation room, Ethan could see just how tired they were. He'd spent most of the time looking at the back of their heads. Now that he was facing them, he could see the dark bags under their eyes. Neither spoke as they propped themselves against walls.

"They'll talk," Ethan said. The confidence in his voice almost made him believe it.

Verne snorted in response, but he just stared at his feet.

Ethan looked at Soto, expecting her to at least have something snarky to say in response but she, too, just stared blankly at the wall.

"You clearly hit a nerve with Howard and you're on to something with Lisa. She didn't ask for a lawyer either, so there is still a chance she'll be willing to confess. Don't let one bad night of questioning make you give up."

Soto's eyes locked on Ethan's, making him wish he could put more space between them.

"That's easy enough for you to say. We didn't hide shit from you and then put you in the position to have to clean it up. To make it worse, Camilleri is expecting us to magically fill in the gaps between what you and Fiona already figured out. We look like clowns in there with that stupid hospital log that proves literally nothing, basically a story about a new missing girl, and some mito-fuckery DNA."

Verne had looked up from his feet to stare wide-eyed at Soto, and Ethan just stood there, taking her outburst because it was justified. He had screwed them over, and now, they had to jump through hoops to figure this out when they barely had momentum with the limited evidence at hand. In different circumstances, he might have laughed at this seriously screwed-up game of Clue it felt like they were playing. They probably had their who, and maybe their where, but that was about it.

Soto's laugh brought him out of his head. "This is actually a joke," she said between heaving laughs.

Verne joined in, tears beginning to stream down his face as he repeated her "mito-fuckery DNA."

Before he knew it, Ethan was laughing along with them. The ridiculousness of the situation—every bit of it, from Fiona day one down to this very moment of him hiding in an observatory watching his in-laws being interrogated—finally broke him.

The three of them all ended up in tears, Ethan having slid to sitting on the floor against the wall, laughing with his head resting on his knees.

"What a fucking mess," Soto said in a sigh that brought her own laughter to an end.

Ethan looked up at her and nodded, sobering back up to the reality they were facing. Verne wiped his face on the back of his hands, grunting in agreement.

"What are you going to do?" Ethan asked.

Soto glanced at Verne, who shrugged in response. She looked at Ethan and seemed to be searching his face for something before she answered him.

"We'll keep pushing them. We only have a small window to hold them if we don't press charges—as you know, obviously. But Camilleri is beyond pissed."

"I know."

"I should probably sneak you out before too many people show up," Verne said, pushing himself away from the wall.

Ethan nodded as he pulled himself off the floor. His entire body protested and reminded him he wasn't young and flexible anymore.

He was about to apologize to them both when his phone started vibrating in his pocket. He pulled it out in case it was Ness, having woken up to find he wasn't there. Instead, a number he didn't recognize was on the screen.

"Detective Ethan Dumas."

"Hi, this is Dr. Petrowski from Rothbury Hospital. I'm calling as you're listed as the emergency contact for Vanessa Dumas."

Ethan felt like his heart had dropped into his stomach. There was a ringing in his ear, and the voice on the line suddenly sounded like they were whispering through a tunnel to him.

"Sir, are you still there?"

"Yes," Ethan got out, even with his tongue feeling like it had turned to cotton.

"Mrs. Dumas was brought in by ambulance. While she was being brought to the hospital, the fetal heart rate dropped drastically and was showing signs of distress. Your wife's heart rate became erratic, and we had to rush mom and baby into surgery as soon as they arrived. They're currently still in surgery, so I don't have any further updates, but the surgeon asked we get you here as soon as possible. Are you able to come to the hospital?"

Ethan looked at Verne, who was frowning and had stepped closer to his side. Of course, he'd go to the hospital. But the words to say as much fought to get past his cotton tongue and pressed lips.

"Sir?"

"Yes," his voice hushed. "Yes. I'm on my way."

He hung up before he realized he hadn't properly ended the conversation. Maybe the hospital had more to tell him. He stared down at the dark screen on his phone, forgetting he was not alone until Verne put his hand on Ethan's back.

"Is everything okay?" Verne asked.

Ethan looked up to see the concern clearly twisting both Soto's and Verne's expressions.

"I have to go. Vanessa," he said, not bothering to finish his sentence. His thoughts were too scrambled for anything coherent to come out.

He forgot about hiding his presence at the station. He tore the door open and took off down the corridor. He heard footsteps behind him, but he didn't look back. If someone spotted him, so be it. He would deal with Camilleri and his wrath later.

"Dumas!" Verne hissed.

He was almost at the door Verne had let him in when Soto bodied him into the wall. His breath caught in his throat as Soto's shoulder pushed the air out of his lungs. They both grunted as Ethan's back took the brunt of the force.

"Stop," Soto said, both her hands pushing on his shoulders to keep him leaned back on the wall.

Verne caught up a second later. "I said stop him, not hurt him. He's an old man."

"I'm forty-two," he said in between deep breaths, his lungs needing a second to recover from Soto's blow.

"Old," Verne reiterated.

"He's fine," Soto said, and gave Ethan's shoulder a gentle pat as she unpinned him.

"I need to get to the hospital. Vanessa is there. She's in surgery. Oh god, the baby," he said, as he pushed himself off the wall. He tried to push through them to the door, but this time, Verne pushed him back.

"You're in no state to drive. Let me—"

"Verne, I don't have time for this—"

"Shut up, I was saying let me drive you," Verne said, as he held up keys to a cruiser.

Verne led the way to the cruisers and put his hand on Ethan's head, like he was a suspect, as he guided him into the passenger seat. Ethan's burst of energy had subsided to a numbness, making him nearly useless.

She'd been fine when he left. As fine as a woman whose life had just been torn apart could be. She'd been emotionally exhausted, but physically, she'd seemed fine.

He squeezed his eyes shut; his head pushed back against the headrest. Their baby was supposed to make it this time. She'd gotten so much further than her brother and sister before her.

"I'll stay back and distract Camilleri if he gets in before you're back," Soto said, her hand holding the passenger door open.

"I might have to stay with him at the hospital for a while."

"I'll just tell him you're following up with Vanessa. Seeing if she has anything to say."

Ethan listened to them talk about him through the open passenger door. He knew he should say something to them, at the very least thank them, but he couldn't form words. Fear for Vanessa and the baby had his entire body tremoring. All he could do was hold back his urge to demand Verne hurry. He peeled his eyes open to see Soto shut the door, and Verne jogged around to the driver's seat. Verne turned on the lights and sirens, warned Ethan to brace himself, and then threw the car in drive, tires screeching as he tore out of the parking lot toward the hospital.

CHAPTER FORTY-NINE

WEDNESDAY, APRIL 24TH

Ethan managed to collect himself by the time Verne came to a stop outside the hospital. Verne left the cruiser in the parking spot for police and ran in with Ethan as he headed for the first desk he saw.

"My wife, Vanessa Dumas, she's in surgery or was in surgery. She's pregnant," he blurted out as soon as he crashed into the side of the desk.

The nurse looked up at him with arched eyebrows and an alarmed gaze. He wasn't sure anything he'd said had been coherent enough for the nurse to understand.

"I.D. please." The nurse held out his hand expectantly.

"Yes. I.D. My I.D.," Ethan said, fumbling as he patted his pockets for his wallet. He hadn't appreciated how much his hands were shaking until it took a few attempts to pull out the card. Verne had stepped up, probably to offer help, but Ethan managed to pull it free and practically flung it in the nurse's face. "Sorry."

"Can you confirm her date of birth?" he asked, as he typed something on the computer and handed Ethan back his I.D.

"5, 17, 81."

The voice in the back of Ethan's mind reminded him that Anne Griffin's birthdate was June 13th, but he pushed it back. This was not the time for that, he reminded himself.

"She's still in surgery, but you can wait in the post-op waiting room on the third floor. The elevator and stairs are to the right," he said, pointing them out to Ethan.

Ethan took off running and heard Verne thank the nurse before his footsteps echoed Ethan's. Ethan opted for the stairs, not willing to stand there waiting for an elevator, only to be trapped inside with other people. He took the stairs two at a time and practically launched himself onto the third floor. He only gave himself a moment to find the post-op waiting room on the directory and see the arrow pointing left to take off running again.

"Dumas, slow down!" Verne shouted behind him.

It brought him to a halt, and almost sent him face-first into the tiled floor as his body went to keep moving forward. He turned to see a red-faced Verne slowly jogging up behind him.

"Man, you're in much better shape than I give you credit for," Verne said in between gasping breaths. He dropped his hands to his knees and wheezed a little before he straightened up.

"You heard him say she was still in surgery, right? Why are we running?"

Ethan stared at him for a moment, blinking as if he was waking up from a nap and needed his eyes to adjust. Why was he running? Besides the fact his wife and daughter were in surgery, and he hadn't been there for them when they needed him.

"I don't know," he answered sheepishly.

Verne nodded and slapped a hand on his back.

"We're going to walk the rest of the way," Verne said, falling in step beside Ethan.

Neither spoke as they walked to the waiting room. Verne found a seat, and Ethan went to the desk to let them know he was there for Vanessa Dumas when she got out of surgery. He joined Verne in the uncomfortable green vinyl chair. Silence continued to hang between them, and Ethan just stared at the tan-and-white checkered floor, trying to ignore the spot where the pattern was broken.

* * *

"Mr. Dumas."

Ethan stirred, his neck aching from resting on Verne's shoulder while he slept. Verne stretched, clearly having fallen asleep too. Ethan hadn't meant to sleep. He hadn't thought it even possible with how stressed he was, but it seemed to be his body's defense to all the shit that was piling up.

He looked up at the sober-faced doctor standing before them. She had a clipboard clasped in her hands. He sat up a little straighter.

"Yes, that's me. Vanessa?" He couldn't bring himself to say more.

"I'm Dr. Gutierrez, Vanessa's surgeon. She has been moved to post-op. You'll be able to see her once she's awake. However, the baby—" The doctor's words were drowned out by ringing. Ethan swallowed and tried to hear, but the words became jumbled, and his mind wouldn't let him comprehend.

Verne's hand on his arm brought him back. He looked at his partner's face and saw the wateriness in his eyes and pouting bottom lip. No. This could not be happening. Not again.

Ethan looked back at the doctor, whose expression had molded into that of sympathy and compassion.

"We had to perform an emergency hysterectomy due to the blood loss your wife was experiencing."

"Wait, a hysterectomy? What?" He looked from the doctor to Verne and back again. "I'm sorry, can you say that again?"

The doctor started from the beginning, and this time, Ethan forced himself to hear every single word of it. Vanessa was brought in after suffering a fall at home. She was taken into surgery when she arrived due to fetal distress and a uterine rupture likely caused by her fall. By the time they got to their baby, the umbilical cord had wrapped around her neck and constricted breathing. A team attempted to resuscitate her, but she'd gone too long without oxygen, and they weren't able to save her. The surgical team attempted to mend the ruptured uterus, but Vanessa had already suffered extensive internal bleeding, and her vitals had become unstable. The surgeon chose to perform a hysterectomy to increase Vanessa's chances.

The doctor offered condolences and asked if Ethan had any questions. All he could do was shake his head. He could see the break in the pattern behind the doctor's leg. It was stupid they hadn't managed to continue a simple checkered pattern.

"Ethan?" Verne's voice sounded distant. He managed a grunt in response as the doctor walked away from them. All the tilers had to do was switch the tan and white tiles and the pattern would have been right.

"I'm so sorry." Verne placed a hand on Ethan's back and patted it a little.

Why had no one asked them to fix the tiles? Did it not bother anyone that something that simple couldn't be done right? How was anything supposed to go right if they couldn't even get the damn tiles right?

Ethan stood up and turned to look down at Verne, who sat with his hand still hovering in the air where Ethan's back had been a moment before. Verne had tears running down his cheeks, and he gave Ethan a look that made Ethan want to throw up. He hadn't imagined it. That was what Verne's face told him. He hadn't heard wrong. He wasn't in a delusional state.

Ethan shook his head, his own tears beginning to blur Verne where he sat.

"No. No," Ethan choked out. He pressed his fist against his mouth to stop the sobs escaping. He should have been home. He should have stayed away from the station like Camilleri said. He should have been home and helped her, so she didn't fall. He should have been with her, and then their daughter would be alive.

Verne stood up and guided Ethan back into the chair. He said something about going to find Ethan a drink, but Ethan couldn't process the words, his body was so wracked with sobs. He let his head fall into his hands, his elbows on his knees the only thing stopping him from rolling forward out of his chair.

He'd let Vanessa and their baby down. It was all his fault.

"Ethan."

And hers.

Ethan wiped the tears away to look up at Fiona Griffin standing over him, Gregory Griffin just behind her. It was her fault.

"How—why are you here?" he asked, beyond baffled at the sight of them.

"I went to your house to see Vanessa, and your neighbor kindly told us she'd been taken away by an ambulance this morning," Fiona said, a bite to her tone like she was angry.

"And why would you come to my house? Again. Haven't you done enough?" He stood up, his own voice rising.

Fiona took a small step back, and Gregory shifted to stand beside her. Ethan only had an inch or so on Gregory, but he felt like he towered over them in this moment.

"She is our daughter; we have a right to see her." Fiona stood firm now.

Under different circumstances, he would have laughed in her face. Now, he had to remind himself not to lay a hand on either of them because being arrested for assault, while on suspension, would be the final nail in the coffin of his career.

"You've got to be fucking joking."

"We are not, and we demand to speak to a doctor about our daughter," Gregory said, turning to the desk, where several nurses had gathered to watch their argument unfold.

"No! You don't get to show up and make demands. You're not her family. They're not her family," he shouted at the nurses, who dropped their gaze and busied themselves behind the desk.

Fiona laughed. She laughed in his face. At the hospital. Where his daughter had just died. Ethan's mouth fell open as he looked down at the tiny old woman who had ruined everything.

"Ethan, I got you a—oh shit." Verne rounded the corner back into the waiting room.

"Jay, they need to go," Ethan said, dropping back into the chair, too drained to be dealing with this.

Verne set the two cups of watery brown liquid on the side table next to Ethan's seat and stood up as straight as he could. Barely eye level with Gregory's chin. "I'm going to have to ask you folks to leave."

Gregory rolled his eyes, waving a dismissive hand in Verne's face. He grabbed Fiona's arm to turn her toward the desk.

"The patient is part of an open investigation, and you two are not permitted to have contact while the investigation is ongoing," Verne said, pulling his badge out of his pocket. He flashed it for the nurses too, who had stopped pretending they weren't watching. "They're not allowed access to the patient without my say-so."

"This is ridiculous!" Gregory's face was turning red, and he stormed up to the desk. "I demand to know the status of Vanessa Dumas."

The nurse gave him a once-over before looking back at Verne, who still had his badge in hand. "Do you need me to call security?"

Verne looked at Ethan, and Ethan shook his head. That would only make this so much worse later. Verne was using his power on shaky grounds. Add in the Griffins being escorted out by security, and it would only worsen the repercussions later.

The nurse turned back to the monitor, ignoring Gregory standing over the desk. When it became clear no one was going to give in to their demands, Gregory practically stomped his way back to Fiona.

"Let's go," he said, grabbing Fiona's arm. He practically dragged her toward the exit before turning back to jab a finger in the air at Ethan and Verne. "You'll be hearing from my lawyers."

Verne trailed behind them, standing in the doorway for a few minutes before he came back to sit next to Ethan. He silently handed Ethan one of the cups he'd brought back, which faintly smelled like it was supposed to be coffee. Ethan held on to it but didn't bring it to his lips. The idea of trying to eat or drink made his stomach churn.

The silence between them was broken by liquid spraying onto the floor. Ethan looked at Verne as he was wiping his tongue on his hand.

"Don't drink that, it tastes nasty," Verne said, setting the cup down. He reached over and took the cup back from Ethan. "They've got some balls."

"The hospital?" Ethan asked, staring at the cups of coffee.

"The Griffins," Verne spoke gently. It was unnerving.

"Oh. I'm not surprised. Fiona hasn't bothered to respect boundaries so far. Her showing up at my house again was going to happen. I'm surprised she bothered to tell Gregory who Vanessa was, and that he actually believed her."

Verne's phone buzzed from a text. He pulled it out of his pocket, reading the message before putting it back.

"Soto has stalled as much as she can, but Ed wants me back at the station. Are you going to be okay?"

Ethan was far from okay, but he nodded, too tired to do much else. Verne seemed to hover, as if he expected more from him, but when Ethan didn't say anything, Verne pushed himself out of the chair and told him he'd check on him later. Ethan listened to Verne's footsteps as they echoed through the hospital corridors.

The silence was deafening. He could hear a clock's obnoxious ticking. The phone on the desk rang every so often, and a nurse would answer, letting them know they'd reached post-op in Rothbury Hospital. The coffee Verne had misted over the floor dried into a brown blood spatter pattern. People came and went from the chairs around him. Doctors came out to give families updates, all more uplifting than a dead baby.

"Mr. Dumas?"

His head snapped up to see the nurse who was standing in front of him. He didn't know how long ago Verne had left, but his neck ached from how long he'd sat with his head hung.

"Mr. Dumas, your wife is awake if you'd like to come see her."

He stood up, nodding.

The nurse led the way, explaining what he could expect and that she'd still be sleepy from the anesthesia. Before she opened the door, she paused and looked Ethan straight in the eye.

"She hasn't been told about your baby or her emergency surgery. The doctor's going to come in and explain everything, but because she still has the anesthesia in her system, she might react differently than you'd expect, or you may have to tell her again in a few hours."

Ethan could only continue to nod. He just wanted to see her. The nurse pushed the door open and led the way. When she stepped around the bed and gave him a clear view of Vanessa, he had to stop himself from crying. He had to be strong for her. Her face looked pale, and so many tubes and cables seemed to be coming off her body. A nurse was in there cleaning up from removing her breathing tube, discarded on a tray beside the bed.

He moved closer, doing his best not to get in the way of the nurse as he reached for her hand. With the IV in place, he was concerned he'd hurt her if he held her hand, so he awkwardly held just her fingertips, to let her know he was there.

He dragged the chair to the side of her bed as the nurse helped her take a few sips of water. Her eyes slowly opened and trailed his way.

"Ethan," she said, her voice hoarse from surgery.

"I'm right here, Ness."

"The baby?" she asked, trying but failing to lift her hand to her stomach.

He blinked fast to stop the tears from forming. He looked up at one of the nurses, who held up a finger before leaving the room. He kept holding Vanessa's fingers but couldn't bring himself to answer her question. Selfishly, he didn't want to be the bearer of the most devastating news she'd possibly ever receive. She couldn't hear that from him first.

The nurse came back with Dr. Gutierrez, who had spoken to Ethan earlier. He couldn't bring himself to look up, so he focused on Vanessa. On how frightened she looked. Her green eyes fighting to close from the drugs but kept forced open by her need for answers. Her hair was matted to her head, and she smelled of sweat and the sterilizing substance they put on people before they cut them open.

The doctor spoke gently and slowly. It was the same as before—no more or less than what he'd been told. The doctor apologized for their loss and left.

"Ness," he said, reaching up his free hand to stroke her hair. "I'm so sorry."

Tears poured down her face, but her body was still. She hadn't made a noise or tried to move the entire time the doctor spoke. The nurses finished what they needed to do and left the room without a word.

"I'm so sorry," he whispered again. He didn't know what else to say. He brought her hand up to his face, continuing to mumble the words.

"Leave."

He lifted his head, sure that he'd misheard her.

"Leave," she repeated, her voice more forceful. Her green eyes were turned away from him. She wiggled her fingers as if she were trying to pull away from him.

"Ness," he pleaded.

"Leave!" Her voice cracked as she shouted as loud as she could with her dry throat and cracked lips.

Ethan sat frozen. He hadn't expected this reaction. He was her husband. He was supposed to be here to comfort her. They'd lost their baby girl. She'd lost her chance to carry another baby.

A nurse came in, holding the door open. "Sir, I am going to have to ask you to leave. The patient is—"

"I heard her," he snapped. He stood up and looked down at Vanessa. She wouldn't look at him. "I'll come back later."

She didn't respond. The nurse stood there waiting for him to leave, like he was a threat to Vanessa. He slowly walked toward the door, glancing back to see if he could catch her eye, but she'd turned to look where he'd been sitting.

The nurse escorted him back to the waiting room, on the other side of the keypad access. She left him there without a word. His phone vibrated with a text. He pulled it out to see Verne had texted to ask how he was doing. Soto had also texted to say she hoped everything was alright. Verne must not have filled her in. He stared at both messages on the lock screen, before clearing them. He didn't want to think about work or talk about how shit had gotten so much worse.

He dialed Riley Robinson's number, flinching at how cheery she sounded when she answered the phone. He filled her in and left no room for her to interject. He begged, more than asked, her to come be with Vanessa at the hospital. She was choked up but said she'd be there as soon as possible.

Ethan hung up and headed for the stairs. It would only take him twenty minutes to walk back to his car near the station. He didn't want to be there to see the pity on Riley's face when she arrived.

CHAPTER FIFTY

WEDNESDAY, APRIL 24TH

By the time he got close to the station, he couldn't feel most of his body anymore. It was unseasonably cold for late April, and the wind that had picked up as he walked only made it worse. Verne had called him while he was walking back, and he'd reluctantly answered. It was the least he could do given everything Verne was doing and risking for him. Verne wanted to fill him in, and when Ethan explained where he was headed, Verne said he'd meet him at his car so that they wouldn't be spotted. Last thing he needed was Verne or Soto kicked off the case too.

"There you are! I was starting to get worried. Soto's blowing up my phone to hurry up." Verne was leaned against Ethan's car.

"Has something happened?" He unlocked the car and climbed in while Verne climbed into the passenger seat.

"It obviously has to be followed up on, because we can't just take her word for it."

"Whose word? For what?" Ethan asked, frustrated with, and far too tired for, these vague and roundabout answers.

"One of the Ashbys' neighbors came forward this morning, while we were at the hospital. She claims, all hearsay until we can get a team out there, but—"

"Just spit it out!" Ethan immediately regretted the harshness of his tone. He rubbed at his head, wishing he could be in darkness right now.

"She told us what we already figured out, about there being a different Vanessa Ashby, and she believes she saw something to support her claim that the Ashbys killed her." Verne's sentence trailed off.

Ethan just stared at him, processing what Verne had said. Kidnapping was one thing and, of course, he'd considered that something must have happened to their biological daughter. However, hearing Verne say that Howard and Lisa had been accused of murder was different. Not even he'd been willing to conjure up that possibility. They had raised Vanessa, his Vanessa. He'd known them for over a decade. They weren't his favorite people, far from it, but he would have known if they were killers, surely.

Ethan found himself shaking his head. "It has to be a bogus witness. Maybe there's some bad blood there? Or she's nosey and decided to insert herself into the investigation because she has nothing better to do?"

Verne arched an eyebrow but only pretended to lock his lips and throw away the key. Ethan wanted to point out it was a little late for Verne to decide not to share case information with him. Instead, he kept his attention on the supposed witness.

"They have three direct neighbors, and only two of them have a woman living there, so I've got a fair shot of guessing."

"I can't tell you."

"Is it the old one, with the big glasses and bejeweled cane?"

Verne kept his mouth shut, but the flare of his nostrils and wrinkling of his nose gave away his annoyance that Ethan had guessed right.

"She's in her nineties. Is she seriously being considered a reliable witness? She hasn't been allowed to drive for almost three decades. Vanessa said she was always crashing into things and claiming she was lost when Vanessa was a little kid!"

"Well, what she claims to have witnessed happened nearly four decades ago, so she'd have been driving still. Not that that has anything to do with anything!" Verne sounded defensive, which surprised Ethan.

They stared each other down, both more worked up than was warranted from the interaction. Ethan didn't want to admit why he was defensive over what this neighbor claimed. It seemed like everything was becoming a reminder that he failed to protect Vanessa.

Ethan stayed quiet, staring out the windshield. A few cars drove by, but no one glanced their way as they passed. Too busy in their own worlds to notice those around them falling apart. When Verne didn't speak up after a few minutes, Ethan stole a glance his way to see him staring out the passenger window, a heavy frown reflecting in the glass.

"I'm sorry you got dragged into this mess."

"And that you didn't trust me sooner."

"And that I didn't trust you sooner," Ethan repeated.

Verne turned to face him again. His eyes roamed Ethan's face, and Ethan resisted the urge to look away. He was embarrassed how everything had unfolded. He wasn't a bad detective; he knew that, even if he didn't quite believe it right now. He didn't hide evidence, shape cases to fit the narrative he wanted. He didn't break laws in the name of justice. He sure as hell didn't try to fight the truth and stop a case from being solved. Yet he'd done all those things this time. He'd let it get to him, let the connection he had to the case cloud his judgment and hurt everyone.

"For what it's worth, I don't think she's lying," Verne said.

"Yeah, probably not." He looked back to the road, forcing himself to sit with the fact the Ashbys might go down for more than just kidnapping.

"I can show you the statement she gave."

Ethan looked over surprised, as Verne pulled out his phone and opened to a picture of the statement. He zoomed in so Ethan could read it. He gave Verne one last questioning look, a chance to back out of showing him even more case material he wasn't supposed to share, but Verne didn't stop him.

In July 1982 I watched out my upstairs window in the early hours before dawn as Howard Ashby went in his backyard with a shovel. A tree blocked him from view, but he went back in their house after a while and came back outside. He had something small wrapped up in a blanket or sheet. He was gone out of view for a while, until the sun started to come up and he left his backyard with his shovel and he was covered in dirt. They had a different baby they called Vanessa, but it wasn't the same baby. The first baby had brown eyes and a scar. The new baby had bright green eyes and no scar.

He felt like he was going to be sick. Verne didn't say anything as he put his phone away, at least giving Ethan a second to process.

"I know the evidence is pointing in that direction, but my head can't wrap around the fact Lisa and Howard may have killed their child. Have you questioned them again?"

"No, Soto sent a team to the Ashbys' to excavate the backyard. I mean, we are assuming it's a body since Constance—I mean, the neighbor, spotted a difference in appearance. No one told her about the eyes."

Ethan thought back to Lisa working in the backyard garden when he'd been over there, the day he stole the medical records for their biological daughter. "Oh shit."

"What?"

"Lisa and Howard have a little memorial spot in their garden that Vanessa always said was for their dog that died before she was old enough to remember. I always thought it was kind of weird because they didn't have a little headstone or anything to mark the dog's grave. Plus, I swear Howard hates dogs."

Ethan looked at Verne, who was staring at him wide eyed. He seemed to understand what Ethan had concluded. Before either of them voiced their conclusion, Verne's phone rang with an incoming call. He sent it to voicemail, a text immediately coming in.

"I've got to go. Ed noticed I'm gone," Verne said, as he pulled the passenger door open and climbed out.

"Verne, wait."

Verne bent down so he was looking at Ethan sitting in the driver's seat.

"Why did she not say something sooner?"

"Soto asked her the same thing. She said she saw them get put in the cruisers last night and had a feeling it was time. She'd been too afraid to speak up all these years, living so close and all by herself."

Ethan exhaled, slumping into the driver's seat. That wasn't promising for the Ashbys and made the likelihood of her telling the truth that much stronger.

"I've got to head back in, but I'll keep you updated. If I can, I'll try and get you back into the station when we question them again."

Ethan watched Verne jog across the street and around the corner to head back to the station. He sat there for a while, letting his mind wander through all his memories with Howard and Lisa. Nothing about them screamed murder. Nothing screamed child abductor either, but he already knew that to be true, so his judgment of them was clearly off.

Once he felt he could focus enough to drive, he threw the car in gear and headed back toward the hospital. He knew Vanessa didn't want him there, so he'd stay in the waiting room and make sure the Griffins didn't try to bother her. It was the best he could give her right now.

CHAPTER FIFTY-ONE

SATURDAY, APRIL 27TH

The days following Vanessa's surgery were excruciatingly uneventful for Ethan. Verne and Soto had made enough progress to charge the Ashbys with kidnapping, which allowed them to keep them in custody and build the rest of their case. Ethan felt useless.

Vanessa let him sit in her room, but she refused to talk to anyone. It made him feel slightly better to know it wasn't just him she couldn't bear to speak to. Riley spent all her free time at the hospital. The only time she wasn't there was when she had to take care of her kids, and then she'd rush back to Vanessa's side as soon as she was done.

The doctor expected she'd recover physically in six to eight weeks, with necessary checkups once she was discharged, but Ethan had been pulled aside to speak about her mental health. He was handed pamphlets on late-term loss, infertility, and other options for growing a family. They all felt inappropriate to bring back into Vanessa's room, so he'd put them in the glove box of the car, where they would likely remain until he remembered to throw them away in a few months.

He spent as little time at home as possible. He'd stopped by after the first night Vanessa spent in the hospital to grab himself a change of clothes, some items of comfort for Vanessa, and to clean up the blood a little better than he had during his middle-of-the-night attempt.

When he couldn't be in the room with Vanessa, he slept in the car in the parking garage. It was closer to the station anyway, if Verne called with an update or opportunity for him to come in, which came in handy on the morning of Vanessa's fourth day in the hospital.

Ethan was reclined all the way back in the driver's seat when Verne's name lit up his phone, and he all but threw it in his eagerness to answer.

"Did you find something? Did someone confess?"

"Desperate much? You're sounding like an ex I had one time in—"

"Verne!"

"Right, sorry. So, we excavated the entire backyard and found no canine skeletons."

"So, nothing?"

"And one human skeleton."

"Verne!"

"I needed to do it for dramatic effect! Stop yelling at me."

Ethan grunted in response. It would be very unlike Verne to deliver news without making some show of it. It simply wasn't in his nature to behave appropriately, even when delivering news that they found a body.

"Have you got lab results back?"

"You're really stealing my thunder on this one," he sighed as he said it. Ethan could only imagine the physical sign of deflation Verne was putting on to match his accusation.

"Yes, we were able to get a rush on it, and as I'm sure you've already guessed, we have on our hands the skeletal remains of a toddler estimated to be between the ages of one and two years old. We have a familial match to both Howard Ashby and Lisa Ashby. And, for the finale, I have a cause of death listed in the report being due to a broken neck."

"Well, shit," Ethan said. He didn't know what else there was to say to that. It was damning evidence that the body of their child was buried in their backyard where their neighbor saw Howard with a shovel and covered in dirt.

Ethan heard someone talking to Verne in the background, and Verne's several responses of "hmm" and "yeah" before he came back clear on the line.

"Ed told Soto we're good to press charges and to lay into the Ashbys hard. He wants confessions, and he wants them by the time the evening news airs so he can, and I quote, 'fix this shit storm.'"

Ethan looked at the clock on the dash; it was a few minutes past ten in the morning. Howard might hold out on them, but if they could get Lisa to break, then that would be plenty. They just needed one of them to fill in the missing pieces of the story.

"Don't even bother with Howard."

"Really? I mean, he was the one that was seen digging. Kind of—"

"Trust me on this. You'll waste your time. I'd bet every penny to my name he'll go to the grave before he talks about this. You'll be better off going after Lisa."

"I don't know, Soto says she wants a crack at Howard because she thinks she can get under his skin," Verne said, though Ethan could already hear the doubt in his voice.

"She can't. I've known him almost thirteen years. He won't crack unless he wants to, and he's not going to want to. You have to focus on Lisa, but it's important it's Soto and Barnett."

Verne laughed like Ethan had just delivered the punch line of a joke. He kept going, not acknowledging Ethan repeating his name to get his attention, until his laugh trailed off.

"No."

"Yes."

"Nope. Nada. Hell to the no."

"Verne."

"Dumas! She is a backstabbing piece of shit who was happy to get you suspended if it meant she earned brownie points with Ed," Verne said. He sounded serious now, and even mad, which surprised Ethan. He'd been the one most affected by Barnett's call, and he didn't feel that strongly about what she'd done, but he was touched by Verne's sense of loyalty.

"Objectively, she's a good detective, and she's a mom. You need someone who can try to genuinely relate to Lisa and get in her head. You need two female detectives, so she won't feel as threatened, especially now that she's already sat with you once."

Verne didn't speak. He needed Verne to trust him, and to listen. He knew he was right, and he needed Verne to see that, so that they'd get the results they wanted. Otherwise, they were going to get nothing from either Ashby.

"Okay, I'll talk to Soto. She's not going to like it though."

"She doesn't have to like it; she just has to do it."

"Ed might want to watch, so I'm not sure I'll be able to sneak you in. Listen, I've got to go, but I'll keep you updated."

Verne hung up before Ethan could reply. He'd figured he wouldn't get another chance to sit in. They'd gotten lucky the other morning that Camilleri hadn't shown up. This time though, this was going to make or break their case. They had enough to charge them, but if Camilleri, Mayor Chippley, and anyone else with a stake in this wanted to see a hefty sentence secured, then they were going to need at least one confession.

He considered if he should drive over to the station anyway and wait outside for any in-person update Verne could give him, but that felt like a waste of time. Verne would call or text if there was something. Waiting outside like a begging dog wasn't going to speed things up.

Instead, he calmed himself before heading back into the hospital. Riley had run out to take her youngest to a doctor's appointment, so Vanessa was alone in her room.

He knocked softly on the door as he walked in, catching her eye as he rounded the bed to the chair in the corner. She looked better than she had even the day before. There was more color in her cheeks, and Riley had brought some dry shampoo to help her "freshen up" a bit.

"The nurse said I can go home today," Vanessa said, her voice still sounding hoarse.

Ethan paused mid-sitting before he lowered himself the rest of the way. It was the first time she'd spoken to him since telling him to leave the first day.

"That's good. When are you being discharged?"

Vanessa looked up at the clock on the wall. "She said I can leave whenever I have a ride."

Ethan stood back up. "I can go get someone now then."

"Are they home?"

Ethan considered pretending not to hear her, or not know who she meant, but she'd only just started acknowledging him again. He made himself look her in the eye.

"No, they're still being held."

Vanessa stared at him, but she had no reaction. He wasn't sure she'd heard him. He went to say it again, but she nodded. She didn't ask a follow-up question, and he decided not to tell her the details. There was no point upsetting her further. Once Verne confirmed one of them confessed and they were slapped with the additional charges he knew would follow, then he'd rip the bandage off.

He found a nurse to get the discharge process started, and Vanessa signed all the appropriate paperwork. He stayed in the room while the nurse helped Vanessa change, helping where he could and when Vanessa had no choice but to accept it.

The nurse wheeled her downstairs while he'd gone ahead to get the car. Carefully, she eased herself in, thanking the nurse while remaining stone-faced with Ethan. Even on the drive home, she had nothing to say. He almost wished she'd scream at him, then he could know what was going through her head.

"Do you want to shower?" Ethan asked, as he helped her in the front door and out of her coat and shoes.

"Yes, please," she said softly. She freed herself of his hand and used the wall to guide herself toward their bathroom. She moved slowly, and a few times she inhaled sharply, stopping to lean more on the wall before she started moving again.

Ethan followed behind her just in case. Once she'd made it as far as their bed and stopped to lean, he left her side and got the shower ready. He cleared the bench in the shower in case she needed to sit, and moved all her bottles onto the shelf so she wouldn't have to bend down. He gave the bathroom a final look to make sure there were no tripping hazards.

"Okay, the bathroom is ready for you," he said, going back into their room.

He'd expected to see her still leaning on the bed, but she'd moved to a bag by her nightstand. He moved closer and saw the top of a floral-patterned onesie sticking out over the edge and swallowed down the lump that formed in his throat. She just stood over the bag.

"Ness?"

"Where were you?" Her words came out in broken sobs, her back still to him. He could see the shudder in her body from her crying.

"What?"

"Where did you go after you brought me home?"

He didn't want to say it. To tell her he picked work over being there for her. That even when he was suspended, he couldn't stay away. That he hadn't chosen to be home with her when she was hurting. But she would know. Even if he lied, she'd know that he'd put his work first.

"The station."

Those two words sent her crumbling to the ground, her sobs no longer controlled. He ran to where she lay on the floor, pulling her into his lap even as she made a feeble attempt to push him away. He pressed his lips to her hair, repeating an apology over and over that wouldn't change anything.

"I was so scared, and you weren't here," she choked out, thrown into another wave of body-shaking sobs.

His own tears ran down his face, stinging his still-healing nose on their way to her hair. "I'm so sorry, Ness. Please forgive me. I'm so sorry."

He hugged her for what felt like hours, a shower forgotten. She cried, and his heart broke some more. He watched her fall asleep in his arms as tears continued to streak down her cheeks and occasional sobs wracked her exhausted body. Ethan stayed on the floor and leaned against the bed, where he held her and whispered his already broken promise to not leave her, his mouth salty from his own tears.

* * *

After a while, when his back began to ache, he helped her climb into bed instead of lying on the floor. He quietly moved to the bathroom and splashed water on his face. The exhaustion in his eyes startled him. He looked a decade older to himself than he had seven months ago, before he'd ever set eyes on the name Anne Griffin.

Ethan coaxed Vanessa to put something in her stomach by making her peppermint tea and toast. He helped her into her coziest clothes and fuzziest socks. He gave her the correct dosage of medicine, just as the doctor had instructed. He read the occasional updates from Soto and Verne but stayed off his phone as much as possible. He needed to put Vanessa first and be present.

Still, he wanted to know if one of them confessed. Vanessa needed that news to come from someone she trusted, not see it on the TV or read it online.

It was already into the afternoon though, and if Camilleri wanted it on tonight's news, they had little time left. Not that there was a "they" that included him now. He was on suspension. He wasn't supposed to be part of any of it, he reminded himself.

He grabbed a random book from Vanessa's bookshelves, wanting to find something to distract himself while he waited for a call because Verne would call when it was big enough. But the book was on educational philosophies, and Ethan couldn't even bring himself to pretend he understood or cared what they were trying to explain.

He gave up after the first two pages and set it on his nightstand, glancing over at Vanessa on her side of the bed. She was looking at him with a bemused expression.

"Have you suddenly found a passion for teaching?" she asked, as she slowly shifted her body more toward him.

"I was considering a potential career change; don't you think teaching suits me?"

She went to say something but cut herself off with a small gasp, wincing as her hand went to her lower abdomen.

"It hurts," she said, once her face had relaxed again.

Ethan nodded, not sure what to say. He couldn't imagine how much pain she was in, and he felt foolish continuing to apologize anytime she was in pain, even if he did feel like it was his fault.

"What are they like?"

"Who?" Ethan asked, pulled out of his thoughts.

"My biological parents—Fiona and, well, I don't even know his name."

Ethan couldn't help the surprise that probably showed on his face. It was the first time she was acknowledging what he'd told her a few days earlier. He quickly schooled his features as he took in her pained grimace. He tried to gauge if she really wanted to know. She'd already met Fiona, even if only briefly, but he hadn't expected her to ask about them or even acknowledge them.

"Well, you've met Fiona."

She frowned and made a soft "hmm" noise, as if she was considering that. "Under false pretenses though. Unless you're implying how I met her says a lot about her."

"You've been watching too many crime shows. Since when do you say, 'false pretenses'?"

"I'm a history teacher, I can use phrases like that," she said, before her face twisted into a grimace. The momentary lapse from reality was gone, as her pained expression reminded him of everything they'd lost.

"But what are they really like? I know you know Fiona, probably better than I realize. You mentioned her enough during the investigation to give me some idea."

Ethan drew his mouth tightly closed, considering what to tell her. He could paint different pictures of Fiona: the loving mother who never gave up on her daughter, the overbearing hindrance to investigations, the conniving sneak who ruined so much, the criminal stalker determined to get her way. But as he looked back at Vanessa, her green eyes intently searching his face, probably trying to guess what was going through his mind, he thought back to the first time he'd gone to the Griffins' home. The way Fiona's green eyes had seemed so fierce. The same fierceness he realized he so often saw in Vanessa's.

"Fiona is strong, like you."

She rolled her eyes, but he kept going. He'd tell her everything he could before she asked him to stop. He owed her as much.

"She never gave up looking for Anne—for you. She blamed herself for you being taken, and she never believed anyone when they said you were dead. She wears a little 'A' necklace. She's determined and did lots of investigating on her own when the police wouldn't help her." He stopped, unable to admit out loud that he hadn't helped her either.

He'd stared off at the wall while he spoke and dared to look back at Vanessa. She seemed lost in thought, eyes in his direction but not actually seeing him. He watched her until she snapped out of her thoughts, bringing her eyes up to meet his.

"Most people would have given up."

"Yeah, probably."

"What about her husband, my biological father?" She stuttered as she said it, and Ethan could only imagine the internal turmoil of trying to grasp a new understanding of her identity.

"Gregory. Fiona calls him Greg. He's a lawyer."

"Did he believe I was still alive?"

He recalled Gregory Griffin's mockery of his wife, of the entire situation. The ease with which he wrote Verne and him off when they'd initially reached out at the beginning of the investigation. It felt like a lifetime ago. He hadn't liked him from that first moment. Nor did Ethan respect him when he found out about his second family, the mistress and the sons, Vanessa's half-brothers. He'd keep that one to himself for now.

He chose his words carefully. "He believed the detectives when they told him you were likely dead."

Vanessa nodded once, her eyes drifting down to her hands crossed on her stomach. He wanted to ask her how it felt, but it was an insensitive question. She'd lost the baby and her uterus in one go. It had to feel strange, emotionally and physically.

"Are they kind?"

Not particularly, he thought. Definitely not Gregory, but he didn't want to say as much.

"They came to the hospital. They'd stopped by the house that morning, and one of the neighbors told them you'd been brought to the hospital. They came to see you, to talk to you."

He found himself holding his breath as he waited for her reaction. She deserved to know, but now that the words were out of his mouth, he wondered if it was too soon to tell her. Maybe, like other things he was holding back, he should have waited.

"I—" She stopped, frowned, opened her mouth to start again, and then promptly closed it.

He didn't push. If she needed time to sit with her thoughts, then he'd give her all the time she needed.

"I don't know how I'm supposed to feel," she whispered. "I've read stories over the years, you know, kind of like this. No one talks about how the victim feels. I don't know if I even feel like a victim."

Ethan went to say something generic, the type of statement he'd offer victims during investigations, but Vanessa kept going.

"It doesn't even feel like it's happening to me. I know it is, and every morning I've woken up hoping it was just a weird dream. And I know it's not, but I just kind of feel numb about it all. Like Mom and Dad aren't bad. Can I even call them Mom and Dad anymore?"

Ethan tried to shrug at the same time he jerked his head in a nod. There was no protocol for all of this, comforting a spouse going through finding out her parents weren't actually her parents because she was kidnapped. She didn't seem that bothered that he didn't have all the answers though.

"They never hurt me. I swear. They love me. I really believe they do."

"I believe you."

Her bottom lip stuck out as she went quiet again. He wanted to tease her about her thinking face, try to put a smile on her face, but he didn't think he had the right words to do it.

His phone ringing snapped him out of his self-pitying spiral and drew Vanessa's questioning gaze to him. He grabbed the face-down phone from his nightstand to see Verne's name on his screen. He showed Vanessa before answering.

"Hey, you're on speaker," Ethan said, cutting Verne's initial greeting off.

"I'm on my way over. I've got a lot to tell you. Also, hi, Vanessa. I'm really sorry about the baby. I know you'd have been a great mom."

Ethan cringed at Verne's directness and looked at Vanessa, panic rising in his chest. But she didn't look on the verge of losing it. She looked sad, but she spoke clearly when she thanked him.

"Camilleri let you step out?" Ethan asked, to change the topic.

"He doesn't know I left yet, and if he asks, Soto is going to tell him I got lunch from that sketchy food truck that parks around the corner from the station—you know the one you tell me I shouldn't eat from. Don't worry, I didn't. But Soto's going to tell him I did, and that I'm taking a massive dump."

Vanessa let out a tiny gasp that almost sounded like a laugh and then winced. "Jay, you can't say funny things. My body still hurts."

"I can't help myself. You know I'm unbelievably gifted with humor."

Ethan rolled his eyes but was glad to see his Vanessa was still in there and that she could still enjoy Verne's personality and candor.

"Well, I'll meet you outside when you get here," Ethan said, prepared to hang up.

"Wait! I want to hear it too. I have a right to hear it," Vanessa cut in as Verne went to agree with him.

Verne didn't say anything, and Ethan locked eyes with Vanessa. He wanted to argue against it. He didn't know what the news would be, but if Verne wanted to drive all the way over to deliver it, then he knew it was important. She was right, he couldn't throw her physical state back in her face as a reason for why she couldn't be privy to the information firsthand.

"Okay, then when you get here, I'll let you in," Ethan said.

Vanessa gave him a single nod before she took a deep breath and closed her eyes.

CHAPTER FIFTY-TWO

SATURDAY, APRIL 27TH

Vanessa insisted Ethan help her move to the couch. She didn't want Verne to see her laid up in bed, and no matter how much Ethan insisted he wouldn't care, she wouldn't hear otherwise. She also had him bring the bowl of Easter candy she had left over from the week before, familiar with Verne's sweet tooth. He opted not to point out that Verne was about to deliver life-altering information, and bunny-shaped chocolate didn't fit the narrative.

Verne arrived faster than Ethan expected, though knowing how Verne drove, it shouldn't have surprised him.

"Ness is waiting in the family room," Ethan said, by way of greeting.

They joined Vanessa in the family room. Ethan took a seat beside her, and Verne grabbed the armchair she usually occupied. A silence fell over them. Verne tapped his foot on the carpet, creating a rhythmic thump. Vanessa had drawn a pillow into her lap and was picking at the floral embroidery on the cover. Ethan was absentmindedly cracking each knuckle as he wondered how much worse this situation with the Ashbys was going to get.

"Just say it," Vanessa whispered.

Ethan looked up at Vanessa, who'd set her mouth into a thin line, her eyebrows sinking in as she stared expectantly. Ethan rested a hand on her leg, giving a gentle squeeze of comfort. No matter what came next, he was there for her.

He looked to Verne, who looked somewhere between being ready to cry or spew the contents of his stomach all over them. He'd lost the enthusiasm he had on the phone. He caught Verne's eyes and gave him a slight nod. For everyone's sake, they needed to just get on with it.

"As you'd called it," Verne motioned at Ethan, "when we questioned Lisa further, and brought forward the new evidence, she cracked."

"Sorry, already interrupting, but what new evidence? More than what you'd already told me?" Vanessa asked, turning to Ethan. He saw her try to hide the wince as she moved.

"Your par—uh, Lisa and Howard's neighbor. She came forward and said around the time you were taken, she saw Howard in the backyard with a shovel in the early morning hours. He'd carried something into the backyard wrapped in a sheet."

"I mean, my parents lost their dog when I was little. They buried it in their backyard." There was a tightness to Vanessa's voice, and Ethan had to swallow his objection.

"We dug up the yard and we found a body, which we believe is who the neighbor saw him bury. It was their child's remains," Verne spoke softly, but he'd at least composed himself enough to look at them while he spoke.

Vanessa didn't say anything. Her mouth fell open in a slight "oh" before she gave a curt nod and pressed her lips tight again. Ethan could hear her audibly swallow, as if the truth had gotten stuck in her throat.

"We did like you said, Soto and I. She and Barnett did the questioning, and Lisa confessed. She told us everything." Verne paused and looked at Vanessa. "I can stop, if it's too much right now?"

"I need to hear it, and eventually, I'll hear it whether I want to or not. So, I'd rather it be from you," Vanessa said, her determined expression back as she looked to Verne.

He sat up straighter, grabbing a chocolate from the bowl. He tossed the foil wrapper onto the coffee table, popping the chocolate into his mouth.

"Alrighty. Well, I gave you an out, so please don't hold this against me. Like I said, she confessed to everything. Barnett talked to her mother to mother, which I think killed Barnett a little bit because she didn't see Lisa as a comparable mother."

Vanessa shifted slightly beside Ethan, but she didn't interrupt. He couldn't look at her. If he saw even an ounce of pain on her face, he'd tell Verne to stop, and she needed to hear this. It was her story.

"We had her start from when they brought Vanessa, the real Vanessa, not to say you're not real—"

"Just keep going," Ethan cut in before Verne dug himself into an awkward hole.

"Right, well, I'll call her the first Vanessa. They brought her in because she'd been sick, which was an issue with her weakened heart. She'd been keeping them up for days, and they were exhausted and overwhelmed. I guess the first Vanessa could really scream her head off when she didn't feel well."

Ethan gave him a warning glance to rein in the storytelling a bit. Verne paused when they made eye contact but didn't react or slow his roll, just altered his tone to seem less enthused to be telling Vanessa how the couple who raised her were killers.

"Lisa stayed in the little curtained-off area the first Vanessa was seen in while Howard went to sign the papers and have her discharged. It was prior to the Griffins arriving at the hospital. While Howard was gone, the first Vanessa started crying and screaming again. Lisa was tired, and she said she picked her up by her shoulders and she just…" Verne recreated the motion with an imaginary baby, but Ethan knew what came next.

Ethan gave Vanessa's leg another squeeze and glanced her way to see her hand pressed flat against her lips, her face ashen. He thought back to training they'd had to do last year on analyzing the mental damage that could occur when discussing cases with victims and non-case-related individuals. A psychologist would definitely say hearing about a baby's murder so soon after losing one was not the right course of action, but nothing about this situation would really please a psychologist. Vanessa was going to become a walking case study at this rate.

"She didn't mean to, so she says. She said the first Vanessa just went still in her hands. I truly don't think she even understood what she'd done at the time. Not right away, because even saying it to us, she looked dazed. She said she tried to wake her up and she panicked because Howard came back, and he was apparently speechless from horror. He picked the first Vanessa up and just held her to his chest and cried."

Ethan swallowed the lump in his throat because, for once, he understood Howard to some degree. It was never Vanessa's fault, and Ethan had never felt blame toward her in those moments when they'd lost their babies, but he knew the heartbreak at least a little.

"The next things are kind of choppy, and we'll need Howard to cooperate and corroborate Lisa's story, but she said when Howard did this, she ran. She said she didn't know what came over her, but seeing Howard holding the first Vanessa scared her. So, she went and hid in the hospital."

"He's not violent."

Ethan looked at Vanessa, surprised to hear her voice. She'd been so silent, he hadn't even realized she'd started crying until he saw the tears running down her face.

"He isn't violent. He never laid a hand on either of us," she repeated. She was staring down Verne, as if to dare him to say otherwise.

Verne cleared his throat. Ethan and Verne made eye contact. Verne looked stressed.

"I don't think Verne was saying that, were you?" Ethan said.

"No, not at all. Lisa didn't say anything about him being violent either."

Both turned to Vanessa, and she stared them down a little longer before nodding, seemingly satisfied with their verdict of Howard.

"Well, when Lisa went and hid, that's when we believe Howard left the hospital with the first Vanessa. Otherwise, the hospital would've found out she was deceased—dead, sorry, I was trying to sound all technical and that felt worse." Verne grimaced at his own detour and then waved himself on. "So, Lisa is hiding, Howard has presumably left—"

"Wait, sorry," Ethan said, waving a hand to call a timeout. "Lisa doesn't know? Have her and Howard never discussed it?"

"I'll get to that later. Don't rush art. Oh, sorry, Vanessa."

"It's fine," she said, though the strain in her voice was clear that the entire situation was anything but fine.

"Well, Lisa wasn't sure how long she was hiding for, but she'd just hid in a bathroom for a few hours, and when she came out, she was still on the patient side of the hospital. So, she started walking toward the exit. She said she felt like she was in slow motion because, you know, she hadn't come to terms with what she'd done a few hours earlier. She was walking through the curtained-off beds, and she heard a baby start crying. She said she convinced herself it was the first Vanessa, and so she went to the bed…and found you." Verne's voice trailed off toward the end. He was looking at Vanessa, and Ethan turned to look at her too.

"What?" she snapped.

Verne shifted in the chair, but Ethan kept his eyes on Vanessa. She finally met his gaze, and she clenched her jaw.

"We can stop if you don't want to hear more," he offered, in case she was afraid to say as much.

"No."

"Are you su—"

"Ethan, I said no. This is my life. I need to know."

She said it with such conviction, Ethan didn't think there was anything left to say. He wouldn't try to convince her otherwise.

"She just soothed you at first. Fiona stirred a little, and it spooked Lisa, so she picked you up and ran with you. She just carried you right out the front door of the emergency room, and no one stopped her. The hospital staff hadn't even noticed Lisa, and the detectives had asked. Right?" Verne looked at Ethan for confirmation.

He nodded, recalling the fact there had been no witnesses of Anne being taken. Lisa had walked right out with her, and no one even noticed.

"She walked all the way home, and Howard was there when she got there."

"He really just left and didn't even try looking for her?" Vanessa asked, her voice near yelling.

"Uh...yeah."

"Howard was also likely in a state of shock," Ethan said, not sure why he was defending him now.

He'd gotten to know Howard enough in thirteen years to know he didn't like the guy, and he wasn't surprised he'd abandoned his wife in a crisis, but he couldn't help himself when Vanessa sounded so shocked. The man had just lost his baby, and not from his own doing. It seemed slightly unfair she was so appalled by his actions when Lisa was the one who confessed to murder and kidnapping. Not that he was going to say that, at least not right now.

"Should I?" Verne asked.

"Yes," Vanessa and Ethan said at the same time. Despite them agreeing, Vanessa's frown suggested he'd done something wrong. He turned back to Verne, making sure his face was out of her line of sight before he arched his eyebrows as a silent "I don't know" to Verne.

"When she got home with you, Howard was mad. He apparently shouted that she'd messed up and they were going to go to jail. She said the first Vanessa was wrapped up in her blanket in her bassinet they kept in their family room. Lisa said she doesn't really remember the conversation because she was crying and you were crying, and then she was comforting you. But she said, at some point, Howard went outside with the first Vanessa, and when he came back, he was dirty and she wasn't with him."

Verne shifted in his seat again. The neighbor's statement filled in the gaps of what happened when Howard went outside with the first Vanessa.

"Is there more?" Ethan asked, when it seemed like Verne had paused longer than just getting more comfortable.

Verne nodded, but his eyes went to Vanessa beside Ethan. Ethan turned, too, and saw she had moved to hug the throw pillow to her body. Her chin was resting on top, and her eyes were unfocused. Ethan considered asking if she wanted to continue, but, given the last time he'd asked, he figured they should just give her a minute. Rushing her through hearing how her entire existence was a lie didn't seem wise or appropriate.

"Well, the rest is more fine details of how they got away with it," Verne said, filling the silence.

"I want to hear it. I need to hear everything," Vanessa said softly.

"Of course, yeah," Verne said, clearing his throat before he continued. "Lisa said they didn't leave the house with you for weeks after because they were paranoid. Barnett asked if they ever thought to turn you back over to your family, but Lisa said no. It was never something they discussed. Howard went through every photo album they had and removed most pictures of the first Vanessa. The medical records were all paper back then, so they just removed any reference of a heart defect from the records to pass the rest off as yours. Everything that referenced the first Vanessa was hidden in the basement. Lisa said they only kept the pictures from her birth accessible because you couldn't really tell what she looked like from those pictures. And then they bought a camera and started taking pictures of you to fill up the albums they'd emptied."

Ethan was surprised they hadn't even contemplated turning themselves in, reuniting Vanessa with the Griffins. The hairs on the back of his neck felt prickly as he remembered bringing up the case at dinner months ago and Lisa had mentioned Fiona's pleas for Anne's return. For Vanessa's return. She watched a mother in pain, begging for her missing child, and didn't ever consider reuniting them. He'd been staring at his hands again before he looked up at Vanessa's tear-streaked face.

"That kind of sums everything up. We still want to try and take a crack at Howard, but he's a stubborn jerk—he just doesn't want to confess, but we can charge them both regardless."

Ethan gave him a discreet thumbs-up. He wanted to congratulate Verne, but it could wait for a more appropriate time. Instead, he stood up and took Vanessa's hands in his from where they lay limp in her lap.

"Ness, let me get you back to bed."

She nodded, not even looking up at him as he pulled her to her feet. He started guiding her toward the doorway when she stopped, gripping the wall for stability.

"Thank you, Jay."

Verne stood up and gave Vanessa a wonky smile. Ethan held up a finger, to signal he'd be back, before he walked Vanessa the rest of the way to their room. He tucked her in and made sure she had everything she needed. She didn't say anything beyond a mumbled claim that she wanted to sleep. He drew the curtains closed for her and pulled the door closed behind him.

Verne was on the phone when Ethan went back to the family room. Ethan stood in the doorway listening to Verne's side of the conversation.

"Yeah, wrapping it up. Just stall twenty more minutes.—Obviously, I can make it in twenty minutes.—Okay, bye."

"Camilleri questioning how long you take to shit?" Ethan asked.

"Doesn't know the strength of this body."

"If he shared an office with you, he wouldn't question this hour-long bathroom break." Ethan dropped his voice a little lower. "I remember something because of Lisa's confession. You remember how I told you I saw that nurse, Kathryn Manson. I know she was unreliable, but she said, 'The baby died, and then she was gone.'"

Verne's eyes widened a little as Ethan reminded him of what he'd told him just days before, despite it feeling much longer since Ethan had confessed almost everything to Verne.

"You think maybe she saw what Lisa and Howard did?"

"Maybe, I mean, then it raises questions of why she didn't speak up that night. I know she may have thought it unrelated to Anne's disappearance, but if she really believed she saw a baby die and didn't say anything…" Ethan let his sentence trail off.

"Sometimes, people do the wrong thing but reason with themselves it was right," Verne said with a shrug.

Ethan nodded, and silence fell between them. Verne could have been describing him, with how he handled everything.

"You probably have to get going then," he said, breaking the silence.

"Yeah. Soto isn't going to cover much longer. Ed is breathing down her neck."

"So, listen," Ethan started, but Verne shut him down with a dismissive wave.

"You don't have to."

"You're risking your badge too. Maybe because you're too stupid to consider the consequences," Ethan teased, as Verne tried and failed to scowl. "But I think you're a really good detective, and I underestimated you a lot. So, I'm sorry, and I really appreciate everything you've done for Ness."

Verne looked down at his feet, rocking back and forth on his heels. Ethan wasn't sure he was going to acknowledge him, but he looked up, and Ethan was surprised to see the tears welling up in his eyes. Ethan opened his mouth to say something to stop him from full on crying, but Verne stepped forward and wrapped his arms around Ethan, trapping his arms at his side.

"Thank you," Verne said into his shoulder.

Ethan patted Verne's back the best he could with his arms trapped. They'd gone from Ethan sometimes feeling like he was babysitting Verne more than working with him, to Verne risking his own career for Ethan in seven months.

Once it had teetered close to too long of a hug, Verne let him go and straightened himself. He ran both hands down his dress shirt to fix himself and sniffed a little. Ethan didn't look at his shoulder, but he swore he could feel the spot where Verne's face had just been.

"I'm gonna go," Verne said with a nod at Ethan. He'd put on his serious expression, which Ethan always thought made him look constipated, but he wasn't going to ruin a moment clearly special to Verne by saying so.

"I'll update you if anything else happens, but hopefully, you'll see this on the news tonight."

"Truly, thank you," Ethan said, as he opened the door.

Verne jogged out to his car. He almost made it and would have probably looked as smooth as he liked to dress if his foot hadn't caught in a crack. He stumbled the last few feet before he slammed against the driver's door. Ethan stepped out, but Verne spun around and gave Ethan two thumbs up with a giant grin plastered on his face. Ethan shook his head as he closed the door, genuinely smiling for the first time in quite a while.

CHAPTER FIFTY-THREE

FRIDAY, MAY 10TH

The reporters began their vigil outside the house the same evening Verne stopped by and became a staple for the next few weeks, following the press conference he and Vanessa hadn't watched. Ethan did his best to ignore them and keep them out of Vanessa's face when they had to leave the house.

The morning of the funeral, his face was essentially back to normal, besides a new bump on his nose that Vanessa insisted wasn't even noticeable. He tried not to think about it because, in the grand scheme of things, it seemed fairly irrelevant as he stood in front of the mirror and redid his tie for the third time. It felt too tight, then too loose, and now, it just looked wonky.

"I'm ready," Vanessa said from the doorway of the bathroom.

He looked over and felt a lump form in his throat. She was the image of ghostly beauty, and it squeezed at his heart. She looked exhausted. He heard her crying every night when she thought he'd fallen asleep. She had commented earlier in the week, when she'd tried on the same dress she wore now, that her stomach felt too empty, and as she stood there with a hand pressed to it, he wished he could turn back time.

She didn't have to say it, but he knew they both blamed him. He also knew that Vanessa would forgive him much sooner than he'd forgive himself, if that day ever came. Now, they had to bury her. Bethany. He couldn't bring himself to say her name out loud still. They'd never gotten this far with the others. But Vanessa had asked, the morning after Verne had visited, to have a proper funeral, and so Ethan had made the arrangements.

He picked out the smallest coffin he'd ever seen. Said okay to the floral arrangements the funeral home suggested. He'd told Verne, Soto, and the Robinsons. He didn't know who else to invite. He hadn't asked Vanessa for names.

"Okay, let's go," Ethan said, giving his tie one last feeble tug. It was still crooked.

He walked her out the front door and tried to use his body to shield her from the cameras. They were relentless, even if their numbers had slowly dwindled from the first evening they appeared. They repeated themselves like a broken record as they shouted their questions at Vanessa about the Ashbys, the Griffins, and being a prisoner. That was what they had reduced her life to; she had been a prisoner.

She remained stoic until she was in the passenger seat. As he rounded the car to get in the driver's side, the questions switched to him and his fumble as a detective.

"How long did you know your wife was the victim?"

"Do you think there will be consequences for you obstructing justice?"

"Do you have a comment on the Griffins' statement from yesterday?"

He didn't see who asked the last question, but it did stop him in his tracks for a moment. He was unaware of the statement they were referring to, but his reaction seemed to send them into a new frenzy. He shut the driver's door firmly and adjusted his expression back to the blank stare he'd mastered for interrogations.

He laid on the horn as he reversed, not in the mood to add murderer to his reputation for running over a reporter. They rode in silence to the church, Vanessa fidgeting with the hem of her dress while he drummed his fingers absentmindedly on the wheel.

Everyone was already at the church when they arrived. It seemed Riley had taken it upon herself to invite a few more people, which Ethan didn't mind. Vanessa needed her friends, and he was in no state to be reaching out to everyone repeating the same rehearsed invite over and over.

He wasn't religious. He was pretty sure the last time he'd set foot inside a church was for his wedding. He held Vanessa's hand through the entire service and returned the soft squeezes she gave throughout. Verne was seated to his left, sniffling throughout the service.

Ethan knew people would expect him to cry, and he expected himself to cry, but he just felt numb sitting there staring at the coffin. It looked like a morbid doll toy. The pink flowers the funeral home picked felt too cheery now. He didn't even understand why funerals had flowers. He'd thought it was weird at his parents' funeral too, but now, he couldn't even remember what flowers were picked. He had probably let the funeral home decide then too.

When the service was over, he released Vanessa's hand so he and Tom Robinson could carry out the coffin. He couldn't bring himself to look at it again as he held one of the handles. When they got it in the back of the hearse, he let go like it was burning him. It felt too light.

"Ethan," Robinson said, as he reached out and put a hand on his arm. "I am so sorry."

Ethan looked at him, tried to speak, but could only muster a nod. He hated that people kept saying that like they had been responsible for what happened to Vanessa and Bethany. That was on him.

Robinson gave his arm a pat, like he understood Ethan's silence, and walked away as Vanessa walked up to him. She slid her hand back into his, and he held on tight.

"Are you ready to head over?" he asked.

"Yeah."

"It's nice your friends came," he said, then immediately felt stupid. Nothing about today was nice.

Vanessa didn't seem to hear what he'd said anyway. She just stood there staring into the hearse. He gave her hand a tug and helped her to their car, already parked in the line directly behind the hearse. When everyone had gotten situated, the hearse led the way as they made their slow crawl from the church down the road to the graveyard.

He'd had to buy burial plots, which he'd never done before. When his parents died, they were buried next to his dad's parents in plots gifted to them in his granddad's will. Ethan had joked it was messed up since his parents were still so young when he was fifteen. Naïvely so, given that just a few years later, it was one less thing he'd had to do when burying them.

When he'd gone to purchase the plots, they asked if he wanted to purchase a family bundle, a deal, they explained. Four spots for the price of three. The overly perky salesman had been overjoyed to tell him they offered special financing, so it was less of an upfront cost.

So now, he had four spots, even though they were just burying one very tiny coffin. One very tiny coffin he and Vanessa watched get lowered into one very tiny hole and then covered slowly, a single digger with a shovel left to fill it in.

They had opted not to hold a luncheon after. Riley had offered to host, but neither wanted to spend time hearing platitudes meant to somehow ease their pain. Instead, Ethan drove them home and guided Vanessa back inside.

"The flowers were lovely," Vanessa said, as she moved about their room and removed her jewelry and black dress.

"The funeral home picked them. I don't even know how much they cost," Ethan said.

"Does it matter?"

He threw his tie into a drawer and closed it, his jacket already discarded on the foot of the bed as he worked the buttons of his shirt open.

"No."

"When will the headstone arrive?"

"Sometime next month," he answered. His own body felt robotic as he finished changing out of his suit into sweatpants and a shirt.

He was still suspended while he was under review. Verne and Robinson both did their best to keep him updated on when he might hear something, but he knew neither played a part in the final decision.

He sat on the edge of the bed and felt exhausted. The weeks since Fiona Griffin had revealed the DNA test to him had piled on, one after the other, and he just wanted it to be over.

"Ethan?"

He shifted to see Vanessa, sat on her side of the bed looking at him.

"I don't blame you. I know we haven't really talked about that morning...that you were gone." Her voice trailed off at the end, like she couldn't fully embrace the meaning.

"I—" He choked up as he tried to tell her he blamed himself. He wished more than anything he hadn't gone to the station that morning. He had beaten himself up knowing that things could have been so different if he hadn't left her. He turned away, resting his elbows on his knees and his head in his hands. It was all becoming too much.

He felt her climb over the bed and sit behind him, her arms encompassing his chest as she rested her chin on his shoulder.

"It's not your fault, Ethan. None of it. You were doing what you know how to do. You tried. I know you were just trying to protect me," she whispered in his ear.

He'd spent so many weeks trying not to cry in front of her. He'd had to be strong for her. She'd been through so much, and he'd only made it worse. But to hear her say she didn't blame him, and feel her comforting him, broke the last thread of strength he'd been clinging onto. He let the tears he'd been holding back go. Vanessa's soft "I love yous" whispered in his ear as the weight he carried poured out of him.

CHAPTER FIFTY-FOUR

MONDAY, MAY 13TH

The following Monday after the funeral, Ethan got a text from Camilleri to come to the station. Vanessa helped him pick out a suit that she said perfectly balanced "I stand by my decision" and "I'm really, really sorry and want to keep my job." He texted Verne the news before he headed to the station and got two thumbs up emojis followed by a gif of a little kid dancing.

When he got there, Camilleri had him wait outside his office for exactly thirty-nine minutes and forty-three seconds. Ethan watched the clock the entire time.

"Dumas," Camilleri shouted from his office.

Ethan stood up, took a deep breath, and walked in, surprised to see Tom Robinson sitting in one of the two seats in front of Camilleri's desk. Robinson must have been in here the entire time because no one had come or gone from the office since Ethan had arrived.

"You know Lieutenant Robinson from homicide," Camilleri said, waving a hand toward him.

Ethan wasn't sure if Camilleri was trying to be funny or was just oblivious that they used to be partners, but he decided not to push him today, so he went with a simple "Yes, sir" as he took the empty seat.

"Well, to start, you are very lucky we had capable detectives able to clean up your mess."

Ethan nodded. He held his tongue because, when it came down to it, it had been his mess, whether Fiona Griffin had started it or not.

"Since we were able to throw the book at Howard and Lisa Ashby, Mr. Griffin has stopped his threats to sue and stopped demanding that you be fired."

Ethan sat up straighter in his chair. He hadn't been aware Gregory Griffin had pushed for him to be fired. If Verne knew, he'd probably been wise to keep that from Ethan. That might have gone down poorly if he'd let his anger get the better of him while he was suspended.

"Your case was reviewed, and thanks to glowing remarks from detectives you've worked with, the overall spotless record you'd kept up to this point, and Lieutenant Robinson's groveling on your behalf, your suspension is lifted."

Ethan looked at Robinson, who looked pleased with himself. Under different circumstances, with an entirely different audience, Ethan would have hugged him because apparently he was a hugger now. Instead, he settled for a smile and a nod.

"Thank you both. This means a lot. I truly am horrified with how this all came about and wish I had conducted myself better." He'd practiced with Vanessa what he might say if forgiven. He'd also practiced his argument if they fired him, but he was grateful to be able to forget that particular speech already.

"Not so fast," Camilleri said, as he pulled Ethan's badge and gun out of his desk. "You can be reinstated on one condition, suggested by Robinson. He vouched for you, and in doing so, he also said he'd take responsibility for you while you're in your probation window following this suspension."

"I'm not sure I'm following."

"I've requested you be transferred back to homicide to work under me," Robinson said, the self-rewarding smile still on his face.

"Wow. Thank you," he managed to say without sounding overly strained. He knew he ought to be kissing Robinson's feet. He could be in a far worse position, but there was a part of him that couldn't help but resent this change in stature. He'd gone from being Robinson's equal, for many years, and would now be working under him.

"Now, in terms of your probation, it's rather simple. You mess up, you're out. You're out of strikes. So, I advise you, Dumas, to keep your head down and do your job." Camilleri slid his badge and gun toward him.

Ethan took them both, hesitant to say what was on his mind, but if he didn't speak up now, he may never get the chance.

"Sir, I have an unusual request."

"You're not really in a position to be making requests." Camilleri had leaned back in his seat, arms crossed, as his expression fell into his standard disapproving glare.

"I understand, but if you'll just hear me out, I'd really appreciate it." Ethan knew he was pushing his luck, but he had to try. He just hoped Verne wouldn't be mad.

CHAPTER FIFTY-FIVE

MONDAY, MAY 13TH

Verne jumped and fist-pumped the air for the third time in the few minutes Ethan had been back in their office. He never thought he'd miss the broom-closet room, but it felt right to be back, even if only to pack up his stuff.

"I can't believe we're going to homicide. I've wanted to be in the squad since I became a detective." Verne had switched to punching an imaginary bag in front of him, still amped from when Ethan had told him the news.

Camilleri had been surprised by Ethan's request that Verne be transferred with him to homicide, as his partner. Robinson had looked equally as puzzled when Camilleri then asked him if he wanted both detectives. Ethan liked to think it was his pleading eyes that won Robinson over, but he knew it was far more plausible that Robinson was well aware that getting the captain's approval for more detectives wasn't easy, so he would take what he could get while he could get it.

Camilleri had grumbled something along the lines of needing more cold case detectives, but Ethan had been too busy internally celebrating the fact they had both, much to his surprise, agreed to his request.

"I owed you. Plus, I couldn't leave you here alone. You'd go crazy," Ethan teased, emptying the contents of his desk drawers into banker boxes.

"They might have stuck me with someone who does nothing."

Ethan generously chose not to point out that, at one point, Verne was someone who did nothing. He was glad Verne had come around though. It was much more enjoyable to work beside him than do both of their jobs.

"You should be packing," Ethan said and put one of the empty boxes on top of Verne's messy desk. He'd work on that in homicide. Baby steps.

Verne had been about to say something, likely complain about packing, when Ethan's phone ringing interrupted him. Ethan pulled the phone out of his pocket and immediately hit decline, his heart racing as he did.

"Fiona Griffin," Ethan said, not needing to look up to know Verne was watching him.

"She still calls you?" Verne had started to shove random piles into the box, much to Ethan's horror. He wasn't even attempting to stay organized.

"That's the first time since everything happened. I haven't seen or heard from her since the hospital."

"You could just block her."

"There's no point. She'd just find another way." He hadn't even given himself time to decide to answer. He wasn't ready to hear what she had to say. He wasn't sure he'd ever be, but he also knew on a deeper level he wouldn't block her because of Vanessa. It didn't feel like his call alone to make.

"Do you think you'll ever answer? Even just to tell her to fuck off?" Verne had found his rubber band ball and abandoned his packing. He bounced the ball from hand to hand while Ethan watched.

"I don't know. Vanessa and I haven't talked about what she wants. Sometimes, she asks a question about them, but I don't want to push her. I don't know if she'll ever want to meet them. Well, properly meet them. I don't think how Fiona tricked her that day counts."

"I feel like curiosity will get her. Especially since the Ashbys are probably going to get max sentences." Verne tossed the rubber band ball into the box and threw some more papers on top.

Ethan shrugged, not sure what to think. He would ask her eventually, but not yet. He wasn't going to rush her process. She was almost back into a routine. She'd texted him that she decided, upon hearing he wasn't fired, to teach summer school after missing the end of the term with her medical leave. She was going to cook a celebratory dinner tonight. Ethan wanted to let her have some semblance of normalcy. When she was ready to face the Griffins, he'd be right there beside her, but he wouldn't suggest she do it a moment sooner.

EPILOGUE

TUESDAY, OCTOBER 6TH, 2020

Ethan was hunched over crime scene photos at his desk, now in a large space surrounded by other desks and detectives. It had been strange to move back to a busy environment after he and Verne had established a routine in their closet. Still, even with so many other detectives around, uniformed officers coming and going, no one ever seemed to pay anyone else any mind.

When his phone rang with Fiona Griffin's call, he almost, without having to think, declined the call. His finger hovered over the red before he froze. He wasn't sure why he hesitated. It may have been the fact two days ago marked two years since Fiona became a presence in his life he'd never forget. It might be she'd finally worn him down with the random calls over the last eighteen months he'd always ignored, the voicemails he deleted without listening to, even when the curiosity was there.

Whatever the reason his subconscious was guided by, he picked up his phone, hit the green, and pressed it to his face before he could process exactly what he was doing or what he wanted to say.

"Hello?" Fiona sounded breathless, no doubt taken aback that the ringing had stopped so soon, so unexpectedly, after months of calling.

He tried to decide if she sounded like Vanessa. Probably not, since she didn't raise her, but he didn't know how that worked. Maybe voice was genetic.

"We need to talk," he said, when he finally found his voice.

"I'm rather shocked you answered."

"Me too." He was surprised by his own candor.

"What do we need to talk about? Is Anne—Vanessa alright?"

She sounded genuinely concerned and, though it shouldn't have surprised him, it was odd to hear. Yes, she was her biological mother, and she'd searched decades for her. Yet, since finding out Vanessa was Anne, she'd only managed to hurt Vanessa.

"Meet me at Gardens Park in thirty minutes."

He hung up before she could argue or try and take control of the situation. He sat back in his chair and let out the breath he hadn't realized he'd been holding. The park was right around the corner from the station. He didn't need more than five minutes to walk down there, but he'd need the other twenty-five to pull himself together.

He had questions, though he wasn't sure he'd ask. He knew he had to tell her to stop calling. He would break it gently that Vanessa didn't want contact with Fiona or Gregory Griffin. He'd make it clear that, if Vanessa changed her mind, they'd reach out, but otherwise, Fiona needed to stop calling. It was the best thing to do, he decided as he pulled on his coat and scribbled a note to Verne that he was taking his lunch break.

* * *

He walked through the wrought iron arch at the entrance of the park. It was chilly; fall in Connecticut was gorgeous but biting. He followed the asphalt path that wound through the park and, if he continued, would dump him at the other end with a matching wrought iron arch, but he didn't have to walk far.

Fiona Griffin sat upright on a bench off to the side. The formality of her appearance reminded him of when he met her two years ago. She had her small purse clutched to her stomach, and she wore a black dress with a matching jacket.

As he approached, she didn't look his way, her gaze locked on the playground she'd chosen to sit across. There weren't any kids playing, likely due to the weather or the time of day.

"Fiona."

He took a seat on the other end of the bench without looking at her. He followed suit in watching the playground, vaguely recalling how he used to love when his dad took him to the park on weekends. He hadn't thought about those trips in years, but this park looked a lot like the one they used to visit.

"How is she?"

"Well," he responded dryly. Despite having answered the call, he felt like he really shouldn't talk about Vanessa.

"I had to do it. I'd waited so long already, and there was never going to be a good time to expose the truth."

It sounded rehearsed, and he imagined she had probably said it to herself hundreds of times. Easing her own conscience, given that she had caused irreversible damage.

"Why did you wait to say something if you knew where she was? Why not just go to the police when you found out?" He hesitated before adding, "I know you knew for years. I saw the hidden space in Anne's nursery."

He saw her turn out of the corner of his eye, but he didn't look at her. He wasn't quite ready to look her in the eyes again. Wasn't ready to, potentially, see Vanessa there. There was still a deep part of him that was angry with Fiona for everything. While he had accepted the role he'd played in how it all came out, he felt like Fiona had not been duly punished, and in part, it was his own fault. He'd never told anyone what he'd seen when he broke into the Griffins' home, or admitted he'd done as much.

After what felt like minutes of silence, Fiona spoke up. "I suspected you'd seen it. My neighbors told me they'd seen someone in my backyard and called the cops. They said the man flashed a badge and everyone left. You never said anything; the police never came and questioned me about it."

"I was in enough trouble," Ethan said, knowing that was not entirely his motivation behind not saying.

There was a part of him, buried under all the anger he carried for her, that pitied Fiona. As messed up as everything was, including her stalking and meddling in their lives, he wanted to believe he understood her to some degree.

"I'm divorcing Greg."

The sudden shift in focus threw Ethan, and all he could muster was a feeble "oh" in response. Fiona didn't seem to notice though.

"He's allowing me to keep the house, and he's even going to continue to pay me a monthly stipend. He's already proposed to *her*."

Ethan knew from the way Fiona said "her," that she was referring to Sheila Waterford, the mother of Gregory's two sons. The half-brothers Ethan had eventually told Vanessa existed, though like her biological parents, she had no immediate desire to know them.

Silence fell over them. Ethan wasn't sure how long they sat there. His nose felt numb from the wind, and he watched a tree shed vibrant orange leaves, watched it scatter them all over the ground surrounding its trunk.

"It might be pointless to ask now, but how did you find her?" Ethan asked. He didn't really care about why she took so long to come forward, why she chose to have it all come out the way she did, but the detective in him needed to know how. How she did what police failed more than once to do.

"I hired a private investigator to look into everyone on the hospital log. When he showed me a photo of Anne—Vanessa, I knew."

She spoke so matter-of-factly that Ethan surprised himself with the sharp bark of laughter that escaped him. That was all it took. Something the original investigation failed to do. Something he and Verne failed to do. After all, they'd been quick to dismiss the patients who'd been gone before the Griffins had arrived at the hospital.

Ethan watched as a mother with her little girl approached the playground from the opposite side of the park than he'd entered. The mother pushed the girl on a swing, the little girl's squealing laughter reaching where they sat on opposite ends of the bench.

"Was it worth it?" Ethan asked.

Fiona didn't answer him, and he finally caved and looked at her. She was crying. He wouldn't have known if he couldn't see the tears that fell silently down her face and onto her jacket.

"She doesn't want to meet you." He knew it was harsh, but he needed to tell her. Whatever Fiona's reasoning for her elaborate scheme, he did believe she'd just wanted Anne back in her life.

"Maybe, one day, she'll feel differently."

She didn't sound as confident as she normally did, and despite everything, he found that he hoped she was right. He couldn't forgive her for the role she played in losing Bethany, because he couldn't bear to carry that burden alone, but he hoped, for Vanessa's sake, she'd one day get to know the woman who never gave up on her.

The mother helped her daughter off the swings, and they walked back the way they'd come into the park. He couldn't hear what they said, but the laughter of the little girl poked at the unhealed wound in his heart that he'd forever have for Bethany.

"I suppose, in the end, you, me, the Ashbys…we all ended up the same," she said, breaking the silence that had fallen between them again.

He contemplated her words and tried to imagine the reality she saw them all in together. Finally, he gave in, "What do you mean?"

"In the end, we all remain childless."

She stood up, brushing off her dress. She looked down at him, and he had to squint against the sun behind her to look into her eyes. Vanessa's eyes.

She looked as if she had more to say to him, but then, she abruptly turned and walked away. Ethan watched her go. He sat by himself for a few minutes and stared over the desolate playground. Her voice pounded through his head like a drum with the sole purpose to drive him mad. He stood up and slowly walked back to the station. He had cases that needed his attention.

The rhythm of his own step eventually fell in line with Fiona's voice echoing through his mind. A single word beat inside of him. *Childless.*

ACKNOWLEDGMENT

There are so many people who have helped me along the way. I regretfully can't list all of them but just know even if you're not explicitly listed, I appreciate the support and energy behind helping me make this book possible.

Of course, the biggest thank you to my parents for believing in me always. (Also, for being *Criminal Minds* fans so I could sneakily watch it from the kitchen when I was supposed to be upstairs.) Without them I never would have become the person, and writer, I am today. They gave me my undying love for reading and writing, the confidence to believe in myself, and most importantly, their support when even I thought I was crazy for chasing my dream.

I need to give a particularly special shout out to my mom who has read every single version of *Childless*, and even when we have argued about edits and revisions, has still sat there for hours to re-read the book again when I asked.

While he came in later in the book's development, I owe a big thank you to my partner. He immediately supported and believed in me without an ounce of doubt that I could do it. He has been my cheerleader since the day we met and made my writing as important to him as it is to me.

I also want to thank all the people who helped me shape *Childless* from the short story it started as during my undergraduate degree to the novel it became. From my college days, Dan and Christy for helping me learn my craft. My numerous workshop groups who had to read and re-read the same thing over and over until I got it right. My Creative Writing friends who may have had to suffer through some of the worst writing I've ever done so I could get to the good stuff. A big thanks to my beta readers: Anna, Maryanne, Yashira, and Lily. To my writing support duo, Kit and Madi, for hyping me up with every idea I brought to them (or existential crisis). The GIFs helped every time!